TRIPLE CROWN

TRIPLE CROWN

A Dick Francis Novel

by

FELIX FRANCIS

**SIMON &
SCHUSTER**

London · New York · Sydney · Toronto · New Delhi

A CBS COMPANY

First published in Great Britain by Simon & Schuster UK Ltd, 2016
A CBS COMPANY

1 3 5 7 9 10 8 6 4 2

Simon & Schuster UK Ltd
1st Floor
222 Gray's Inn Road
London WC1X 8HB

www.simonandschuster.co.uk

Simon & Schuster Australia, Sydney
Simon & Schuster India, New Delhi

A CIP catalogue record for this book
is available from the British Library

Hardback ISBN: 978-1-4711-5547-5
Trade Paperback ISBN: 978-1-4711-5548-2
eBook ISBN: 978-1-4711-5550-5

Typeset in Sabon by M Rules
Printed and bound by CPI Group (UK) Ltd, Croydon, CR0 4YY

Simon & Schuster UK Ltd are committed to sourcing paper
that is made from wood grown in sustainable forests and support the Forest
Stewardship Council, the leading international forest certification organisation.
Our books displaying the FSC logo are printed on FSC certified paper.

In fondest memory of my dearest friend
Diana Patin
so much missed

With thanks to my neighbour
Andrew Higgins, MA, VetMB, MSc
for his veterinary help and advice,

and, as always, to Debbie

The Federal Anti-Corruption in
Sports Agency, FACSA, as depicted
in this novel, is fictitious. But it
could exist. Perhaps it should.

To capture the Triple Crown of
American racing, a horse has to win
the Kentucky Derby, the Preakness
Stakes *and* the Belmont Stakes.

The races are for three-year-olds only,
so a horse gets only one chance.

Three championship races in a period
of just five weeks.

In more than 140 years since the first
running of all three races, only twelve
horses have managed the feat.

Between the Triple Crown being won
in 1978 and 2015, thirteen horses
won the first two legs but then failed
in their attempt to capture the most
elusive prize in world sport.

PROLOGUE

United Kingdom

April

I

'Where are those goddamn cops?' Tony Andretti said it under his breath, quiet as a whisper, but it was full of frustration nonetheless.

'Calm down,' I murmured back. 'They'll be here soon enough.'

Tony and I were lying side by side, out of sight in the bushes, next to a lay-by off the A34 trunk road north of Oxford. We'd been in position for several hours, getting ever wetter thanks to the persistent rain.

'Call them in now, Jeff,' Tony hissed at me angrily. 'Or we'll lose them.'

I ignored him and went on watching through my binoculars.

Two men were standing in the lay-by, between the cars in which they had recently arrived, their heads bent close together as if they didn't want to be over-heard. Not that there was much chance of that, I thought, not with a line of heavy lorries thundering past noisily on the dual carriageway only a dozen or so yards away.

One of the men, the shorter of the two, removed a white envelope from his trouser pocket and handed it to the other, who then turned away from the road, conveniently facing directly towards me, as he counted the banknotes it contained.

I used the camera built into my binoculars to take a couple of still shots as the man thumbed through the wad, then I switched to video mode and zoomed in, first on the money in the man's hands and then up to his face. The light wasn't perfect but my top-of-the-range digital system would be well able to cope.

Obviously satisfied with its contents, the taller man stuffed the white envelope into his anorak and then handed over a small flat package. I filmed it all.

'Now, Nigel,' I said quietly but distinctly into the microphone taped to my left wrist.

I went on filming as the two men briefly shook hands and then started to return to their respective cars.

'We're losing them,' Tony said to me in an irritated tone.

I was beginning to think that he might be right, that I'd left it too late, when a couple of police squad cars arrived at speed, screeching to a halt and blocking in the vehicles in the lay-by. Even before they had come to a complete stop, the doors were flung open and four uniformed officers spilled out.

The shorter of the two men stood stock still, open-mouthed in disbelief, but the taller one turned and ran – away from the police, and straight at me, at the same time removing a long-bladed knife from his coat pocket.

'Knife!' Tony shouted loudly from beside me, as he struggled to stand up.

The man changed from looking back at the police to looking forward to where Tony and I had been hiding. He saw Tony, who was now on his feet, and turned slightly to go directly for him, the blade facing upwards in his left hand in a manner that suggested to me that he knew exactly how to use it.

I rolled over, grabbed Tony by the ankles and pulled hard.

He came down on top of me, his considerable bulk sprawling over my legs.

'Let go of me,' Tony shouted angrily, trying to kick out towards my face.

I hung on tight.

The man with the knife hurdled the two of us and ran off into the trees behind, pursued by a pair of the policemen.

They're welcome to him, I thought, even with their anti-stab vests. I'd been on the wrong end of a carving knife once before and had no wish to repeat the experience.

I released Tony's legs and we clambered to our feet.

'What the hell were you doing?' Tony shouted at me, his face puce with rage. 'I could have had him.'

'He'd have had you, more like,' I said. 'Better to live to fight another day.'

Tony stood staring at me, his hands bunched into fists, adrenalin still coursing through his veins. I stared back at him.

Slowly he relaxed and his fingers uncurled.

'I suppose you're right,' he said. 'Thanks. But I'd have taken him down if I'd had a piece.'

'Tony, you're no longer with the NYPD.'

As a younger man, Tony had been a cop, one of 'New York's Finest'.

'I can't get my head round you Brits and guns. Not even your cops carry them. You're just asking to get yourselves killed.'

I resisted pointing out to him that, in the previous ten years, only a handful of British police officers had been killed on duty, whereas hundreds of American cops had died in the same period.

The remaining two police officers had arrested the shorter of the men and were applying handcuffs to his wrists while relieving him of the package, which was then carefully enclosed in a plastic evidence bag.

Nigel had followed the police in his own car and was now standing to one side watching. Tony and I went over to join him.

'Well done,' I said, slapping Nigel gently on the back.

'You're certainly a cool one, and no mistake,' Nigel said, smiling at me. 'It was as much as I could do to stop the boys in blue turning up as soon as they knew the men had arrived.'

I smiled back at him. Nigel Green was a colleague of mine in the integrity service of the BHA, the British Horseracing Authority, and we had together spent several weeks setting up this operation after a tip-off. We had been surprised that the police had been so cooperative, agreeing to wait in a farm lane with Nigel until I called them in. Word of our past successes, when they alone had previously failed, had clearly filtered up to the powers that be.

'Damn right he's cool,' Tony said. 'Nerves of steel. I'd have called the cops in far sooner.'

'I'm not cool,' I said jokily. 'At least, not in that sense.' In temperature terms, I was extremely cool, and very wet. I shivered. 'If the posse had turned up before the package was handed over we wouldn't have been able to implicate both men. That's all.'

'Do you think those guys will get their man?' Tony asked in his rich New York accent, looking over his shoulder towards the woods.

'Eventually,' I said. 'If not today then sometime soon. I have all the evidence we need on disc.' I tapped the binocular-camera round my neck.

The arrested man was frogmarched past us towards the police cars by two tall officers who made him look even smaller than he actually was.

He stared at me with hatred in his eyes.

'Hinkley, you're a bastard.' He said it with feeling.

'You shouldn't get mixed up with drugs, Jimmy,' I said.

The man was placed in the back of the police car.

'He knows you, then?' Tony said to me.

'Indeed he does,' I said. 'Jimmy and I have crossed swords before.'

Jimmy Robinson was a jockey, quite a good jockey,

who had previously tested positive for cocaine and been banned from riding for six months as a result. That had been two years ago but he had clearly not learned his lesson.

'I thought you always worked undercover.'

'I used to, but things change.'

It was a consequence of being a long time in the job. When I'd first started as an investigator at the BHA, fresh out of the army, I worked my entire time incognito, often using false beards and glasses to ensure that, even if I were seen, no one would recognise me again. But gradually, over time, my name and face were slowly put together by the racing fraternity and my covert work was now limited, although I could still occasionally get away with it provided I employed some of my more elaborate disguises.

It was a situation I was not happy with. I had enjoyed living in the shadows, rather than in the spotlight.

For some time I had even considered leaving the BHA altogether, packing up and moving abroad, possibly to Australia, to start again where my face was unknown.

The two policemen returned from the woods empty-handed, which didn't please Tony.

'They should have caught him,' he said to me. 'Your cops need to be fitter.'

I thought that was rather rich coming from him. Tony could hardly run fast enough to catch a cold.

He had clearly put on far more than the odd pound since his days on the force.

'We'll have to call the dogs out,' one of the policemen said. 'They'll soon find him.'

'Get a helicopter up,' Tony said, almost as an order.

The policeman shook his head. 'No point. Even their heat-seeking cameras can't see through that lot.'

I looked past him into the trees. It was, in fact, more of a plantation than a natural wood, with evergreen firs standing cheek by jowl for as far as I could see, which wasn't very far at all due to a lack of illumination beneath the trees. If visible light couldn't penetrate the cover, it was no surprise that infrared would be unable to do so either.

'Do you need us any more?' I asked.

'Not here,' said the senior officer. 'But you will each need to give a statement concerning this operation. Can you do that on a Section 9 Form?'

'No problem,' I said. 'I have one on my laptop.'

Section 9 of the UK Criminal Justice Act 1967 allowed written statements to be accepted by a court as evidence, provided they obeyed certain conditions. The Section 9 Form wasn't absolutely essential but it contained the necessary declarations of truthfulness and I was happy to oblige. The police had been uncharacteristically helpful so far and I had no wish to upset them.

'Come on, Tony,' I said. 'Let's go home.'

Tony was my shadow, as he had been for the past two and a half weeks. His official title was Deputy

Director at the Federal Anti-Corruption in Sports Agency (FACSA) based in Washington, DC, and he was on a fact-finding mission to the UK to learn how the integrity service operated at the BHA.

He and I had instantly liked each other and I had enjoyed having him around, while he, in turn, had developed a love for British steeplechasing, and especially for the Grand National.

Ten days previously, Tony and I had travelled north by train from London to Liverpool for the big race.

He couldn't get over the excitement that a single jumping race could generate in the population as a whole, with everyone discussing the relative merits of the forty runners, and every workplace running its own sweepstake.

'At home in the States, steeplechase racing is mostly a small-town affair, run by farmers out in the boondocks. You'd be lucky to have more than a couple of tents in a field somewhere with some temporary bleachers. Nothing like this.' He had waved his hand expansively at Aintree's towering grandstands and the impressive media centre.

'Over seventy thousand will be here today,' I'd said, as Tony had shaken his head in disbelief, 'with tens of millions more watching live on television.'

And the Grand National itself had certainly lived up to all the hype with the eight-to-one favourite catching the long-time leader on the line to win by a nose in a photo finish.

'Amazing,' Tony had said repeatedly, as the victor

was loudly cheered all the way to the winner's circle, flanked by two police horses. 'Is all your jump racing like this?'

'No,' I'd said, laughing. 'You should try a wet winter Wednesday at Hexham. Two men and a dog if you're lucky.'

I had gone to the National not for any specific reason but simply to watch and listen, to gather intelligence and, maybe, to defuse any trouble before it started. At least that's what I'd told myself, although I had mostly wanted to show off one of the great showpieces of British racing to my American guest.

He had not been disappointed.

Back in the lay-by, a police van arrived with a pair of vicious-looking German shepherds barking loudly through the rear windows.

Nigel, Tony and I stood watching as the excited, snarling dogs were removed from the vehicle by their handler, a mountain of a man with hands as large as any I had ever seen. He crouched down to cuddle each dog in turn, allowing them to nuzzle their snouts into his neck, sharp teeth and all.

Rather him than me, I thought.

After this moment of tenderness, it was time for work.

The dogs were first taken over to the car that belonged to the fugitive and given a few moments to register his scent. Then they were off into the woods, the strain on their leads almost pulling over the handler. A smaller man would have had no chance.

'I'm glad I'm not the one they're chasing,' Nigel said. 'Did you see those bloody fangs?'

We all laughed but with a slight nervousness – it was really not a joking matter.

'I'll miss all this excitement,' Tony said to us with a smile as we climbed into Nigel's car. 'I'm back to being stuck at my boring desk from next Monday.'

'Don't you get out into the field at all?' I asked.

'Not much any more. I'm getting too old. And too fat.' He guffawed loudly and clasped his hands round his substantial midriff. 'Nowadays I have a team of young pups like you to do all my legwork.'

He remained unusually quiet and pensive all the way back to London, a smile never leaving his face. He didn't elaborate on what was occupying his mind and I didn't press him. He would tell me if he wanted to.

He didn't. Not then, anyhow.

2

'Diuretics!'

'Yup. Mostly diuretics together with a few laxatives.'

'No cocaine?'

'Not even a dusting.'

'Amphetamines? Or ecstasy?'

'Nope. Nothing.'

'Bugger!'

It was the following morning in my office at BHA headquarters in Central London. Nigel was giving Tony and me the bad news about the contents of the handed-over package.

'The cops aren't very happy about it either, I can tell you,' Nigel said. 'My contact says they've dropped the investigation and released Jimmy Robinson with no charges and an abject apology. The chief superintendent is really angry and intends to call Paul Maldini to give him what for.' Paul Maldini was Head of Operations at the BHA – our boss. 'He claims we've made them look like foolish amateurs.'

To be fair, I suppose we had. But we had also made fools out of ourselves.

Nigel had received a tip-off from one of his regular cluster of covert informants that Jimmy Robinson was again dealing in drugs. Perhaps I had been naïve or careless in assuming that the drugs in question were unlawful, but Jimmy had previous form in that respect. I had called in the police and, with much pushing on my part, the matter had eventually gone right to the top with the Director General of the National Crime Agency applying to the Home Secretary for a communication intercept warrant on Robinson's mobile telephone. That's how we knew where and when to wait for the hand-over.

'Couldn't they indict Robinson for *anything*?' Tony asked.

'Purchasing medicines without a prescription?' Nigel raised his eyebrows. 'It's hardly grand theft auto. You or I could do the same on the Internet.'

'Then why all the cloak-and-dagger stuff in some deserted lay-by?' I asked. But I already knew the answer. Whereas the drugs purchased may have not been illegal according to the Misuse of Drugs Act, both diuretics and laxatives were banned substances for jockeys under the Rules of Racing.

'Does Jimmy Robinson have trouble with his weight?' I asked.

'Doesn't every jockey?' Nigel replied.

It was true.

Rises in racing weights had never kept up with the increasing height and bulk of the population as a whole. Before diuretics were added to the list of banned substances in 1999, their use had been widespread by jockeys of all abilities to control their weight.

One former champion jockey once joked to me about taking a handful of pee-pills every day as his only breakfast. 'The trouble was,' he said, 'they made me so dehydrated I got dreadful cramps. On one occasion I remember being given a leg-up in the paddock and being unable to get my left foot into the iron because of it. Had to bump-trot the horse all the way to the start before it eased.'

Another told me he regularly used laxatives, taking them by the packet-full. 'Explosive decompression,' he'd said with a laugh. 'I'd pebbledash the ceiling if I wasn't careful.'

I'd asked him what the jockeys did now that those drugs had all been banned. 'Fingers down the throat, mate,' he'd said. 'Eat to ease the hunger pain then throw it all back up again so as not to put on any weight. Not clever really.'

'Can't do much for their teeth.'

'Teeth?' He'd laughed again. 'Bugger the teeth. Most of those get knocked out in falls anyway.'

I dragged my mind back to the matter in hand.

'Surely Jimmy would know we would test him for diuretics,' I said.

'The police lab says this is something new. Still a thiazide, whatever that means, but a synthetic version. Perhaps Jimmy thought it wouldn't show up in a test. And maybe he's right.'

'Why do these bloody drug firms keep muddying the water with new compounds?' I sighed. 'Don't they realise we're trying to stop the cheats?'

'Apparently millions of people take diuretics every day for heart problems and high blood pressure.'

'I'm one of those,' Tony said meekly, tapping his jacket pocket.

I suppose I couldn't realistically blame the drug companies for making our life difficult, not if they were doing good for millions.

I sighed again. 'So why did the supplier run? And why pull a knife?'

'He claims he didn't know what was in the packet,' Nigel said.

'So they caught him then?'

'My police contact said the man walked out of the woods with his arms in the air when he heard the dogs coming. He'd got rid of the knife by then, of course, and the cops weren't about to launch a massive search for a weapon that hadn't been used. The man claimed he was only an intermediary, delivering a sealed package for a friend.'

'So why did he run?'

'He says that he was told the package contained drugs and he'd assumed they were illegal.'

He hadn't been the only one.

I was now even more relieved that Tony hadn't had a 'piece' in the lay-by. I could imagine the furore that would have followed the shooting of a man who was supplying perfectly legal medication.

'It seems odd to me that he just happened to have a knife in his pocket. Surely that's not normal.'

Tony waved a dismissive hand as if to say that it was quite normal where he came from.

The man's car had been removed to a forensic laboratory to be searched and, according to Nigel's police chum, no illegal substances had been found. The man was free to pick it up whenever he wanted to.

The phone on my desk rang. I answered it.

'Jeff, it's Paul Maldini,' said a voice down the line. 'I need you in my office, right away.'

Oh God, I thought. The chief superintendent must have called.

'On my way,' I said.

'And Jeff, bring Tony with you.'

'And Nigel?' I asked.

'No. Only you and Tony.'

How odd, I thought. It had been Nigel and me who had been responsible for setting up this sorry affair, not Tony. He had simply been an innocent observer to the disaster. It didn't seem fair that he should be facing the firing squad alongside me.

Tony and I made our way along the corridor to Paul's office. It felt to me like we were two miscreant schoolboys who had been summoned to the headmaster's study after having been caught smoking behind the bike sheds – hugely apprehensive and not a little frightened.

'Ah, come in, come in, both of you,' Paul said as I knocked and opened his door. 'Sit down.' He waved at the two chairs in front of his desk.

I thought the condemned always had to stand to receive their punishment.

Tony and I sat down.

'Now, Jeff,' Paul said, smiling and nodding at Tony, 'Tony here has something to ask you.'

'Eh?' I was unsure what was going on.

'I'd like you to come to the States,' Tony said, half turning towards me.

'Eh?' I said again. 'Isn't this about the Jimmy Robinson affair?'

'No,' Paul said. 'It is not.'

'Didn't the police chief superintendent call you?' I asked.

'As a matter of fact, he did,' Paul replied. 'And quite cross he was too. So I reminded him of all the things we had done right in the past and that we had acted in good faith in asking for their help in this case. I told him we had nothing to apologise for.'

'What did he say to that?' I asked.

'Not much.' Paul laughed as if amused by the memory. 'I suspect they might not be so helpful in future, but we can live with that. Now, let's move on. Tony spoke to me last evening and I've just had a meeting with the chief executive and the chairman and they have given their approval for his proposal.'

'What proposal?' I asked, confused.

I felt like I was living in a parallel universe. I had been expecting to get a severe telling-off and yet here was Paul Maldini, a man with an infamous temper, smiling and joking as if I was flavour of the month.

'I would like you to come and work for me,' Tony said.

I turned in my chair and stared at him.

'Permanently?'

'For as long as it takes,' he replied.

'For as long as what takes?'

'Let me start from the beginning,' Tony said. 'But what I'm about to tell you is highly confidential and cannot be discussed outside the three of us. Not even the BHA chairman and chief executive have the full picture. Do I make myself clear?'

'Absolutely,' I said, even though I thought he was being rather melodramatic. As an ex-army intelligence officer, one thing I *did* know was how to keep a secret.

'You are aware that I am Deputy Director at FACSA, an agency dedicated to preventing corruption in sport.' He pronounced it 'Facsa', as a word rather than speaking out each of the letters in turn.

I nodded.

'We have the particular task of keeping US horseracing free of organised crime. As you may know, unlike here in the UK with the BHA, there is no national racing authority in the US. Each of our states has its own rules and is responsible for enforcing them. My federal agency was set up to provide a nationwide focus on anti-corruption, and the Thoroughbred horse industry, both racing and breeding, represents a significant part of our efforts. We even have a special section dedicated to it.'

'Yes,' I said. I knew most of this from discussions Tony and I had had during the last fourteen days. 'But where do I fit in?'

Tony looked around him as if making sure no one was lurking and listening. He also lowered his voice.

'For some time I have had my suspicions that we have an informant in our ranks.'

'Mmm,' I mused. 'Corruption within the anti-corruption agency. Not good.'

'Indeed not,' Tony said.

'How do you know?' I asked.

'I don't *know*,' Tony said. 'I only have suspicions. My racing team have initiated several operations only to discover that the target has got rid of the evidence just before we turn up. At first I thought it was bad luck, but it has happened too often.'

'What sort of operations?' I asked.

'We recently raided the barns of a trainer who we believed was employing illegal immigrants as grooms, mostly Mexicans, paying them well under the minimum wage and in cash to avoid federal payroll taxes and Social Security dues. We had done our homework and were pretty sure we had the trainer dead to rights. All we needed was to catch the illegals in the act.'

'But you found none?' I said.

'Not one. Vanished like mist in the morning sunshine.' Tony held his hands out, palms uppermost. 'On another occasion we received a tip from a disgruntled ex-employee that a Maryland horse farm was using an unlicensed antibiotic together with equine growth hormone on a newly born foal in order to determine if they made the foal grow faster and larger. This practice would be unlawful under the US Animal Welfare Act, but we were involved because it would also constitute a fraud on the future buyer of the foal. So the team arrived one day at dawn to search the premises and take blood samples for analysis.'

'What did they find?' I asked.

'That the foal had been euthanised and the carcass cremated.'

'Did the farm give a reason?'

'They tried. Some hooey about the animal kicking out and breaking its leg. But the pit was still red-hot from the fire. They must have incinerated the poor thing through the night.'

'It could have been a coincidence,' I said. 'They do sometimes happen.'

'If it were only those two I might agree but there have been more, like a fire that conveniently destroyed all the computers in the office of an illegal bookmaker hours before they were to be seized.'

'Arson?'

Tony rolled his eyes. 'Not that anyone could prove.'

'Have you had a leak inquiry?' I asked.

'Not officially. But the Director and I initiated a review of our internal and external communications. In the process, we covertly examined the email and phone records of all of our staff who knew about the operations ahead of time, but it turned up nothing of any use.'

'How many people knew about these operations beforehand?'

'About twenty.'

'Why so many?'

'There are eight field agents in the horseracing team with a half a dozen backup support staff. Then there are three or four senior personnel, myself included, who would be fully briefed. Plus the Director. All would know about an operation ahead of time. Most would be involved either in the planning or in the decision to give it the green light.'

'That's far too many,' I said. 'A true secret stops being secret when two people know it, let alone twenty. Planning should be done by only two or three key decision makers, with those taking part in the raid briefed about the operation and told the target only immediately before the off, when it's too late for the information to be leaked.'

Tony looked down at his hands as if somewhat embarrassed.

'We are a relatively new agency,' he said. 'We clearly still have much to learn.'

'So you want me to come and teach your people how to do it,' I said rather flippantly.

'I suppose that would be nice eventually,' Tony said seriously, 'but what I really want you to do now is to come and find our mole.'

'Why me?' I asked.

Tony and I were safely back in my office with the

door firmly shut. Even so we kept our voices to a murmur.

'A number of reasons,' Tony said. 'Mostly because you know what you're doing and, because you are an outsider, you are above suspicion. I came to London specifically to recruit you but I needed to be sure. Hence I've watched you closely over the past two weeks and I *am* sure you are the right man. You are determined and single-minded and, most important, you are unflappable. Yesterday you demonstrated admirably that you can keep your head when all around are losing theirs, and that includes me.'

'I try,' I said.

As an army intelligence officer in Afghanistan, it had been my task to acquire information from local tribal leaders, most of whom hated the Taliban only fractionally more than they hated the British. Meetings were always fraught with danger, and a wrong word or action could result in an all-out shooting response. Keeping one's head at all times was essential, metaphorically and literally.

'But surely there is someone else in another part of your organisation who is better placed to investigate the leak?'

'I need someone who understands the racing industry.'

'I know British racing,' I said. 'not American.'

'No matter,' Tony said. 'I've realised during my stay that horseracing here is much the same as in the

US and the potential for trying to beat the system is identical.'

'I'm not so sure,' I said. I'd been to the United States before, on holiday, and everything had seemed very different – bigger, brasher and more ballsy.

But Tony wasn't giving up that easily.

'Jeff, I need your help. Having a corrupt component in an anti-corruption organisation is like having a cancer. It has to be excised and destroyed, otherwise it will grow and spread, killing the whole body.'

I knew what he meant more than most – my sister had cancer.

'But I know nothing about how your organisation operates.'

'I consider that a plus. You won't be blinded by procedure and protocol. You will be able to look at things afresh while being someone who knows what to look for. I can hardly ask one of my own racing team – I might be approaching the very person we're looking for.'

'Don't you trust any of them?'

'I thought I did. I picked them all myself. Nearly half are ex-military and the rest are ex-cops. I'd have trusted each of them with my life six months ago. Now I wouldn't walk down a dark alley with any of them.'

It never ceased to amaze me how wafer-thin and fragile trust can be. All relationships, both work and play, rely on trust as their foundation, yet that trust can be dispelled so quickly by a single word or

24

a casual action, anything that plants a seed of doubt in the mind. And once trust has gone, it is difficult, if not impossible, to re-establish. Ask any divorce lawyer. It's not a lack of love that drives most marriages apart, but a lack of trust.

'But there must be other people you could ask, someone from another agency like the FBI or CIA?'

'Maybe,' he said. 'But would they know what to look for? Also, we at FACSA value our independence. It took much persuasion in Congress for our agency to be set up outside of the FBI rather than as a subsection of it, against the wishes of their then Director. Neither my Director nor I have any wish to go to the FBI now and admit we were wrong.'

'And were you wrong?' I asked.

'Not at all. FACSA reports directly to the Attorney General and the Department of Justice, the same as the DEA and ATF do, and I want to keep it that way.'

'DEA and ATF?'

'Drug Enforcement Administration and the Bureau of Alcohol, Tobacco and Firearms.'

'You Yanks do love your acronyms,' I said with a laugh.

'Be grateful you don't work for the Navy's Bureau of Medicine. Its official acronym is BUMED.'

'You're kidding me.'

'I'm not. Its headquarters building is on Arlington Boulevard. I pass it every day on my way into work.'

'In Washington?' I asked.

'Across the Potomac in Virginia. We're in Arlington,

near National Airport. Real estate in DC has now gotten too expensive for the government. Even the FBI is currently looking to move out.'

Did I fancy some time in Virginia during the spring? I'd heard of the Washington Cherry Blossom Festival. I wondered if it would still be out.

'OK,' I said. 'Tell me what you want me to do.'

LEG 1:

THE KENTUCKY DERBY

'The Run for the Roses'

A mile and a quarter
Churchill Downs, Louisville, Kentucky

First Saturday in May
Run every year since 1875

3

'America?'

'Yes.'

I was on the telephone to Faye, my sister. Her with the cancer.

'How long for?'

'I don't really know,' I said. 'But not for too long, I hope.'

For as long as it takes, Tony had said.

'On holiday?'

'No. I'm going to be on attachment to the American anti-corruption agency. It's like an exchange. Their Deputy Director has been here with us at the BHA for three weeks and I'll be doing the same over there.'

'When do you go?' she asked.

'I'm already at Heathrow. My flight leaves in an hour.'

'That was rather sudden.'

'Yes,' I said. 'I only knew about it myself two days ago. I should have called but, you know how it is, I've been busy getting everything done ready to leave.'

'Is Henrietta with you?'

'No,' I said.

There was a silence from the other end of the line as Faye waited for me to expand my answer. I didn't.

'It is over then?' she asked finally.

'Pretty much,' I said. 'We live in different worlds.'

Henrietta had been my girlfriend for the past few months. An initial whirlwind romance that had cooled almost as quickly as it had started. Such was life.

'Does she know you're going away?' Faye asked.

'I told her last night,' I said. 'I think she was relieved.'

'I'm sorry.'

Yes, so was I. But it was no good trying to go on if it didn't work.

'You'll also miss Quentin's birthday.'

Quentin was Faye's husband, my brother-in-law, and missing his birthday was not something I would be losing any sleep over, unlike Henrietta.

'When is it?'

'Next weekend,' Faye said. 'I was going to ask you over.'

'I'll send him a card.'

'Right.'

She seemed distant, as if thinking of something else.

'Is everything OK?' I asked.

'Absolutely.'

There was something about the way she said it that convinced me that things were absolutely not OK.

'Are you well?' I asked.

A simple question with so many unspoken nuances. There was another silence from her end.

'Faye, what's wrong?' I asked earnestly.

'I'm told it's nothing to worry about.'

'*What* is nothing to worry about?' I asked, with dread in my heart.

'I've been feeling a bit under the weather recently.' She forced a laugh. 'Not that that's been unusual these past few years. So I went to see my oncologist and he did some tests and a scan. I received the results yesterday.'

She paused.

'And?'

'There's another spot on my liver.'

Oh dear God, I thought, will this bloody disease never leave her alone?

'What precisely did the doctor say?' I asked.

'He told me it was nothing to worry about but, naturally, I do. I've got to have another round of chemo and maybe some radiotherapy. I can't say I'm particularly looking forward to it.'

'My dear Faye, I'm so sorry. Perhaps I shouldn't be going.'

'Nonsense. Of course you must go. The chemo won't start for at least another week anyway as I have a touch of flu and they want me to recover from that first. It seems the damn chemo drugs also reduce my white-cell count and I need those to fight the infection. You'll be back before things get really bad. I'll be fine. I promise.'

Was she trying to convince me or herself?

'I can always fly home if you need me. You only have to call.'

'Thank you, but I'm sure I won't need you. I'm a

31

big girl and I can look after myself. You go and enjoy yourself.'

I was pretty sure it wasn't going to be a fun trip, but I didn't say so.

'I'll call you as soon as I know where I'm staying. The agency's head office is in Virginia, near Washington, DC.'

'Say hi to the President for me.' Faye laughed again, this time with a little more genuine amusement.

'Sure will.'

My flight landed at Dulles Airport at a quarter past two, Washington time, on Saturday afternoon.

I had looked up the climate for Virginia on an American weather website. The temperature averaged from sixty-two degrees Fahrenheit at the beginning of the month to seventy-two at the end. But it regularly varied from below fifty to almost ninety.

I'd decided I would have to take everything from shorts and T-shirts to a scarf and gloves, in fact the whole shebang other than my skiwear. I had also packed my collection of disguises. You never knew when they might be useful. Fortunately the luggage allowance in business class was fairly generous.

Tony had worked miracles at the US Embassy in London and had fixed within twenty-four hours both a letter of introduction and the required non-immigrant work visa. Consequently, apart from the usual lengthy queue, I had no difficulty in clearing US Immigration and Customs.

There was even a driver waiting for me in the arrivals hall with HINKLEY written in large letters on an iPad screen.

'That's me,' I said, going up to him.

'Welcome to America,' he said, taking my luggage trolley. 'I'm parked across the road in the lot.'

I followed him out of the terminal into bright sunshine.

Today must be one of the nearly-90-degree days, I thought, as I rapidly started to perspire under the intense rays. It is easy to forget how much further south Washington, DC is compared to London. Apart from Alaska, not a single part of the United States is as far north as any part of the United Kingdom, with Washington at the same latitude as Lisbon in Portugal. Perhaps I wouldn't need my scarf and gloves after all.

Thankfully, the car was air-conditioned and the driver also knew where we were going, which is more than I did. He took me to a hotel in Arlington where the reception staff were expecting me.

'Someone called Mr Andretti made the reservation this morning,' said the young woman behind the desk. 'He didn't say when you were leaving.' She raised her eyebrows in a questioning manner.

'That's right,' I said. 'I don't yet know.'

My accommodation was more of an apartment than a regular hotel room, with a small kitchen plus sitting room as well as bedroom and bathroom. It overlooked the Pentagon, Arlington National Cemetery and the Potomac River, with the Lincoln

Memorial and the rest of Washington's iconic buildings clearly visible in the distance.

As I stood by the picture window taking in the spectacular view, I had mixed emotions. Part of me was excited to be here in a new place, with a new task among people who did not know me, just as I had longed for, but I was suddenly overwhelmed by the undertaking ahead of me.

I had done some research on FACSA and had been amazed to discover that it had over 800 federal agents and nearly 2,000 other employees, most of them at its Virginia headquarters. Even the horseracing team, one of the smallest sections in the agency, was larger than I was used to at the BHA.

How was I going to discover a mole in that lot?

A knock at my door brought me back from my daydreaming. It was Tony.

'Welcome, Jeff,' he said, shaking my hand. 'Everything OK?'

'Fine,' I said. 'Good flight, and this is very comfortable.' I waved my hand around.

He smiled. 'Anything you need?'

'Yes,' I said. 'I need information. In particular I need copies of the personnel files for all your racing team and the results of your communication inquiry.'

He nodded but looked troubled.

'I'm not sure I can get the personnel files.'

'You're Deputy Director,' I said. 'Surely the files are not confidential from you.'

'It is not the confidentiality that's the problem,

34

although they are, it's that I don't want anyone to know why you are here, not even the personnel team.'

'Tony, I really need that info. Otherwise I'll be wasting my time. I should really have the opportunity to study it before I arrive at your offices on Monday.'

'I'll get on to it. Anything else?'

'Yes. I also need details of all the operations that you have launched, including those that you feel were compromised. There has to be a common link. And I need direct access to you at any time.'

'I'll give you my private cell number,' Tony said. 'Never ever contact me at the agency, either in person or by using agency comms.'

'I thought I was here as your guest, as you were mine at the BHA.'

'My trip to the BHA was made without the knowledge of anyone at FACSA other than the Director. As far as anyone else at the agency is concerned, I was away on annual leave travelling in Europe with my wife, Harriet. Your cover is that you are here under our international exchange scheme for law-enforcement agencies simply to observe our methods of operation.'

'But the British Horseracing Authority is not a law-enforcement agency.'

'I know but it is as good as. The exchange scheme was the best excuse the Director and I could think of. All federal agencies have observers from other national police forces, mostly from those where the US is helping to set up law enforcement such as in Afghanistan and Iraq. So our staff are used to visitors but, as such, you would not have direct access to the Deputy Director. Therefore you must never contact me except through my private cell. And never refer to anyone about my time in London. That's essential. I do not want to give our mole friend any cause for alarm.'

There was something about the way he said it that made the hairs on my neck stand up.

'What are you not telling me?' I looked him directly in the eye.

He turned away.

'What is it?' I asked.

'It might not be connected.'

'What might not be connected?'

He looked back at me.

'You are not the first person we have approached to assist us.'

He paused.

'Who is the other person?' I asked.

'Was,' Tony said. 'He's dead. He was killed last December in an auto wreck on I-95 south of Baltimore.'

'Accident? Or deliberate?'

'There was a thorough investigation by the Maryland State Police. Their conclusion was that he went to sleep while driving home late at night. His vehicle left the road, hit a tree and caught fire. Toxicology tests showed he'd been drinking.'

'Didn't your agency initiate its own investigation?' I asked.

'How could we?' Tony said. 'It was outside our jurisdiction.'

'Who was he exactly?'

'His name was Jason Connor. He was a journalist who wrote about horseracing for a magazine called *Sports Illustrated*.'

I nodded. I'd heard of it.

'How did you come to use him?'

'Initially, Connor went to NYRA last October because he was concerned about blood doping in racehorses at Belmont during their fall meet. He had seen some transfusion apparatus at a training barn at the track that he felt was suspicious.'

'NYRA?' I pronounced it as a word in the same way as Tony had.

'New York Racing Association. They control horseracing at the three tracks in New York State. It was NYRA who contacted us. We initiated a raid on the barn and we found absolutely nothing. The whole place had obviously been steam-cleaned. I have never seen a barn so spotless and disinfected. You could have eaten your dinner off the stall floors. And the horses had been sent away to Kentucky for what was described as a *vacation*. I ask you. Some of them had been due to race at the track that week. The whole thing was a farce.'

Tony shook his head.

'Jason Connor was furious. What he was really after, of course, was an exclusive for his magazine and now he wouldn't get one. He blamed both the agency and NYRA for leaking the information. At first we dismissed his notions as just the ranting of an angry man, but then I started looking at how often our operations were being compromised. That's when I went back to him to ask him for help.'

'And you now think his death was to do with that?'

'The Chief Medical Examiner for Maryland declared his death was accidental but I've never liked coincidences. On the very day Jason Connor died, he'd been to Laurel Park racetrack to question a groom who had previously been working at the barn at Belmont.'

'What did the groom say?'

'I don't know. Connor never got to report back and the groom has since vanished. Not that that's particularly unusual. It happens all the time. He was probably an illegal alien who was frightened away by the attention.'

'Didn't you try to find him?' I asked.

'Of course. But trainers' record-keeping is not always great at the tracks. Turns out the groom had a work permit issued on forged paperwork in the name of a 26-year-old Mexican called Juan Martinez. That may or may not be his real name. Martinez is by far the most common surname in Mexico, much more so than Smith is here. And they didn't even have a photo.'

'Who did the looking?' I asked.

'What do you mean?'

'Was it someone from your agency?'

'I did it myself,' Tony said. 'I was once a detective in the Bronx. I reckon I still know the moves but this one was a dead end.'

'So who at the agency knew about Jason Connor?'

'Everyone in the racing section knew he'd been to NYRA with the original concerns. That was common knowledge. It was with the help of his information that we set up the operation.'

'Who knew he'd also been approached to help find your leak?'

'Supposedly only the Director, the chief of the horseracing team, and me.'

'Who is the chief of the horseracing team?'

'Norman Gibson. He's an ex-cop from Chicago.'

'Do you trust him?'

'I would say so, yes.'

'Does he know about the real reason I'm here?' I asked.

'No. He does not.'

'So you don't trust him that much,' I said. 'How about the Director of FACSA? Do you trust him more?'

'I'd trust him with my life,' Tony said.

'How about with mine?'

It felt like the stakes had suddenly been raised dramatically.

It was clear to me that, whatever the Maryland Medical Examiner might say, Tony believed that the death of Jason Connor and the investigation into the agency leak were connected. And I didn't like coincidences either.

'Why didn't you tell me all this in London?' I asked.

Tony looked uncomfortable. 'I don't know. Maybe I was afraid you wouldn't come.'

He clearly didn't know me very well.

'OK,' I said, clapping my hands together. 'In the light of all that, we need to beef up our security. First, you shouldn't be here now, it is a risk we ought not be taking.'

'I told no one I was coming here, not even Harriet.'

'No matter,' I said. 'You are Deputy Director of an agency that employs over two thousand people. Your offices are up the road from here. Even on a Saturday, one of those employees might have seen you arrive as they walked their dog. Then they might mention it to a colleague, just in passing, and so on. You never know who is watching or listening.'

Tony nodded.

'Also,' I said, 'it was a mistake to give your name when you made the hotel reservation. The front desk staff told me it was made by a Mr Andretti.'

'I had to use a credit card to confirm.'

'Your private card?'

'The agency's.'

'Who has access to the statements?'

'I have to sign them off for the finance team.'

'Won't someone question a charge for a hotel so close to the offices?'

'I'll say we were entertaining a guest,' Tony said.

'And the next question would be who and why. What are you going to do? Lie? Lies get you into trouble if only because someone in the finance team will think you're having an affair – getting a little bit more than only a ham sandwich during your lunch break.

I will pay for the hotel with my own credit card. You can reimburse me at a later stage.'

Tony nodded. 'I'll give you my cell number.' He reached for the notepad and pen next to the hotel phone.

'No,' I said. 'Not secure enough. I will buy two pay-as-you-go phones. One will be delivered by courier to your office marked for your attention only. We will only use those to talk to each other. You must not use that phone for any other reason.'

Tony looked rather sceptical that such a thing was needed.

'Tony,' I said firmly, 'this is important. We must take no unnecessary risks. Get the personnel files and have them delivered to me here, preferably by tomorrow. Pay cash for the delivery and arrange it yourself well away from Arlington. And don't use the agency address on the paperwork.'

'OK,' he said. 'I'll get on it.'

'Now, who do I report to and what have they been told?'

'Norman Gibson is expecting you on Monday morning. He's been told you are from England and are part of the international observer scheme.'

'Does he know I work for the British Horseracing Authority?'

'All he's been told is that you are from England and you are to be shown the workings of our horseracing section.'

'I think that I'll say I am from the BHA. It's too

dangerous otherwise. Am I supposed to be sponsored by the British Government?'

'Yes,' Tony said, 'through the Embassy. That's how exchanges have been organised in the past.'

'Let's hope your mole doesn't have a friend who works at the British Embassy.'

'Do you think he will check?'

'I would if I were him,' I said. 'I'd be hugely suspicious of anyone turning up unexpectedly. I expect him to verify my story down to the very last detail. That's why it is essential he can find me at the BHA.'

I was reminded of the advice I'd been given in the army by an MI6 operative – a spook. 'Lie only when it is absolutely necessary,' he had said. 'Make your cover story as true as it can be. Otherwise it will be the little things that catch you out while you are concentrating only on the big ones.'

'I'll get on to Paul Maldini in London to warn him,' I said.

'What about the Embassy?'

'If Norman Gibson has already been told that it has been arranged through the Embassy then we'll have to take the chance. Changing things now will draw more attention.'

'Norman may not have told anyone else,' Tony said.

'No matter. Leave it.'

I did not want anyone else knowing the truth.

My life might depend upon it.

4

On Sunday morning I walked down the street to the Fashion Centre at Pentagon City, a vast shopping mall over four floors with everything from major international department stores to a shop dedicated only to the finer art of men's shaving.

I was searching for a mobile-phone store. There were two and, in one of them, I found what I was looking for.

'This one won't go on the Internet.' The young sales assistant was doing his best to direct me towards one of his more expensive models.

'I know,' I replied patiently. 'It's for my mother and she doesn't really understand technology.' In fact, my mother had died when mobile phones were still the size of a brick, but the young man wasn't to know that. 'This is the model I have been recommended by her care home. I'll take two of them.'

'Two?' He shook his head. 'I don't know if we have two. No one ever wants phones like this any more.'

He went off into the back still shaking his head but triumphantly returned holding two boxes from which he blew off the dust.

'You're lucky,' he said. 'These are the last ones. The

company is discontinuing this item when they've all gone.'

'It will still work though, won't it?' I asked with mild concern.

'Sure,' he said. 'It'll work fine for calls and texts, but it is not 4G. It's not even 3G and doesn't have Bluetooth, GPS or even a camera. Are you sure you still want it? The iPhone 6 does far more. That's like a full-blown computer in your pocket and very good value. We have it on special offer.'

His enthusiasm was almost infectious.

'These are just perfect,' I said, touching the two boxes in front of me on the counter. Perfect, I thought, if you wanted phones that weren't 'smart'. Smartphones might be great for accessing the Internet and for using the thousands of apps available for download, but they could also be tracked and hacked.

'Right,' said the young man, slightly deflated. 'Do you want them on a contract?'

'No. Pay-as-you-go.'

'It is cheaper on a contract,' he said, 'in the long run.'

'But I'm not sure my mother has a long run,' I said, smiling at him. 'Pay-as-you-go will be fine.'

'For both?'

'Yes,' I said. 'For both. My mother has a habit of mislaying things so I'm buying her two.'

He clearly thought I was mad but he inserted SIM cards into the phones before topping them up with a hundred dollars each of credit. More than enough, I thought, for calls and texts between Tony and myself over the next few weeks.

I paid for it all with cash and gave a made-up name and address to the young man for the guarantee – just to be on the safe side.

Next I went into a computer store and bought a desktop colour printer, spare ink cartridges, a USB connecting lead and some paper.

Finally, I went to the FedEx Office Print-and-Ship store on Crystal Drive, conveniently open on a Sunday, and arranged for one of the phones to be delivered early the following morning to Tony Andretti at FACSA.

'Any message?' asked the young woman behind the counter.

'No,' I said. 'Only the box, thank you.'

I again paid in cash and gave a false return address. The transaction might have been anonymous but I had noticed the CCTV camera in the corner of the store, silently recording the faces of everyone who entered. I wondered whether I should have used one of my disguises, but perhaps I was being paranoid about secrecy.

But it was better to be paranoid, I thought, than dead.

I spent some of Sunday afternoon sightseeing.

To be precise, I took a taxi from my hotel across the Potomac to the Thomas Jefferson Memorial.

My first disappointment was that the cherry

blossom was well past its prime, with much of it now decaying on the ground beneath the trees that surrounded the memorial. But there was enough remaining to give me some idea of how magnificent it must have been only a week or so earlier.

I climbed the circular marble steps and walked between the classical Ionic columns. In the centre, under the shallow marble-clad dome, stood a nineteen-feet-high bronze statue of the third president of the United States. I looked up at the face of the man after whom I had been named.

Jefferson Hinkley.

As a child I had hated my name. I was made fun of at my junior school because of it and I had vowed at the time that, thereafter, I would be known only as Jeff.

Curiously, in the presence of his likeness, I felt a slight affinity towards the man. Not that he was buried here. His final resting place was on his family plantation at Charlottesville, about 100 miles south-west, and this memorial had been built more than a hundred years after his death.

Jefferson was perhaps best known as the principal author of the US Declaration of Independence and part of his preamble was cut into the marble: *We hold these truths to be self-evident, that all men are created equal, that they are endowed by their Creator with certain inalienable rights, that among these are life, liberty and the pursuit of happiness ...*

Strange, therefore, that Jefferson had been such

a strong supporter of slavery. Indeed, he'd even had African slaves working in the White House during his presidency and, after his death, 130 slaves from his plantation were sold at auction to help pay his debts.

All affinity gone, I walked away without a backward glance across the bridge into West Potomac Park and on to the memorial of my other presidential namesake.

In full, I was officially Jefferson Roosevelt Hinkley.

I was never able to ascertain the reason why my parents had named me after dead American presidents. By the time I realised where my strange forenames came from, my mother had died and my father claimed it had been her idea and he couldn't remember the reason. In truth, he couldn't remember much, other than where he had hidden his whisky.

I had always imagined that the Roosevelt after whom I had been named was Franklin Delano, the hero president of the New Deal and the Second World War, rather than his fifth-cousin Theodore – he of teddy-bear fame – who only became president due to the timely assassination of his predecessor.

The memorial to FDR was very different to that of Jefferson, being very much a creation of the mid-1990s. It lacked the grandeur of the earlier structure, consisting of four outdoor 'rooms' depicting the four terms of his presidency.

One of the many inscriptions on the memorial caught my eye, an extract from Roosevelt's inaugural speech on first becoming President in 1933.

The only thing we have to fear is fear itself.
I hoped he was right.

'Mr Hinkley,' called the young woman at Reception as I walked into the hotel, 'package for you.'

I signed for a small plain-white padded envelope with my name written on the front in pencil. It had to be from Tony, I thought. No one else knew I was at this hotel.

The envelope contained two USB flash drives and a short handwritten note:

Here are the agency personnel files, the communication inquiry and the operation reports. I had them copied from the off-site data backup server so no one at the agency should be aware. I've asked my wife to deliver the package.

He'd clearly been busy in the twenty-four hours since we'd met.

The flash drives were each sixty-four gigabytes and they were both crammed with data.

I sat at the desk under the picture window and opened the first drive on my computer. It contained the personnel files of not only the racing section but all 2,631 employees of FACSA, as of the previous Friday. They were listed alphabetically by last name and it took me some time to navigate my way around the index to access them by section. But, before long, I had found the files of the eight agents working specifically on horseracing, together with their section head and six support staff – two intelligence analysts, one IT specialist and three admin assistants.

I connected the new printer to my computer with the USB lead. I had purposely not bought one that worked wirelessly and, furthermore, I ensured that both the Bluetooth and Wi-Fi capabilities on my laptop were switched off. Unlikely as it might be, I did not want someone else remotely snooping on *my* snooping.

I printed out the front page for each of the fifteen files and laid them out on the floor in a large semi-circle round my chair. Fifteen faces stared up at me like arrest mugshots. I stared back at them.

Was one of these faces really that of a mole – someone who was prepared to forewarn wrongdoers of an impending raid? And if so, why? For financial gain? Or out of some misplaced sense of mischief?

Six of the fifteen were women – two of the agents along with four of the support staff.

Where the hell did I begin?

I spent the next four hours cross-referencing the names of the fifteen with their phone and email records that Tony had provided.

It was a mammoth job and I had barely scratched the surface by the time the figures began swimming in front of my eyes from tiredness.

By then I had discovered only one thing of interest.

I had no absolute proof, no smoking gun, but I was pretty sure that two of the agents were engaged in a secret relationship. It was something about the tone of their emails, together with the number and timing of the phone calls between them that left little doubt.

I looked more closely at their files.

Robert Wade, known as Bob, was forty-two, a former DC Metro-area traffic cop, married with two teenage daughters. He had been recruited into FACSA at the time of its creation sixteen years previously and was now considered to be one of its senior agents. According to comments in his assessments, he was being tipped as a future head of the horseracing section.

Steffi Dean was a recent recruit, having been a field agent for only a year. A graduate of the United States Air Force Academy, she had spent seven years in the service as a logistics officer, rising to the rank of captain before quitting the military to join the agency. At twenty-nine, she was thirteen years younger than Bob Wade, and single.

I leaned back in the chair and yawned.

I wasn't here to pass judgement on the morals of the agents, just on their honesty. We all have our little secrets. It was only those that harboured corruption that I was after.

I went on through the lists but my concentration levels were dropping so much that I was wasting my time.

I glanced at the brightly lit red digits of the hotel alarm clock – 10.02 p.m. Hardly time for bed, but it was 3 a.m. back in London and I could hardly keep my eyes open.

I would have to continue in the morning.

As requested, I presented myself at the Federal Anti-Corruption in Sports Agency at nine o'clock on Monday morning dressed in my best Armani suit plus silk tie. First impressions were important and an Englishman abroad would be expected to be smart.

The agency was housed in what appeared to be a normal, modern, glass-and-concrete office block, whose architect had clearly devoted only a minimum of imagination to its design.

But there was nothing normal about the security arrangements.

The building and its associated parking lots were surrounded by an eight-foot-high steel fence topped with razor wire, and the main gate would not have looked out of place at a top-security prison.

When I arrived on foot there was a line of vehicles being checked through, each of them having to first negotiate a tight chicane of large concrete blocks before being searched by the guards, some of whom had machine carbines slung across their chests.

'Papers?' demanded one of the guards in a manner that reminded me of a Gestapo officer in a war film.

I handed over the letter of introduction I had been given from the US Embassy in London together with my passport. The guard left me standing outside the pedestrian gate as he went into the guardhouse to check my credentials.

I waited.

There was a large notice on the guardhouse wall that declared that all firearms were prohibited on these premises unless authorised by the Attorney General of the United States. Beside it was another that announced that it was unlawful for more than twenty-eight persons to occupy the guardhouse at any one time, by order of the US Department of Homeland Security.

I was attempting to count the guards, to ensure there were fewer than twenty-eight, when the Gestapo man returned and handed back the letter and my passport together with a FACSA-branded lanyard attached to a rectangular pass with 'VISITOR' stamped diagonally across it in large red letters.

'Use the front door,' he said, letting me through the gate and pointing across at the building. 'Report to security inside.'

More security? What are they hiding?

I had to empty my pockets and then pass through a metal detector before I was directed towards the building's main reception desk where again I had to produce my letter of introduction.

'Norman Gibson is expecting me,' I said.

I was asked to wait.

The receptionist made a telephone call and, presently, a man in his late forties appeared from the lifts and strode purposefully towards me.

'Jeff Hinkley?' he asked. 'I'm Norman Gibson.'

We shook hands.

'Delighted to meet you,' I said.

'Let's go up.'

He used his lanyard pass to activate yet another security barrier and ushered me through.

'It is like getting into Fort Knox,' I said.

'Blame Timothy McVeigh,' Norman replied.

In April 1995 Timothy James McVeigh had detonated a 5,000lb bomb outside the federal office building in Oklahoma City, killing 168 people, including nineteen young children in a day-care centre. Needless to say, security since then had been greatly beefed-up at all US federal buildings.

'I'll fix it so you get your own pass,' Norman said. 'Then it'll be easier for you to get in. Security is a bore but I suppose it's better than being dead.'

'Much,' I agreed. 'And the threats seem to be ever-increasing.'

'You're so right. We have more than our fair share of nutcases who blame the government for everything. Plus we have the anti-abortionists and the animal liberation lot to contend with – both worthy groups, I'm sure, but they seem to attract extremists. And don't even mention the Islamic militants . . .'

I thought about the security arrangements at my office in London – or rather the lack of them. There was a reception desk in the lobby by the front door of the building but it was usually unmanned. The main reception for the horseracing authority was on the second floor and that was dead easy to bypass.

We took the lift up and I followed Norman along a corridor and through two more security doors before we reached his office, a glassed-off corner of an otherwise open-plan space.

'Welcome to the racing section at FACSA,' he said.

'Thank you.'

'Who are you with?'

'The BHA,' I said. 'The British Horseracing Authority.'

'Is that a government agency?'

'No,' I said. 'It was set up by the British Jockey Club and is wholly funded by the racing industry. We're responsible for the regulation of all horseracing in Great Britain.'

'We could do with something like that here. American racing is still regulated by the individual states, each of them with different rules. Everyone agrees it would make sense to have a nationwide authority but the states are reluctant to give up their power bases. They all think they know best. That's why we at FACSA act as the de facto upholder of common standards using federal anti-corruption legislation.'

It sounded like a line he'd used often before.

'But it is a bureaucratic nightmare.' He rolled his eyes. 'Everything to do with governments is.'

'The BHA gets no financial support from the British government, nor do we answer to it.'

'Lucky you,' Norman said. 'Now, how can we help you?'

'I've really come only to watch and listen,' I said. 'To study how you do things and compare them to our own methods. To see if there's something for us to learn.'

He nodded. 'I hope there is, but you have far more racing over there than we do here. Perhaps we should be the ones taking lessons.'

I smiled at him. 'Maybe there will be something I can spot that would be beneficial to us both.'

'Fair enough,' Norman said, although my smile was not reciprocated and I detected a slight annoyance that an outsider was here at all, let alone a foreigner with more experience of racing.

'I'll try not to get in your way,' I said.

'Good. We've not had a foreign observer in this section before. Most go to the FBI anyway, although I think our baseball team had someone from Japan last year.'

'How many sections are there in FACSA?' I asked.

'Lots,' he replied somewhat unhelpfully. 'The major sports each have their own – baseball and basketball are the biggest. Then there's the Olympic Games section. That's where it all started. There was such a hoo-ha over allegations of bribery to get the Winter Olympic Games at Salt Lake City back in '02 that the Department of Justice set up FACSA to ensure it could never happen again.'

I had a vague memory of all the fuss at the time.

'You should have a FIFA section,' I said with a laugh. 'That would keep you busy.'

'We do,' he replied seriously. 'We pass our findings on to the FBI as we have no jurisdiction outside the US. Hence it was FBI agents who made arrests with the Swiss police at FIFA headquarters back in May 2015.'

'Have you been with the agency long?' I asked.

'I joined twelve years ago,' he said. 'Moved from Chicago. The winters were too long and cold up there.' He smiled but it didn't really reach his eyes.

And I knew the real reason why he'd left Chicago.

I'd been up early and studied his personnel file.

He had been a high-flying detective in the Chicago Police Department, promoted young to be commander of the 26th District on the city's South Side. However, his glittering police career had stalled somewhat when five of his junior officers had been arrested for planting incriminating evidence to secure a conviction. Even though the investigation by the FBI had concluded that Gibson had not known about or been involved in the conspiracy, he had done the honourable thing and resigned.

That principled action had been rewarded by the call to set up the racing section at FACSA.

There was a knock on the office door. Norman looked over my head and stood up. 'I've arranged for you to spend time with one of our special agents, Frank Bannister.' He waved the man in. 'Frank, this is Jeff Hinkley, from England.'

I stood and shook Frank's hand while we both looked each other up and down. He was taller than me by at least four inches, and broader too. He squeezed my hand hard as if to make sure I knew that he was also stronger. He smiled down at me and I smiled back without a waver. If he wanted to play silly games, so be it, but I wouldn't rise to his bait.

'Frank will show you the ropes,' Norman said. 'Stick to him like glue.'

Frank didn't look best pleased at the prospect but he was civil enough – just.

He showed me round the office and I met the other staff.

'Bob Wade,' one of them said, smiling warmly and offering his hand. 'Welcome to the madhouse.' He laughed with a distinctive rapid-fire guffaw.

'Thank you,' I said.

Steffi Dean sat at the desk next to his. Not conducive, I thought, to hard work. I also shook her hand and wondered what she saw in Special Agent Wade, who appeared somewhat older in the flesh than in his personnel-file mugshot.

'Are you all *special* agents?' I asked.

'Sure are,' Frank said. 'All FACSA agents are special.'

I wasn't sure if he was being facetious.

'Ignore him,' Steffi said. 'But he's right. Special agent is a rank and all FACSA agents are special agents. We're all L-E-Os, just like the special agents in the FBI and DEA.'

'L-E-Os?'

'Law-enforcement officers.'

'Does anyone have only regular agents?' I asked.

'Not here,' Frank said loudly. 'Nothing regular about this lot.' He laughed expansively at his own joke while Bob and Steffi looked slightly embarrassed.

'Does everyone carry a gun?' I asked.

It was difficult not to notice the automatic pistols that each of them had in holsters either on their belts or under their shoulders. The Attorney General had clearly been busy with his authorisations.

'Only the special agents,' Steffi said. She patted the gun as if it were a family pet. 'Never leaves my side. I even sleep with it under my pillow.'

I wondered if there were two guns under her pillow when she slept with Bob Wade.

'Have you used yours much?' I asked her.

'Only on the range. We all have to pass a marksman test every year in order to keep our special-agent status. But I've never had to use my weapon in the field. Not yet, anyway.'

'Is it loaded?'

She smiled at me as if I was an imbecile. 'Of course it's loaded. No point in having it otherwise.' She removed the gun from the holster. 'Glock twenty-two-C, point-four-zero-calibre automatic.' She pushed a latch on the pistol grip and slid out the magazine, visibly full of shiny brass bullets. 'Fifteen rounds per mag. Smith and Wesson hollow-nosed expanding ammunition. And I have a silencer plus two more full mags on my belt.'

'A silencer?'

'In case we need to be covert,' she replied. 'But we don't use it as a general rule. It upsets the balance of the weapon in the hand. Tends to make the shots go high and right.'

She snapped the magazine back in and returned the pistol to its holster in a single movement. She clearly was completely at ease with such deadly apparatus.

'I thought expanding bullets were illegal,' I said. 'Aren't they against the Geneva Convention?'

Expanding bullets would flatten out or fragment on impact with anything hard, like human bone, causing serious trauma over a much wider area than a normal bullet. They had been much feared during the American Civil War due to the horrendous wounds they produced.

'It was the Hague Convention,' Bob Wade said. 'But it only applies to warfare, not to law enforcement. All US police forces use them.'

I must have looked somewhat aghast that ammunition banned in war as being too brutal and cruel was standard issue on the streets of America.

'Expanding bullets,' Bob said in explanation, 'are less likely to pass right through suspects and into innocent bystanders behind them. They also have more stopping power.'

Nevertheless, I was still not convinced that using them was ethical. No wonder more than a thousand members of the American public were shot dead by police each and every year.

Tony Andretti had said in the lay-by near Oxford that he couldn't get his head round Brits and guns.

Well, I couldn't get my head round Yanks and guns either. Statistics showed that, in all circumstances, you were seventy times more likely to be shot to death in the United States than in England. And that must have something to do with the number of guns at hand.

And what worried me most was that the section mole was likely to have a Glock 22C holstered on his hip with fifteen .40 expanding bullets in the magazine, plus a silencer and two more loaded mags on his belt.

I really *would* have to watch my back.

5

By the end of the day I had been round the whole office and met all the section staff except for the most junior admin assistant, who was away on maternity leave.

I had a good memory for faces and facts and I had been easily able to match the individuals to their life stories as outlined in the personnel files. The only difficult thing was not appearing to know something that I hadn't been told. For example, I nearly asked one of the two intelligence analysts if he liked working for FACSA more than for a bank when he hadn't actually mentioned his previous employment.

'Monday is a good day for you to start,' Frank Bannister said over coffee in the FACSA cafeteria at lunchtime. 'It's when all the special agents try to be in the office for meetings and such. Mondays and Tuesdays are usually dark at the major tracks, unless they're public holidays.'

By 'dark', he meant there was no racing.

'Do you go to the tracks a lot?' I asked.

'I usually go somewhere every week,' he replied. 'All of us do. It is as important for us to be seen as it is for us to see what's going on. I tend to concentrate on the northeastern tracks but I love going to the smaller ones too, especially those that race only for a few days each year. Over the years I've been to almost all of them.'

'It must do wonders for your frequent-flier miles.'

'We don't get them,' he said. 'We often travel on government jets. Even when we are on commercial flights, federal-service rates don't earn you miles.'

'Where are you going this week?' I asked.

'Highlight of the year,' he said with a big smile. 'Louisville for the Derby. You coming?'

'You bet,' I said.

For years I had wanted to go to the Kentucky Derby but it was run on the first Saturday in May, usually on the same day as the 2000 Guineas at Newmarket, and my presence had always been expected at one of the biggest days of the English racing season.

Now I was free of that obligation and the prospect of going to Churchill Downs thrilled me.

'How do I get there?' I asked.

'The whole section is going Wednesday. Make sure the boss puts you on the manifest.'

'I sure will.'

Overall, it was an interesting but somewhat frustrating day.

Whereas I was welcome to wander round and speak to the section staff throughout the morning, I was sidelined for much of the afternoon as all but three of them gathered in a room for a meeting on the second floor. A meeting from which I had been specifically excluded.

'What's going on?' I asked one of the non-participants, one of the two intelligence analysts, who sat resolutely at his computer throughout.

'Planning and briefing for an operation.'

'Why aren't you there?'

'No point,' he said. 'The op is not based on any intel I've looked at, and I don't get involved with planning.'

'When is the op?' I asked hopefully.

'Sorry. I can't say. It's a secret.'

I suppose I shouldn't really have minded. Back in London I'd given Tony rather a hard time for letting too many people know about FACSA operations so I could now hardly expect to be one of them.

Mind you, to my sure knowledge, there were at least eleven at the meeting, which was still far too many for something so secret.

'Where does most of your intelligence come from?' I asked the analyst.

'Information comes from a variety of sources. It is analysis that turns info into intelligence.' He sounded rather full of his own importance.

'What sort of sources?' I asked, ignoring his second comment. 'In England we have a network of covert informants from within the racing industry.'

He nodded. 'Us too. But they're mostly disgruntled grooms who have a score to settle with their employers either for being fired or being overlooked for promotion. Much of the stuff is just malicious lies with no substance. It's my job to apply contextual knowledge to sort the truth from the trash.'

Perhaps he *was* important after all.

The operational planning meeting went on and on, and there was a limit to the amount of time I could hang around doing nothing.

The hands on the clock moved slowly round to four-thirty.

'Tell Frank I've gone, will you?' I said. 'I'll see him in the morning.'

The analyst simply waved an acknowledgement and went on studying his computer screen.

After escaping the security cordon, with the photograph on my new shiny identity pass scrutinised at every door and gateway, I walked back to the hotel via a 7-Eleven store, where I picked up a few essential supplies like coffee, milk, cereal and so on, as well as a ready-meal of cheese and pasta for my dinner.

Back in my room, I called Paul Maldini. It was ten in the evening in London but he picked up straight away.

'You were right,' he said. 'There was a call to the office from the US asking about you.'

'What time?'

'At five, just as I was leaving.'

Midday in Washington.

'Man or woman?'

'Man.'

'What did he say?'

'He asked for you by name. I'd had Reception direct any calls for you to my phone.'

'What did you say?'

'I told him that Jeff Hinkley was away and was not available and could I help him. Then he asked me where you were so I told him you were in the United States.'

'Did he say anything else?'

'He asked what you were doing in the US and how long you'd be away. I told him you were visiting another racing authority and I didn't know for how long. Just as you told me to. Was that right?'

'Yes, Paul, it was. Thank you. Did you happen to ask the man for his name?'

'I did but he said that didn't matter, then he hung up.'

'Any clues about his voice?'

'He had an American accent,' he said. 'Other than that I can't help you. I couldn't tell you which part. All Yanks sound the same to me.'

Must be his Italian heritage, I thought. Tony Andretti would have been appalled.

I thought back to what I'd been doing at midday.

Even though Norman Gibson had told me to stick to Frank Bannister like glue, I'd been intent on meeting as many of the section staff as I could and, at midday, I had been moving from desk to desk introducing myself as a member of the BHA Integrity Department.

I couldn't be exactly sure when I'd rejoined Frank

to go down to the cafeteria. Probably nearer 12.30. So any of the men in the section could have made the call. And why shouldn't they? Other than a letter from the US Embassy in London and my passport, I had no documents confirming my bona fides.

Had I called FACSA when Tony had turned up in London to check up on him?

No, I hadn't. But these guys were attached to the US government and far more security-minded than the BHA.

Maybe the call had been merely an innocent check-up.

But why then had the caller not given his name when asked?

I used my new pay-as-you-go phone to call Tony.

He answered at the second ring.

'The phone arrived safely then?' I said.

'First thing this morning. Where are you now?'

'Back in my hotel. Where are you? Can you talk?'

'I'm in my car,' he said. 'Still in the parking lot at FACSA. I'm leaving for the day.'

'Are you alone?'

'Yes.'

'Good. Stay and listen. I need a couple of things.'

'Shoot.'

'First, someone from here made a call today to the BHA offices asking about me. It may have been an innocent check or it might have been our friend being suspicious. The person declined to give his name. Can

you access the section phone records? Can you find
out if anyone called London at midday today?'

'I'll try,' he said, not sounding particularly hopeful.

'But don't tell anyone else. If it was our friend who
made the call, I don't want to spook him.'

'What's the other thing?' Tony asked.

'I was excluded from an operational planning meeting today. If this is another operation where the details
are likely to be leaked, I need to know what's going
on. I can't do this job if I'm to be kept in the dark.'

There was a pause from the other end.

'Tony?' I said.

'I'm thinking,' he said. 'When Jason Connor first
came to me with his suspicions, I sent a memo to
all staff reminding them of the need for secrecy and
not to let any non-agency personnel be aware of our
operations. It would be a bit hypocritical for me to
now insist you were brought into the loop.'

'I agree,' I said. 'And it would flag up to our friend
that I'm more than just an observer. But I still need
the information. You'll have to get it for me. And
Tony, could you make a list for me of everyone who
knows about the operation?'

'No problem,' Tony said. 'I was at the meeting
today so I already have the details. How shall I get
them to you?'

'Could your wife deliver them? After dark.'

'No problem,' he said again. 'I'll go back in and
make copies of the paperwork.'

'Tony,' I said. 'Be careful. If FACSA is anything

like the BHA, you can't make copies without entering your personal code on the copy machine.'

'OK,' he said with a resigned sigh. 'I'll use the small copier in my PA's office.'

As far as I was concerned no precaution was too minor to be ignored. In my experience, it was usually the accumulation of small clues that added up to create the big picture rather than any single dramatic revelation. The fewer traces we generated regarding the true purpose of my visit the better.

'I also need account details for all the racing section staff, preferably recent bank statements. Whoever is leaking information may be being paid for it. If so, we need to find those deposits.'

'That'll need court subpoenas,' Tony said.

'Then get them. But will the staff then know their statements are being looked at?'

'They shouldn't. I'll deal with it personally and the banks will get the subpoenas, not the staff. The need for discretion will be emphasised.'

'Good.'

'Anything else?'

'Yes,' I said. 'I want to go to the Kentucky Derby this Saturday. Frank Bannister told me the whole racing section is going to Louisville on Wednesday. Can you fix it so that I go with them?'

'Absolutely,' Tony said. 'The operation we were discussing today will be executed at Churchill Downs this coming weekend. I'll ensure you are included on the flight.'

'Carefully,' I said. 'You don't know me, remember.'

'I'll have a quiet word with Norman Gibson.'

'He's not in the loop,' I said. 'I'd prefer it to remain that way.'

'Don't you trust Norman?'

'I trust nobody to keep a secret that my life might depend on.' Not even you, I thought, but I decided not to say so.

The package from Tony arrived at nine o'clock as I was again studying the FACSA personnel files.

Out of curiosity, I had looked up Tony Andretti's own record.

He was 64 years old, having been born on Staten Island, New York, in the 1950s. He was not named Anthony, as I had assumed, but Antonio after his Italian father, and he was married with three grown-up sons. He and his wife Harriet now lived in Fairfax, Virginia, a few miles away from his office.

He had joined FACSA as a special agent direct from the NYPD when the agency had been first established. He had worked his way up through section chief to assistant director in charge of administration, and then finally to Deputy Director three years previously.

He had reached the pinnacle of his career. Simple research on the Internet showed that the Director was a political appointee, determined by the US President and, as with the FBI, the position was invariably awarded to someone outside the organisation.

Tony would not get to be Director.

I opened the package. It contained details of an operation to raid a trainer's barn at Churchill Downs to check for the improper use of medications in horses.

Unlike in the United Kingdom, where horses were trained 'at home' and then only taken to a racecourse by horsebox on the day of their race, racehorses in the US were trained at the track, living in barns on what was known as the backside or backstretch. Each individual trainer had a barn and there were accommodation blocks for the grooms.

The main reason for the difference lay in the way races were scheduled and that, in turn, was largely due to the differing surfaces on which the horses competed.

In the UK, the vast majority of races were run on turf rather than on dirt whereas in the States it was the reverse. Dirt tracks could take far more use than turf as they didn't cut up and were simply harrowed back into pristine condition after each race.

Consider Santa Anita Park, one of the major tracks in California. During the first six months of each year, there were eight, nine or even ten races a day on four days of every week. That was nearly nine hundred races in only half a year.

Compare that to Newbury racecourse, one of the busiest tracks in the UK, where twenty-nine days' racing were spread evenly across all twelve months. With seven races each time, at Newbury there were far less than a quarter of the races of Santa Anita over twice the time.

But the real difference was that the Santa Anita backside barns were also home to some two thousand racehorses that were also exercised on the dirt track every day. No turf racecourse could stand up to such punishment.

I read through the paperwork for the proposed raid and the details were surprising to say the least – *horrifying* might be a better word.

6

I was familiar with the British regulatory structure that had a simple but all-embracing rule in relation to drugs being present in a horse during a race – they aren't allowed and, if detected, severe penalties would follow.

In addition, certain substances were not permitted to be introduced into a horse's system at any time. They included all anabolic steroids, hormones, and any metabolic moderators such as insulin.

Reading one of the background briefing papers for the Churchill Downs raid, it became very clear to me that the situation in the United States was very different.

Anyone connected with racing worldwide was well aware of the widespread use in America of the drug furosemide, sold under the trade names Lasix or Salix. It is a potent diuretic and is used in horses to prevent bleeding in the lungs under extreme exertion, a condition known as EIPH, exercise-induced pulmonary haemorrhage. Whether they actually need it or not, almost every horse that races in North America has 500mg of the drug injected intravenously four hours before they race.

The diuretic effect is dramatic, with the horse producing ten to fifteen litres of urine in the first hour after administration of the drug. This in itself has a two-fold effect. First, it makes the horse ten to fifteen kilogrammes lighter, and second, it tends to flush out of the animal's system any other drugs, which then become impossible to detect in a post-race dope test.

And, boy, according to what I was reading, there were plenty of other drugs.

American racing was seemingly rife with them, and most were allowed by the various state rules, even though there were attempts to reduce the dependence.

In some states, the administration of any legal medication was permitted up to twenty-four hours before a race, while in others the period could vary from a few days to a few weeks before racing.

A particularly worrying aspect of drugs in American racing was the widespread use of anti-inflammatory and painkilling medication such as phenylbutazone, known as 'Bute', which was often administered intravenously, allowing a horse to race when otherwise it would be unable to do so.

In the UK, the racing authority warned trainers that such painkillers should be discontinued a minimum of eight days prior to a race. In practice, most trainers stopped any course of treatment at least two weeks beforehand so that no trace remained. Otherwise they would be liable to large fines and lengthy suspensions. However, in the US, use of such drugs right up to race day was common, and a 'positive' post-race test for Bute was not against the rules.

According to the briefing paper, the disturbing effect of this was that the drugs allowed horses to compete when really unfit to do so, masking injuries such as sprains and even slight cracks. This could result in catastrophic collapse, an all-too-frequent occurrence on American tracks, where the rate of horses fatally injured in flat races was twice that of the UK.

However, the purpose of the proposed raid at Churchill Downs was not to look for Lasix or Bute. Finding those would be expected. It was to test recent runners for anabolic steroids, in particular stanozolol, a drug that promotes growth of muscle and hence improves performance.

I knew all about that drug.

Back in 2013, the BHA had expelled trainer Mahmood Al Zarooni from all racing for eight years for giving it to horses in his care. And the discovery of stanozolol in his urine had been the reason Ben Johnson was stripped of the hundred-metre Olympic gold medal in Seoul, bringing disgrace on him and his sport.

In UK racing the rule was crystal clear. Anabolic steroids were banned in horses at any time. But in the United States things were not so straightforward. Their use had not been regulated at all until 2010 and, even since then, several anabolic steroids were permitted for therapeutic treatment up to thirty days before racing.

But, it seems, some old trainers found it difficult to learn new tricks.

FACSA had received intelligence that one such trainer, Hayden Ryder, based at Churchill Downs, was still using the methods of the past and injecting his horses much closer to race time than was permitted, relying on a hefty dose of Lasix on race day to wash traces of the illegals out of their system.

And who could really blame him. The potential gains were huge and typical penalties for getting caught very modest – a fifteen-day ban and a maximum fine of one thousand dollars.

The date of the raid was set for very early on the coming Saturday morning, the day of the Kentucky Derby, the aim being not so much to remove a miscreant trainer from the sport as to get maximum media coverage to demonstrate that horseracing will not tolerate cheating.

It was to be a major media moment.

Today was Monday. The raid was due in five days. That would give Ryder plenty of time to get rid of the evidence if he was made aware of what was going to happen. It might even give him the opportunity to arrange transportation of horses elsewhere to prevent them from being tested.

I read through everything in the package twice, including Tony's handwritten list of those present at the planning meeting.

I recognised most of the names. Section chief

Norman Gibson was on the list, as was Frank Bannister, together with the other seven FACSA special agents I had met earlier in the day. In addition there were two others from the section: one of the intelligence analysts plus an admin assistant.

Tony had told me he had been present at the meeting but there had been two other senior agency staff there as well – the head of the resource planning office, and the assistant director in charge of security.

Would one of these fourteen people really pass on information to Hayden Ryder?

And, if so, why? For what gain?

'Bring the op forward,' I said. 'Do it tonight or first thing tomorrow morning.'

It was late, well gone eleven, and I was speaking to Tony using our non-smart phones. I think I had woken him.

'That's logistically impossible,' he said, suppressing a yawn.

'Why?' I asked.

'Our raid team is still here in Virginia.'

'Have you no one in Louisville?'

'The nearest FACSA regional office would be Cincinnati, but that's concerned only with baseball and football. We also have one in Indianapolis but they deal with the NCAA.'

'NCAA?' I asked.

'College sports – sadly, no horseracing.'

'You surely don't get much corruption in college sports?'

'You must be joking,' Tony said. 'It's huge business. College football has three times as many spectators per annum as the NFL.'

'There must be someone else in Louisville who could act for you,' I said. 'How about the FBI?'

I could almost hear the cogs turning in his brain.

'Difficult, if not impossible,' he said. 'Use of anabolic steroids in horses close to a race may be a corrupt practice, as we see it, but does it actually break any federal law? The FBI would be unable to act unless they also suspected racketeering, such as making or taking illegal bets as a result of the steroid injections. And they would be most unlikely to mount a raid so quickly just on our say-so anyway.'

'Then get the FACSA team from here to Louisville tonight. Do the raid in the morning. If details of this operation are leaked to Hayden Ryder then you can expect to turn up at his barn on Saturday morning to find the place cleaner than a priest on Sunday. You'll find nothing. Even the drugged-up horses will have been moved out. Rather than being a media coup for FACSA, it will be a media disaster. You will be a laughing stock.'

There was a lengthy silence as if he had never considered the possibility.

'Tell me what to do,' he said finally.

In the end, Tony convinced me that he couldn't rouse the troops from their beds and arrange for them to be transported more than 450 miles in the dead of night.

'The raid is simply not important enough,' Tony said. 'I'd never get the authority for the cost. It is not as if the President's life is at stake or anything. It's only a few drugs.'

Yes, I thought, and drugs that weren't even illegal. Maybe if it had been a stash of cocaine or heroin, I'd have had more chance, but anabolic steroids occurred naturally in the human body and were regularly prescribed to thousands of citizens for the treatment of cancer and AIDS.

'I'll try to bring forward the move to Louisville from Wednesday to tomorrow,' Tony said. 'I'll also arrange to do the raid on Thursday morning.'

'Do it on Wednesday morning,' I said. 'The sooner the better. And don't tell anyone.'

'I'll have to tell them something. Everyone is expecting to be travelling on Wednesday.'

'Make up a reason,' I said. 'Say that flights are full on Wednesday so they have to go earlier.'

'We're due to travel on a government-owned aircraft out of Andrews.'

'Air Force One?'

'I wish,' Tony said with a laugh. 'Just a regular jet. I'll have to check if it's available tomorrow.'

'If not, get them onto commercial flights. Say the government plane has broken or something, but don't say anything about moving the raid forward. Say you need to gather them together for a rehearsal or something on Wednesday morning then, at the last minute, switch it for the real thing when it's too late for the information to be leaked.'

'I ought to discuss this with someone. For a start I would have to inform the US Department of Agriculture.'

'What on earth for? Don't you have the authority yourself?'

'It is not that,' Tony said. 'USDA provides the accredited veterinarians we need to take the blood samples. Also I have to liaise with the local Kentucky law enforcement. They're expecting us to go in on Saturday, not Wednesday. I don't want to start a shooting match between our agents and the Louisville Police Department.'

'Then do what you have to do,' I said wearily, 'but stress the need for confidentiality. Ask them not to even tell their wives and husbands. Secrecy is essential if we are not to waste our time, and far too many people know about this raid already.'

Add the vets from USDA and the local police force to those from the agency who knew and I was quite surprised it wasn't already on the Kentucky tourist information website as an upcoming attraction.

'I'll also have to talk it through with the Director,' Tony said. 'And I ought to consult Norman Gibson. He *is* the section chief.'

'But what if he's also the mole?'

*

The calm of Monday morning in the FACSA racing section had been replaced by a hive of activity twenty-four hours later.

'What's going on?' I asked.

'Ask the damn government,' Frank said crossly, as he collected papers from his desk and stuffed them angrily into a briefcase. 'I've been informed that our delightful private jet trip to Louisville is off. Some member of Congress has requisitioned the aircraft – probably to take his mistress on a vacation to Hawaii. So we've got to go commercial – and we're flying coach.' He threw his hands up in disgust. 'My flight leaves from National in two and a half hours and I've got to get home first to pack.'

'I thought we were going tomorrow.'

'We were but, apparently, there are no seats left tomorrow due to everyone else going to the Derby.'

'Is everyone going today?' I asked, all innocently.

'As far as I know,' Frank said. 'But not on the same flight. We're on all sorts. Some are having to go through Atlanta or Chicago, for God's sake. Atlanta is completely the wrong direction.'

'How about me?' I asked.

'Go see the boss,' Frank said. 'Maybe he can help you. I can't.'

With that he rushed off towards the exit.

I walked over and knocked on Norman Gibson's door.

He looked up and waved me in.

'Frank tells me he's off to Louisville,' I said.

'So am I. The whole section goes to the Derby.'

'How about me?' I asked.

The look on his face told me that he hadn't thought about me.

'Sorry,' he said. 'Er ... I don't know.'

'There's no point in me staying here if you are all in Kentucky.'

'No, I suppose not. I'd assumed you were coming with us on the jet but that's all changed.'

'Is there somewhere for me to stay in Louisville if I make my own way there?'

'Sure. No problem. We have use of a dorm block and mess hall at the Kentucky Air National Guard. It's not quite the Brown or the Seelbach but it's good enough. We always stay there for the Derby.'

'Where is it?' I asked.

'At Louisville Airport. On the eastern edge, away from the civilian side. It's real close to Churchill Downs.'

'Right,' I said. 'I'll see you there.'

'If you can get a flight,' Norman said. He spread his hands wide. 'I'm sorry there's nothing I can do.'

'Don't worry. I'm sure I'll get there somehow.'

He seemed relieved.

Not as relieved as me, I thought.

I had been afraid he would say that I couldn't go at all.

And what Norman didn't know was that I was already booked on a flight from Washington to Louisville that afternoon. I had made the reservation the previous evening, after I had spoken to Tony and before the FACSA logistics team had filled up all the available seats.

I was due to leave National Airport somewhat later than Frank, at 3 p.m. local time, and I *was* packed, with my suitcase ready for collection on my way to Check-in.

7

National Airport, or Ronald Reagan Washington National Airport to give it its full title, was only a couple of miles from the FACSA offices and I was there in good time for my flight.

As I waited at the gate for boarding to commence, I discovered that I was not alone among strangers. Three of the FACSA special agents were there too.

'Hi, Jeff,' Bob Wade said, walking over to where I was waiting. 'How did you get on this flight? I thought all seats were taken. Steffi is having to go through Chicago.'

Oops!

I thrust my boarding pass for seat 8C into my trouser pocket.

'I'm a standby,' I said. 'I get on only if there's a no-show.'

Bob seemed to accept my hastily made-up explanation.

He came and sat down next to me while the other two took the seats opposite.

'You've met Cliff Connell and Larry Spiegal?'

'Sure,' I said, leaning forward and shaking their hands. 'We met yesterday.'

'What is it yer do?' Larry asked in a deep Southern drawl.

'Much the same as you,' I said, 'but in England.'

'I went to England once,' he said slowly. 'With a friend when I was in college. Absolutely loved it. The best thing was y'all being able to drink booze at eighteen without a fake ID.' He laughed. 'I remember we made the most of that. Sadly, now, I reckon I can't remember much else.' He laughed again and Bob joined him, producing his rapid-fire guffaws.

The flight was called and Bob, Cliff and Larry went to board. I remained seated.

'Good luck,' Bob said. 'See you in Louisville.'

I watched them go through the gate and down the jetway to the plane.

I waited until the very last minute to board and then made my way down to 8C only to find that I was seated right next to Cliff Connell.

'Made it then?' he said.

'Yes,' I replied sitting down. 'Must be my lucky day. Where are Bob and Larry?'

'Farther down the back.'

I strapped myself in and we taxied out to the runway for take-off.

The flight was scheduled to take two hours, not enough for a full meal service, but about half an hour in the flight attendant came through the cabin with a trolley offering drinks for purchase.

'Fancy a beer?' I said to Cliff.

'I can't,' he said.

'On duty?'

'Armed,' he said quietly in my ear while lightly touching his jacket beneath the left armpit.

'Really? Don't you get stopped at security?'

'I have authorisation to carry a concealed weapon at all times. All federal special agents do.'

'I thought guns and planes didn't mix.'

'I wouldn't really want to use it while airborne,' Cliff said with a smile. 'But I always have it with me, just in case.'

The flight landed at Louisville on time at five o'clock and I was quite surprised to find that, in spite of being so far west, we were still on Eastern Time.

'The time zone changes west of Louisville,' Cliff informed me. 'About half of Kentucky is on Eastern, the rest on Central.'

'Doesn't that make things rather complicated for the state government?'

'Time zones are decisions for individual counties not states, although they have to be approved by the US Congress,' he said. 'But there are still a few crazy anomalies in some places – towns on Eastern Time that are farther west than neighbouring towns on Central.'

Tempus fugit, I thought, whatever the time zone.

Cliff and I joined up with Bob and Larry at baggage reclaim. Each of the agents had checked two large bags compared to my one, and theirs appeared to be much heavier than the fifty-pound airline allowance. But I suspected that they hadn't had to pay any excess charges.

I hitched a lift in their pre-arranged transport from the civilian terminal round to the Kentucky Air National Guard facility.

Getting in was easy for the others but less so for me.

My new security pass, it seemed, was only valid for FACSA headquarters in Arlington. Fortunately I had three special agents with me to vouch for my integrity and soon all four of us were drawing up outside the dorm.

There was a list pinned to a noticeboard near the entrance showing names and the allocation of rooms. At least someone was expecting me, even if my name had been written in by hand on an otherwise typed sheet. I had been assigned Room 304 on the top floor, next door to Steffi Dean who was in 303.

Alongside the rooming list was another sheet of paper with NOTICE TO ALL FACSA SPECIAL AGENTS printed large and boldly across the top. Beneath, it stated that all agents must immediately read the briefing papers placed in their rooms.

I went up the concrete stairs to the third floor. The key was in the door.

I had imagined the dorm would be a large room with iron bedsteads arranged down each side, as in *Tom Brown's School Days*, but that couldn't have been further from the truth.

The dorm was, in fact, a block of twenty-four

identical self-contained apartments, eight on each of the three floors. Each apartment consisted of a bedroom, an en-suite bathroom and a kitchen-cum-living room, that came fully equipped with furniture, large refrigerator and a microwave oven. There was even a wide-screen TV bolted to the wall with a bracket.

And these were enlisted men's barracks, not those for officers.

I thought back to some of the accommodation I had been required to live in during my time in the British Army. I don't think I'd ever had an en-suite bathroom, let alone a government-issue television.

I went back out into the corridor.

The key was also in the door of Room 303.

Steffi is having to go through Chicago.

That's what Bob Wade had said to me at Washington National.

Surely she wouldn't be here yet.

I looked up and down to check there was no one else in the corridor, then I opened the door to 303 and went in, removing the key while I did so.

There was a large white envelope on the bed with 'Steffi Dean' written on the front. The envelope was sealed shut.

Damn it.

I picked up the envelope and took it back to my own room. Then I searched the kitchen area and found what I was looking for in a cupboard – an electric kettle.

I hadn't steamed open an envelope since I was

89

thirteen, when I'd opened my school report before my father could see it. I had been particularly worried about what my history teacher had written concerning my poor behaviour in his class, and with good reason. I had removed the offending piece of paper before resealing the doctored report back into its envelope. My father had never known and I, of course, had never told him.

I did, however, discover one difficulty now that I hadn't had the last time. Due to the development of more modern technology, this kettle kept switching itself off as soon as it started to boil, cutting off the flow of steam from the spout.

I solved the problem by tying a dishcloth around the kettle that held down the switch in the 'on' position and, before long, the white envelope was lying open on the worktop.

I scanned quickly through the briefing papers, ever conscious that Steffi could arrive at any time.

Much of the details I already knew from Tony's earlier package. However, this time there was a detailed map of the barns at Churchill Downs with Hayden Ryder's outlined in red, together with the raid timetable and a list of actions specific to Steffi Dean. I noted that she was to secure the northeastern corner of the barn on arrival.

The briefing papers also stated that the track opened for training at dawn, which was at 6.45, so the raid would take place at 6.30 a.m. on Saturday. They also gave details of the raid personnel and their specific roles, as well as the transport arrangements. All eight FACSA special agents would be involved together with Norman Gibson, the section chief, who was to be in overall control.

My name was not included on the raid personnel list.

Local Kentucky law enforcement would be present on-site immediately after the raid was initiated in order to limit disruption for trainers in other barns. In addition, three veterinary surgeons from the US Department of Agriculture would travel on the transport with the agents to secure samples from each of the twenty-four horses known to be stabled in Ryder's barn.

The papers went on to say that there would be a full-scale rehearsal on Wednesday morning using an unused barn on a local horse farm. Special agents should study and fully assimilate the map of the real Churchill Downs barns prior to the rehearsal. All personnel were to be fully kitted with their firearms readied, as if for the real thing, at 0600 hours on Wednesday. The Deputy Director would be attending the rehearsal and making an assessment of individual performances.

Tony had obviously followed my advice to the letter.

I put the papers back in the envelope and resealed it. Then I slipped it under my arm beneath my coat and went out into the corridor.

I could hear voices in the stairwell at the far end.

I quickly reinserted the key into the handle of Room

303 and went in, placed the envelope back where I'd found it, and made a hasty retreat.

I was only just back in my own room when I heard Bob Wade's distinctive laugh coming down the corridor.

That was much too close for comfort, I thought, and my thumping heart agreed.

I took a couple of deep breaths and stepped back out into the corridor. Bob and Steffi were kissing and they jumped apart as if they'd had an electric shock. Silly people. Why not wait until they were inside?

'Hello, Jeff,' Steffi said with a nervous laugh. 'I didn't realise you were coming.'

'It'd be a waste of my time to remain in Arlington with you all here,' I said. 'I'm off to explore.'

I walked past them and on towards the stairwell without looking back. I smiled to myself. Perhaps they would be so engrossed in each other for a while that they wouldn't notice that the white envelope still had a slight dampness to it due to the steam.

Dinner was at six-thirty, served in what Frank Bannister called the chow hall, a large building close by the accommodation.

I personally thought it was a little early to eat but some of the others bemoaned the fact that it was so late, and they didn't seem to worry that two of the agents who'd had to fly via Atlanta hadn't yet arrived.

'I'm sure they'll get something on the flight,' Frank

said, helping himself to a second serving. 'I would if I were them.'

'It won't be long 'til breakfast anyway,' chipped in Trudi Harding, the second female special agent, sitting alongside Steffi Dean. 'Why do we have to be up so damn early? Why can't the rehearsal be at a more reasonable hour?'

'That's government service for you,' Frank said, laughing. 'They never take your comfort into consideration.'

He was so right. In the army, I'd regularly risen at five, ready to be at work by six or six-thirty. And that was in the UK. On operations in Afghanistan it was a matter of catching an hour's sleep whenever and wherever you could. Only since joining the BHA had I grown fonder of my bed.

After eating, everyone drifted back to their rooms 'to check kit, clean weapons and to memorise their individual action plan' according to Frank. 'It's not often we get a Deputy Director's assessment,' he said. 'Failing can result in loss of special-agent status.'

'Does that happen often?' I asked.

'I've never known it at FACSA,' he said, 'but there are stories from other agencies. And no one here wants to be the first.'

He rushed off, no doubt to oil his Glock 22C and polish his expanding bullets. I, meanwhile, wandered over to a quiet open space to make a call to Tony.

'Where are you?' Tony asked.

'In Louisville,' I said. 'How about you?'

'I've just landed.'

I instinctively looked over to my left towards the airport runways. Crazy really. There was not a chance in hell I'd be able to see him.

'Any luck with the staff bank statements?' I asked.

'The subpoenas have been issued and served on the various banks. We should have everything by tomorrow.'

I was impressed. The wheels of government agencies could spin fast after all.

'Good,' I said. 'Now about tomorrow morning. I am not on the list of raid personnel.'

'Have you seen it?'

'Yes. I borrowed the briefing papers from one of your agents.'

'Someone showed them to you?' He sounded troubled.

'Not exactly,' I said. 'I borrowed them without their knowledge.'

'But those papers are highly confidential.'

'Then people shouldn't leave them lying around for others to look at, even if they were in a sealed envelope in a locked room. It was plain careless to leave the key in the lock. I couldn't help myself.'

Tony laughed. 'You see, I do have the right man.'

'But what can you do about it? I need to be there for the raid.'

'Why don't you ask me in the morning?'

'I'm asking you now,' I said, slightly irritated.

'No. I mean ask me formally in the morning with

the others listening. I'm sure Norman Gibson will introduce you to me if you ask him. I will just say – why not? – and you'll be in.'

I supposed it was a better plan than him going directly to Norman to request it.

'OK,' I said, 'I will.'

'See you in the morning, then.'

'Yes,' I replied.

I was excited about the raid but also quite apprehensive.

Who wouldn't be with eight special agents running around in an enclosed space with their firearms readied? A space that was also shared by two dozen highly strung Thoroughbred racehorses.

While not necessarily a recipe for disaster, there was ample scope for things to go wrong.

8

And they did go horribly wrong. At least, I thought so, although the others seemed to be remarkably happy with the outcome.

Everyone was ready well before the 6 a.m. call and it quickly became apparent why the agents' baggage had been so heavy – body armour.

Each special agent was wearing a dark blue bullet-proof vest with FACSA in large yellow letters on the front and back. In addition they were all in matching uniform of dark blue trousers, a lighter blue shirt and black baseball cap, again with FACSA embroidered in yellow above the peak.

There was no attempt now to hide the weapons, their Glock 22Cs visible in full sight in gunslinger-style holsters attached to the agents' belts and tied around their legs above the knee with black straps.

They were also wired with personal radios, with earpieces on curly wires, and microphones attached to their non-gun wrists.

The final touch was a shiny gold badge with 'Department of Justice' and 'US Federal Anti-Corruption in Sports Agency' embossed around the edge and a large 'Special Agent' stamped across the middle. Secured to the front of each agent's bulletproof vest above the heart, they reminded me of the toy sheriff's star I'd pinned to my cowboy outfit as a child.

The sky was still totally black as Norman ushered the eight special agents into a line on the dot of six o'clock.

'Does everyone know their roles?'

He received eight thumbs-up.

'Justin and Mason, are you sure you're happy?'

Justin Pickering and Mason Rees were the two agents who had arrived late via Atlanta the previous evening.

They both nodded. 'We're ready, boss,' one of them said.

At that point, a black Chevy Suburban pulled up in front of the line and Tony Andretti climbed out from the back seat. He was wearing a dark suit as if for a day at the office, save for the earpiece already in his ear.

Norman Gibson stepped forward to greet him and the two men shook hands.

I, meanwhile, was hovering at the far end of the line, having previously asked Norman to introduce me to the Deputy Director.

Tony walked briefly along, stopping once or twice to talk to the agents. Then he came straight towards where I was standing.

'Deputy Director,' Norman said, 'can I introduce Jeff Hinkley? He's an international observer from England.'

'Delighted to meet you,' I said, shaking Tony's offered hand.

'What organisation in England?' he asked.

'The British Horseracing Authority.'

'Then this operation should be up your alley.'

'So can I come with you?' I asked.

'I don't see why not,' Tony said. He turned to Norman. 'What do you think?'

'Sure. It is only a rehearsal,' Norman said. 'No problem.' He looked down at his watch. 'OK, everyone, let's load up.'

Even though there was a fleet of half a dozen black vans available, identical to the one in which Tony had arrived, the transport on this occasion was a military vehicle, identical to the ubiquitous American school bus, but painted dark blue rather than the regular bright yellow.

The three USDA veterinarians were already on board and no one had told them it was a rehearsal – because it wasn't.

I had recommended to Tony that he should wait as late as possible before informing his special agents about the switch from rehearsal to real thing, so that no one would have the opportunity to make a call or send a warning text. But I hadn't expected him to leave it as late as he did.

The journey from the Kentucky Air National Guard facility to the backside barns of Churchill Downs was only four miles.

We had turned off I-264, with the iconic twin spires

of the grandstand almost visible in the pre-dawn twilight, before Tony stood up at the front of the bus.

'Listen up, please, ladies and gentlemen.' He spoke loudly and had the instant attention of all. 'The operation has been brought forward. This is *not* a rehearsal. I repeat. This is *not* a rehearsal. We will arrive at Hayden Ryder's barn at Churchill Downs in precisely two minutes. I trust you will perform your duties with the usual FACSA expertise and proficiency. Good luck.'

I was trying to watch their faces to see if I could detect any emotion, perhaps a touch of panic that information given to Hayden Ryder in good faith had now been rendered inaccurate.

From the look of his eyes, Norman Gibson was not at all happy. I couldn't blame him. He was meant to be in charge of this operation but he, too, had been unaware of the switch. There was also some surprise among the others and a couple of murmurs of disapproval, but nothing particularly obvious in the way of panic.

Cliff Connell, sitting right opposite me, simply shrugged his shoulders and removed his Glock 22C from its holster. He checked once again that the magazine was full, and then cocked the weapon by pulling the slide back sharply and releasing it.

He saw me watching him and smiled. 'Don't worry,' he said. 'The safety's still on.'

But I did worry, and I was beginning to wish I had a bulletproof vest like the rest of them.

*

To say that the Churchill Downs raid was different from similar operations I had conducted in the UK would be an understatement.

Only the previous September, I had led a team of three BHA integrity officers to a training stables in Newmarket after an anonymous tip-off that certain horses were being given a concoction of bicarbonate of soda by tube into their stomachs before racing. The process, known as 'milkshaking', has the effect of making the blood and muscle less acidic, and hence reducing fatigue.

Milkshaking was a serious breach of the Rules of Racing.

The three of us plus a veterinary technician had appeared unannounced at the stables to carry out a search and to take blood samples for analysis. The trainer in question had been understandably concerned by our arrival but he had assisted us in identifying the correct horses and, all in all, he had cooperated in every way without the need for coercion or threats.

There had been no question of us turning up then in the same manner employed here today by the FACSA agents – before dawn like a posse in a Wild West movie with their guns drawn.

The bus swung in silently through the backside gates, helpfully opened by a Kentucky police deputy, and came to a gentle stop at the designated spot at the end of a line of barns. If I remembered correctly from Steffi's map, Hayden Ryder's was the third one down.

'All set?' Norman said it in a whisper but each of the agents heard it clearly through their earpieces. 'Final radio check.'

Again there were eight raised thumbs.

'OK,' Norman said, checking his watch. 'The op is on.' He withdrew his own weapon from its holster and cocked the mechanism. 'Get into your positions and wait for my call before going in. Good luck, everyone.'

He started to go down the steps but turned to look straight at me. 'Jeff, you can use this.' He tossed me a spare radio. 'But you wait on the bus with the Deputy Director and the veterinarians. You do not come forward until I tell you to do so. Do you understand?'

I nodded.

The raid team followed Norman off the bus with a mixture of enthusiasm and apprehension showing in their faces. Trudi Harding smiled down at me wanly but her eyes betrayed her anxiety. She was the most nervous. Cliff Connell, meanwhile, was clearly excited and raring to go.

The seven men and two women each knew their starting positions and moved silently towards them. Although it was still before sunrise, there was plenty of light both from the brightening sky in the east and from numerous security lights set high on poles, and I watched through the bus window as the team spread out.

Even though the track wouldn't be open for another fifteen minutes, there was already much activity in the barns with horses being readied for their morning exercise.

'I'm going closer,' I said to Tony.

'But Norman said you were to wait on the bus.'

I looked at him with my head cocked to one side as if to say, 'So what?'

I went down the steps and moved slowly past the first barn in the line, stopping close to the second one. Hayden Ryder's barn was the next one down and appeared quite normal, with several internal lights visible through the open sides.

All was still quiet.

'Listen up,' Norman's whispered voice said in my earpiece. 'Anyone not in position?'

There was no responding call from the agents.

'Good. Count down – three, two, one – go!'

The stillness of the dawn was suddenly broken by seemingly all nine armed agents shouting at the same time.

'Armed federal officer! Stand still with your hands up.'

I watched as Steffi Dean made her way towards the northeastern corner of the barn, her two arms stretched firmly out in front of her, her right hand locked around the grip of her Glock 22C, with her left hand holding her right wrist for added stability.

No silencer, I noted. This was not a covert operation.

Back in the offices in Arlington, she had told me

that she'd never fired her gun other than on a range, but now she looked more than ready, moving her whole torso from side to side with her head so that the barrel always pointed directly where she was looking.

As I crept closer, there was more shouting from within the barn and then, quite suddenly, a series of shots rang out – at least ten in rapid succession.

'Man down! Man down!' was shouted loudly through my earpiece by a high-pitched female voice.

Oh shit!

Even I knew that 'Man down' meant that one of the special agents had been injured, or worse.

I inched forward and peered around the side of one of the huge steel skips that were dotted around the site for the collection of manure.

I could see Steffi Dean standing in the exit at the corner of the barn, her gun held out straight in front like a natural extension of her arm.

'Who's down?' Norman asked in my ear.

'Bob Wade,' came the reply. It was Trudi Harding who spoke.

I watched as Steffi buckled at the knees and almost went down to the dirt floor.

Her gun dropped to her side and, even from my hiding place some ten yards away, I could clearly hear her gasp with despair.

'I think Bob's fine,' Trudi went on. 'I shot the assailant. He's down too.'

From somewhere over my right shoulder I could

hear the rhythmic raising and falling siren of an approaching ambulance.

'Are we secure?' Norman asked. 'Anyone else need assistance?'

There was no reply.

'Suspects?' Norman said.

'Only the one down here,' Trudi replied.

'All others lying face down in the dirt and cooperating,' a male voice added. 'Secure on the south side.'

'And on the north,' chipped in another agent.

'All clear,' called Norman. 'But stay vigilant, everybody. Conduct a full search.'

In front of me, Steffi Dean had recovered her composure somewhat and again had her Glock 22C up at the ready. She moved into the wooden building and started to move forward, looking into each horse-stall in turn.

Hayden Ryder's barn was identical to most of the other barns at Churchill Downs. About seventy yards in length, it contained twenty-four wooden-built horse-stalls, arranged in two rows of twelve, situated back to back, with wide, open walkways running along in front, bounded on the outside by a half-height wall. At either end were more substantial, two-storey, block-built structures containing the trainer's office, equipment and feed stores, together with the stable dispensary.

The whole thing was covered by a green shingle-covered roof that stretched from the structures at either end over the total length and width of the barn, supported above the half-walls by white-painted vertical wooden beams.

From the direction of the shots, it seemed that all the action had taken place at the far end of the barn.

I walked up alongside and went in.

Three of the special agents, Larry Spiegal, Cliff Connell and Mason Rees, stood looking down at a man who lay in a crumpled heap on the ground.

No one made any attempt to help him, because he was beyond help.

The back of his head appeared to have been entirely blown away.

Norman appeared from the far side of the barn. He took in the scene, together with the fact that I was standing there. He pursed his lips.

'Anyone know who it is?' he asked.

None of the agents replied.

'I think it's Hayden Ryder,' I said. 'The trainer.' They all looked at me. 'I did some research on the Internet. I think that's his face, or what's left of it.'

We all looked down again at the mangled bloody mess at our feet.

'Cover him up,' Norman said to no one in particular.

Larry Spiegal took a horse rug that was hung over the half-wall and draped it over the body.

'Where's Bob?' Norman asked.

'Down there,' Mason Rees said, pointing.

I glanced to my left. Bob Wade was sitting on the floor with his back up against one of the stall walls and his legs stretched straight out on the dirt. Trudi Harding was crouching down next to him.

'What happened?' Norman asked.

'This guy came at Bob with that fork,' Mason said, indicating the long-handled, two-pronged pitchfork lying close to the body. 'I saw it happen. He came out of that door, ran straight at Bob, and stabbed him in the chest.' He made a two-handed stabbing motion. 'Trudi took him down.'

Norman walked over towards Bob.

'You OK?' he asked.

Bob Wade looked up at him and nodded. 'A bit shaken up but I'll be fine. One of the prongs hit my badge.' He fingered the groove that the fork had made in the metal.

'You were lucky,' Norman said. 'How come he got close enough to stab you?'

'He came from behind me. I heard him and turned but he was too close. He was on me before I had a chance to react.'

Norman was far from happy.

It was clear that Trudi was still shocked by what had happened.

'He would have killed Bob,' she said, speaking with a nervous timbre in her voice. 'I'm sure of it. He was lining up for a second attempt with the fork so I shot him.'

'You did the right thing,' Norman said.

Two uniformed paramedics ran into the barn weighed down with medical kits. They took a brief look at the body under the rug, and then went over to Bob Wade. They could only help the living.

Norman walked a little bit away and signalled for me to follow.

'I told you to remain on the bus.'

'I heard you say "all clear" over the radio so I came forward.'

He didn't like it but there was little else he could do.

'Go back to the bus now,' he said firmly. 'I will try to sort out this damn mess. It might take some time as I have to call in the Louisville Police to investigate the shooting.'

'Can I help in any way?' I asked hopefully.

He shook his head. 'Get back on the bus and wait for me there, or else I will have you arrested.'

That seemed to be a fairly definite no, then.

I went back to the bus.

9

I sat on the bus for the next two hours, by which time the whole area round Ryder's barn had been cordoned off with bright yellow 'POLICE – DO NOT CROSS' tape by the Louisville Police.

From my vantage point, I watched as a black van with 'County Coroner's Office' painted in white lettering on its side arrived and drove up to the barn.

A little while later, the van departed, carrying, I presumed, the mortal remains of Hayden Ryder.

Soon after that the three veterinary technicians were called forward to collect blood samples from the horses.

That left me alone on the bus. Even the driver had deserted me and I hadn't seen Tony since before the raid had gone in.

Meanwhile, life on the Churchill Downs backside went on as usual with horses being prepared from the other barns for their daily workout on the track.

True, there were more members of the media on site than might be normally expected three days before a big race, and the crews were from the TV news networks rather than from the sports channels, but the welfare and training of the horses still had to go on. It seemed it would take more than the shooting of a trainer to derail the Kentucky Derby juggernaut.

With over 170,000 spectators expected for the main event, some having paid in excess of $6,000 for a single ticket, it was *the* big annual occasion for Louisville. Every hotel room was full for a hundred miles around, and you had more chance of walking on water than getting a dinner reservation in a city-centre restaurant.

But only for the first Saturday in May.

For the rest of the year, Louisville returned to its regular, sleepy existence where the tourist highlights included an educational visit to the Louisville Slugger baseball-bat factory, or nostalgic trips to the birth-place and grave of Muhammad Ali.

Eventually Norman returned. He came up the steps into the bus and sat down on the seat opposite me.

'Who the hell *are* you?' he asked.

'You know who I am,' I replied. 'Jeff Hinkley, from the BHA in London.'

'What are you doing here?'

'I'm on the international exchange scheme.'

'Don't give me that bullshit. I reckon you're here to spy on us. I just don't know yet who sent you.'

He'd clearly been a pretty good detective.

'Whatever gave you that idea?' I said, trying my best to control my voice and be all innocent.

'You know things you shouldn't, and you also do things you shouldn't.'

'Like what?' I asked.

'Like how did you get here from DC?' he said. 'Every single seat was taken on the direct flights. I know because I was trying to use my position at FACSA to get more without any success. The airlines told me they were already oversold, yet you made it here easily.'

'I must have been lucky.'

'I don't believe in luck.' He said it without a trace of humour in his voice. 'But, most of all, how did you know it was Hayden Ryder who was shot?'

'I told you,' I said. 'I recognised him.'

'How?'

'I'd researched him on the Internet.'

'Why?' he said slowly. 'You shouldn't have known anything about this raid. You certainly shouldn't have known we were after Hayden Ryder.'

That had been careless of me.

I stared at him.

'Who told you?'

'I think you had better speak to the Deputy Director.'

'I'm speaking to *you*.' He said it with some real menace in his voice. 'Who told you?' he asked again.

I didn't answer.

He removed his Glock 22C from its holster, cocked the mechanism, and pointed it right at me, somewhere between my eyes, from a distance of only a few inches.

'I'll not ask you again,' he said calmly.

Was this really happening?

My head told me that he wouldn't possibly pull the trigger, but my head hadn't informed my heart, which was pounding away so fast that it felt in danger of bursting out of my chest altogether.

I'd had loaded guns pointed at me before but I'd never seen the business end of one quite so close up. I almost had to cross my eyes to focus on the .40-calibre black hole at the end of the barrel.

My mind started playing silly tricks, like wondering if I would have time to actually see the expanding bullet appearing before it took off the back of my head.

I decided it was time to come clean.

'I was asked to find a mole in your organisation, someone who has been leaking confidential information to those you were meant to be investigating.'

The Glock 22C didn't move a fraction of a millimetre.

For a moment I was worried that it was Norman who was the mole, and I had just signed my own death warrant.

'So who told you about the raid?'

'Tony Andretti,' I said. 'He gave me the details after your meeting in the offices on Monday.'

He dropped the gun down onto his lap and I breathed a quiet sigh of relief.

'I wondered why he let you come on the bus when he knew it wasn't a rehearsal.'

'It was my idea to bring the operation forward to

this morning. To reduce the chance that the information would leak or, at least, to reduce the time any leak could be acted upon.'

'Why wasn't I told?' Norman said, but he was smart enough to work out the answer. I just looked at him.

After a few seconds, he nodded. It didn't seem to make him any happier.

'So who is the mole?'

'I have no idea,' I said. 'Not yet.'

'Will you go on looking?'

'Yes, I suppose so. If I'm asked to.'

But I was now a little worried. It had been my carelessness that had allowed Norman to work out that I'd been highly economical with the truth.

I wondered who else might have come to the same conclusion.

By the time Norman finally allowed me off the bus, Tony had been summoned to Louisville City Hall to explain to the mayor why one of FACSA's special agents had shot dead a prominent Kentucky racehorse trainer on his patch. And in the week of the Derby, too, when the entire world's horseracing media was focused on Churchill Downs. It was the wrong kind of publicity, and most unwelcome.

My release from the bus, however, did not provide me with access to the barn at the centre of the action. That was still cordoned off by the yellow tape and the local police were proving far too vigilant at keeping me out.

Hence I was still standing close to the bus when a huge eighteen-wheel truck and trailer pulled up alongside.

'Which one is Hayden Ryder's barn?' the driver called, leaning out of the window towards me.

'The one behind the police tape,' I said. 'You can't get there at the moment.'

'What's going on?'

'Someone got shot,' I said.

The driver didn't seem unduly surprised or worried. Shootings were commonplace.

'I've come to pick up Ryder's horses.'

That was quick, I thought. Hayden Ryder hadn't yet been dead for four hours and someone was already here to take away his horses.

'Where are you taking them?' I asked.

'Chattanooga.'

'Where's that?'

'Tennessee,' said the driver. 'Three hundred miles south.' He looked at his watch. 'Is this going to last long? I'll have to get going by midday at the latest, or I'm stuck here overnight. I'd be out of hours.'

I looked at the side of his truck. 'CHATTANOOGA HORSE TRANSPORT' was painted in large black letters on the white side of the trailer.

'Have you come from Chattanooga this morning?' I asked him.

'Sure have,' he said. 'I've been on the road since five.'

'Five this morning?' I asked.

He nodded. 'Made really good time up I-65 from Nashville.'

'How many horses are you collecting?'

'A full load,' he said. 'Fifteen for me. There's another truck behind me for another nine.'

All twenty-four horses.

Hayden Ryder's whole barn of Thoroughbreds would have been shipped out of Churchill Downs 300 miles south to Chattanooga only three days before the planned FACSA raid.

Could that be a coincidence?

I didn't like coincidences.

'When were you booked for this trip?' I asked the driver.

'Yesterday,' he said. 'Rush job. I've had to postpone a trip down to Tampa to fit it in.'

'Which racetrack are you taking the horses to?'

'It's not a racetrack – there's no horseracing at all in Tennessee. They're going to Jasper, west of Chattanooga. To a horse farm.'

No horseracing in Tennessee.

How convenient, I thought.

There would be no state racing commission to authorise any testing. And Jasper might be far enough away not to bother to send someone from Louisville.

'Do you have a name?' I asked the driver.

'Elvis,' he said.

I laughed.

'It's true. Elvis O'Mally. My dad came over to Tennessee from Ireland as a boy. He was a huge fan of the King.'

'Well, Elvis,' I said, 'you wait here. I'll try and find out when you can get the horses.'

I wandered a little away from his listening ears and called Tony on the non-smart phone.

'I can't talk,' he said quietly. 'I'm in a meeting with the mayor.'

'Don't hang up,' I replied quickly. 'Listen. Two horse trailers have arrived here to collect all Hayden Ryder's horses and take them to Tennessee. The trailers left Chattanooga at five o'clock this morning. They were booked yesterday.'

I allowed time for the significance of the information to sink in.

'And another thing,' I said. 'Norman knows.'

'Knows what?' Tony said.

'He knows the real reason why I'm here. I had to tell him or I'd have been arrested.'

Or shot.

'I'll get back there as soon as I can,' Tony said.

He hung up.

I walked back to Elvis the driver, who had climbed down from his cab.

'You'll have to wait,' I said.

'For how long?'

Good question.

Tony returned shortly after midday, by which time Elvis and his fellow Chattanooga Horse Transport driver had given up waiting.

'It's a damn shame,' Elvis had said. 'I should have

been sunning myself on the beach in Tampa, not hanging around up here.' He climbed up into his cab. 'I'll be back tomorrow morning for this lot.'

I doubted it.

I wasn't certain what would happen now to the twenty-four horses still standing in the barn, but I was pretty sure they wouldn't be going to Jasper, Tennessee.

It would be up to their owners to find them new trainers, either here at Churchill Downs or at another track.

Elvis was backing up his truck. I went over and banged on the driver's door. He lowered the window.

'What time yesterday did your trip to Tampa get postponed?'

'I don't know,' he said, uninterested. 'Must have been in the morning. My boss told me when I got back to the depot around one.'

He turned his eighteen-wheeler around in a space I'd have had trouble turning a dinghy trailer. Then he drove off, followed by his mate.

I was still standing by the blue bus when Tony came over to me, with Norman Gibson in tow.

'On the bus,' Tony ordered.

The three of us climbed aboard.

Norman started to complain to Tony that he hadn't been told the true purpose of my visit but Tony cut him off.

'Tell Norman what you told me.'

'Hayden Ryder's horses were due to be removed from here today and taken to Tennessee.'

'How do you know?' Norman said.

I told him about Elvis and his Chattanooga Horse Transport van.

'Is he still here?' Norman looked out of the bus windows.

'No. He's gone. He'd run out of time to drive all the way home today. He told me he'd be back in the morning.'

'Why didn't you tell me this while he was here?' Norman was not best pleased.

'I couldn't get through the police line to find you,' I replied in my defence. 'But I do have the company's phone number.'

I handed over a piece of paper. I'd copied it off the side of the truck.

Tony was more interested in the significance of Elvis being there in the first place.

'It means that Hayden Ryder must have been aware of the raid by one o'clock yesterday at the latest.'

Norman nodded. 'The stable dispensary has also been packed up in boxes ready to be shipped out.'

'So who told Ryder?' Tony said.

It was the all-important question.

Sadly, we could no longer ask the man himself for the answer.

IO

There was a debriefing for the FACSA raid team at four o'clock that afternoon, back at the mess hall of the National Guard facility.

Most of them had spent some of the preceding eight hours being individually interviewed by detectives from the Louisville Police Department's fatal-shooting investigation team.

'It is perfectly routine,' Tony told me on the phone when I called him well away from the others. 'There's a standard procedure for all officer-involved shootings. Such events bring intense media scrutiny and we have to guard against any damage to the agency's reputation. Hence the local police conduct a detailed enquiry and interview everyone involved.'

'I wasn't interviewed,' I said.

'The fatal-shooting investigation team is only concerned with events up to the moment the shots were fired. You were not a witness to the actual shooting so I didn't give them your name. I thought it was best to keep you out of it.'

'I agree,' I said. 'Thanks. So what happens next?'

'The evidence may have to be presented to a grand jury to confirm the killing was justified, although that's most unlikely in this case.'

'So you think the killing was justified?' I asked.

'Without a doubt,' Tony said. 'Ryder attacked a law-enforcement officer with a deadly weapon. That in itself is enough reason for him to be shot.'

'But surely not ten times.'

'It can often take more than one shot to bring down a suspect. Our agents are trained to fire multiple rounds in case some of them miss.'

'I was told your agents are all hotshots,' I said. 'Surely they don't miss.'

'You'd be surprised,' Tony said. 'They may be OK on the range but operational situations are very different. A Miami police survey showed that of thirteen hundred bullets fired at suspects, more than eleven hundred missed. And NYPD found barely a quarter fired from under six feet hit their target, with less than a fifth at ten feet.'

'How many hit Hayden Ryder?'

'I don't know yet. The autopsy will tell us. The important thing is that at least one did, and that one was enough to disable him.'

It had done more than that, I thought.

I had spent the day trying to erase from my mind the grisly image of Ryder's head completely torn apart by an expanding bullet.

I'd seen more than my fair share of killings during my time with the army in Afghanistan but nothing really prepares you for the sudden finality of violent death, the instant wiping out of an active, vivid and cognisant existence, to be replaced by ... nothing. Nothing more than a useless rotting corpse.

'What will you do now?' Tony asked.

'I'm not sure,' I said. 'I'll stay on here for the Derby. I wouldn't want to miss that, but I feel I'm approaching the problem from the wrong end.'

'How do you mean?'

'These guys are smart – they don't get to be federal special agents if they're not. I can't hang around forever on the off-chance that our friend will make a mistake. He won't. And I'll have wasted my time, and yours. I feel we have to tackle things from the opposite direction.'

'Explain.'

'I work best undercover but I'm not using those skills here. Everyone at the agency knows who I am and that severely limits my scope.'

I took a deep breath. In for a penny ...

'I need to get a job on a track backside, maybe as a groom or something, with one of the trainers. FACSA then has to plan a raid on that trainer for some reason and hope our friend somehow tips him off.'

'Would the trainer be made aware of your existence?' Tony asked.

'Best not, at least to start with. I know from experience that being undercover is fraught with danger. It is ten times worse when somebody is aware of the truth. Body language can be a real giveaway.'

'But how would you know if the trainer had been forewarned about a raid?' Tony asked.

'Hayden Ryder couldn't have packed up the whole of his stable dispensary and arranged to ship out his horses without the help of his staff. Racehorses have to have grooms accompanying them – they would hardly walk onto a truck on their own. Ryder's whole team had to be involved in the preparations even if they didn't know the reasons why.'

'But *how* will you get a job? Do you have any experience working with horses?'

'Loads,' I said. In truth, I'd only had a little. But I was confident around racehorses and that was half the battle.

'And you're hardly the right size,' Tony said.

I was five feet ten inches in my socks, but I was lean and fit. Maybe I was a bit tall and perhaps a tad too heavy to ride young Thoroughbreds, but not to work as a groom.

One thing I had discovered while I'd been waiting at Churchill Downs all day was that, unlike in the UK, the grooms did not ride the horses. That was the preserve of the exercise riders, up-and-coming riders or retired jockeys who would often move from barn to barn, exploiting their skills for more than one trainer.

The grooms were simply there to, well, groom the horses, to muck out their stalls, and to fetch and carry their feed and water. On race days they might get to lead one of their charges over to the saddling boxes and the mounting yard but, in truth, the life of a backside groom was far from glamorous.

Tony wasn't finished. 'Most grooms are Latino or African-Americans. An Englishman would surely stick out like a sore thumb.'

He was right.

'How about an Irishman?' I said.

I had always been good at speaking with an Irish accent. While at school, I had entertained my classmates by mimicking our headmaster, who had come from County Cork.

'I can easily pass as an Irishmen,' I said. 'I've done it before, and I know you have Irish grooms over here. I've heard their banter.'

'Will you try to work at Churchill Downs?' Tony asked.

'That might be a bit of a risk. Almost all of the Churchill Downs backside staff came over to Ryder's barn to have a look at the action at one time or another today and many of them asked me what was going on.'

'Where then?'

'How about at Pimlico?' I said. 'Isn't the Preakness run there in two weeks?'

'It sure is,' said Tony. 'But Pimlico isn't used any more as a regular training centre. Their barns are only open for seven weeks during their spring meet. Better to try Belmont in New York. That's where the third leg of the Crown is run. There are plenty of full-time trainers at Belmont.'

'Isn't Belmont where the *Sports Illustrated* journalist thought someone was blood doping?'

'Yes,' Tony said. 'Jason Connor.'

'Right, then I'll try there. Can you get me a list of Belmont-based trainers, especially those you may have doubts about?'

'Sure,' Tony said. 'No problem. Anything else?'

'Yes. You told me in London about a raid on a trainer who employed suspected illegal immigrants as grooms. Where was that?'

'Aqueduct Racetrack. Also in New York, near JFK. Back in February.'

'Is the use of illegal-immigrant grooms widespread at all tracks?'

'Cash gambling tends to make racing a cash-rich business. Wherever cash is used to pay staff there will always be illegals working.'

'Could you therefore send an official letter to all the trainers at Belmont advising them of the severe consequences of employing illegal immigrants?'

'What for?'

'If you can fix me a legal work visa, it might help provide a vacancy for me to fill.'

Tony laughed. 'The letter would be better coming from ICE – Immigration and Customs Enforcement. It's part of the Department of Homeland Security. They're responsible for tracking down illegal immigrants. I know the Deputy Director, we've been to conferences together. I'll get him to write the letter.'

'Best not to tell him why.'

'I'll say it's a follow-up from FACSA's raid earlier in the year. I'll recommend he sends the letter to all registered racehorse trainers across the country threatening them with jail for employing illegals.'

'Is that true?'

'Unlikely,' he said. 'But it could happen in extreme cases.'

'Would your man be prepared to cover the cost of sending a letter to all trainers?'

'Sure he will,' Tony said. 'It's peanuts compared to what else they spend. Their budget is over five billion a year. I'll get it sorted straight away – have it done this week.'

'How about the work visa?' I said. 'Preferably in a false name.'

'What name?'

Think of a common Irish name. 'How about Patrick Sean Murphy?'

'Shouldn't be too much of a problem,' Tony said. 'I'll have a quiet word with someone I know in the State Department.'

'Great,' I said. 'And how are the bank statements coming along?'

'They should be with me this evening. How shall I get them to you?'

'Can we trust Norman?' I asked. But it was a rhetorical question. He already knew the true purpose of me being there. If we couldn't trust him my cover was totally blown anyway, and my future prospects were likely to be severely limited.

'We have to,' Tony said.

'Then give the statements to him to pass on to me.'

'He'll want to know what they are.'

'Then tell him. But best not to say that his bank statements are there too. He might not like that. In fact, you'd better remove his in case he checks, but scan them yourself first for any suspicious deposits.'

'You don't really trust him, do you? Not even now.'

'I trust no one,' I said.

'Not even me?' Tony asked.

'Not even my mother,' I said.

And she'd been dead for twenty-five years.

Back in the National Guard mess hall, Trudi Harding was being hailed as a hero.

She was applauded and cheered by the other agents when she finally arrived back after a lengthy interview with the Louisville police.

Bob Wade embraced her warmly, which didn't particularly endear him to Steffi Dean, who looked on stony-faced.

Everyone was in good spirits, as if the whole raid hadn't been blighted by the shooting dead of Hayden Ryder.

Some of them even thought it was a bonus.

'Saves all the expense of a trial,' Cliff Connell said openly with a huge grin.

The debriefing turned rapidly into a self-congratulatory celebration.

There was even a short emotional address by Norman Gibson, who thanked his staff for 'a job well done'.

None of them seemed to entertain the notion that death had been rather an extreme penalty for Ryder's alleged wrongdoing, even if he had been shot for attacking Bob Wade rather than giving his horses prohibited drugs.

I personally found all the backslapping and high fives a bit tasteless, what with Hayden Ryder's body still cooling in the county coroner's morgue.

Hence I left them to it.

Instead I went up to my room and watched as a local Louisville TV newsreader echoed the same sentiments, blatantly accusing the dead trainer of serial drug abuse and the wilful maltreatment of his horses.

I knew that freedom of speech and honest opinion were enshrined in the First Amendment of the US Constitution but, even so, the claims seemed somewhat outrageous.

I had a political journalist acquaintance who once told me that there was nothing better than finding out that some detested fat cat had died. 'You can't libel the dead,' he would say, while gleefully filling his column with some lurid tales of wrongdoing that may have been mildly suspected of the deceased, but were far beyond any actual proof.

'Do you have no compassion?' I'd said. 'Surely it's disrespectful to speak ill of the recent dead?'

'Maybe,' he'd replied with a smile, 'but it sells papers.'

No wonder some people tell you never to believe what you read in the newspapers.

I used the remote control to flick through the other TV news channels and found much the same fare on all of them. In the end, I lay on my bed watching a quiz show where, bizarrely, the contestants had to give the question, having been shown the answer.

It wasn't long before it caused me to drift off to sleep.

I was woken almost immediately by someone hammering on the door.

I opened it to find Norman Gibson standing there with a large brown envelope in his hand, but he didn't hand it over. Instead, he pushed past me and marched through into the apartment living room, where he stood in the middle of the space with his feet firmly set about eighteen inches apart as if ready for action.

He was far from a happy man. Steam was almost emanating from his ears and he had obviously been working himself up into quite a fury.

'Now, fella,' he said loudly, jabbing at my chest with his right index finger, 'you had better explain to me what the fuck's going on here.' He emphasised the expletive with raw anger in his voice. 'What makes you so important that you can get to see all our bank statements, while I get to look like a fool?' He waved the brown envelope right into my face.

He was so furious that I seriously thought he might hit me, and I was considerably relieved to see that he didn't still have his Glock 22C holstered on his hip. But, no doubt, it would be hiding somewhere beneath his jacket.

I'd had to deal with this sort of confrontation before, in Afghanistan, when boiling-over tempers of local village elders could easily end up messily with bullets flying around. I had been trained to keep control of my emotions and to maintain my composure, but I knew from experience that nothing provoked an angry response more than belittling or ignoring someone's grievance.

I had found that an apology usually helped to defuse difficult situations, even if there was nothing for *me* to actually be sorry for. Consequently, I was a serial apologiser and had, over time, expressed my personal remorse and sorrow for everything from Adam's consumption of the forbidden fruit to the Nazi Holocaust.

'I'm so sorry,' I said to Norman, doing my best to sound sincere. 'You should have been made aware of the true purpose of my visit.'

I didn't mention that it had been my idea not to tell him.

'Won't you sit down?' I said, indicating towards one of the armchairs.

Norman hesitated. Sitting down clearly had not been on his agenda, but he slowly lowered himself into the seat. I relaxed a little. It was far more difficult, if not impossible, to hit someone from a seated position in a deep armchair.

I then sat down opposite him, making sure I was well out of reach.

How much did I really trust him?

Enough, perhaps, to talk about being invited by

Tony Andretti to try to find the section mole – he already knew that by now – but maybe not enough to apprise him of my future plans.

'Tony Andretti approached my boss in London and requested some help in finding a mole in your organisation. It clearly was a mistake not to involve you and, for that, I am very sorry.'

My apology tactic seemed to be working. Norman's ire was placated and the high-pressure steam in his head slowly abated.

'So what *have* you discovered?' he asked, his voice full of sarcasm.

'Precisely nothing,' I said.

I wasn't able to read in his face whether he was pleased or disappointed. Either way would not have been incriminating. In his place, I wouldn't have been particularly happy if the new kid on the block had found out something in just three days when he'd been trying without success for months.

He simply nodded knowingly. He hadn't expected anything else and I wondered if Norman actually believed there was a mole in the first place.

'Mr Andretti asked me to give you these.' He tossed the envelope he had been carrying into my lap. 'What do you want them for anyway?'

'To see if anyone in FACSA's racing section is receiving money from someone they shouldn't. Payment in exchange for a tip-off.'

'Do you really think one of us is selling confidential information?'

'Why else would someone be forewarning your targets?'

He shrugged. 'Maybe out of cussedness.'

I thought that most unlikely. Especially if Tony was correct and Jason Connor had been killed because of it. It was my belief that sane people didn't kill just out of cussedness; they did it for one of four other reasons – money, revenge, jealousy, or a political cause.

Which one was it here? Surely it had to be for money.

'So what are you going to do now?' Norman asked.

'Keep my eyes and ears open, and enjoy the Derby.'

I'd also be watching my back.

11

The rest of my time in Louisville was considerably less stressful, although equally exciting, but for different reasons.

The Kentucky Derby was the most hyped sporting event I think I had ever attended and easily outshone the Epsom version for glamour and glitz.

While the Derby at Churchill Downs could not match the pomp and circumstance and the genuine royalty of the original, it attracted the Hollywood 'royalty' in abundance, complete with red-carpet entrance where the public was encouraged to stand and idolise the screen superstars as they made their way to Millionaires Row, as the upper level of the grandstand is officially known.

I reflected on the differing attitudes to money that existed on either side of the Atlantic. In the UK, serious wealth is mostly played down by those who have it. To do otherwise is considered rather vulgar. In the United States huge riches are to be applauded, and flaunted at every opportunity.

And Kentucky Derby Week was certainly one of those.

Accompanying the two minutes of the race itself were several days of celebrations with a succession of parties and dinners to satisfy every taste and wallet. Those in the inner circle, and those with the greatest wealth, could secure an invitation to the exclusive black-tie eve-of-Derby gala, an event that regularly creates a lengthy traffic jam of stretch limousines throughout downtown Louisville.

For my part, I spent most of my time shadowing Frank Bannister and, fortunately for me, he enjoyed the good things in life and was not averse to using his federal-special-agent status to gain entry to occasions and activities where his presence was hardly warranted.

Early on Friday morning, Frank drove the two of us in one of the Chevy Suburbans from the National Guard facility to the backside of Churchill Downs, to see the Derby hopefuls in their morning exercise.

Hayden Ryder's barn was still cordoned off with yellow tape but the local police no longer guarded the perimeter. The horses had gone too, quickly snaffled by other trainers eager to fill their own barns. The police did, however, guard the Derby runners, with a sheriff's deputy standing watch outside each stall.

'To stop them getting nobbled,' Frank said.

I considered it was more of a token presence than true security. Any determined nobbler would have found it dead easy to get past the deputy's laissez-faire attitude, chatting and joking with the stable staff with only half an eye at best on the actual horse. But it was good for the cameras, as TV crews from all the local stations were invited from barn to barn to observe the stars 'at home'.

Frank and I joined the racing press on a small bleacher-seat viewing stand as the twenty Derby contenders made their way out onto the track. By this stage, with less than thirty-six hours to the race, the hard training work was done and now it was only a matter of maintaining peak condition and not over-tiring the young equine athletes.

'Come on,' said Frank after fifteen less-than-exciting minutes of watching the horses gallop. 'I've seen enough. Let's go to Wagner's before the rush starts.'

'Wagner's?'

'Wagner's Pharmacy.'

'What do we need a pharmacy for?' I asked.

'You'll see,' he said with a laugh, leading me back to the Suburban.

Wagner's Pharmacy was on South 4th Street, across from the entrance to the Churchill Downs infield. And it was not a pharmacy as I knew it.

True, it sold its own proprietary racehorse liniment in gallon containers for the treatment of bumps, bruises and strains, but it was most famously known as *the* place to have breakfast during Derby week.

Frank and I sat down on the only two free stools at the long counter.

'Two orders of bacon, eggs over easy, toast and grits,' Frank said to the waitress behind the counter. 'Plus coffee and orange juice.'

'Grits?' I asked.

'Boiled ground corn,' Frank said. 'I was raised on the stuff in Alabama.'

The waitress poured our juice and coffee and, shortly after, delivered two enormous plates of food – two fried eggs each, four or five rashers of crisp bacon, two rounds of toast, a mini-mountain of fried potatoes, plus a side bowl of grits – a white sloppy concoction akin to lumpy wallpaper paste, complete with a dollop of melting butter on the top.

I sampled a small amount and pulled a face.

Frank guffawed loudly. 'I reckon it's an acquired taste.'

I concentrated on the eggs and bacon.

'Eat up yer grits, man. They're good for you,' he said, shovelling another great spoonful of the white stuff into his mouth. 'Full of iron.'

I'd have rather chewed on a rusty nail for my iron than eat grits, but the rest of the meal was excellent and I was soon fit to burst.

'It's a tradition,' Frank said, forcing in yet another mouthful. 'It wouldn't be the Derby without a break-fast at Wagner's.'

Clearly everyone agreed with him and soon a line had formed out on the sidewalk as people waited their turn to get in. As it was, not a spare inch of floor space was wasted with horsemen, media and a few brave tourists crammed together at tables so close together that no one had enough elbow room to cut their bacon.

And it was noisy too, with most of the banter being about the chances of the various horses in the following day's big race.

'Fire Point, that big chestnut colt of George Raworth's, will surely canter up,' said one man on my left. 'Destroyed the field in the Gotham Stakes at Aqueduct in March.'

'He's no chance,' called the waitress as she delivered more breakfasts. 'He's drawn in Gate One and everyone knows that being on the rail is not good. He'll be swamped in the early running.'

Racing really was the religion in these parts come early May.

'Did you hear that Ryder was shot seven times,' said someone behind me. 'Twice in the head, poor man. Killed him instantly, apparently.'

'He shouldn't have tried to stick one of them Feds with a pitchfork,' said someone else. 'He had it coming, if you ask me.'

Nobody did, and most of the sympathy was clearly with the dead trainer. Overall, however, I was amazed that Ryder's death hadn't caused greater disquiet among the racing fraternity. They seemed to take it in their stride, almost as if sudden violent death was an expected part of the business. Of course, it was, but not often for the human participants.

'I fancy Liberty Song for the Derby.' The man on the other side of us said it to no one in particular. 'He was truly brilliant in the Blue Grass Stakes at Keeneland last month. Won by five lengths easing up.'

'But he had no competition,' claimed a man sitting further beyond him. 'I reckon it will be one of those two West Coast horses that'll clean up this year.'

Racing chat was the same the world over as punters tried to pick a winner.

The truth was that the starters in the Kentucky Derby were all potential champions. They were the best three-year-old horses in North America, each of them having had to qualify through outstanding performances in some of thirty-five other major stakes races held at tracks all over the country. Points were awarded for the first four home in each race and the top twenty points holders were entitled to a place in the Derby starting gate.

This year there were four horses with far more points than any of the others but that was no guarantee of success. In 2009, the $1.4million prize was carried off by a gelding called Mine That Bird, which had been bought as a yearling for only $9,500. His career before the Derby had not been spectacular, finishing last in the Breeders' Cup Juvenile, but he scraped into the Derby field with a win in the Grey Stakes at Woodbine and a fourth-place finish in the Sunland Derby in New Mexico.

No one gave the horse a chance, the press being far more interested in the trainer, Chip Woolley Jr, who had driven the horse himself the 21-hour, 1,700-mile trip from his home to Louisville in a horse trailer attached to a pickup truck, and with his broken foot in a cast to boot.

Yet, Mine That Bird, stone last and so far out of the running for the first half of the race that he didn't even appear in the TV coverage, slipped through an opening on the rail at the top of the final stretch and romped home to win by six and three-quarter lengths, the longest margin of victory in over sixty years, and at a price of fifty-to-one. It was a lesson in not writing off any of the starters.

Frank and I finished our breakfast and gave up our seats to the next two in the ever-growing queue. He had been absolutely right about beating the rush.

'Where to now?' asked Frank as we climbed back into the Suburban.

'You're the expert,' I said. 'I've never been here before.'

He drove us round to the front entrance of Churchill Downs.

'You'll never find anywhere to park,' I said. 'It's the Oaks today.'

The Oaks was sometimes called the Fillies' Derby. It was raced over the exact same course and distance some twenty-four hours earlier, but was reserved for three-year-old female horses.

Frank just smiled at me. Oaks Day was second only to Derby Day itself as a crowd-puller, not least because if you wanted to buy a Derby ticket, you had to buy one for the Oaks as well. Most racegoers, therefore, made a two-day trip of it.

But that didn't seem to worry Frank.

A quick flash of his 'FACSA Special Agent' metal

badge and we were welcomed into the restricted parking lot with open arms.

The same tactic allowed us not only to gain entry to the public enclosures but also to jump the sizable line, and to get in for free. It seemed that the simple words 'security check', together with the badge, was an automatic 'Open Sesame' to every cave of treasures.

'He's with me,' Frank said, when one of the staff asked for my non-existent ticket. I could get used to this, I thought but, to be fair, I too had an 'access all areas' pass for every racecourse in Britain.

Even though it was still well before nine o'clock, Churchill Downs was beginning to fill up. The entrance gates had opened at eight and many had been queuing for several hours before that for general admission tickets. Indeed, even twenty-four hours ahead, there was already a line for Derby Day with some hardy folk staking their place early so they could be first through the gates the following morning.

General admission ticket holders did not get a seat and were not able to get much of a view of the track itself, but that didn't seem to dampen their spirits. They were there to see, and to be seen with, the rich and famous.

'General admission tickets also give access to the infield through the tunnel,' Frank said. 'About seventy thousand will cram into there tomorrow and hardly any of them will even get to see a horse, let alone the race. Most come only to drink and get laid. It's like a big frat party. The bars open at eight in the morning and everyone's drunk by lunchtime.'

'It must be hell if it rains,' I said.

'It is hell anyway,' Frank said, laughing. 'When it rains the women wrestle in the mud. When it's dry, they just wrestle. It's a complete nightmare.'

It was far removed from my mental image of Kentucky Derby Day, with gentlemen in seersucker suits and ladies in haute couture and fine hats, all of them sipping traditional Derby mint juleps.

'Come on,' said Frank. 'Let's go check out the upper echelons.'

The metal special agent badge again worked wonders as we rose in a special VIP elevator directly to the top floor of the clubhouse, to Millionaires Row and the even-more-exclusive 'The Mansion at Churchill Downs', where the admission charge was so high that, if you queried the $700 tab for a single bottle of bubbly, you plainly couldn't afford it.

We wandered round on the deep-pile carpet between the lush leather seating of the dining area, and then out onto the spectacular terrace doing our 'security check'. The view was indeed as stunning as the price.

Frank and I completed a full sweep of the clubhouse and the grandstand without finding anything out of place.

'Do you and the others have a specific job to do here?' I asked as we went through the private suites on the fifth level.

'Not really,' he said. 'They like us to provide a presence and react if necessary. But we won't get into these sections tomorrow. The Vice President is coming and his security is the job of the Secret Service. They'll have the place sealed up as tight as a tick.'

'It must be confusing having so many law-enforcement agencies all working at the same place. Is there an accepted hierarchy?'

'Not officially, but the Secret Service act like they're the top dogs.'

'And are they?'

'I suppose so. They're here to protect the Vice President, and what they say goes. They won't be interested in the racing, only in the people.'

'While you'll be busy watching the horses?'

'I keep an eye out for everything. But the racing integrity work is the responsibility of the state racing commission. They'll contact us only if they think anything suspicious is going on.'

'Have they done that before?'

'A few times. Betting matters, mostly. Especially when someone is trying to avoid paying the tax on their winnings.'

'Are racetrack winnings taxed?' I asked with surprise.

'Sure are,' Frank said. 'All gambling winnings are considered to be taxable earnings. Even if you win a car or a trip on *Wheel of Fortune*, you have to pay income tax on its market value.'

'So how do people try to avoid it?'

'Multiple identical bets,' he said. 'Any payout over five thousand bucks is subject to hefty withholding tax by the track. So big bets are rare. Much more sensible to have several smaller identical bets on separate tickets. Then, if they win, you collect from lots of different windows, keeping each one below five grand, and don't tell the IRS anything.'

'Clever,' I agreed.

'Yeah, maybe it is, but it's also dishonest. And we're getting wise to that tactic. The IRS is busy installing cameras at the track payouts windows to record faces.'

'Spoilsports.'

He laughed. 'Whose side are you on?'

'Not the taxman's,' I said, 'that's for sure.'

'It's my job,' he said. 'Anyway, some big gamblers now get their friends and family to collect for them so that no one individual collects more than five grand. But then those people are required to declare it on their own 1040s, or Uncle Sam might come knocking. There's nothing as certain as death and taxes.'

'It still seems unfair to tax a slice of good luck.'

'Lotto and casino winnings are taxed too. You know those people who put a dollar in the big slot machines in Vegas, pull the handle, spin the reels and win a million? You see it sometimes on the TV.'

I nodded.

'The IRS takes a quarter straight off the top, there and then. And there's more to pay the following April fifteenth.'

I shook my head in disbelief.

'What happens in England?'

'There is no tax on racetrack winnings. Whatever it says on the ticket, that's what you get. It's the same for all gambling. All payouts are free of any form of tax.'

'Even the lottery?'

'Absolutely. Every sort of winnings.'

'Wow,' he said. 'I think I'll move to England.'

On Friday evening, with Frank Bannister still acting as my chaperone and mentor, I went to the Fillies and Lilies party at the Kentucky Derby Museum before moving on to one of the other Derby-eve events in downtown Louisville.

The only problem was that we couldn't have anything to drink.

'Not while on duty,' Frank explained. 'Not with this baby on my belt.' He tapped the Glock 22C under his jacket. Although unarmed myself, I felt obliged also to be teetotal for the evening.

There were several other FACSA special agents at both events.

'Are y'all havin' a good time?' Larry Spiegal asked in his deep Southern drawl at the Fillies and Lilies event.

'Sure are,' Frank said. 'But there are more menfolk here in hats than I've seen outside a rodeo.'

I looked around and it was true. Most of the men were sitting at tables either in small narrow-brimmed straw trilbies or large ten-gallon cowboy hats. I thought it bizarre to wear hats indoors but my new colleagues thought nothing of it.

'A true cowboy always wears his hat,' Frank said, 'except when greeting a lady.'

Clearly, they didn't consider that the scantily dressed young fillies at this party were ladies.

'But we're inside,' I said.

'Inside and out,' Frank said, 'makes no difference.'

'He'll wear it even when taking a shit,' Larry added unnecessarily.

'Especially then,' Frank confirmed. 'Keeps it off the floor.'

Yet another reason why I concluded that Americans were a rum lot.

12

I finally turned out my bedside light at almost two in the morning. Not that I'd been partying the whole time.

Frank and I had returned to our quarters about eleven but I had spent the next three hours continuing my examination of the bank statements of FACSA's racing section.

In the first pass, I had discovered not a single suspicious deposit into any of the accounts. But I hadn't really expected to. Someone who had been clever enough so far to avoid detection would not have been so stupid as to make large payments into their own personal bank account.

They might, of course, have a second bank account, which they hadn't declared. But that wasn't as easy as it sounds. Every US bank is required to disclose the names of all account holders to the tax authorities, together with their dates of birth and Social Security numbers.

Maybe the mole was using an offshore account.

However, that option was also fraught with danger. Under the new Foreign Account Tax Compliance Act, the US Treasury forced a deal with over a hundred other countries compelling their banks to report the names of all US citizens holding accounts with them directly to the IRS. Even the traditional offshore tax havens such as the Cayman Islands, Bermuda, the Isle of Man and the Channel Islands had all signed up.

Basically, hiding illicit money in a bank anywhere is now extremely difficult, and is getting more so every year as governments bring in new anti-money-laundering measures.

So what is the alternative?

Cash.

We all use cash at some time – for burgers at McDonald's, taxi fares, milk at a convenience store, even a wager on the horses. Sure, these days, we could probably pay with plastic if we had to, but no one blinks an eye at our using cash.

How about if we also paid cash to fill the car with fuel? Or for the weekly groceries? Even buying an expensive Christmas present for the wife or kids?

Still no one would question our cash in hand.

Indeed, under US law, it was not necessary to report any cash transaction under ten thousand dollars.

So I started to search through the bank statements again, looking for an account that had absolutely no cash withdrawals, no ATM records, and where other transaction activity was sparse, perhaps indicating that utility and other bills were also being settled with cash.

The columns of figures finally drove me to sleep.

But it felt like I had been dead to the world for only a short while when I was woken by a furious slamming of doors and the sound of feet running along the corridor.

Bleary-eyed, I stuck my head out.

'What's going on?' I asked Steffi Dean as she appeared from her room fully dressed in her FACSA uniform, including bulletproof vest and holstered Glock 22C.

'We've been scrambled,' she said. 'There's trouble at the track.'

I dressed in record time and made it onto the last of the black Suburbans to leave, one driven by Cliff Connell and also containing Special Agents Trudi Harding and Justin Pickering.

'What's the trouble?' I asked.

'We're not sure,' said Cliff over his shoulder. 'Norman got an urgent call from the State Racing Commission saying they needed our help.'

We raced past a large lit-up sign on a pole that showed it was 6.15 a.m. and 52 degrees. I must have slept longer than I realised. The sky was even becoming light in the east.

The backside was a hive of activity when we arrived, with sheriff's deputies, Louisville Police and the FACSA agents all pacing around the barns not really knowing what they were looking for.

I came upon Norman standing next to one of the Suburbans.

'What's happening?' I asked.

'Three Derby horses are sick,' he said.

'Is that all?' I said. 'With all this fuss, I thought someone else must have died.'

'They're three of the most favoured runners. The trainers are claiming they've been got at.'

'Is that what you think?' I asked.

'I'll wait for the test results,' Norman said. 'The veterinarians are taking samples. There's a rumour it might be EI.'

EI, or equine influenza, was a much-feared disease in the racing world, and for good reason. Highly infectious through the air, and with an incubation period of only a day or two, it could spread through a horse population like a bushfire in a drought. Its appearance at a major centre like Churchill Downs, where the training barns were packed so tightly together, could easily shut down racing here for weeks.

In August 2007, four stallions arrived in Australia from Japan, where there had recently been an outbreak of EI. As was normal practice, the stallions were transferred to a quarantine centre near Sydney Airport.

On the twenty-fourth of August, tests confirmed that several horses at the quarantine centre were infected with the H3N8 subtype of the equine influenza virus.

Even though the affected animals were supposed to be isolated from the general horse population, new cases of the same subtype were simultaneously reported at a nearby equestrian centre. Although never proven, the official report assumed that the virus had been transferred accidentally on the tools of a farrier who had attended to horses at both sites.

The following day some eighty horses were found to be sick and, by the end of August, just one week after the first instances, 2,000 horses were unwell with the disease. Movement of horses throughout Australia was banned without a permit and many equestrian events were cancelled, including the Sydney spring racing festival. At the peak of the outbreak, more than 47,000 horses across New South Wales and Queensland were infected and horse-industry operations did not return to normal for almost a year.

To lessen the likelihood of such epidemics, all racehorses in the United States and Europe have to be vaccinated and then given regular six-monthly boosters but, as in humans, the influenza virus can mutate, rendering the vaccine useless.

The outbreak of a new variant, even this close to the race, would put the Derby itself in jeopardy. No wonder the Kentucky Horse Racing Commission was running round in panic mode.

All morning exercise on the track was cancelled and the media circus, which had arrived to cover it, instead spent their time speculating as to what might happen next. Multiple TV crews busily set up at various locations between the barns, much to the alarm and dismay of everyone else, who worried that they might help spread the plague yet further.

An impromptu press conference was called for eight

o'clock and everyone crammed into the tented press centre situated next to the track to listen.

The nervous-looking racing commissioner sat alone at a table with a microphone set up in front of him. 'Ladies and gentlemen,' he began, 'let me start by assuring you that the Kentucky Derby will go ahead later this afternoon as planned.'

There was a collective sigh of relief from the assembled media, and a round of applause from the many owners, trainers and jockeys who were squeezed in at the back.

The commissioner waited for silence before continuing. 'Early this morning, at around five a.m., three horses that had been due to run in today's Derby didn't eat up their food and were found to be showing signs of sickness. The horses in question were immediately placed in isolation and, as of just now, no further cases have been reported. However, on veterinary advice, those three have been scratched from the Derby. As it is now past the deadline for replacements, only seventeen runners will go to post.'

'Is it equine influenza?' shouted one reporter from the front row.

'As yet, we have no indication of the disease,' said the commissioner, 'but we wish to remind you that all US racehorses are routinely immunised against equine influenza.'

'So are you saying it is not influenza?' asked the reporter.

'Er ... no, I'm not. It may be a new strain. We will all have to wait for the results of blood tests.'

He didn't exactly exude confidence, but he changed direction by then naming the scratched horses and, as Norman had indicated, they were three of the four most favoured for the win.

Was it just the way my mind worked, or was that rather convenient for the fourth?

Life in the backside returned to normality, if that was the right term for the excitement generated by Derby Day morning at Churchill Downs.

The remaining seventeen Derby hopefuls were trotted up in turn in front of the state senior veterinary officer for him to decide whether each animal was sound and also, in the light of what had occurred earlier, for them to have their temperatures checked. Fortunately, after a thorough inspection, all were declared well and fit to race.

After the medical examination each was then presented to the press in what can only be described as a beauty pageant for horse and owner.

Occasionally, in England, especially at the Cheltenham Festival, connections of a particular horse might wear a necktie in similar shades as their racing silks, or perhaps a knitted scarf in comparable tones – nothing too ostentatious, you understand.

There was clearly no such restraint in Kentucky.

One of the Derby owners was decked out in a three-piece suit cut from cloth boldly printed with his green-and-yellow racing colours, complete with matching tie, baseball cap and even coordinating green-and-yellow-striped shoes. The poor horse looked positively embarrassed to be standing next to him for the photographs. But there was more. The owner's wife and family were similarly attired in green and yellow and, in case you couldn't work it out, each of them wore a huge button badge with the name of their horse printed large across it.

And the man was as brash as his outfit, telling all the assembled press that his baby was a certainty to trot up and collect the trophy. None of them really believed him as the horse in question was one of the rank outsiders, but that didn't seem to dampen the owner's enthusiasm.

Meanwhile, away from the limelight of the press parade, I watched behind the media tent as another owner, inconsolable in his grief, was trying to come to terms with the fact that his prized Thoroughbred star, strongly tipped to be a Triple Crown winner, would now not even get to the starting gate of the first leg.

It is not generally polite to stand and watch a grown man cry, but I felt sorry for him. Only a handful of racehorse owners ever have the privilege of owning a potential champion and this man's dream of glory had been snatched away by a virus so small he would need an electron microscope to see it.

And there would be no coming back next year to have another go. The Kentucky Derby, like all the 'classic' races, was for three-year-old horses only. This might have been the unfortunate man's only chance in life of owning a Derby runner, let alone the favourite – no wonder he was in tears.

Horseracing history is full of heartbreaking 'if only' stories and this one, like all the others, would quickly be forgotten by everyone except those whose lives it touched most closely. The victor that afternoon would be hailed as the conqueror of all and, in future years, no one would ever mention the three who failed to line up at the start.

Such was life.

But for this moment, it was almost too much for the desolate owner to bear and he sobbed openly. Fortunately for him, all the TV crews and photographers were busy snapping the fancy suit and striped shoes around the other side of the tent.

At ten o'clock the focus of attention for some switched from the backside barns to the racetrack proper.

The Derby was far from being the only race of the day. In fact, there were twelve additional contests scheduled, ten before and two after, and, for the owners, trainers and jockeys, the support races were clearly worth winning too. In addition to the Grade 1 Derby itself, there were three Grade 2 stakes, plus two other Grade 1s, each with purses in excess of half a million dollars.

But for the enormous crowd already teeming into the public enclosures there was only one race that mattered, the one due off at precisely twenty-six minutes to seven in the evening. Everything about the day was building up to the moment when the starting gates would swing open and the 'most exciting two minutes in sport' would begin.

Fortunately, there was still plenty of time for eating and drinking before then, especially drinking, with the sickly sweet mint juleps on sale in special commemorative glasses from the moment the entrances opened at eight am.

Frank and I tried to get another breakfast at Wagner's but decided the line was too long, stretching out the front and right round the corner of the street, so we found a drive-thru burger outlet and sat in the Suburban munching our way through English muffins filled with bacon and eggs.

'No grits today, then?' I said with my mouth full.

'We're not far enough south. They have it at home in Alabama.'

'McGrits?' I said, laughing at my own joke.

Frank didn't think it funny in the slightest.

13

As Frank had suspected, our movement throughout the grandstands was much restricted compared to the previous day. Indeed, I was lucky to be able to get in at all as I didn't have a magic badge and a simple 'I'm with him' didn't seem to work with the gateman today.

'No ticket, no entry,' he kept repeating.

Fortunately, Frank was able to rustle up Norman Gibson on his mobile phone, and he soon arrived, together with the racetrack head of security. Eventually the gateman relented and allowed me through, but he clearly didn't like it. Perhaps he thought I looked a bit shady, and he was probably right. I hadn't had a shave for four days, not since I'd decided to go undercover as a groom, and I was already sporting some substantial stubble.

If I thought that the Gold Cup at Cheltenham or the Grand National at Aintree were jam-packed, it was nothing in comparison to Churchill Downs on Kentucky Derby Day.

At least at Cheltenham and Aintree it was just about possible to move from the grandstands to see the horses in the paddock and then get back to the stands to watch the race. Here, it was virtually impossible.

Several hundred of those with general admission tickets had no intention of ever seeing the race itself. They had arrived early to bag a preferred spot on the paddock rail from where they would not budge, couples taking turns to elbow their way to the restrooms and the beverage outlets, so as not to lose their place. In the grandstand boxes, suites and glass-fronted restaurants, meanwhile, the patrons wore their tamper-proof, colour-coded wristbands with pride and tended to stay where they were between races, venturing only as far as the nearest bar or betting window.

As the afternoon progressed, the excitement built, with rock bands playing in the infield and a string of A-list celebrities swaggering along the red carpet. At two o'clock, the Vice President arrived in a bullet-proof limousine with much fanfare and the playing of the 'Star-Spangled Banner'.

There was some general dismay among the crowd that three of the best horses had been scratched from the race but it didn't seem to diminish people's enjoyment unduly.

Frank and the other FACSA special agents were assigned to assist with enhanced security measures for the Derby horses, so I made my way through the grandstands to find somewhere to watch the racing. That sounds easier than it actually was because, unlike on British racecourses, there was no standing concourse at the front. Rather, the ticketed seating went right down to the running rail.

I managed to talk myself past another gateman and into a spot in front of a temporary grandstand on the clubhouse turn, but it lacked any shade and, boy, it was getting hot, with the sun baking down from a cloudless sky. I began to wish I had one of the straw hats that were clearly popular all around me.

But I couldn't leave my position to buy one or to find some other shade. With only a few hours to go to Derby post time, every vantage point had been seized by the tens of thousands without a reserved seat. If I left my spot now, I'd never get back, even if I could again talk myself past the gateman.

I started seriously to envy those upstairs in the air-conditioned luxury of The Mansion at Churchill Downs, enjoying a five-course Derby lunch while imbibing their seven-hundred-buck vintage champagne.

As in the UK, the first few races of the day were scheduled at half-hourly intervals, but here, as the afternoon progressed, the periods between races became longer. There was more than an hour between the ninth and tenth races and then almost a two-hour break before the Kentucky Derby itself.

I thought the crowd might have gone off the boil a bit during this extended period but the excitement was cranked up by the 'Derby walkover', when the seventeen equine participants were led from the barns on the backside round the track to the paddock to be saddled.

Each horse was accompanied by its owner and

trainer, along with their various family members, friends and, of course, a sheriff's deputy, all of them cheered to the rafters by the expectant spectators.

The full green-and-yellow brigade was there in force, the striped shoes getting covered with dirt from the track. The brash owner looked far more circumspect now as the nervousness had set in with fifty minutes to post time.

Fire Point, the big chestnut colt trained by George Raworth, was now the only one of the top-four points scorers still in the field and he was the overwhelming favourite.

I watched as he was walked past me led by a groom wearing a huge white bib with the number '1' emblazoned large on both back and front.

I remembered back to what the waitress had said at Wagner's.

He's drawn in Gate One and everyone knows that being on the rail is not good. He'll be swamped in the early running.

According to the race-day programme, which contained every Kentucky Derby statistic known to man, the race had been won eight times by a horse drawn in Gate 1, although the last of those had been over thirty years ago.

Would Fire Point break the mould?

We would soon find out.

At six-fifteen precisely, a rotund huntsman, clad in a bright scarlet jacket and black riding hat, stood in front of the grandstands and played 'The Call to Post' on a long silver trumpet to announce the arrival back onto the track of the seventeen hopefuls, now saddled and mounted by their brightly silked jockeys.

One could almost cut the mounting tension as the 170,000 crowd joined together to sing 'My Old Kentucky Home' before the horses made their way down to the starting gate at the far end of the finish straight.

I had attended all the big races in England and some others around the world but there was something unique about the atmosphere here today at Churchill Downs. Hysteria would hardly be too strong a word to describe the excitement that had gripped those around me. Two people on my left were openly praying and a man to my right almost collapsed from hyperventilation.

There was a lull in proceedings as the horses went behind the starting gate to be loaded. It was as if everyone was taking a deep breath, but then the bell rang and the gates swung open. The race was on.

I am sure there was a track commentator somewhere calling the race but I had no chance of hearing him over the shouting and cheering from the crowd as the seventeen runners broke in an even line.

My vantage point, low down on the clubhouse turn, was not ideal but there was a huge-screen TV across the track giving me a perfect view.

As predicted, Fire Point was indeed swamped by the others in the early running as they all moved left towards the rail to take the shortest route, but he wasn't impeded, passing the finish line for the first time in sixth place, well tucked up behind the leading group.

They came into view around the turn, sweeping past right in front of me at a terrific speed. Then they were off down the back straight where the field began to spread out as the breakneck pace caused some of the lesser animals to tire.

Fire Point was not among them.

The chestnut colt hit the front coming off the final turn and was never again headed, striding away from the chasing pack down the stretch, in the shadow of Churchill's famed twin spires, to win by three lengths.

As the horse passed under the wire, his jockey, Jerry Fernando, stood tall in the stirrups, saluting the crowd with his whip hand held high, while those in the enclosures roared back their approval.

I noticed that the green and yellow silks finished fourth, collecting a hundred grand for the man in the striped shoes. Perhaps he'd be happy but, in this race, as in every other, winning was everything. Unlike in Formula One, there are no trophies in horseracing for coming second.

The jockeys pulled up their exhausted mounts right in front of me, each of them bar one with a hard-luck story of how they maybe didn't get a clean run down the stretch, or were hampered on the rail in the turn, or the track was too dry, or a hundred other reasons why they didn't win.

But for the connections of Fire Point, all their Christmases had come at once, as their champion racehorse was led to the Kentucky Derby winner's circle to be draped across the withers with the traditional three-metre-long garland of red roses.

The race wasn't called the 'Run for the Roses' for nothing.

LEG 2:

THE PREAKNESS STAKES

'The Run for the Black-Eyed Susans'

A mile and three-sixteenths
Pimlico Race Course, Baltimore, Maryland

Two weeks after the Kentucky Derby
First run in 1873

14

'Can you ride?'

'To be sure, sir, I can,' I answered in my best ex-headmasterly Cork accent.

'You're a bit tall.'

'I blame my parents, sir,' I said. 'They fed me too well when I was a wee lad.'

My interviewer laughed. His name was Charlie Hern and he was the assistant to George Raworth, the Derby-winning trainer of Fire Point. I took him to be in his mid-thirties but he looked older, having already lost most of his hair.

'You won't have to ride the horses anyway,' he said. 'We have exercise riders for that. But it might be a bonus.'

He looked again at the slightly battered Green Card he was holding in the name of Patrick Sean Murphy complete with my picture and thumbprint. A Green Card's official name was a United States Permanent Resident Card (USCIS Form I-551) and Tony Andretti had worked a miracle with the State Department to have mine delivered to his home the previous day.

It meant that I, as Patrick Sean Murphy, had the right to work legally in the United States.

Not only was the name on the card false but so

was the date of issue, as it stated that I had been a US permanent resident for the past three years. Consequently I had spent some time the previous afternoon 'aging' the card by rubbing it under my shoe on a concrete floor.

The man shuffled once again through my equally fake testimonials while I stood in front of him without speaking, waiting.

'Why did you leave Santa Anita,' he asked, tapping one of the references.

'Too hot, sir,' I said. 'Especially in the winter. I prefer me winters cold, same as at home, like.'

He was silent for a moment, then he shuffled the papers together.

'OK, Patrick,' Charlie said finally. 'You'll do. We've just had to let a groom go, so we're shorthanded here at present. Can you start immediately?'

'Indeed I can, sir,' I said, smiling broadly at him. 'And please call me Paddy.'

'All right, Paddy,' he said, handing me back the Green Card. 'You'll be paid minimum wage and half of it will be withheld for your room and board.'

I had looked up the minimum wage. I hadn't been particularly impressed.

'Where do I sleep?' I asked.

'Keith will show you. He's the barn foreman so you do as he says.'

Keith had been standing next to me throughout the short interview.

We were in an office at the end of a training barn

on the backside of Belmont Park Racetrack in New York. It was Wednesday morning, four days after the Kentucky Derby in Louisville, and two days after every racehorse trainer in the United States had received a strongly worded letter of warning from Immigration and Customs Enforcement concerning the employment of illegal immigrants.

'And Paddy,' said the assistant trainer as I turned to leave, 'Mr Raworth expects absolute loyalty from his staff. You will do as you are told without question. You will not discuss your work with others, and you especially will not speak to the press about any of the horses. Do you understand?'

I turned back to face him.

'Yes, sir,' I said.

Keith and I went outside.

'Where's your stuff?' Keith asked.

'Me life's all in here,' I said, indicating the canvas holdall over my shoulder.

Keith led me round the side of Raworth's barn to a two-storey building that was desperately in need of a coat of paint.

'In here,' he said, pushing open the door. 'Do you want to share with a Mexican or a Puerto Rican?'

'You keeps half me wages and then you makes me share a room?'

'Take it or leave it. We have others after jobs, you know.'

'The Mexican,' I said, for no particular reason.

Keith showed me into a room that reminded me of

a prison cell as depicted in a British TV sitcom of the 1970s. It was uniformly grey with a set of bunk beds taking up almost half the available floor space. In the corner, at the foot of the beds, were two wooden lockers stacked one upon the other, plus a hard, upright wooden chair. And overlaying everything was the smell of cheap disinfectant mixed with the characteristically pungent ammonic 'horsey' aroma.

There was no sign of my roommate.

'Yours is the top,' Keith said.

'Bed or locker?' I asked.

'Both.'

'And the jacks?'

He looked at me quizzically.

'The jacks, man?' I said. 'The bleeding lavvies?'

'If you mean the bathroom, that's down the end of the corridor. You share it with four other rooms.'

It made my former life in the army look rather luxurious.

'Dump your kit and I'll show you the rest of the place,' Keith said.

I tossed my bag onto the top bed and followed him out.

The 'backside' at Belmont Park was not actually in the back of the racecourse but to the side, situated around a second exercise track set close to one end of the main racetrack.

The barns were similar to those at Churchill Downs insofar that they were long thin structures, but these were enclosed at the sides rather than open, perhaps reflecting the fact that New York was further north than Louisville. And, whereas Churchill barns were white with green roofs, those at Belmont were the opposite.

Keith and I walked down alongside George Raworth's barn. There was little chance of confusing his barn with any other. The initials GR were emblazoned everywhere and there was already a workman screwing a white sign to the green outside wall that read, *Home of Fire Point. Winner of the Kentucky Derby.*

'That was a great day last Saturday,' Keith said. 'Now for the Preakness.'

'Is Fire Point here?' I asked.

'Sure is,' he said. 'We flew back together from Louisville on Sunday afternoon. He'll stay here now until he goes down to Maryland.'

'Will he fly there?' I asked.

Keith shook his head. 'He'll go by truck. It's only two hundred miles from here. We could probably go down only the day before the Preakness but Pimlico demands that all the horses are down there earlier. It helps them market the race to the public. I expect we'll go Monday. That would be usual.'

'Does Mr Raworth have his own barn at Pimlico?' I asked.

'No. He did once but they've closed the barns there now, except for during the actual meet. I expect we'll use the Stakes Barn.'

A Stakes Barn was where a trainer would keep a

horse brought in especially for a big race when he didn't have a barn of his own at the track. It would normally be shared by several trainers.

'Do you think Fire Point will win?' I asked eagerly.

'Sure, he'll win,' Keith replied with unshakable confidence. 'He's in great shape. He'll win the Belmont too.'

We walked over to a blue pickup truck.

'Get in,' Keith said. 'I'll show you around and get you registered.'

First we went to the backside office where I was issued with a groom's photo ID card on a lanyard that I was expected to wear round my neck at all times, and handed a printed sheet of rules and regulations that mostly consisted of dire warnings not to smoke anywhere near the barns.

Next, we set off round the site. The backside at Belmont Park was considerably bigger than that at Churchill Downs, the barns being more spread out and separated from each other by smart white railings. It was like a small town with a recreation hall, learning centre, chapel, medical facility, even a bank branch where employees could cash their pay cheques and wire money home. But there was also the quirky side to the place – roosters pecking at undigested oats on the dungheaps, tethered goats acting as lawnmowers on the grass between the barns, and dogs and cats lying out, warming themselves lazily in the mid-afternoon sun.

Add the occasional neighing of the horses and it

was more like a tranquil rural oasis than the actual reality, squeezed as it was between a busy suburb and a six-lane highway of a major metropolis.

'You eat here in the track kitchen,' Keith said as we pulled up in front of it. 'You get tokens from me for basic meals. If you want extra, you pay for it.'

We went inside and Keith introduced me to Bert Squab, the manager. 'Paddy here has just joined Raworth's,' Keith said to him. 'Usual system.'

Bert nodded at him and at me. 'Supper at six-thirty,' he said without much friendship in his voice. 'Don't be late or it'll be gone.'

I smiled at him, trying to break through his icy exterior, but without response. In spite of working in a hot kitchen, Bert was solid permafrost.

Keith and I went outside and climbed into the pickup. He drove us back to Raworth's barn.

'Here, take these.' Keith counted a number of plastic discs into my hand. 'These are meal tokens. These will last you until Sunday. You'll get more then with the others.'

I put the tokens in my pocket.

'Evening stables are from four to six,' Keith said.

'Which horses do I do?'

'That'll be decided by Mr Hern.'

'How many?'

'Four or five horses to a groom, it depends on how many we have in. Our barn is one of the larger ones here. It has thirty-two stalls and we're usually pretty full – today's count is twenty-eight. We also have two other permanent barns, one at Del Mar in California and the other at Gulfstream in Florida. Mr Raworth splits his time between the three, the fall at Del Mar, winter in Florida and the rest of the time either here or upstate at Saratoga where we all go for six weeks in the summer.'

'So he's here right now?' I asked.

'Certainly is,' Keith said. 'Arrived back from Louisville last evening for today's racing.'

'Here at Belmont?'

He nodded. 'We race here throughout May, five days a week. Mr Raworth is coming over from the track to see everyone at four, so don't be late.'

I could see that 'don't be late' was going to be my mantra as long as I was here.

I went back to the bunkhouse and lay on my bed to do some thinking.

The full FACSA team, including Tony Andretti and myself, had flown back to Washington on Sunday morning as originally planned, on the government-owned jet, a converted Boeing 737 fitted out with thirty business-class seats. It wasn't quite Air Force One but it was very comfortable nonetheless.

I purposely sat well away from Tony, with him up near the front and me down the back next to Larry Spiegal.

On the flight I had gone round to most of the agents individually to thank them for their hospitality and to say goodbye.

'You leaving us already?' Larry had said. 'You've hardly had time enough to spit.'

'I'm afraid I have to,' I'd replied, smiling. 'I can't spend my life gallivanting around the world in private jets like you lot. I have work to do in London.'

We had landed at Andrews around midday and most of the agents had dispersed immediately to their homes, eager to catch up with wives and children for what remained of the weekend.

I had hung around until the last of the agents had departed then I'd called Tony Andretti. He, meanwhile, had been collected by Harriet, but they now returned to where I was waiting at a secluded spot outside the base main gate.

I slung my suitcase onto the back seat and climbed in after it.

'Where to?' Tony asked.

'No idea,' I said. 'Where do you suggest?'

'Our place?' Harriet asked.

'Do you have neighbours?'

'Sure,' Tony said. 'Why?'

I had always been obsessed with my own security, to the extent of being paranoid. But that paranoia had helped keep me alive through three long tours in war-ravaged Afghanistan and subsequently, working undercover for the BHA.

'I don't want anyone to see you and me together. You never know who's watching or who they will talk to.'

'The neighbours don't need to see you,' Harriet

175

said. 'We can drive straight into the garage. You lie down on the back seat.'

'OK,' I said.

So, perhaps against my better judgement, I had gone home with Tony and Harriet to Fairfax, Virginia, where I had spent the next two days hiding from their neighbours, studying bank statements, growing my beard and making plans to become a groom.

'Why Raworth's?' Tony had asked when I'd told him where I was going for a job.

'Partly because George Raworth trains at Belmont Park. Do you remember telling me that FACSA had conducted a raid on a barn at Belmont last October but had found nothing, the whole place having been steam cleaned?'

'Of course,' Tony had said. 'That was the raid that Jason Connor was so furious about.'

'Can you recall the name of the trainer?'

'Man called Mitchell, Adam Mitchell. But he's now gone from Belmont permanently. He went back to Florida after that trouble and NYRA were glad to see the back of him. We interviewed him in Miami about Jason Connor and how he had been tipped off regarding our raid, but he wasn't talking. It was a total dead end.'

'How about his grooms?'

'They mostly went down with him to Florida. We interviewed some of them too, but they all said they knew nothing. I think they were frightened of Mitchell. That's why Connor tracked down the one at Laurel, he didn't go with the others and was apparently prepared to talk, but now even he's disappeared.'

'And what that groom said to Connor is anyone's guess.'

'Exactly.'

'There may still be some of Mitchell's past grooms at Belmont, working for other trainers. I could try to find them.'

'Seems like a long shot to me,' Tony had said. 'Is that the only reason to work for George Raworth?'

'No. I also want to go there because he won the Kentucky Derby and he has since indicated that he intends to run three horses in the Preakness, including the Derby winner, Fire Point.'

'What difference does that make?'

'To start with, it means I may have more chance of getting to Pimlico, but mostly I'm curious as to whether his other two will actually be trying to beat Fire Point, or will they only be there to spoil the chances of the other runners.'

'You're a cynic.' Tony had laughed.

'Maybe I am. But I believe there is something very fishy about the way those three competitors conveniently all fell ill on the very morning of the Derby.'

'The track veterinarian didn't think so,' Tony had said. 'He said that it was not uncommon for horses to go off their food and run a fever, especially when being moved around. But, I grant you, it looks a bit suspicious for those three to have fallen ill on that particular day.'

I'd read the vet's interim report. Not that I'd really understood much of it. It had all been a bit too scientific for me and it didn't answer the most important question, which was what was wrong with the horses. One of his paragraphs had stuck in my mind: *Antigenic drift of antigenically heterologous viruses may reduce the degree and duration of protection conferred by previous infection or vaccination.*

The phrase 'blinding with science' came to mind. At least I could understand the last bit.

'Does he think it may have been a new strain of equine influenza?'

'He doesn't know yet,' Tony had replied. 'Apparently he has to wait for the horses to produce antibodies and then test for those, rather than for the virus itself. It takes a few days.'

But, if it was equine influenza, one of the most infectious diseases around, why hadn't it infected more of the horses? What was so special about those three? Other than, of course, they were three of the most fancied runners in the Kentucky Derby.

I thought that fact alone was sufficiently suspicious for me to go to work in Raworth's stable, in order to find out.

My roommate returned from wherever he'd been at about ten minutes to four as I was still lying on my bed. He rushed into our room, grabbed some boots from his locker and was pulling them on before he even noticed me.

He was a short man that I took to be in his fifties. He looked up at me.

'*Hola*,' he said, totally unfazed to find another man in his bedroom. '*Mi nombre es Rafael Diaz. Y tu?*'

'Paddy,' I replied. 'Paddy Murphy. From Ireland.'

'*Mexicano*,' Rafael said, pointing a finger at his chest. '*Vine aquí hace diez años.*'

I shook my head. 'No *Español.*'

He had exhausted my Spanish by asking my name.

He smiled broadly, exposing the few teeth that still remained in his head, which themselves appeared to be in need of some urgent dental treatment.

'Mexican,' he said in heavily accented English. 'I came to here ten years.'

I climbed down from my bunk and shook his hand. He grinned some more. 'We go work. No late. Mr Keith say boss come.'

'Yes,' I said, looking at the watch on my wrist.

It was five minutes to four.

Don't be late, Keith had said.

Rafael and I rushed along from the accommodation block to the barn.

'Come on, you two,' Charlie Hern shouted at us. 'Hurry up and get in position.'

We quickly lined up with seven others, including Keith who stood on the end. It reminded me slightly of the FACSA special agent parade at the National Guard facility on the morning of the Hayden Ryder raid.

But that is where the similarity ended.

The FACSA team had been a crack outfit while this motley crew appeared anything but. Instead of a smart uniform, the nine of us wore a variety of T-shirts, jeans and assorted footwear ranging from Rafael's ankle-high jodhpur boots to my off-white trainers.

George Raworth appeared from the office in which I had been interviewed earlier, and walked over to where we were paraded. He was casually dressed in blue jeans and a polo shirt, in contrast to the last time I'd seen him wearing a suit and tie on the giant TV screen at Churchill Downs as he'd led Fire Point into the Derby winner's circle.

During my stay with Tony and Harriet, I had used the Internet to do some research on Mr George S. Raworth.

He had been born near El Paso in western Texas where his great-great-grandfather had established a longhorn cattle ranch in the 1890s, just as soon as the railroad had arrived to transport the stock to markets in the north.

The 100,000-acre ranch was now run by two of George's cousins, primarily producing beef for the California market, but also raising American Quarter Horses, a strong muscular breed with a compact body, favoured as cowboys' working horses, and named for their prowess as the fastest equine breed over a quarter of a mile from a standing start.

George had started his adult life training the young Quarter Horses from the family ranch, racing them at the Lone Star racetrack near Dallas, before graduating to the more lucrative Thoroughbred circuit.

Initial successes had marked him as a new golden-boy of American racing but his reputation had been tarnished over the years by several cases involving the misuse of medications, especially steroids.

He was now in his mid-fifties but looked somewhat older, with a head of prematurely white hair and facial skin ravaged both by teenage acne and by too many of his former years having been spent in the harsh Texas sunshine.

He walked along the line of his staff and stopped in front of me.

'And who are you?' he asked in a voice that didn't have as much drawl as I'd been expecting.

'I'm Paddy, sir,' I replied in my best Cork accent. 'I has only started today.'

'Well, Paddy,' he said. 'Welcome to the most successful training barn in the United States. Did you see the Derby on Saturday?'

'Indeed I did, sir,' I said, 'On TV.' I smiled broadly at him.

He smiled back and moved on down the line.

Satisfied by the inspection of his staff, he faced us.

'Well done all,' he said. 'Now for the Preakness and then the Triple Crown.'

George turned and went back into the office.

Charlie Hern scowled at the line. 'Go on then, the lot of you, get to work. Paddy, you go with Maria. She'll show you what's where. You'll do four horses to start with until we see how you go. Maria, show him Stalls One to Four.'

Maria was the only female in the line-up. Slim and young, she was wearing a skimpy, olive-green T-shirt above tight denim jeans with mock-designer holes in the knees. She was beautiful, with high cheekbones under a bronze skin, and she clearly knew how to display her body to maximum advantage, but she didn't seem too pleased to be asked to look after the new boy.

'I should not be treated like common hot-walker,' she said with a slight Spanish accent, tossing her thick dark hair from side to side in displeasure. 'I am *not* hot-walker, I should be groom.'

She was certainly hot, at least to my eye.

15

I very quickly slipped into the routine of George Raworth's barn.

Other than Keith, the barn foreman, there were seven full-time staff, including Maria, plus a yard boy who was clearly the oldest of us all, using his ever-present broom more as a support than for actual sweeping.

Maria showed me where the stable equipment was stored.

'Have you been here long?' I asked her, trying to be friendly.

'I came here January as hot-walker,' she said haughtily, still unhappy, 'but I should be groom by now. I have done my study.'

A hot-walker was someone employed simply to lead the horses around as they cooled after exercise. It was the lowest rung on the horse-care ladder.

'But I am still treated by boss as mere hot-walker.' She sighed and drew herself up to her full height, posing and pouting with obvious irritation. Her facial expression reminded me of a flamenco dancer.

I berated myself slightly for fantasising about Maria cavorting around a dance floor in high heels. I was not here to chase the female stable staff.

'Is being a hot-walker all that bad?'

'I want better,' she said. 'How come you are groom already when I be here much longer?' She turned and walked off, gyrating her hips in an overly belligerent manner. I found it rather sexy, and she knew it.

I sighed and went to work.

I cleared the soiled bedding in stalls one to four and replenished the straw for the equine residents, placing the waste into the huge grey metal skips that were earmarked for the purpose at either end of the barn.

I was quite surprised to see that straw was in widespread use, the preference in the UK having moved towards wood pellets, shavings or shredded newspaper.

As Keith had told me earlier, the barn had thirty-two stalls – two blocks of sixteen built back-to-back down the centre – with a wide covered walkway called a shedrow that ran right around the building inside the exterior walls.

The stalls, like the rest of the building, were constructed from wood and they opened onto the shedrow so that the horses were able to look out over half-doors.

At each corner of the barn was an exit with a sliding door. During the day the doors were left open with only a single bar across the gap to prevent any loose horses from escaping.

The doors were slid shut at night but not locked. The wooden structures, together with large quantities of straw and hay, meant that fire was always uppermost in people's minds and large signs with 'No Smoking/Prohibido Fumar' hung from the rafters every twenty feet or so along the shedrow.

The barns at Belmont were fitted with sprinkler systems but, nevertheless, locked exit doors would hamper the evacuation of the horses if the worst was to happen, as had occurred in 1986 when forty-five top Thoroughbreds, collectively worth several million dollars, had all died one night when fire destroyed barn 48 on the eastern edge of the site.

George Raworth, accompanied by Charlie Hern, made a tour of his stable, stopping at each stall to inspect the occupant and discuss progress. We grooms had to remove the bandages from the horse's legs and stand, holding the animal's head, while both George and Charlie ran a hand down the back of each equine limb, feeling for unwanted heat in the tendon or ligaments.

Like many others, the Raworth's horses all wore leg bandages as a matter of course, not because they were injured but to add support and to hold cotton pads that prevented nicks and bruises caused by kicking into themselves. The bandages were also used to hold medications and liniments in place, often used after racing to ease any slight sprains.

'Everything OK, Paddy?' Charlie asked as he and George came into Stall 1 where I had a firm grip of the headcollar of a four-year-old gelding called Paddleboat.

'Fine, sir, thank you,' I replied.

'Which part of Ireland are you from?' George asked.

'From the south, sir,' I said. 'County Cork.'

'My mother's father was Irish.'

I hadn't spotted that in any of my research.

'He came from a bit further north. From Thurles in County Tipperary.'

'I know it,' I said. 'I went to the racecourse there as a kid.'

'I've never been able to get there myself,' George said. 'Maybe one day.'

I breathed a small silent sigh of relief. I hadn't been there either.

I stood and listened as the two men turned their attention to Paddleboat.

'He ran Thursday in a seven-eighths-mile, fifteen-grand claimer,' Charlie said. 'Finished sixth of eight. Never in with a chance and not claimed.'

'Is he on Clen?' George asked.

'Has been,' Charlie replied. 'Came off it to go to the track.'

'Put him back on it. Up the dose.'

Charlie wrote something down in a notebook.

'If he shows no improvement soon,' George went on, 'we'll have to get rid of him – maybe in an even lower claimer. Ship him down to Philly Park if necessary.'

Unlike in the UK, claiming races made up the bulk of contests at US racetracks. Before the start, any horse in the race could be claimed by a new owner for a fixed amount as determined by the race conditions.

Title in the horse was transferred as the starting gates opened, although the former owner was entitled to any purse-money earned in that particular race.

It would clearly not be sensible to run a really good horse in a race in which the claim figure was very low. The horse would be sure to be claimed by a new owner and, even if it won the purse, the original owner would lose a valuable animal for a fraction of its true worth.

However, if a horse was valued around the claim figure then, if it were claimed, the original owner would recover his initial investment, plus he has the chance of picking up a substantial purse on top if it won the race.

In this way, racetracks used claiming races to encourage horses of roughly equal value, and hence of a comparable standard, to race against one another. This made the racing more competitive and thus boosted the 'handle', the total sum of money wagered by the public. The handle was what ultimately determined the tracks' income, which was what they really only cared about. Each day's programme would have claiming races with a range of claim amounts and horses were entered accordingly.

Claiming races were popular with some owners but usually less so with the trainers, as they had little idea if a horse that was in their care in the morning would be residing in someone else's barn come evening.

Not that all horses were entered in claimers. The top-class ones, those that contested the major stakes races, never had their ownership so easily changed, but for the journeyman horses, those that made up the majority of the backside population at Belmont Park, they lived a merry-go-round life in the barns, being repeatedly claimed by new owners and sent to different trainers.

Paddleboat was clearly not going to remain in Raworth's barn for much longer. If a new owner didn't claim him soon, I feared he'd be off to the knacker. However, I was much more interested in what drugs George was planning to give him in the interim.

Clen was short for clenbuterol, a drug used extensively in certain parts of the world to treat asthma in humans but also as a decongestant to help clear an unwanted build-up of mucus from a horse's respiratory tract.

But I could hear Paddleboat's airways. They were as clear as a bell – not even a hint of a wheeze.

I'd once done some research on clenbuterol for the BHA. Although not in fact a steroid, it had similar anabolic effects in horses, such that it helped to build muscle. It was rumoured to have been widely used in US training barns for many years almost on a daily basis, like a feed supplement. Only recently had new regulations been introduced requiring that clenbuterol use be suspended at least fourteen days prior to racing.

'See to it he also gets a five-millilitre shot of HA in each hock joint and five hundred milligrams of

Adequan into his hindquarters,' George said to Charlie, who wrote again in his notebook.

HA is hyaluronic acid, a component of synovial fluid found naturally in healthy joints, while Adequan is an osteoarthritis drug. Both are used for the treatment of degenerative joint disease, something that really shouldn't affect a horse that was only four years old. Paddleboat's future prospects were looking worse by the minute.

George and Charlie moved out into the shedrow.

I quickly closed the stall door and moved on to my next horse, a five-year-old gelding called Debenture. The trainer and his assistant repeated the process of feeling his legs and discussing his future.

'He's still getting the vitamin shots,' Charlie said. 'I've given him two already this week and I'll do one more tomorrow. They should set him up well for the Spring Handicap.'

'Good,' George said, before moving back out into the shedrow and on to the next horse.

And so on, down the full line of stalls.

When the inspections of my four horses were complete, I returned to each one in turn, replacing the protective pads and bandages on their legs and removing their halters.

George Raworth and Charlie Hern were still on their tour when I'd finished, so I walked round the shedrow towards Stall 17, which was at the other end of the barn, next to the office.

Stall 17 was the home of the barn star.

Fire Point had his head out over the half-door and he seemed to be taking a special interest in everything around him. Horsemen often talk about a horse having an intelligent head, by which they mean it is broad with eyes set far apart, a straight profile with ample nostrils. Fire Point's head was none of those things. It was narrow, slightly dished, and with a small muzzle. However, his eyes were bright and alert.

'Wonderful, isn't he?' said a voice behind me. I turned. It was Keith. 'I love redheads,' he said. 'He's like a reincarnated Secretariat.'

It was quite a statement. It was true that both Fire Point and Secretariat were chestnuts, but Secretariat was a legend in racing. Big Red, as he had been nick-named, didn't just capture the 1973 Triple Crown, he destroyed it, completing his trio of wins with an astonishing 31-length victory in the Belmont Stakes, a feat so extraordinary that it reportedly made those watching it cry.

And now, more than forty years later, Secretariat still held the record times for all three of the Triple Crown legs. He had been quite a horse, maybe the best ever.

I went over to stroke Fire Point but Keith put a hand out to stop me.

'Mr Raworth doesn't like anyone going near him. Other than me, that is. I look after him.'

I remembered that it had been Keith I had seen leading Fire Point over from the barns before the

Kentucky Derby. Now he looked at the horse almost in awe. Certainly in adoration.

When the trainer's tour of the barn was over, the grooms lined up at the feed store for Charlie Hern to issue the correct amount of concentrated mixed horse nuts for each animal.

As a general rule, racehorses eat one pound in weight of mixed feed for every hand high they stand at their withers. Most Thoroughbreds are around sixteen to seventeen hands high so they eat sixteen to seventeen pounds a day, plus some hay for fibre.

'Paddleboat,' I said, getting to the head of the line.

Charlie scooped two large measures of nuts from the feed bin into a black plastic bucket with a large number '1' painted on the side in white. He then poured some thick syrup onto the food from a stubby brown glass bottle with a white label.

The syrup contained the clenbuterol – it said so on the label. Next, he measured more feed into the buckets marked 2, 3 and 4, for my other horses.

'Make sure they eat it all up,' Charlie said.

I took the buckets back to the appropriate stalls, gave the feed to the horses and waited while they ate it. I then checked they all had fresh water before returning the equipment to the appropriate store. My first evening's work as a groom was done, and I hadn't messed up.

*

Raworth's six grooms plus Maria and the yard boy went together to the track kitchen for supper.

'Food good,' Rafael said to me on the way. 'Plenty.'

'Don't listen to him,' Maria said. 'It is garbage. Always full of chilli. Mexicans will eat anything.'

'Where are you from?' I asked.

'Puerto Rico,' she said.

Hell, I thought. I hope I hadn't turned down the chance to share a room with her.

'Are there many Puerto Ricans here?' I asked.

'Lots,' she said. 'Diego, my cousin.'

She indicated towards one of the others in our group. I smiled at him but it wasn't reciprocated. He simply glared back at me with cold black eyes.

The eight of us did not eat together as a single unit. Having individually swapped a meal token for food with Bert Squab at the service counter, most went off to sit on their own or with grooms from other barns. Maria, however, sat down right opposite me.

Cousin Diego clearly wasn't happy.

He moved to our table, taking the chair right next to Maria. He continued to stare at me, eating his supper without ever looking at it once. I found it rather disconcerting, and Maria wasn't happy with him either.

'Go away,' she shouted at him in English.

He didn't like that.

'*Habla Español*,' he shouted back at her. '*Mantente alejado de este gringo.*'

'*Púdrete!*' She stood up and raised her hand as if

to strike him but stopped short. She sat down again. '*Por favor vete.*'

Diego reluctantly moved away across the gangway, but still he continued to stare.

'I sorry,' Maria said, looking down at the table. 'Diego speak very good English, much better than me, but he still act like he in San Juan. All his friends here from Puerto Rico. They like control of women. He not like me speak to men not from Puerto Rico.'

'Do you speak to men not from Puerto Rico often?' I asked.

She looked up at me and smiled broadly. 'Only every day.'

I smiled back at her and sensed Diego getting agitated to my left.

We ate for a while in silence. Maybe the food was a little too hot for Maria's taste, but I liked things spicy and, as Rafael had said, there was plenty of it.

Attached to the track kitchen was a recreation hall and Maria and I went through there after eating. Diego followed. In the hall were some casual seating, a jukebox, two pool tables and five computer workstations. There was also a large TV currently showing a baseball game between the New York Yankees and the Kansas City Royals.

'Where's the bar?' I asked.

'No here,' said Maria. 'Sometime boys go out to bar but drinking not allowed on backside, although some still do.' She smiled as if implying that she was one of those.

'Is there much else to do?' I asked.

'We have classes. English most, but also reading and math.'

'Hey, Maria,' shouted one of the young men watching the baseball, 'come and give us a kiss and a cuddle.'

She raised her middle finger to him but she wandered over to join them nevertheless. Maria clearly enjoyed being the centre of attention.

If possible, Diego looked even less happy.

I, meanwhile, went over to another group of eight grooms gathered at the far end of the hall.

'May I join you?' I asked in my best Cork accent.

None of them said anything but two shifted along a bench to make some room. I sat down.

'I'm new here,' I said. 'Name's Paddy. I'm Irish. I started today, on Raworth's crew.'

All I received was a few nods.

'I've come from working the barns at Santa Anita,' I went on, 'in California.'

I received a couple more nods.

'How about you?' I asked, turning to the boy sitting right next to me. 'Been here long?'

'A while,' he said nervously, glancing across at an older man.

'Where do you come from?' I asked him.

'Why do you want to know?' the older man said sharply. He was probably in his early forties, with slicked-back black hair and a matching goatee, and was clearly the group's leader.

'I'm only being conversational,' I said.

'Well, don't be,' the man said abruptly. 'We don't like people asking questions. Especially about who we are and where we come from. Too many of us are trying to forget.'

I could see that finding any of Adam Mitchell's previous grooms was going to be difficult, if not impossible.

This was not the first time I'd come across those with such a sentiment.

I thought of them as victims of a 'here-and-now' syndrome – people that exist only for the here and now, without any consideration of their future, and without learning any lessons from their past.

Many habitual criminals have it. It is not that they enjoy going to jail, they just persistently ignore previous experience and mistakenly believe that it will not happen to them again this time. The notion that long prison sentences act as a deterrent against criminal behaviour simply does not apply to such people.

In many respects, steeplechase jockeys have exactly the same here-and-now mentality. History should have taught them that future mounts *will* fall and they *will* be seriously injured, but they live only for the here and now, for the thrill of the race, not contemplating for one second the inevitable agony of broken bones or dislocated shoulders. Once they do, it is time to retire.

I stood up and went outside to find a quiet corner to call Tony Andretti.

16

'Equine viral arteritis,' Tony said. 'EVA.'

'What is that?'

'It's a disease caused by a virus. The three horses at Churchill have tested positive for antibodies in their blood. There's no doubt. It seems it is quite common in some breeds but less so in Thoroughbreds.'

I'd never heard of it

'How did they get it?' I asked.

'Strictly speaking, according to one of the veterinarians I spoke to, EVA is contagious rather than infectious,' Tony said. 'It is a respiratory disease but horses have to have their noses in contact to pass it on, as the virus exists in their nasal discharges – snot to you and me – rather than in the air. But it can also be transmitted via any nasal droplets left on shared tack or feed bowls, anything that is moved from one animal to another, as long as it is done immediately.'

'How long is the incubation period?'

'Anywhere from three to fourteen days depending on the strain of the virus and the amount transmitted.'

'That means that one of them couldn't have given it to the other two because all three went down with it on the same day. So where did it come from initially?'

'Maybe there was another horse with a mild case

of the disease,' Tony said. 'It seems that some horses don't show any clinical symptoms when infected but they still shed the virus and so can infect others.'

'Can you find out when those three horses arrived at Churchill Downs and where they stayed when they were there? If you can, find it out for all the Derby runners. See if any were together in a Stakes Barn.'

'I'll contact the Churchill backside manager,' Tony said. 'He must have had a list of where each horse was housed to know where to detail the sheriff's deputies.'

'Also try to discover if there's anything else that might be a common denominator for those three. Perhaps they flew to Louisville on the same flight or something.'

'OK,' Tony said. 'I'll get on to it. Oh yes, there's one more thing. We've had the results back from the samples taken from Hayden Ryder's horses after he was killed in the raid at Churchill. At least half of them were dosed to the eyeballs with the steroid stanozolol and had obviously been running with it in their system.'

'That'll be why he was trying to ship them out to Chattanooga.'

'Stupid man,' Tony said. 'Hardly worth dying for.'

I agreed.

'Anything else?'

'Not that I can think of at the moment,' I said. 'I'll call you again tomorrow, same time.'

'I'll be here.'

I went back into the recreation hall. Maria was

now sitting on one of the young men's laps holding court, and cousin Diego was almost beside himself with rage. Meanwhile, the baseball was in the bottom of the fifth inning, not that anyone was taking much notice any longer.

There was now a far more interesting game to watch – sexual electricity.

I left them to it.

One of my greatest frustrations at working under-cover was that I'd had to leave my laptop and iPhone at Tony's house – a groom working on minimum wage would never have such things – and I desperately wanted to do some Internet research on EVA.

I left Maria to her admirers and sat myself at one of the recreation-hall computer workstations, the one at the far end closest to the wall. I angled the screen such that prying eyes could not see what I was reading.

According to a veterinary website, equine viral arteritis had been first isolated as a separate disease in horses in Ohio in the 1950s, although it had been blighting horses around the world for centuries. It was easily confused with other equine respiratory diseases such as influenza or herpes, and could be confirmed only by the detection of EVA antibodies in blood.

Most infected horses, even those badly affected with the associated hives, conjunctivitis and swelling of the legs, made complete clinical recoveries in three to four weeks without any specific treatment other than rest.

I learned that, apart from the snotty discharge

route, it could also be sexually transmitted from stallion to mare.

What's more, the virus was able to remain permanently active in equine sperm, totally unaffected by the animal's natural immune system. It seemed that this was because testicles, both equine and human, are strange organs in immunological terms insofar that they generate proteins that are not present at birth. Nature has had to develop a mechanism to prevent the body's own immune system from reacting against these alien substances when puberty comes around.

And the same process that prevents the immune system from attacking sperm tissue also means that it can't kill off any virus that settles in the testicles. Consequently, stallions that become infected continue to shed EVA virus in their ejaculate for the rest of their lives, whilst otherwise being entirely healthy.

The owner I had seen weeping behind the media tent at Churchill Downs was about to have a fresh reason to cry. His hoped-for future stud-fee gold mine had struck iron pyrite – fool's gold.

Even if the three infected colts recovered sufficiently quickly from the disease itself to become champion racehorses, they would never be permitted to stand at stud for fear of infecting the mares they covered, often resulting in barren seasons or miscarriages.

I also discovered that a vaccine existed against EVA but it was not widely used in the United States or Europe unless there had been a specific outbreak.

The vaccine worked, as did most vaccines, by introducing a quantity of dead virus, which couldn't infect the horse but nevertheless stimulated the production of antibodies in the blood. These antibodies would remain in the system and immediately kill off any live virus that might subsequently appear, so preventing infection.

Because the illness was relatively rare in Thoroughbreds and generally short-lived without any lasting complications, the racehorse population was not routinely vaccinated.

The only animals for which infection was a serious matter were stallions or sexually mature colts destined to be such. But there was an added problem. If vaccinated, a routine blood test of a colt would confirm EVA antibodies and it was extremely difficult, if not impossible, to prove that those antibodies were as a result of the vaccine rather than due to the live virus.

Would you then take the chance of breeding the stallion with your best mare?

Hence colts were also not normally vaccinated as a matter of course. It was only given to valuable stallions, when it could be categorically proven by every single test available that they were free of the virus prior to vaccination.

So where did that leave the seventeen other colts that *had* made it to the starting gate in Louisville the previous Saturday and, in particular, the winner? Any colt that won the Kentucky Derby would be expected to retire to a lucrative career at stud after his racing days were over.

It was now almost five days since the three horses had become ill. With an incubation period of up to two weeks, there were still another nervous nine illness-free days to go before it could be safe to assume that Fire Point and the others had not also contracted the disease.

I clicked off the website and erased the web history. I am sure that some computer whiz kid would have been able to find out precisely what I'd been browsing, and there would definitely be a record on the server, but no one here would casually be able to look.

Next I checked my emails.

Among the usual junk were several messages from work colleagues in London, most of which I was able to ignore.

But there was one from Nigel Green that caught my eye.

He reported that Jimmy Robinson, the jockey nicked for buying banned diuretics in the A34 lay-by, had since been sacked as stable jockey for a top Newmarket establishment. He may not have done anything against the law of the land but British racing valued its integrity.

'Be warned though,' Nigel wrote, 'there's a strong rumour he's off to ride for a trainer called Sidney Austin in New York.'

Nigel was one of the very few people at the horseracing authority who knew where I was, and why. Most of the others believed I was on extended unpaid leave, visiting friends in the Far East and Australia.

I scanned again through the list of emails.

There was nothing from Henrietta.

I hadn't really expected there to be and, strangely, I wasn't sure if I was happy or sad by the omission.

However, there was one from Faye.

She said that her new course of chemotherapy had started and it was making her tired but, as always, she was positive about the outcome and didn't complain – although, God knows, she had enough to complain about.

As usual, she was more concerned with me than herself, asking how I was doing and reminding me that I was to (a) get enough sleep, (b) eat healthily and (c) launder my clothes regularly.

I smiled. She couldn't help herself. Faye had taken over the maternal role when I was eight and she'd been twenty, when our dear mother had died from cancer.

Here we were, twenty-five years later, and nothing had changed.

I wrote back sending her all my love and wishing her success with the treatment. She wouldn't have wanted me to be too emotional about it, so I wasn't. I knew she could just about hold everything together provided everyone else was not wailing and whining on her behalf. We all had to be strong individually and collectively.

I also assured her that I was doing all the things she

asked, even though privately I thought that getting enough sleep might be a problem. Maria had already told me we had to be at work at 4.30 a.m. now that May was here.

It seemed that George Raworth liked the horses to go out for their exercise before the heat of the day became too great. I couldn't think why. All the racing at Belmont in summer was in the afternoon when the mercury was at its highest. Surely part of the training should be to get the horses accustomed to running fast when it was hot.

But it had been made very clear to me by Charlie Hern that my place as a groom was not to question *anything* – it was only to do *exactly* as I was told.

Sleep on the top bunk did not come easily, not least because of my flatulent roommate lying below.

I had returned from the recreation hall at eight-fifteen, as it was getting dark, to find that someone had been tampering with my belongings.

My holdall had been still there on my bed, where I'd left it and, as far as I could tell, nothing had been taken, but I was certain someone had been through it. I had purposely left the zips in a particular position so that I'd be able to tell, and there was no doubt they had been moved. They weren't even close to where I'd left them.

I smiled to myself.

If I'd been working here and someone new turned up out of the blue, I'd have had a look through their stuff too. But that was probably because I was naturally curious.

I emptied the contents of the canvas bag onto my bed.

All my usual smart clothes, including my Armani suit and my silk ties, were safely hanging in the guest-room closet in Tony Andretti's home, along with my polished black-leather shoes, my smart leather toilet bag, my Raymond Weil wristwatch and my suitcase.

I had spent some of Monday afternoon at a discount store at the Fair Oaks mall in Fairfax, buying five ten-dollar T-shirts, two pairs of bargain jeans, plus other sundry items like underwear and a patterned green nylon sweater that I wouldn't ordinarily be seen dead in. I also picked up some discounted sneakers, a pair of faux-leather black loafers, a plastic wash bag, a cheap digital watch with an imitation crocodile strap, and a blue baseball cap with the interlinked LA logo of the Los Angeles Dodgers on the front from a sportswear shop.

I then amused Tony by rubbing the lot of them in the dirt in his backyard and scuffing the shoes against the brick wall of his garage. Next, the dirty clothes all went into his washer, together with the sneakers and the baseball cap, for a couple of cycles without any detergent or softener.

My new clothes hadn't been particularly fashionable to start with but, afterwards, they looked just as I had wanted – drab and rather shabby, with the white underwear now a delicate shade of grey.

I stacked everything in my locker.

At the bottom of my holdall, underneath all the clothes, I had meticulously placed two pieces of folder paper with one of them sticking out from the other by precisely the width of my thumb.

The pieces were still there but now they were folded together in line. Someone had definitely been peeping.

Not that the papers were secret or anything. They weren't. In fact, I had left them there in order for them to be looked at.

One was a handwritten letter, supposedly from my old Irish mother back in County Cork but actually penned by Harriet Andretti, telling me how much she missed me and expressing hope that I might come home very soon. The second was a letter on IRS-headed notepaper, addressed to me at the Santa Anita racetrack, advising me that I was being charged a penalty for late filing of my income tax return the previous April.

Neither was true or particularly important. I had only added them to my kit to augment my story of having previously been an Irish groom working at Santa Anita. And one never knew when an official-looking letter from a government agency might come in useful as a form of ID, even if it had been created on my laptop and run off on Tony's desktop printer.

I climbed up onto my bed and, presently, Rafael returned. He was clearly one of the boys that went out to a bar or indulged in some illicit drinking on the backside. He reeked of alcohol and was so inebriated he could hardly find his bed in a room that was only eight feet long by six wide.

He said nothing to me, as if he hadn't noticed I was there, and eventually he tripped over the wooden chair in the corner, crawled onto his bunk, still half-clothed, and went to sleep.

I had travelled to America in an attempt to learn the identity of a mole in the FACSA racing section. I wondered how the hell I had come to the point where I was lying in the dark trying to ignore a drunken Mexican, farting beneath me?

17

Other than making calls and sending texts, my non-smart phone had one other function that was useful – it had an alarm, and it went off under my pillow at four o'clock in the morning.

The sky was still pitch-black but there was plenty of illumination coming into the room from the electric security lights that constantly lit up the whole barn area. The wafer-thin curtains didn't stretch across the full width of the window and were obviously there more for decoration than to provide greater privacy or darkness.

I swung myself down to the floor from my top bunk.

The occupant of the lower was still out for the count and snoring gently. I was tempted to leave him sleeping – if he was late and got fired, I'd not have to put up with the flatulence. However, my good nature prevailed and I tried to rouse him by shaking his shoulder, but to little effect.

In the end I rolled him off the mattress onto the floor and forced him to sit up but, even then, I wasn't quite sure if he was conscious in the normal sense of the word. I left him there and went down the corridor to the bathroom.

I was, therefore, quite surprised to find Rafael not only upright but dressed and ready for work when I returned, even if his eyes were rather bloodshot.

'*Lo siento,*' he said. '*Bebido demasiado.*'

I smiled at him. I knew *siento* meant sorry and that was enough. I didn't expect him to be able to speak English with a hangover.

'No late,' I said, tapping my watch.

'OK.' He smiled back with his mostly toothless grin.

We went out together to the barn.

Charlie Hern was there ahead of us and he was barking out orders to the other grooms.

'Paddy,' he shouted at me.

'Yes, sir,' I replied.

'All four of yours go out today in stall order. Paddleboat first at five-thirty. Have him ready.'

'Yes, sir,' I said again. 'Sure will.'

I turned and calmly walked away, but I was far from composed inside. I thought I'd done my homework about what being a groom involved but, quite suddenly, I felt I was in the deep end, and wearing lead boots.

I went in search of Maria and found her in the tack room.

'Where are the saddles?' I asked, looking around at walls draped only with bridles on numbered hooks. There were a few metal saddle racks but all but one were empty.

'Exercise riders bring their own, stupid,' Maria said. 'Where you been?'

Stupid was the right word. I had really only spent any time at racing stables in England and, even then, only as a visitor or as an integrity inspector. The stable lads there not only looked after the horses' needs in terms of bedding, feed and water, they generally rode them out to the gallops each morning as well. Hence the stable tack room had racks full of saddles, one for each of the lads plus a few spares.

But it was getting increasingly difficult to find good stable lads who could not only ride well, but were of the right size and weight. It wasn't only jockeys like Jimmy Robinson for whom maintaining riding weight was a problem.

I knew that exercise riders were becoming more popular in the big English racing centres like Newmarket and Lambourn but in the United States, where the training barns were grouped together in clusters at the racetracks, the exercise riders had completely cornered the market. Here a groom could spend his whole life with racehorses and never once sit on one's back.

Maria showed me which of the bridles I needed.

Each horse had his own bridle with the specific style of bit that the trainer had chosen as the most suitable. Most were simple snaffle bits, but a few were special with extended side pieces for controlling excess sideways motion of the head, or with added rings and straps that prevented the animal rearing.

I selected the correct bridle for Paddleboat and turned to leave.

'Why you desert me last night?' Maria asked in an aggrieved tone.

'You seemed to be enjoying yourself with the others,' I replied.

She laughed and batted her long eyelashes at me. 'I only trying to make you jealous.'

Surprisingly, I now realised that she had.

More by luck than judgement, and on the dot of five-thirty, Paddleboat was ready for Victor Gomez, a 44-year-old semi-retired Venezuelan jockey who was employed as Raworth's exercise rider. He had pitched up ten minutes earlier with his saddle over his arm. By then, I had given the horse his breakfast, brushed him down, removed his overnight bandages and picked out any muck from his feet.

Maria helped me with the saddle, fetching me the right pad to put underneath, and assisting with girth adjustments so that everything fitted perfectly.

'No tendon boots,' she suddenly shouted when I thought that all was finished.

'Tendon boots?' I'd never heard of them.

Maria rushed off and returned with two black padded tubes about nine inches long that she strapped to the horse's forelegs.

'Gives tendon support,' she said. 'Horses always wear them for exercise and racing. How come you are groom and not know of tendon boots?'

'We never used them at Santa Anita,' I said.

I'm not sure she believed me but I didn't wait to

find out. Instead, I led Paddleboat out of his stall and round towards the office.

Charlie Hern was there, giving Victor instructions on what work he wanted the horse to do. He broke off to inspect my handiwork. Satisfied, he gave Victor a leg-up into the saddle.

'OK, Paddy,' he said. 'I'll take him along to the training track. You carry on with getting the next one ready.'

'Yes, sir,' I said.

I did as I was told and that was how the morning progressed, with only a short break for a hurried breakfast in the track kitchen at seven.

Each of the horses went out to the track for a work-out lasting about twenty to twenty-five minutes. Not that they ran fast for all that time. I leaned on the rail and watched the last of mine at exercise. Victor Gomez took him through a combination of walking and trotting, interspersed with a few fast gallops over no more than half a mile at a time.

Meanwhile, George Raworth and Charlie Hern stood on a raised platform at the edge of the training track, Charlie with a stopwatch in his hand, recording everything in a notebook. Occasionally Victor would go over to George for further instructions before setting off again.

When its exercise was finished, each horse was handed over to Maria who would first give it a wash to remove the sweat from its coat, and then, as her hot-walker job title suggested, she would walk the hot horse round and round the shedrow until it had cooled, giving it a drink of water every lap or two.

There was another exercise rider also working that day for Raworth and, between him and Victor, they rode all the horses scheduled for track exercise in about two and a half hours.

All except Fire Point.

He was a special case and his Derby-winning race jockey, Jerry Fernando, had made the journey up from Baltimore especially to ride him after the other horses had finished. All the Raworth stable staff, including me, stood and watched as the star of the barn was led out to the track by Keith.

We were rightly proud to have a Triple Crown contender in our midst.

I, however, couldn't help wondering if he'd been given a dishonest helping hand to become so.

Not that the daily grind of a groom was over just because the horses had finished their exercise. There were still stalls to be cleaned, bedding to be laid, coats to be brushed, standing-bandages to be replaced, water to be fetched and carried, plus countless other things that needed to be done for the horses before it was time for any rest.

And then there was the visit from one of the track veterinary surgeons to collect blood and give injections.

I held Paddleboat's head as five different needles were stuck into him. First, about 20ml of blood was drawn from the jugular vein in his neck. Next, a quick-acting sedative went into the same vein to keep the horse calm so that the hyaluronic acid could be injected directly into his hock joints. Finally, an intramuscular shot of Adequan went into his bottom.

'What's the blood for?' I asked.

'Regular weekly testing,' he said. 'We do a quick cell count at our lab here at the track. High white would indicate an infection, while low red is a sign of anaemia.'

I wanted to ask if he also did a test for EVA antibodies but decided against it.

Blood was taken from all the horses in the barn, and most had medications of some sort thrust into them one way or another. Two were running that afternoon and, as was usual, they would both receive their 500mg dose of Lasix four hours before race time.

Next a delivery truck arrived, piled high with bales of straw, all of which needed to be transferred by hand from the vehicle to the bedding store, which was inconveniently situated right on top of the office, in the space below the roof rafters.

And all the moving had to be done by the grooms, while the truck driver stood around watching.

I was sent up to the store, climbing the wooden ladder that was attached to the wall. I then had to bend down to grab each bale in turn after it had been carried from the truck and lifted up towards me by the others. I stacked it in place before repeating the process. Over and over, it seemed to be never-ending.

I had always tried to maintain a pretty good standard of fitness, ever since my days at the Royal Military Academy at Sandhurst, but by the time the last of the straw had been raised my muscles were seriously complaining, especially in my back. I obviously wasn't quite as fit as I'd thought.

I was looking forward to a soothing lie-down on my bunk when Charlie Hern put paid to that idea.

'Paddy,' he shouted into the barn. 'Here. Now.'

'Coming, sir,' I shouted back, running round the shedrow to the office.

'Good,' Charlie said, seeing me. 'Rafael claims he's sick with flu, so you will look after Anchorage Bay today. Stall Eighteen. He runs in race four. Have him at the receiving barn on time and over at the paddock ready for saddling by two o'clock.'

'Yes, sir,' I said.

Flu, indeed.

I'll murder that bloody Rafael.

18

Anchorage Bay ran second in race four, pushing the winner all the way to the line but failing to get up by a neck.

I was just glad he'd made it to the starting gate on time, and that I hadn't somehow messed up.

George Raworth seemed to be fairly pleased with the outcome.

'I reckon he'll win next time out,' I heard him tell the owner after the race. I was holding the horse's head as he was unsaddled on the track in front of the grandstand. 'And he wasn't claimed so we still have him.'

The owner smiled wanly at his trainer but he was enviously eyeing those having their photographs taken in the winner's circle. He had wanted to win *this* time.

'Well done, Paddy,' George said to me. 'He looked nice.'

'Thank you, sir,' I said, although the horse's smart appearance had mostly been down to Maria.

She had come to my rescue again, showing me where the racing bridles were kept, how to prepare the horse to look his best, and when and where I had to take him. In fact, she had stayed by my side all afternoon, walking Anchorage Bay with me through the horse tunnel that ran from the barn area under the main-entrance roadway to the paddock. She also helped take him back to Raworth's barn afterwards.

Even though there was no touching of hands, or lips, it was clear to both Maria and me that some sexual chemistry did exist between us. We laughed and joked as we washed Anchorage Bay, and she sprayed me playfully with the hose.

Don't get involved – I kept telling myself. It was far too dangerous.

'Stop it,' I said seriously, cutting short her antics. 'Let's get the horse back in his stall.'

By which point it was four o'clock and time for evening stables.

I finally finished work at six having been on the go continuously for over thirteen hours. I was exhausted.

'Do we get double-rate for overtime?' I asked Charlie Hern as I collected the feed for my horses.

He laughed. 'Be thankful you have a job in the first place.'

I took that to mean that no, we didn't.

'We're classified as agricultural workers,' said one of the other grooms who had overheard the exchange. 'Overtime doesn't apply until you've done more than sixty hours in a single week, and then they don't count meal breaks or time spent waiting over at the track.'

The European Union Working Time Directive clearly didn't apply here.

I acquired a new-found sense of admiration for the humble stable lad.

'They all travelled to Louisville separately,' Tony said when I called him after supper. 'Two flew in from California, but on different days and from different cities, while the third, Liberty Song, arrived by horse trailer from Keeneland racetrack in Lexington.'

So they hadn't become infected with EVA on the journey.

'When did they arrive?' I asked.

'The two from California came the previous week, one from LA on Thursday and the other from San Francisco on Friday. The one from Lexington also arrived Friday, eight days before the Derby.'

'So they had to have been infected while at Churchill Downs,' I said. 'It would be too much of a coincidence if all three had been infected elsewhere, especially as there have been no other cases.'

'There has now,' Tony said. 'Another horse at Churchill fell sick today. They're doing tests to confirm it is EVA, although it has all the signs.'

It was Thursday. Five days since the others had first shown signs of illness.

'It must be due to secondary infection from one of the original three.'

'Most likely,' Tony said. 'The new horse that's fallen sick had been in the next-door stall to Liberty Song up until last Saturday.'

'Was that in the Stakes Barn?' I asked.

'No. Liberty Song was in his trainer's own barn. One of the two from California was in the Stakes Barn but the other was in a separate barn right at the far end of the site that, ironically, the trainer had rented specifically to prevent his horse catching anything from others in the Stakes Barn.'

'Is there any common denominator at all between the three?'

'Not that I have found. As far as we can tell, they weren't ever in the same place together. They had different training schedules so they didn't even use the track at the same time.'

'There *has* to be something,' I said. 'Assuming the incubation period was the same as for the latest case, they must have all been infected on the Sunday or Monday before the Derby.'

'But how?' Tony asked.

'If there was no accidental coming together of the three,' I said, 'then there has to be another virus carrier that *did* come into contact with each of them on that Sunday or Monday.'

'But other horses would surely also become sick.'

'Not if it was deliberately targeted at those three,' I said.

'How?' he asked again. 'You can't lead an EVA-infected horse over to three separate stalls in completely different parts of the backside and get it to snort some virus into the noses of only those three specific horses. You would have been seen and stopped for a start. And the virus doesn't live long outside the body so, even if you could transfer the infection with nasal droplets, those would have had to come from an infected host, so where's that horse?'

'I don't know,' I said forlornly.

It was frustrating.

The only thing we knew for sure was that the three horses had somehow been infected – there was no doubt about that.

'Anything else to report?' Tony asked.

'Not really,' I said. 'Other than to say that the life of a groom is bloody hard work. I ache all over.'

He laughed.

'It is not a laughing matter,' I said.

'Then let's get a FACSA raid sorted so that you can get out of there. Have you found anything suspicious for us to search for?'

'Not yet. I've been so damned busy doing the job.'

He laughed again.

'Give me a while longer,' I said. 'I've already seen some evidence of the drug regime Raworth uses but I'm not sure if it breaks the rules. I'll have a proper scout round and see if I can spot anything else. It would be much better if I could actually find something dodgy going on rather than you just making it up. If Raworth is tipped off about an upcoming raid, there would only be a major reaction if he was really doing something wrong.'

'OK,' Tony said. 'I'll do nothing yet. Will you call tomorrow?'

'I'll try. If not tomorrow, then Saturday.'

'Harriet and I are out to dinner with friends that night, but you can call earlier if you want. I won't be at work Saturday.'

I would, I thought.

This Saturday was an important day at Belmont Park. It marked the annual running of the Man o'War Stakes, one of the major races of the year for horses aged four or over. It was named after the great champion racehorse and sire of the 1920s, and George Raworth had two runners.

'Enjoy your dinner,' I said to Tony and we disconnected.

I had walked well away from the track kitchen to make the call and now I started to return.

I didn't make it.

There were four of them and Diego was their leader.

The Puerto Rican mob.

'*No toque Maria, gringo!*' Diego shouted at me. '*Dejarla sola!*'

They didn't wait for me to reply.

Instead, they rushed at me before I had a chance to react, two of them grabbing me by the arms and a third placing his arm round my neck from behind. I was trying to crouch down and make the target as small as possible but the man with the headlock hauled me up straight. The two holding my arms then spread my legs wide with their feet.

Diego ran up and kicked me hard in the groin, scoring a direct hit on the family jewels.

The pain was excruciating, running up into my abdomen and right down to my toes.

The three men behind let go and I collapsed to the dusty ground, tucking myself up to try to ease the fire that was now raging between my legs.

'*La próxima vez, te mataremos,*' Diego shouted, and he drew a finger across his throat in case I hadn't understood his Spanish.

As a parting gesture he gave me a kick to the side of the head, then he and his friends laughed, turned away and walked off, leaving me curled up in the dirt.

I lay on the ground for quite a while, unable to do anything other than draw up my knees and wait for the tide of pain to ebb away.

Why people think it is funny when a cricketer or baseball player gets hit in the nuts baffles me. There's nothing funny about it at all, especially when it has been inflicted on purpose, as in this case.

I heard someone approaching and was worried that Diego and his chums were coming back for another go.

'*Estas bien?*' said a voice from above me.

Still holding my knees, I rolled onto my back and looked up. It was Rafael and he stared down at me with deep concern in his eyes, shocked to discover that it was his roommate lying at his feet.

'You OK, Paddy?'

I tried to smile at him. 'Yes, OK,' I croaked.

He held out a hand to help me up but, in spite of it still being quite early, Rafael was already the worse for wear with drink and I almost pulled him over on top of me.

Being on my feet didn't seem to help the pain much, and I was hardly standing upright. Instead I was crouched down on my haunches.

Gradually the intense pain subsided, replaced only by a dull ache and a feeling of nausea that made my skin feel cold and sweaty.

Rafael was still concerned by my appearance.

'You sick,' he said, slightly slurring the words. 'I fetch doctor. You go hospital.'

'No,' I replied quickly. 'No doctor. No hospital.' I forced myself to stand up straight, and then I smiled at him. 'I'll be OK now.'

Rafael didn't look convinced by my bravado and I wasn't entirely sure I was either. I did worry that Diego had done some real damage to my nethers, but doctors and hospital would have required such awkwardnesses as my real name and payment, neither of which I was prepared to give at the moment.

If things didn't improve with time, then I'd seek medical help, but not yet.

Rafael and I made our slow way back to the bunkhouse, me walking delicately with my knees spread wide apart like a cowboy who'd spent too long in the saddle, and him holding on to me for support.

I went along to the shared bathroom and delicately examined my privates. Everything was very tender but at least it all appeared to be in the right place and there was no blood in my pee, which was encouraging.

'Who do this to you?' Rafael asked when I went back to our room.

'I didn't see,' I lied.

'You call *policía*.'

I shook my head. 'No police. It would only make things complicated.'

He looked at me with a quizzical expression.

'More bad,' I said, and he nodded, steadying himself on the bedpost.

Rafael then lay down on his bed and went straight to sleep while I carefully climbed up onto the bunk above him.

Calling the police was not an option. For a start, it would blow my cover, but mostly it would be a waste of time. It would simply be my word against those of the Puerto Rican four who would all swear it wasn't them and each one would give the other three an alibi.

Diego and his chums had actually been rather clever, either inadvertently or on purpose. They had used the right degree of violence to seriously hurt me, but not enough to cause any lasting harm. I didn't think the police would be interested, and I was quite sure they wouldn't have arrested anyone. Indeed, I was convinced that going to the police would have placed me in greater danger of receiving a repeat performance, and I had absolutely no desire for that.

No police.

I would fight my own battles, and I would choose when and where.

19

I had a restless night.

When my phone alarm went off at four, I'd already been awake for ages, and I was sore.

Even the slightest of movements sent shock waves down into my groin.

Gritting my teeth, I swung my legs over the side of the bed and lowered myself gently to the floor.

I dug into my plastic wash bag for a couple of painkillers and hoped they would work quickly. Next I walked gingerly along the corridor to the bathroom, feeling sick.

Using the cracked and tarnished mirror above the sink, I examined myself again as best I could. There was a slight darkening of the skin due to bruising but no major swelling and my pee was still clear of any blood.

I decided that I'd live.

In an ideal world I would have lain still on my bed for a day or two to allow the bruising to come out and for recovery to start. But I wasn't currently living in an ideal world. I had to get to work, not least because I wasn't prepared to give Diego the satisfaction of seeing that I was off sick.

As it was, I managed to get myself dressed and over

to the barn by half past four. Not for the first time, I was glad that Raworth's grooms didn't have to ride the horses. That would have been a step too far for the throbbing orbs between my legs.

I readied my four horses for exercise and spent the entire morning moving slowly round with my knees slightly spread apart. Two more painkillers helped and, gradually, things started to return to normal.

I came upon Diego as we were both collecting feed from the store. He said nothing. Instead he repeated his finger-across-the-throat gesture. I just smiled at him but that made him angry and he tipped the feed bowl I was carrying out of my hands and into the dirt.

I sighed.

I could do without this difficulty. It wasn't that I'd even made a hit on Maria; it was all the other way around.

I did my best to avoid her but she spent most of the morning walking hot horses round and round the shedrow, passing by the stalls where I was working every couple of minutes.

Finally, after I had ignored her for almost two hours, she came in.

'What wrong with you today?' she demanded, standing full square in the middle of Paddleboat's stall.

'Nothing,' I said, not turning round and continuing to lay the straw bed for the horse.

'I watching you,' she said. 'You move like Chuck.'

Chuck was the yard boy, eighty years old if he was

a day, permanently shaking, and only kept moderately upright by his broom. The way I felt right now, I wouldn't want to pick a fight with him – he'd have won easily.

'I caught myself on the bedpost,' I said, still not turning to face her. 'I'll be fine in a couple of days.'

'You want me apply ice?' she asked with a laugh.

'No,' I said. 'I do not.'

But I couldn't help smiling.

I spent the afternoon lying on my bed, alone, for more thinking.

I needed to move things on and, in order to do that, I needed to have a look in Raworth's drug store, and also in the barn office.

But that was easier said than done.

Even though most of the grooms were off duty from about midday until four in the afternoon, the barn was never totally free of humans.

When he wasn't actively engaged in looking after Fire Point, Keith spent most of the afternoons in the office, often watching the live racing on a television connected to the racetrack system. Every hour or so he would do a circuit of the barn, looking briefly into each stall to ensure that the equine resident wasn't stuck down or suffering from colic.

And then there were always the day's runners going back and forth from the track, led by one of the grooms or a hot-walker.

The barn was never deserted.

Even at night, Keith slept in a bedroom adjoining the office, with a connecting door between the two. And, for added security, the door contained a small glass viewing panel.

I considered my options.

If I'd had my top-of-the-range night-vision goggles readily available, I might have gone in at midnight, but how would I have explained them away to whoever had been through my bag on my first day?

The only possibility was to do it during the day, maybe when Keith was having a meal at the track kitchen.

And what exactly was I going to look for anyway?

I'd already witnessed clenbuterol in use on Paddleboat, but it wasn't against the rules provided the horse didn't race until the drug had cleared its system. That alone would not be sufficient for FACSA to mount a raid. I would have to find something else.

The drugs for the horses were kept in a large, walk-in cupboard at one end of the feed store, and it was always kept locked except when Charlie Hern was there issuing items from it. The feed store was also locked most of the time. The keys were on a ring in Charlie's pocket.

Suddenly even the idea of getting in seemed hopeless, never mind actually finding something there that I shouldn't.

The office was slightly better.

As a general rule the office door was left open during the day when Keith or Charlie Hern were in the barn but I'd seen Keith pull it locked when he went to lunch.

All three of the locks, on the doors to the office, feed store and the drug cupboard, were of the pin-tumbler cylinder variety, like those found on many front doors, where the door would lock automatically when pulled shut.

I'd been taught how to pick such a lock by one of my corporals in the army. He had learned it from his father, who had been nicknamed Harry Houdini by the East London criminal underworld on account of him escaping twice from prison by picking all the locks. The son had then perfected the technique and could reportedly open anything, including safes. During the many hours of boredom of an Afghan tour of duty, he had wiled away the time by teaching the art to the rest of his platoon, me included.

All you needed were two simple pieces of kit – a torsion wrench, which was a small L-shaped metal bar inserted in the keyhole to apply tension to the cylinder, and a thin piece of metal called a rake that was moved back and forth inside the key slot to lift the pins. As always, I had both in my wash kit.

It was not the process of getting in that concerned me; it was doing it, and getting out again, without being seen.

I went over to the barn half an hour early for evening stables with the two lock picks in my left sock. But the office door was already open and Keith was in there, tipping an office chair back on two legs, with his feet up on the desk. He was watching the racing on the TV.

I went in.

'Hello, Paddy,' Keith said, taking his eyes from the screen for a mere split-second. 'We have a runner in this. Teetotal Tiger. Gate Two.'

I watched as the starting gates flew open and the horses emerged in a line, Teetotal Tiger easy to spot as his jockey was wearing a white cap.

Belmont Park boasted the longest Thoroughbred track in North American racing with a one-and-a-half-mile dirt oval, but this race was only half that distance, at six furlongs. Hence the start was midway down the back stretch.

As on all US racetracks, the horses ran anticlock-wise round the home turn. Keith took his feet off the desk and leaned forward, concentrating on the screen.

The white cap was clearly visible in third or fourth place out of the eight runners, keeping close to the rail for the shortest trip. As they straightened up for the run to the line, the leading pair drifted slightly to their right, allowing Teetotal Tiger room to sneak through on the inside and win by half a length.

Keith was now on his feet cheering. I was cheering too and suddenly Keith turned and hugged me in his excitement.

'I knew old Tiger would win sometime,' he said, punching the air in delight. 'I've been telling Mr

Raworth so for ages. He's such a sweet old thing. I hope he hasn't been claimed.'

It made me smile to think that a six-year-old was called a sweet old thing. American racing was almost exclusively for horses aged two, three, four and five, and there were very few horses still in training over seven. In England a seven-year-old was a youngster, especially in steeplechasing. No horse under eight has won the Grand National steeplechase since the Second World War, and Red Rum is one of thirteen horses that have won the race aged twelve or older – one was fifteen.

'How long has Teetotal Tiger been here?' I asked.

'On and off since he was two. He's been claimed a few times and has spent short spells in other barns but his owner, Mrs Crichton, always claims him back the next time he runs. She loves him.'

'Then why does she allow him to run in claiming races in the first place?' I asked.

'That's the way the system works, especially for a six-year-old maiden. Not many of them left at the track, I can tell you. Most would have gone for dog meat long ago – old Tiger as well, if it wasn't for Mrs Crichton.'

Keith stepped outside looking for the returning horse, leaving me alone in the office.

Apart from the desk, there were two chairs plus a four-drawer filing cabinet up against the far wall near the corner. Alongside the cabinet, hung on a row of hooks, were a series of multi-coloured racing silks, complete with caps. I presumed that there was at least one set for each of Raworth's owners.

I glanced down at the desk. It was about six feet wide by three deep, kneehole style, with three drawers on either side of the central space. The surface was covered with several stacks of papers, a china mug full of pens and a heavy horseshoe-shaped clock in one corner.

I was tempted to go behind and have a quick look through the drawers but Keith would surely be back soon. Indeed, no sooner had I dismissed the notion than he returned.

'There's no sign of them coming back,' Keith said. 'I'm worried he's been claimed.'

'Maybe he's been sent for testing,' I said. 'Who's over there with him?'

'Diego.'

I'd have been happier if the groom had been claimed instead of the horse.

No such luck.

Shortly thereafter, both Teetotal Tiger and Diego returned to the barn and George Raworth and Charlie Hern arrived with them. Keith and I went out to greet them and there was a party atmosphere in the shedrow with everyone in good humour.

Even Diego grinned briefly at me as I congratulated him, but then he remembered and the smile instantly vanished as he took the horse off to be washed down.

'I told you he'd win eventually,' Keith said to George.

'And about time too. If it hadn't been for Mrs Crichton, he'd have gone to the glue factory years ago.' We all laughed, even though it was hardly funny. 'Now, how are preparations progressing for Pimlico? We have five going down altogether. Fire Point, Classic Comic and Heartbeat in the Preakness, Ladybird in the Black-Eyed Susan Stakes on Friday, plus Debenture in the Maryland Sprint Handicap. Although God knows why we're taking him. He's good enough for claimers but he'll surely have no chance in that company. But his owner has insisted, and he's paying for the transport, so he goes. The truck for the horses is booked for Monday morning, nine o'clock.'

'Are we using the Stakes Barns?' Charlie asked.

'Yes,' George said. 'I've reserved stalls for all five. Pimlico would like to have Fire Point in Stall Forty.'

'We'll need a minimum of three grooms for the Preakness itself, one for each runner,' Charlie Hern said. 'Keith with Fire Point, plus two others. They will be more than enough to cover everything else while we're down there.'

'Hot-walker?' George said.

'The grooms can do most of that but we'll take Maria as well,' Charlie said. 'She's experienced enough by now to act as an extra groom if one of the horses plays up. We'll also have Victor. He'll be getting there Tuesday morning to ride exercise. And Jerry will be riding Fire Point. We have plenty of manpower.'

'Right,' said George, turning to Keith. 'That's sorted then. We have a runner here at Belmont on Wednesday and another on Friday, so Charlie will stay here until Preakness Day itself, overseeing things. He'll come down to Pimlico early Saturday morning. Keith, tell Rafael to sleep in your room Friday and Saturday nights. He'll be in charge when Charlie's gone. No track exercise Saturday. Back to normal Sunday. Got that?'

'Yes, Mr Raworth,' Keith said. 'Any particular grooms you want to take?'

'We'd better take Diego,' Charlie said. 'He does both Classic Comic and Heartbeat. Keith can also keep an eye on him.'

I was still standing in the shedrow nearby, and now I moved forward.

'Paddy,' said George Raworth, looking straight at me. 'You look after Debenture, don't you?' I nodded. 'Want a trip to the Preakness?'

'Yes, sir,' I replied enthusiastically. 'I sure do.'

'But Paddy has been with us only a few days,' Charlie said with doubt in his voice. 'The others won't like it.'

Bugger the others, I thought. I wanted this gig.

'I promise I won't let you down, sir,' I said quickly before George had a chance to reply. 'Please, sir.'

He hesitated.

'Paddy's been very good,' Keith said in a surprising vote of confidence. 'He cheered on Teetotal Tiger with me just now.'

236

'OK,' George said. 'Paddy, you're in. We leave Monday morning.'

'Great,' I said out loud, almost forgetting to use my Cork accent.

Charlie wasn't very happy. Perhaps he thought his authority had been undermined. But I didn't care – I was going to the Preakness. I felt like a child on Christmas morning who finds his stocking full of gifts.

Indeed, the level of my excitement rather surprised me.

I had been to most of the world's major horseraces but, I realised, this was the first time the decision that I should go had been out of my hands, and not as a result of my position within the BHA.

In spite of the ache that still persisted in my groin, I went to work at evening stables with a spring in my step only slightly dampened by the knowledge that Diego would be another of the grooms going to Pimlico.

'Why did Charlie say you needed to keep an eye on Diego?' I asked Keith when I got him alone.

'No idea,' he replied. Something in his tone told me he was lying.

'Will I have to share a room with him at Pimlico?' I asked.

'All three of us will have to share,' Keith said. 'We'll have only two rooms down there and Maria will be in the other one.'

I could always share with her, I thought.

*

'Rafael says no bedpost. He says he find you lying on ground, beat up. Who do this to you?'

Maria was standing in front of me as I ate my supper.

'I didn't see,' I said, lying to her just as I had to Rafael.

'Was it Diego?' she demanded loudly.

'I didn't see who it was,' I said again, looking down at my food.

What would be the point in telling her the truth? She would only have a fight with her cousin and that would hardly make my life any easier. In fact, it would surely make it worse.

'Why you lie to me about bedpost?'

'I didn't want you to worry,' I said. 'I am fine now, so forget it.' I waved a dismissive hand at her without looking up, hoping that Diego had spotted it from where he was sitting with his three chums at the far end of the dining hall. I was uncomfortably aware that he had been watching the whole exchange.

Maria hesitated but then slowly turned and walked away. She had only been trying to help but I'd cold-shouldered her assistance. She was understandably angry at my sudden indifference towards her. I didn't much like myself for doing it, but there was no way I was going to rectify the situation, not with Cousin Diego and his three amigos looking on.

20

I let myself into the drug store using my lock picks. I'd already searched the office without turning up anything out of the ordinary.

Saturday evening stables had been brought forward from four o'clock to three, and everyone had worked extra fast so that we had finished everything by five, ready for the big race of the day, the half-million-dollar Man o'War Stakes. All Raworth's staff not actively involved had rushed off to the recreation hall to view the race on the large-screen TV.

All of them except me. I had volunteered to keep an eye on the barn, plus its residents, while Keith went with Diego and Maria over to the track with our two runners.

I checked my watch – 5.07 p.m.

George Raworth and Charlie Hern would, right now, be readying the two horses in the saddling boxes next to the Belmont paddock.

The race was due off at 5.28.

I had asked Keith to leave the office unlocked so I could watch the race on the television, and he had readily agreed. Being allowed to be in the office meant that searching it was so much easier and far less stressful.

'I reckon we have a good chance with both of ours,' Keith had said before he left, hardly managing to control his excitement. 'There'll be a bonus for us all if we can win this.'

My bonus would have been to turn up something that would justify a FACSA raid but there was nothing incriminating in either the desk or the filing cabinet, only regular papers concerning such mundane matters as deliveries of feed or bedding, plus the personnel files for the stable staff, which included references and testimonials from previous employers.

I skimmed through them looking for anything from Adam Mitchell that might indicate a prior employment, but there was nothing.

I glanced at Maria's file. She had been born Maria Isabella Quintero in San Juan City Hospital, Puerto Rico, some twenty-seven years ago, and this was her first job since coming to the United States the previous January. There was nothing particularly remarkable in that. However, the file for her cousin, Diego Ríos, was much more revealing.

Diego was two years older than Maria, and also hailed from San Juan. He had been a groom at Raworth's barn for a little over a year but he had been in trouble on two occasions in the past four months, since Maria's arrival. Both were for violence against other grooms, and the second had resulted in his arrest.

According to a letter in the file from Judge Davidson of the local district court, Diego Ríos was subject to something called an 'adjournment in contemplation of dismissal', an ACD.

It was a bit like a suspended sentence except that Diego had not yet been convicted of anything.

But he had been charged with one count of assault and the ACD simply meant that his trial had been deferred for six months. The letter went on to say that, provided Diego did not commit another offence of any kind in those six months, the case against him would be dismissed. However, if he did offend again in that time, Diego would go on trial for the assault and, if found guilty, would be jailed for up to one year at Rikers Island, the notorious New York prison.

The letter was dated April 4th. Just one month ago. And it had been sent to George Raworth as the ACD had needed the consent of Diego's employer to give him 'the benefit of the doubt' and to continue with his employment.

So that was why they had to keep an eye on him.

They clearly didn't give him that much benefit of the doubt, and for good reason. My sore groin was witness to the fact that he had not learned his lesson.

I glanced once more at my watch – 5.10. Eighteen minutes to the race.

The drug store was well ordered with packets of powders and bottles of pills in neat rows on the two upper shelves. Below that there was an open box of sterile needles along with small red-, green- and purple-capped glass Vacutainer test tubes used for taking blood. There was also a supply of multi-sized hypodermic syringes in sealed plastic packs.

Several brown clenbuterol syrup bottles were lined up next to them, and also some packs of stanozolol, the anabolic steroid that the FACSA vets had tested for at Hayden Ryder's barn at Churchill Downs.

Was Raworth using them too close to a race, just as Ryder had been suspected of doing? Was that a good enough reason to raid the barn?

I had seen no sign of their illicit use, but I looked after only four of the twenty-eight horses. I was also confident that Fire Point hadn't been on steroids as he'd been tested both before and after the Kentucky Derby and found to be completely clear of any banned substance.

Standing upright on the left-hand side of the second shelf was the stable drug register, a ledger in which all drugs given to all the horses in the barn had to be recorded. At least that is what the New York Racing Association demanded.

I flicked through the pages and looked at the entries for the past few days. The record showed the pre-race injections of Lasix given to Anchorage Bay on Thursday and Teetotal Tiger on Friday, plus the ones given today to the two runners in the Man o'War Stakes. It also recorded the sedatives, hyaluronic acid and Adequan injected into Paddleboat by the vet on Thursday morning. There was also a record of the clenbuterol being administered daily in Paddleboat's feed.

I checked my watch again: 5.16. Twelve minutes to post-time.

Beneath the shelves of drugs were stacked several cardboard boxes and I briefly took a mental snapshot of their positions before looking in them. One had rolls of unused leg bandages, a second had spare saddle pads and a third was full with plastic containers of disinfectant.

Underneath the boxes, in the corner of the store, there sat what appeared at first to be a rather stumpy beer keg – a heavy metal cylinder about eighteen inches tall and a little over a foot in diameter, with two carrying handles welded to the top. I lifted out the cardboard boxes so I could see it more clearly.

The white cylinder had 'CryoBank' painted in blue letters on its side, and it certainly didn't contain beer – far from it.

The lid was much smaller in width than the cylinder, similar in size and shape to the caps on those large bottles of water used in office drinking fountains, except that it was metal not plastic. There was a slight 'pop' sound as I removed it, as if a little pressure had been released. I tried to look in but couldn't see anything due to a white fog that swirled about inside the container.

I'd seen something like this before, at the equine research hospital in Newmarket. This was a cryogenic flask used to store living cells at very low temperatures, immersed in liquid nitrogen. But what was it doing here?

I remembered asking the laboratory staff at the hospital how often the liquid nitrogen had to be replaced due to it evaporating into the air. Every two or three weeks, they had said, depending on how often the flask was opened and how much material was being stored.

So this flask, which clearly still had liquid nitrogen in it, must have been refilled fairly recently.

I glanced again at my watch: 5.20.

I had to get back to the office in time to watch the race. I needed to know what happened.

The flask had a metal rod clipped to the rim that went down into the tank beneath. I went to touch it but it had frost on the handle, so I folded one of the saddle pads from the box and used it as an insulating glove to lift the rod. On the end was a metal cup containing three straws, similar to plastic drinking straws but rather smaller in both length and diameter. Each of the three contained some deep-frozen material.

I would have loved to remove one of the straws for testing but, with only three there, I was worried it would be missed. But, if I couldn't take the chance of taking a whole straw, how about if I took just a bit of one? Or would it then stand out as being shorter than the other two?

I went back into the feed store. Hanging on a hook were a pair of scissors used to open the feed bags. I fetched them and cut about half an inch off the bottom of each of the straws, making sure that the bits contained some of the frozen material. I carefully placed them into one of the red-capped Vacutainer test tubes, which I then slipped into my pocket.

5.23.

Time to go.

I returned the three straws to the metal cup, lowered it back into the liquid nitrogen and re-clipped it to the rim as before. Then I secured the lid, returned the saddle pad and restacked the cardboard boxes. I spent a moment checking they were back exactly as I had found them.

5.25.

Satisfied, I relocked the drug store, silently let myself out into the shedrow and went quickly back to the office.

The ten runners were at the start, still having their girths checked. The Man o'War Stakes was run on the turf course that sits inside the main dirt track. The race was over a mile and three furlongs so the starting gate was in front of the grandstand.

With one eye on the TV screen, and with the outer office door shut and locked, I used the picks to let myself into Keith's bedroom. Maybe I was just naturally inquisitive, but it seemed a shame not to have a quick look in there while I had the opportunity. I might not get the chance again.

Not that there was much to see.

Keith appeared to have very few clothes, hardly enough to fill even half the available locker space.

Indeed, he had more well-thumbed copies of hard-core girlie magazines than anything else, mostly spread across the floor under his bed.

Each to their own.

I went back into the office, locking the door to Keith's bedroom behind me.

'They're in the gate,' called the track announcer through the TV. 'And they're off and running in the Man o'War Stakes.'

Neither of the Raworth horses won the race. One finished a creditable third but the other was always well off the pace, trailing in last of the ten, some twenty lengths behind the winner.

The mood in the camp when everyone returned to the barn couldn't have been more in contrast to that of the previous day after Teetotal Tiger's triumph.

George Raworth was spitting feathers in anger, in particular over the horse that had brought up the rear of the field.

'That damned jockey,' he kept saying over and over to Charlie Hern. 'He never gave the horse a chance.'

I'd watched the race pretty closely on the TV and, in my opinion, a combined reincarnation of both Fred Archer and Willie Shoemaker wouldn't have managed to get the horse any closer. It was sometimes easier for a trainer to blame the pilot than to accept the fact that the horse was simply not good enough.

I slid away from the inquest.

Just as I had been happy to hang around during

the good times of yesterday, I was eager to be away from the doom and gloom of today. I wanted to be perceived as a lucky omen, not a portent of failure.

Instead, I found a quiet spot away from listening ears to call Tony.

'A cryogenic flask?'

'Yes,' I said. 'It's hidden away under boxes in the drug store. There are three straws of material kept in it, frozen solid in liquid nitrogen.'

'Liquid nitrogen?' Tony said. 'Is that toxic?'

'No,' I said, laughing. 'Eighty per cent of the air we breathe is nitrogen.'

'But that's not a liquid.'

'Liquid nitrogen is just like the nitrogen in the air,' I said, 'but it has been made so cold that it liquefies.'

'But how do you get it?'

'It's created as a by-product when air is liquefied to produce oxygen, you know, for medical use and such. Anyone can buy liquid nitrogen from an industrial gas producer. It's storing it that's the problem. You need what is called a Dewar – a bit like a big thermos. That's what a cryogenic flask is.'

'But what's the liquid nitrogen for?' Tony asked.

'To keep the material inside deep frozen.'

'But what is this "material"?'

'I've no idea,' I said, 'but I have acquired some. It is in a test tube in my pocket. It's no longer frozen but we could still get it analysed.'

'How did you acquire it?' Tony asked somewhat sarcastically, as if he could already guess.

247

'You don't want to know.'

He laughed down the line. 'Do you want me to arrange a pickup?'

'Yes, please,' I said.

'We have a FACSA office in New York. They deal mostly with boxing. I'll get the station chief to collect it himself. His name is Jim Bradley. No one at the racing section will know anything about it.'

I still didn't like it. It would mean someone else would then know that I was not who I said I was.

Tony seemed to sense my hesitation.

'I've known Jim Bradley since we joined the NYPD together as cadets some forty years ago. I'd trust him to hell and back. If I tell him it is hush-hush, he'll not tell anyone, I promise.'

'OK,' I said. 'Where and when?'

'It's Saturday. I'll try Jim at home. Call me back in half an hour.'

I used the time to have my supper at the track kitchen, exchanging a plastic token with Bert Squab for a plate of highly spiced chilli con carne with rice.

Fortunately, there was no sign of Diego or his chums as I sat down to eat. I could do without that distraction at the moment.

I called Tony on the stroke of the half-hour.

'Jim says pass it through the chain-link fence on Plainfield Avenue, which runs up the east side of the barn area. Jim drives a black Ford Bronco SUV and he knows the area well. He'll park up exactly opposite the high-school sports field at eight-thirty sharp. It will be dark by then.'

I looked at my cheap watch. It read 6.46 p.m. I had an hour and three-quarters to wait.

'Fine,' I said. 'I'll be there.'

'Do you need him to get anything for you?'

How about a cricket box?

I was next to the chain-link fence opposite the high school sports field at least fifteen minutes before the allotted time, mostly obscured from the barns by a line of trees and some bushes.

The streetlights out on Plainfield Avenue, and the other lights on poles around the barns, did nothing more than throw deep shadows beneath the trees within which it was easy for me to remain hidden.

I crouched, stock still, facing inwards towards the barns, searching for any telltale movement that might indicate the presence of other eyes, there to watch me.

There was nothing. Not even a rabbit or a squirrel.

I waited.

Jim Bradley arrived in the black Ford Bronco right on cue at eight-thirty exactly, and the handover of the Vacutainer test tube through the fence took only a few seconds.

I was already well on my way back to the bunk-house before the Bronco had even turned the corner at the end of the street.

21

'It's semen.'

'What?'

'Semen. Probably equine semen but more tests are needed to confirm it.'

'But that's ridiculous,' I said.

'Quite so,' Tony agreed. 'But that's what it is, nevertheless. I dug a biochemistry professor at Columbia University out of bed early on Sunday morning to test it. He swears to me that the stuff you gave to Jim Bradley was semen. Some of the sperm in it were still swimming.'

It didn't make any sense.

'Why would a training stable need frozen semen?' I said. 'Artificial insemination is not even permissible in Thoroughbreds. All mating has to be done by live cover – the stallion has to physically mount the mare.'

'Maybe George Raworth is collecting semen from his colts and freezing it to breed from later, even if it's not permitted by the rules.'

'I very much doubt that,' I said. 'It's not all that easy to get semen in the first place, not unless you have a mare on heat to get the colt excited. You would also need specialist collecting equipment, and I saw none of that during my search. And what would be the point? He couldn't use the semen for breeding, anyway. Nowadays, every Thoroughbred foal has to be DNA-tested to confirm its parentage before it can be registered into the stud book.'

'Then your guess is as good as mine,' Tony said.

It was Sunday afternoon and I was behind the track kitchen, talking on the telephone. I had purposefully chosen a wide-open space so that no one could creep up to listen to my conversation without being seen. It also had the added advantage that I would be able to see any potential attacker from afar.

I spun through 360 degrees.

No eavesdroppers. And no Diego.

'So what do we do now?' Tony asked. 'Don't you think we have enough for a raid?'

'I think we should wait a while longer,' I said.

'What for?'

'Two reasons. First, I am interested in finding out what the semen is used for, and second, I am off to Pimlico tomorrow. I'll be down there until after the Preakness. There would be no point in planning a raid here at Belmont if I'm not around to see any reaction if Raworth is forewarned.'

'Is his whole operation moving down to Pimlico?' Tony asked. 'We could mount the raid there.'

'He's sending only five horses down in a truck – three run in the Preakness itself, and the other two in different races. The rest of them stay here.'

'How did you manage to get yourself included?' Tony asked.

'I was lucky. In the right place at the right time. Four of the staff are going, including me, plus George Raworth himself.'

'Well, it's your call,' Tony said. 'Can the British do without you for another week?'

'Paul Maldini was not expecting me back for at least two weeks.'

'But it has already been two weeks since I met you at Dulles.'

So it had. Somehow, it didn't seem that long.

'Well,' I said, 'I need a bit longer.'

'Shall you tell Paul or shall I?' Tony asked.

'It might be better if it came from you,' I said. 'Tell him that I'm not coming back just yet.'

'How long shall I say you'll be?' Tony asked.

'You said to me in London that you needed me to work for you for as long as it takes. Paul Maldini was at that meeting. He didn't object.'

I reckoned Paul hadn't objected because he knew I was contemplating leaving the BHA. He was aware of my unhappiness that I no longer had the opportunity to work undercover. Perhaps he thought it was better to lend me to Tony for as long as it took, and then have me back, than to lose me altogether.

'Tell Paul that it might take a little longer, that's all,' I said. 'When is the Belmont Stakes?'

'Not for another four weeks,' Tony said. 'You're surely not thinking of working as a groom until then?'

'For as long as it takes,' I said.

*

253

On Monday morning, after normal stables and exercise, Keith, Diego, Maria and I loaded the special horse-transport that would take us the 200 miles southwest to Pimlico.

I was more used to British-style horseboxes than the huge eighteen-wheel articulated lorry with its massive cab that arrived for us at nine o'clock. It was similar to the one I had seen arrive at Churchill Downs to collect Hayden Ryder's horses on the morning he'd been shot.

Quite apart from the five horses, there was a mass of other stuff to go – feed, tack, buckets, blankets, bedding, pitchforks and brooms – not to mention our own personal effects.

There had been a few murmurings from Raworth's other grooms, but not because I had been chosen to go to Pimlico ahead of them, rather for the reason their individual workloads would increase here due to me being away.

Charlie Hern told them to shut up and get on with it, or leave. 'There are plenty of others wanting your jobs,' he warned them. In my opinion, it wasn't the best example of how to conduct relations with one's labour force, but I didn't say so. I just got on with the loading.

Diego was a pain. Twice he purposely knocked things out of my hands as I was carrying them to the vehicle.

'*Estúpido gringo*,' he said each time. But he was the stupid one, I thought. I wouldn't fancy a year on Rikers Island for any money.

George Raworth drove a white Jeep Cherokee four-by-four right up inside the barn at the far end from the office, next to the drug store.

Charlie Hern had been in there for a while busily filling boxes with pills, potions and other paraphernalia, and these were now put into the Jeep, along with the CryoBank flask.

George and Charlie carried the heavy white metal cylinder out of the drug store together, each holding one of the handles, and then they lifted it into the vehicle, placing it upright behind the front passenger seat. They did it when they thought all the grooms were otherwise engaged and wouldn't notice. But I'd been keeping a special eye out to see if they would take it.

But I still had no idea why.

Finally, when everything else was packed, the five horses were loaded into the trailer.

I led Debenture out from Stall 2, patting him all the while on the neck to keep him calm. Horses generally don't like any changes to their routine. It can make them nervous, and half a ton of skittish horseflesh can cause a lot of damage both to themselves and anyone close by. That's partly why the five-year-old gelding went in first. He was the old man of the five, the other four being three-year-olds, and his presence on board should help settle the younger horses.

Next, Ladybird, the filly, was loaded, going into a stall at the rear of the trailer behind a solid partition. It was not ideal to take colts and a filly on the same transport, as the very presence of the filly could make the colts become excited. Hence the use of a solid partition and the placing of the filly at the rear so that, as the vehicle moved, the airflow prevented the colts from smelling her. I knew of one transport operator in England who sometimes resorted to smearing Vicks VapoRub into the colts' nostrils to overpower the smell of fillies travelling in the same horsebox.

Fire Point was the last of the horses to be loaded.

He appeared to be in perfect condition, the muscles in his neck standing out sharply and those in his flanks rippling gently under his short summer chestnut coat. Keith coaxed him up the ramp and into his travelling stall in the trailer. All the horses had thick bandages wrapped around their legs and rubber boots on their hooves to reduce the chance of injury caused by a bump or kick, but Fire Point went in without anything more than a shake of his narrow head, as if he already knew he was the star of the show.

Keith and I rode in the back with the horses while Diego and Maria were up front in the cab with the driver. It was an arrangement with which I was very happy. I didn't have to keep my eyes on Diego to prevent him niggling me, or worse, and I didn't have to fight off Maria's sexual advances. Not that I really wanted to, but the fallout from Diego wasn't worth the reward.

Our route went right through New York City and I was able to glimpse some of the iconic sights of Manhattan, including the Empire State Building, before it all disappeared from view as we descended into the Lincoln Tunnel under the Hudson River, and on into New Jersey.

Keith lay down on some bales of straw and went to sleep, while I counted the cars on the New Jersey Turnpike, as in the Simon and Garfunkel song.

Was I looking for America?

No, I didn't think so. I wasn't sure what I was looking for. True, I was enjoying the challenge of working undercover again, but my life seemed to be drifting by.

During my time with the army in Afghanistan I'd felt there was a purpose, a goal, even if that goal now appeared somewhat blurred since the British forces had pulled out and everything had started to return to how it was before.

Then, when I joined the BHA, I believed I had enlisted in a righteous crusade to weed out corruption and wrongdoing. I was the standard bearer – prepared to do almost anything in the fight for justice. But, over the years, the shine on my shield had dulled as I became increasingly snowed under with procedures and paperwork.

Even my love life was in tatters.

At twenty-three, and as the youngest captain in the Intelligence Corps, I had felt like a sexual god, an Adonis, with a string of gorgeous young women hanging on my every word and deed. Between operational tours overseas, I had fully satisfied my desires, running up a reputation as a bit of a Casanova.

But, aged twenty-six, I had bucked the trend of my

army colleagues by abandoning the exploits of the past, leaving the service and settling down with a steady girlfriend.

I hadn't regretted either at the time, happy to have some stability in my life while leaving behind the fear and danger of an intelligence officer in war-torn Afghanistan. Among other things, my role had been to determine if the locals in Helmand Province were on *our* side or not, without getting myself killed in the process.

However, recently, I had begun to crave once more the 'high' generated when terror grips one's stomach and adrenalin surges through the body.

On the lover front, things had also gone somewhat pear-shaped. More than a year ago now, the steady girlfriend had left me for another man who had a 'safer' job, the irony being that my own work had been getting less dangerous.

I'd had one serious romance since then, with Henrietta, but it hadn't worked out.

So here I was, thirty-three years old, single and rudderless.

This American sojourn had been a distraction and I was delighted to be able to extend it. It meant I didn't have to face the realities of my future for a while longer yet.

The truck continued on its steady way southwestward on the interstate highways while I checked the horses.

All of them seemed to be taking the journey in their

stride. Fire Point in particular was unperturbed by the noise of the engine and the continuous swaying of the vehicle. But he'd been used to flying so this was a 'walk in the park'.

After a couple of hours, we pulled over into a rest area east of Philadelphia to give the driver a meal break, and us a chance to stretch our legs.

'Leave the horses on board,' Keith said. 'It's more than my life's worth to have Fire Point loose on the highway. They'll be fine until we get to Pimlico.'

We went over to the rest-area café and Keith paid for the four of us to have a burger each with fries.

'Mr Raworth said food only,' he explained. 'Buy your own soda if you want one. The driver has to have a half-hour break, so be back at the vehicle in good time. I'll eat mine while keeping an eye on the horses.'

He went out and walked back towards the truck while the three of us sat down at one of the Formica-topped tables.

'Want a drink?' I said to Maria.

She glanced at Diego. 'Water,' she said.

I collected three cups of water from the cooler in the corner and put them on a table.

I could tell that Diego didn't like me doing him any favours. He moved away, without his cup of water, and sat at a different table, on his own.

Maria sighed. 'Diego very difficult today. He not stop telling me to be good girl all way from Belmont. I very tired of him.'

'Join me down the back,' I said.

What was I saying? Was I mad?

'Good,' Maria said, and gave me one of her flashing smiles. 'I do that.'

In the end, it didn't work out quite as we had planned.

When Diego saw Maria climbing in with the horses, he immediately went in there with her.

Fine, I thought, I'll ride up front in the cab.

Keith also went into the trailer to be near to Fire Point.

I had spent much of the last two hours staring at Diego's bag, stacked as it was in the trailer along with Maria's, Keith's and mine. I had even been through it while Keith had been asleep, without finding anything incriminating. At one point I had seriously thought of throwing it out of a window to pay him back for kicking me but I had managed to resist the temptation, not least because it may have caused an accident.

Diego might not be so considerate with mine, so I picked up my canvas holdall from the trailer and took it with me to the driver's cab, chucking it onto the spare seat.

We set off again.

'God, I'm glad to get rid of those other two,' said the driver. 'They've not stopped jabbering at each other in Spanish since we left Belmont Park. It has nearly driven me nuts.'

I wished he wouldn't mention nuts.

Mine still ached dreadfully.

22

We stopped again briefly just outside Baltimore in order to team up with four motorcycles and two squad cars from the city police department, who traditionally escort the Kentucky Derby winner the last few miles to Pimlico Race Course for the Preakness.

It was not so much about ensuring the horse's safe arrival as getting the event shown on the local TV news channels.

Marketing the race was the key.

It was hoped that in excess of 130,000 spectators would cram into the racecourse on Saturday to watch the big race, and that that one day would bankroll the track for the rest of the year.

With only twenty-eight racing days per year, compared to eighty or more at each of Churchill Downs and Belmont Park, Pimlico had become rather the poor relation of the Triple Crown venues. But it had a proud history, being the first of the three tracks to open in 1870.

The first running of the Preakness Stakes predated the inaugural Kentucky Derby by two years, with the first Belmont Stakes held at Belmont Park being some thirty years after that.

Several TV crews filmed our arrival and there was

quite a crowd waiting, as the horse transport pulled up close to the Stakes Barn, which was situated behind the grandstand in a corner of the racecourse site. I did my best to keep out of camera shot, especially face-on. I had no wish to be recognised, not least by any of the FACSA team who might happen to see the transmission. After all, Baltimore was only some forty miles from the FACSA offices in Arlington.

I had been cultivating my beard now for almost two weeks and the growth was reasonably substantial, but it was always the eyes that would give me away. Consequently, I pulled the grubby LA Dodgers baseball cap lower, so the peak cast a deep shadow over my eyes in the afternoon sunshine.

The media lost interest as soon as Fire Point had walked the thirty yards from the trailer to Stall 40 in the Preakness Barn, the traditional Pimlico home of the Kentucky Derby winner.

Above and to the right of the door was a plaque showing the sixteen previous winners of the Preakness who had been accommodated in that particular stall, including the great sire Northern Dancer and Triple Crown champions Secretariat, Seattle Slew and Affirmed.

In truth, it was rather a basic space about twelve feet square with off-white walls and a dirt floor, no different from any of the other stalls in the barn. But traditions are traditions, even if some Derby-winning trainers have recently flouted the convention because they think that Stall 40 is too noisy.

Fire Point didn't seem to mind, circling a couple of times to investigate his new environment before sticking his head out through the doorway to watch what else was going on.

Keith, Diego, Maria and I then unloaded all the kit plus the other four horses, putting them in their allocated stalls which were not all together, as the barn with Stall 40 was reserved only for those horses due to run in the Preakness itself.

Debenture and Ladybird were in the next barn along and I was told by Keith that I would be looking after them both, a situation that suited me fine as I thought it would keep me away from Diego, at least while we were working.

However, there would be no respite from him at night.

The grooms' accommodation was up an outside staircase above the horses. As Keith had said, we had two rooms allocated, a small single for Maria, and another only a fraction larger for Keith, Diego and me, the metal bedsteads so close together that they would be considered inappropriate in an episode of *I Love Lucy*.

I bagged the bed in the corner furthest from the door and, fortunately, Keith took the middle one. The communal bathroom was three doors along the open-air balcony, and was shared with two other rooms, eight people in total.

George Raworth arrived in the white Jeep Cherokee about an hour after us. He parked his vehicle in a space next to the barns and then proceeded to conduct a tour of inspection of his horses to check they had settled into their temporary homes. While he was busy with Fire Point, I took the opportunity to have a quick look through the windows of the Jeep. The white cryogenic flask was there, still standing upright behind the passenger seat. But what was it for?

I went in search of George in the Preakness Barn.

With only five days to go before the big event, security at the barn was already pretty tight with a uniformed guard posted at either end.

'ID?' one asked as he blocked my path.

I showed him the groom's pass hanging round my neck. He scrutinised the photo carefully before letting me through.

Ten horses were expected to contest the big race, making it about an average-sized field for recent times. Final declarations would be on Wednesday afternoon, ahead of the draw for starting-gate positions, and all bar one of the ten were already in residence.

Even so, only about half of the barn was actually in use, with many empty spaces. The Raworth three were housed in stalls together down one end with Fire Point in the middle.

The fact that a single trainer had three horses in the field was unusual, but not unique. Nick Zito, Hall of Fame inductee who had worked his way up from hot-walker to become a racing legend, had three runners in the 2005 Preakness. They had finished fourth, sixth and tenth.

Could George Raworth's trio do any better?

Life at Pimlico settled down into a routine, although I could hardly describe the Raworth team as cheerful.

I had realised pretty quickly that the lot of a groom was not a particularly happy one.

For me, the total lack of privacy was the worst aspect, with nowhere to call your own to relax in peace – share a bedroom, share a bathroom, communal feeding and, at Pimlico, not even a recreation hall with computers to act as a distraction.

It was depressing.

On top of that, Diego was acting like a petulant child and I was getting pretty fed up with it.

First he emptied my holdall all over the floor of our bedroom before throwing the bag itself onto the roof. Then, at evening stables, he came round to the barn where I was working merely to tip a bucket of wet manure into a stall I had just finished cleaning. As a parting gesture, he then pulled the hay out of Debenture's freshly filled haynet and threw it down into some muddy water.

It was as if he was trying to provoke me into some sort of reaction. Perhaps he thought I would hit him in the same way he had me, and then he could go whining to George Raworth to get me fired.

But I wasn't going to play that game.

I would put up with his puerile tactics of disrupting my work and messing about with my kit. Instead I would wait my chance. Revenge for me would be a dish eaten cold, when he was least expecting it.

Finding a secluded spot to call Tony was more difficult at Pimlico than at Belmont Park.

While the other grooms went in search of takeout joints and liquor stores outside the main gate on Park Heights Avenue, I walked across the lawn in front of the Preakness Barn, through the bushes, and into one of the deserted car parks beyond.

'How did you communicate with the journalist Jason Connor?' I asked.

'Initially he contacted NYRA, and they called in FACSA.'

'Did you speak to Connor yourself?'

'Not at that point. I became involved after the raid on the barn had found nothing but spotless stalls and no horses. Only when I suspected we had a mole in our midst.'

'So you spoke to Connor then?'

'Yes.'

'How?' I asked. 'On the phone or in person?'

There was a pause on the line as Tony tried to remember.

'On the phone, I think,' he said. 'But only the once. After that we used email.'

'Did you know he was going to see the groom at Laurel Park on the day he died?'

'Definitely,' Tony said. 'He informed me by email the previous day.'

'Using the FACSA office email system?'

'No. My private email address. I thought it would be safer.'

I said nothing.

'Are you implying that my private email has been compromised?' Tony asked finally.

'Yes. That's if you're right about Jason Connor's death not being an accident.'

'But how?' Tony asked.

'All email is compromised to some extent,' I said. 'They are checked by the security services for a start. They have automatic scanners that look for certain keywords such as "bomb" or "explosive" or "jihad". I assume your private emails aren't encrypted.'

'No.'

'All it needs is for someone to have your email address and password.'

'But how would they get my password?' he asked.

'How often do you change it?'

'Never.'

'So someone at work may have seen you enter it. Or maybe it's easy to guess. Please don't tell me it's your mother's maiden name, or your wife's.'

There was a long pause from the other end of the line.

'I'll change it right away,' he said rather sheepishly.

'No,' I said quickly. 'Don't.'

'Why not?'

'Two reasons,' I said. 'One, whoever has accessed your private emails would then know that we know, and, two, we might be able to use it to set our mole a trap.'

'How?'

'I'm working on it,' I said. 'In the meantime, do nothing.'

'But someone else is reading my personal emails. I don't like that.'

'Then don't write suggestive emails to your mistress,' I said flippantly. 'At least, not until after we've caught the mole.'

'I don't have a mistress,' he said nervously.

I wasn't at all certain I believed him.

But flippancy aside, it was a serious breach of security.

'Tony,' I said with concern, 'did you tell Paul Maldini that I wasn't coming back yet?'

'I sure did,' Tony replied.

'How?'

'What do you mean, how?'

'Did you use your email?' I asked.

'No,' he replied. 'I called him on this phone, like you said to. Spoke to him myself.'

I breathed a sigh of relief. 'What did he say?'

'He didn't seem that concerned. He said that you could stay for as long as you need, provided you come back eventually.'

'Did he say those exact words?' I asked.

'He sure did.'

Paul clearly did know me better than I realised.

'Any further word on the semen tests?' I asked, changing the subject.

'What further word are you expecting?'

'Is it equine semen, for a start?'

'My biochemistry professor is still doing the DNA tests. Apparently he's had to do a procedure called poly-something chain reaction.'

'Poly*merase* chain reaction,' I said. 'To amplify the amount of DNA.'

'That's the one. It seems it takes all day.'

'They can do it instantaneously on *CSI Miami*,' I said.

Tony laughed. 'Yeah, and they always catch the bad guys, too. Don't believe everything you see on TV.'

Or in the newspapers.

'Can you ask your pet professor if he can tell what breed the semen is from, assuming it is equine? In particular, if it is Thoroughbred semen? I could then take hairs from all the horses in Raworth's barn for comparison.'

'Right,' Tony said. 'I'll ask him. Call me again tomorrow. Same time.'

My first night at Pimlico could hardly be described as restful.

The bed was lumpy and uncomfortable and that, together with an apparent who-can-be-the-loudest-snorer contest between Keith and Diego, had me longing for nights only with the farting Mexican.

Hence I'd been wide awake and up for some considerable time prior to four o'clock, when I was expected to be at work.

With only two horses to deal with, the workload was only half what I had faced at Belmont, so it was easy. Ladybird went out first for her morning exercise, ridden by Victor Gomez, while I cleaned her stall and prepared Debenture.

When Ladybird returned from the track, I walked her round for half an hour until she had cooled, gave her a washdown, and then returned her to her stall for a feed. I repeated the routine for Debenture, thankfully without any interruptions from Diego, who was busy with his two. Meanwhile, Keith and Maria fussed around Fire Point, who was ridden out to the track by Jerry Fernando, his race jockey, under the watchful gaze of trainer George Raworth.

I was through by eight o'clock and went in search of some breakfast.

The white Jeep Cherokee was parked up against the back wall of the Pimlico track kitchen.

I had a quick look to make sure that George was still out by the track watching Fire Point and no one else was about, then I peeped inside the vehicle.

The cryogenic flask was still there behind the passenger seat exactly as before. But did it still contain the frozen semen?

I tried the Jeep's doors. They were locked.

How I wished my trusty lock picks could open them but there was no hope. It was not even worth trying. For a start, the doors had no visible keyholes for the picks to go into. I spent a moment wondering if my ex-army corporal could open cars that were locked by remote control. Probably. But for me, short of breaking one of the windows, I had no chance of getting in.

Just as in Wagner's Pharmacy at Louisville before the Derby, talk in the Pimlico track kitchen over breakfast was all about who was going to win the big race.

'Fire Point will surely trot up,' said one man sitting near me, 'especially with those other three not running.'

The three he meant were the horses diagnosed with EVA. Two had since returned to California to recover, and the third was still in isolation at Churchill Downs.

However, the man's companion disagreed. 'I think that big bay colt of Bryson's has a good chance. What's his name?'

'Crackshot,' said the first.

'That's it. Won the Florida Derby at Gulfstream by five lengths back in March.'

'If he's so good, why didn't he run at Louisville? His win in Florida would have surely qualified him.'

'No idea. Perhaps Bryson was saving him for the Preakness.'

'Don't talk garbage. No one in their right mind bypasses the Kentucky Derby in favour of the Preakness.'

'He might have this year. There's that new bonus

being offered for winning both the Florida Derby and the Preakness. Five million bucks is a lot of money.'

'Even so ...'

The man might have been right, and Crackshot was not the only one of the ten that hadn't lined up for the big race at Churchill Downs.

There were also Raworth's other two, Classic Comic and Heartbeat, as well as a couple of local Maryland colts.

So only half Saturday's expected field in the Preakness had contested the Derby at Louisville. Some had not been eligible for the Kentucky race and were simply after the big prizes on offer here. The $1.5million purse meant that this race alone was well worth winning, even without the bonuses. Even the fourth horse home would collect nearly a hundred thousand dollars for his owner.

The day dragged.

There was not even live racing to watch, as Tuesday was a dark day at Pimlico.

I lay on my lumpy bed for part of the afternoon trying to catch up on some sleep but without much success, not least because Diego had had the same idea.

He spat onto the floor when he saw me.

'Charming,' I said.

'*Qué?*' he replied in an aggressive tone.

'What is wrong with you?' I asked.

'*No comprende,*' he replied, waving a hand at me in a contemptuous manner.

But Maria had said that Diego 'speak very good English', much better than her.

'Yes, Diego, you do *comprende*,' I said. 'So listen to me. You leave me alone. You don't even talk to me. I know about you.'

He stared at me with his black eyes.

'I know about you,' I said again. 'One word from me and you'll be in the slammer for a year on Rikers Island.'

He understood that all right.

But if I thought it would shut him up, I was sorely mistaken. The look of pure hatred in his eyes caused a shiver to run down my spine.

Letting on to him that I knew about his little problem with the New York courts had clearly been a mistake.

I might need to watch my back more than ever.

23

The Preakness post-position draw took place at five o'clock on Wednesday afternoon with all ten of the expected runners declared for the race.

Crackshot had been the last of the contestants to arrive at Pimlico, flying in from Florida only at lunchtime to join the other nine already in the Preakness Barn.

Fire Point had been installed as the favourite in the morning's edition of the *Daily Racing Form* with Crackshot a whisker behind. All the others were outsiders in comparison.

Of the two, Fire Point certainly had the better draw. He would be out of trouble in Gate 8 while Crackshot was drawn next to the rail in Gate 1, with both Heartbeat and Classic Comic immediately outside him in Gates 2 and 3 respectively.

George Raworth was clearly delighted and had a smile on his face as big as the Grand Canyon as he was interviewed by the assembled media.

Suddenly, the Preakness roller coaster was under way and Pimlico Race Course was coming to life. Celebrities and politicians would be flying in to Baltimore from all over the country during the next two days in order to be here for the race.

It may not be quite as grand as the carnival that had

surrounded the Kentucky Derby at Churchill Downs, but it was big enough, especially on an otherwise quiet weekend for US sports.

And the weather was set fair. Indeed, it was getting hot, with afternoon highs in the mid- to upper-eighties Fahrenheit, dropping down only into the seventies at night. It was so hot, in fact, that Keith had installed two electric fans outside Stall 40 to keep Fire Point cool.

There were no such luxuries for the grooms.

Wednesday night was completely still without a trace of breeze. Even with the door and window of our bedroom wide open, the lack of air meant that getting to sleep was difficult, the situation not helped by having ten horses stabled beneath, pumping out energy from their massive bodies like fiery furnaces.

As I tossed and turned, Diego and Keith seemed untroubled by the heat and went back to their snoring games, which only made things worse.

Eventually, at ten minutes to midnight, and wearing only a T-shirt and my boxer shorts, I took my blanket down the outside staircase and lay on the neatly mown lawn in front of the barn, curling up on the ground as I'd done so often before in the army.

I'd had to cope with higher temperatures than this in the past. July in Kandahar had a daily average well into the nineties and here, at least, I wasn't wearing full combat kit including body armour and helmet, plus a twenty-kilo backpack and as much again in weapon and ammunition.

Lying on the grass was surprisingly comfortable.

I found myself a quiet, dark spot in the shadow of a tree and settled down.

I was drifting off to sleep when I was disturbed by the arrival of a vehicle, its headlights lighting up the trees above my head. It pulled up near the end of the barn closest to me and the engine was switched off.

I rolled over onto my knees and slowly raised my head to have a look.

It was George Raworth's white Jeep Cherokee.

What was he doing here at midnight?

I watched as he climbed out of the driver's seat and walked over to the barn.

'Good evening,' I heard him say, presumably to the night guard who was out of my sight on the far side of the barn. 'George Raworth. Here to check on my horses.'

Who was I to criticise a trainer who wanted to check his horses at any time of night? It must be worrying for him to have the favourite in his charge, especially with all the hopes of the nation riding on it as another Triple Crown champion.

I lay down once more and was drifting off again when a noise made me instantly awake.

I recognised that particular noise. I'd heard it before.

It was the sound of the cap being removed from the cryogenic flask, with the slight 'pop' as the excess pressure inside was released.

I again rolled onto my knees and looked towards the Jeep.

George had the rear door open behind the passenger seat. Even though there were plenty of security lights around the barn, I couldn't actually see what he was doing as the vehicle was in the way. But why would he have opened the flask if he wasn't either getting something out or putting something in?

He closed the Jeep and went back to the barn. In his right hand he held an electric torch and in his left what looked like a small cup.

He disappeared into the barn.

I was now curious.

I rose to my feet and moved silently forwards, making sure that I remained deep in the shadow of the trees.

At night, the lights in the barn itself were switched off to allow the horses to sleep, while the glow of those outside seemed to further deepen the darkness of the interior.

At first I could see nothing but then the glow of the torch appeared as George made the inspection of his horses.

I moved down the side of the barn to get a better view.

George spent only a couple of moments with each horse before moving along the line of stalls.

What was he up to now?

I moved as close as I dared, silently padding over the grass in bare feet and keeping as low as I could behind the post-and-rail fence that ran along parallel to the side of the barn, and about five yards from it.

George stopped at one of the stalls near the far end. The torch went out.

I crouched down, looking through the fence, straining my eyes to try and see what he was doing.

There came a noise, a hissing sound like that made when a pump blows air into a bicycle tyre. There it was again.

Then silence.

I waited, listening hard, but there was nothing more.

George then retraced his steps along the barn towards his own three horses, turning the torch back on as he did so.

Maybe the sound had been one of the horses having a snort, or perhaps it had been the security guard blowing his nose, but the noise hadn't been right for either of them.

I tiptoed back to the end of the barn and was about to creep closer when George appeared right in front of me, coming out of the barn into the bright glare of the security lights.

I immediately stepped back into the deep shadow of the bushes so he wouldn't spot me.

'Good night,' he called over his shoulder.

'Good night, Mr Raworth,' replied the guard, who I still couldn't see.

George then walked back to his Jeep and threw something onto the back seat, before climbing in and driving off into the night.

I returned slowly to my blanket and went to sleep wondering what all that had been about.

*

I was none the wiser in the morning.

I woke at three o'clock, slightly chilled, and went back up the stairs to my bed. Diego and Keith were both giving the snoring a rest so I lay down and returned to sleep for another hour.

I didn't mention my nocturnal excursion to the others and especially not to George Raworth when he arrived to watch his horses at exercise.

I prepared Ladybird for Victor Gomez to ride a steady breeze over five furlongs. She would be racing on Friday afternoon in the Black-Eyed Susan Stakes, a graded race over nine furlongs for three-year-old fillies that was named in honour of the yellow perennial daisy with a black centre that is the state flower of Maryland. So all Ladybird needed today was a gentle pipe-opener to maintain her condition, nothing that would overtire.

Just to confuse people, in 1940, the Maryland Jockey Club decided that, in addition to the Black-Eyed Susan Stakes for fillies, the Preakness Stakes itself would henceforth be designated as the 'Run for the Black-Eyed Susans' and a garland of the yellow-and-black flowers would be draped over the winner, to rival the garland of red roses that was draped over the victor of the Kentucky Derby.

However, there was one slight problem. The Preakness is run in May, some two months earlier than black-eyed Susans come into bloom.

Not that such a trivial matter would be allowed to deter the gentlemen directors of the oldest sporting organisation of North America, one that could boast two US presidents among its former members. They decreed that the garland would be made using early-flowering, but all-yellow, Viking daisies, with their centres hand-painted black in order to resemble black-eyed Susans.

Nowadays, yellow-and-black flowers of the chrysanthemum family are used but, in all its 140-plus years of existence, the Run for the Black-Eyed Susans has never once seen an actual black-eyed Susan.

Victor Gomez came back on Ladybird to swap his saddle onto Debenture.

'Ladybird good,' he said to me. 'She win tomorrow, yes?' He gave me a thumbs up and grinned, not that it was a pretty sight with several of his teeth missing.

'Yes,' I replied, raising my thumb back at him. 'Hope so.'

I walked the horse around for ten minutes for her to cool off before giving her a washdown with soap and water. Next I dried her using a large towel and then brushed her coat until it shone.

I wanted Ladybird to look her best in the paddock, not least because Tony Andretti had told me the previous evening that he would be coming to Pimlico for both Friday and Saturday and I didn't want him giving me any grief about poor standards of grooming, even in jest.

'How about the tests on the semen?' I had asked him.

'Still waiting,' he'd replied. 'Full results should be in tomorrow. All I can tell you at the moment is that it is definitely horse semen but not from a Thoroughbred. My professor is still doing DNA similarity tests for other equine breeds.'

So, if it wasn't from a Thoroughbred, there was no point in me taking hair samples from the colts in Raworth's barn for comparison. None of them could have been the donor.

I continued grooming Ladybird, brushing out her tail and then trimming a straight edge at the bottom.

As I worked, I thought about the next two days.

It was not only Tony Andretti who would be coming to Pimlico, other members of the FACSA racing section would also be in attendance, and I didn't want them spotting me as a ringer.

It would be twelve days since I had left them at Andrews Base and, in spite of the fairly vigorous hair growth on my chin and upper lip since then, I was concerned that federal special agents should be well enough trained in recognition techniques to identify me easily, not least because my beard had not grown dark and concealing as I had hoped, but rather blond and wispy like my hair.

Since first arriving at Belmont, I had taken to always wearing my LA Dodgers baseball cap, with the peak pulled down low. Here at Pimlico, there were too many press and TV cameras around to avoid completely, so it was better to be as incognito as possible at all times. So tomorrow, I decided, I would also wear my cheap dark sunglasses to cover my eyes. With luck, the sun would shine so I wouldn't look too out of place.

I finished with Ladybird as Victor Gomez returned on Debenture. With two days before his race, he had been given a far sterner workout and Maria walked him round the shedrow for a good twenty-five minutes to cool.

While she did so, I went over to the Preakness Barn to fetch some more straw.

George Raworth's white Jeep Cherokee was again parked close by. The man himself was out at the track so, having swivelled round on my heel to check no one else was watching, I went to the far side of the vehicle and tried the door handle.

It opened.

The cryogenic flask was still there but it was now lying on its side behind the driver's seat with the cap off. I tipped it up. It was completely empty both of liquid nitrogen and of the semen.

I had a quick look around the rest of the Jeep. On the back seat sat an electric torch and a small cup, along with what looked like a miniature red rubber rugby ball. The ball was about three inches long, with a short blue plastic pipe extending from one end, and it had 'Polaroid' stamped into the rubber on one side.

I knew exactly what it was. I'd once owned something very similar.

It was an air duster, designed to blow a stream of air to remove dust from the lens or the inside of a camera. I squeezed the ball and was rewarded by the same hissing pump sound that I had heard the previous night.

I was sorely tempted to put the air duster into my

pocket but I could see George Raworth in the far distance, coming back towards me from the track with Victor Gomez, and it wouldn't do to be caught with it.

I left things as they were, closed the Jeep door as quietly as I could, and moved quickly away. Thankfully, George had been too busy talking to Victor to notice me.

'ID?' said the guard at the barn entrance.

I showed him my groom's pass and he let me through.

The place was a hive of activity, with veterinary staff from the Maryland Racing Commission taking blood samples from each of the Preakness runners for pre-race drug testing.

I stood and watched as one of them inserted a hypodermic needle into Fire Point's neck just behind his head. The horse was well used to this procedure. He made no movement as the needle went into his jugular vein and blood was collected into two Vacutainer test tubes, identical to the one I'd passed through the chain-link fence to Jim Bradley at Belmont.

I picked up the straw from the bedding stockpile but, instead of going straight back to my horses, I walked along the line of stalls until I came to the one where George Raworth had stopped during the night. I took a step forward and looked inside. It was empty.

'What do you want?' asked a deep angry voice behind me that made me jump.

'Nothing,' I replied automatically, turning round.

284

The voice belonged to a tall man with ebony skin who was standing in the shedrow, the whites of his prominent eyes standing out against a dark face as he stared at me accusingly.

'I'm Paddy,' I said with a broad smile, putting down the bale of straw and extending my right hand towards him. 'I'm here with Raworth's crew. My first time at Pimlico.'

'Tyler,' the man replied. 'I'm with Bryson.'

He slowly shook my offered hand and even grinned at me, exhibiting a fine collection of gold teeth. My overtly friendly approach had completely disarmed his anger.

'I'm based at Belmont,' I said. 'Only here for the big race.'

'Gulfstream,' Tyler said, pointing a finger at his own chest. 'In Miami. Too damn cold up here, for my liking.' He shivered.

Cold? He must be joking. But I could see from his thick woollen sweater that he wasn't.

'Who do you look after?' I asked.

'Crackshot,' he replied with another flash of the gold teeth. 'He's out at exercise right now.' He waved a hand towards the empty stall. 'I'm doing his bed.'

Crackshot.

What had George Raworth been doing in the middle of the night outside the stall of the only other horse in the Preakness that most of the pundits gave any chance to other than Fire Point?

My suspicious mind was working overtime.

24

I led Ladybird from the barn to the paddock about thirty minutes before the Black-Eyed Susan Stakes and walked right past FACSA Special Agent Trudi Harding, the shooter of Hayden Ryder at Churchill Downs.

She ignored me, not giving me a first glance let alone a second. She was standing with Frank Bannister on a raised platform near the track entrance and they were too preoccupied scanning the faces of the large Friday crowd to notice the groom passing by right under their noses.

Uniquely in my experience, the paddock at Pimlico was indoors, and not at all what British racegoers would expect. Here, instead of being a parade ring where the horses would walk to be inspected, the paddock was an area where the horses stood to be saddled in numbered stalls that corresponded to their post-draw positions.

I held Ladybird's head as George Raworth and Keith made her ready.

First they placed a thin chamois cloth onto the horse's bare back to prevent slippage. That was followed by the saddle pad, weight cloth, numbered saddle cloth and finally the saddle, all of them held in place by a wide strap passed under the belly and secured tightly to buckles on either side of the saddle. Over the top of everything, for added safety, went a three-inch-wide webbing over-girth.

Satisfied, George gave Ladybird a friendly smack on her rump as Keith and I led her up the ramp under the jockeys' room, back into the daylight, and onto the track. George issued jockey Jerry Fernando with some last-minute instructions and a leg-up into the saddle before I handed the horse over to one of the outriders.

Unlike in England, where a horse runs free to the start under the control of its jockey alone, those in the United States are led to the gate by an outrider on a 'lead pony', one pony to each runner.

Whereas a 'pony' is properly defined as a member of an equine breed in which normal mature horses stand less than fifty-eight inches tall at the withers, the lead ponies at racetracks are often retired Thoroughbred racehorses, and therefore are not ponies at all.

But no one seemed to care as the excitement built.

I watched on the big screen as the horses, plus the ponies, circled behind the starting gate that was situated right in front of the grandstand.

The crowd for the Preakness the following afternoon was expected to be three times bigger but, nevertheless, there was a loud cheer as the gates flew open and the nine runners in the feature race of the day surged forward.

Victor Gomez had been right.

Ladybird was good. Very good.

She led from start to finish, holding off a late challenge to win by a neck.

Understandably, George Raworth was delighted, coming out onto the track with me to lead the horse into the winner's circle.

I could see both Bob Wade and Steffi Dean standing by the rail. I pulled the peak of my cap lower and kept my eyes down but I think the special agents were more interested in each other than in anyone else.

I had realised that being a groom was, in fact, a very good undercover persona. Grooms were invisible, even more so than waiters in restaurants. Anyone looking my way was staring into the eyes of the horse rather than into those of the man leading it.

I knew of one trainer in England who could readily identify every horse in his hundred-strong yard just by looking at it, even in the rain, but he couldn't tell his stable staff apart, one from another. Irrespective of their real names, he simply called all his lads 'John'.

While Ladybird's owner, trainer and jockey were receiving their trophies from the star of a TV soap opera, Maria and I walked the horse from the winner's circle to the post-race testing barn.

Here we waited with the horse for almost an hour, whistling and pouring water until Ladybird finally acquiesced and supplied the urine sample the testers required.

Maria was not her usual ebullient self, not speaking to me once during the wait.

'Cat got your tongue?' I said, but she didn't understand the idiom. 'Are you OK?' I asked slowly instead.

She nodded. 'OK.'

'Then why don't you say something?'

This time she shook her head. 'No talk.'

I thought she almost seemed frightened.

'What has Diego said to you?' I asked.

'No talk,' she repeated. 'Diego, he say no talk.'

'Or what?' I asked.

She definitely appeared frightened this time. She looked all around her with wide eyes and then whispered. 'Diego say he cut me if I talk to you.' She traced a fingernail down her cheek from a tearful right eye all the way to her chin.

Diego was getting to be more than just a nuisance. He had clearly decided that it was easier to intimidate his cousin than me, and he was probably right. The sooner he was dragged off in chains to Rikers Island the better.

George Raworth came into Ladybird's stall when I was still brushing her down after washing away the sweat of her exertions.

'Well done, my girl,' George said, patting the horse on the neck in love and gratitude. 'Great job, Paddy. Now for the Preakness tomorrow.'

He even patted me on the back as well.

'Yes, sir,' I said. 'Let's hope so.'

'Hope doesn't come into it,' George said with a laugh. 'I believe Fire Point is a sure thing.'

He should know, I thought.

*

290

'The professor thinks the semen is probably from an American Quarter Horse,' Tony Andretti said when I called him at eight o'clock on Friday evening. 'The DNA doesn't match that of any known stallion held by the National Quarter Horse Registry but it closely resembles other Quarter Horse DNA records that are available, as if the source was possibly related.'

'Quarter Horse semen?' I said. 'Why on earth would anyone want that around a Thoroughbred?'

'Your guess is as good as mine.'

A notion was stirring in my mind. Something I'd read was hovering somewhere just beneath my consciousness.

Was it to do with Quarter Horses?

Suddenly, like a switch being turned on, I remembered what it was.

George Raworth had grown up on a ranch in Texas that bred Quarter Horses. It was still run by two of his cousins.

Was that where the semen had come from?

Other things also floated to the surface .

'Tony?' I said. 'Are you still there?'

'Sure am,' he replied.

'Could you ask your professor if he can do one more test for me?'

'He says he can't do any more than he's already done. If the DNA of the semen doesn't match anything that's registered, then there's no way of telling exactly which horse it came from.'

'No,' I said. 'I'm happy with that. The test is for something else.'

'What?'

'EVA,' I said 'Equine viral arteritis.'

There was a long pause from the other end.

'What are you implying?' Tony said eventually.

'Nothing,' I lied. 'I'd just like to know if the EVA virus exists in the semen sample. I read on the Internet that stallions that have been infected shed the EVA virus in their semen for the rest of their lives. Could you also ask your professor if freezing infected semen would kill the virus or does it preserve it in the same way it preserves the sperm?'

'I'll ask him,' Tony said. 'But I can't think why. The infected horses at Churchill Downs were all colts. Surely infected semen would only infect mares during mating.'

I thought back to the sound of the air being expelled from the air duster, the sound that had come twice from the Preakness Barn on Wednesday night.

'How about if you squirted it up a colt's nostrils?' I said.

'But why would you?' Tony said. 'Semen up the nose wouldn't do any good.'

I laughed. 'Not for reproduction, I'll grant you, but EVA is primarily a respiratory disease. Ask your prof if inhaling EVA-infected semen would make a horse sick.'

'I'll call him straight away,' Tony said.

'Good. I'll call you back in an hour.'

We disconnected.

If I was right, and it was a big *if*, then Crackshot should also come down with EVA in the days ahead. And *if* that occurred, George Raworth might have some difficult explaining to do.

For the time being we had to sit tight and wait.

'The professor will do the EVA test tomorrow,' Tony said when I called him back. 'He wanted to leave it until Monday but I convinced him otherwise. In fact, I asked him to go into the lab to do it tonight but he's hosting a birthday dinner for his daughter.'

'Tomorrow will do fine,' I said. 'Did you ask him the other things?'

He laughed. 'The professor says that he doesn't know. It seems that no one has ever done any research that involves squirting EVA-infected semen up a horse's nose. But he did say that some sexually trans-mitted diseases in humans could be caught if infected semen gets into the eyes, so he doesn't see why not, especially as EVA is a respiratory illness. And he also says that, if the semen does contain EVA, freezing it would not kill the virus. It would still be active when thawed.' He paused. 'But are you seriously suggest-ing that the three colts that became ill with EVA at Churchill Downs had been purposefully infected by squirting semen up their noses?'

Was I?

'Yes,' I said. 'I am.'

'By whom?'

'George Raworth,' I said. 'And I think he's done it again here at Pimlico to a horse called Crackshot.'

'That's quite an accusation,' Tony said. 'Are you sure?'

'No,' I said. 'I'm not sure, but everything seems to fit, at least it will if the professor finds EVA virus tomorrow.'

I now wished I had taken the air duster from the Jeep. I could have had it tested for traces of semen. But it would have been a huge risk. George Raworth might have seen me next to the vehicle, and what would I have said if he had discovered the air duster was missing, only for it to reappear from my pocket during a search.

'So what do we do about it?' Tony said. 'Should we arrest Raworth?'

'We can't. You and I may believe it is true but, at the moment, it's all speculation and circumstantial. Raworth would deny it, cover his tracks, and there would be nothing we could do. We need proof.'

'Surely the semen sample is all the proof we need,' Tony said.

'But would it stand up as evidence in court? Raworth would deny that it had ever been his. Indeed, the sample might not even be admissible as evidence in a trial because I stole it in the first place. We need something more.'

'And how are we going to get that?' Tony asked.

'I'm working on it,' I replied.

'That's what you said about my emails.'

'Yeah, well, I'm still working on that too.'

'Can't we stop Raworth running his horses in the Preakness? Surely it isn't right that he can nobble the opposition and still be allowed to participate.'

'I agree that it doesn't seem fair,' I said, 'but if we make a move now, all we would be doing is fore-warning Raworth and any remaining evidence would disappear faster than jelly beans at a children's party.'

'So what *do* we do?'

'Nothing for the moment,' I said. 'And we don't tell anyone. Not a soul. Does your professor know where the semen came from?'

'No.'

'Then let's keep it that way,' I said. 'Ask him to keep everything confidential unless we tell him otherwise.'

'OK. Is there anything else?' Tony asked.

'Yes,' I said. 'Find out what you can about the Raworth family ranch in Texas. In particular, are there any veterinary records of an EVA outbreak?'

'I'll see what I can manage.' He didn't sound too confident. 'What will you do?'

'Continue with my job as a groom,' I said. 'We have three runners in the Preakness tomorrow.'

'I thought you looked very professional with the winner of the Black-Eyed Susan Stakes this afternoon. I was watching you through my binoculars.'

'Thank you,' I said.

'If anything you looked rather too adept and alert, compared to some of the other grooms.'

'I'll be more careful,' I said, making a mental note.

'I saw a number of your racing team here today. I walked right past Trudi Harding and she didn't recognise me. She didn't even look at me twice.'

'I'll have to have words with her,' Tony said.

'Not yet,' I said with a laugh. 'I don't want her shooting me.'

Tony didn't think it funny and, I suppose, neither did I.

25

Preakness morning dawned bright and warm without a cloud in the sky, not that I had waited for the sunrise before starting my day's work. I'd been hard at it for two hours by the time the fiery globe made its appearance in the east.

I had risen earlier than usual to give Debenture his breakfast. His race, the Maryland Sprint Handicap, was due off at half past one in the afternoon and George Raworth had told me that he didn't want the horse eating within eight hours of race time.

I arrived at the barn at 3.30 a.m. to find Debenture standing upright in the corner of the stall with his eyes closed, gently snoring. I stood silently watching him, marvelling at the fact that such a large bulk could be fast asleep and yet not fall over, especially as he was actually using only three of his legs to stand on, the fourth being slightly bent up with only the toe of the hoof resting on the floor.

Horses are not the only creatures able to sleep standing up. Elephants can also nap on their feet, and flamingos famously do it on only one leg.

In horses, it is due to what is called the 'stay apparatus', a natural locking of the limbs that keeps the animal upright while also allowing the muscles to relax. It is thought the ability evolved because early equines were prey, as zebras still are, and the time taken to get up from a lying position before running could mean the difference between life and death.

Not that horses always sleep standing up. They occasionally lie down for deep body sleep, so comfy bedding and enough space are essential.

I waited. I didn't want to wake Debenture. He was going to have a tiring enough day as it was.

I knew that horses do not normally sleep for very long at a time. In all, they need only about three hours' sleep in any twenty-four, mostly taken in short naps. And, sure enough, the horse soon woke on its own, snorting twice and shaking his head from side to side.

I gave him his regular breakfast of horse nuts plus feed supplements, and then refilled his bucket with fresh water.

Next I brushed Debenture's coat, starting with a stiff dandy brush and then finishing with the softer body brush, working backwards and downwards from his head to his feet on each side until his hide was polished to perfection.

Over the past ten days, I had discovered that there was something quite therapeutic about grooming a horse. All of one's troubles faded away with the strong rhythmic motion of the brushes over the animal's skin. Even the horses seemed to love it.

I began to understand how a mother could spend so long brushing her daughter's hair. It probably wasn't so much for the shine it created but for the relaxing sensation the movement generated in herself.

For a while in the quiet I was even able to forget my ongoing troubles with Diego.

True, we hadn't had a face-to-face confrontation since I'd spoken to him on Tuesday afternoon, but that hadn't stopped him trying to disrupt my life at every available opportunity, sometimes in the most childish of ways. I had no proof, but I was quite certain that it had been he who had squeezed my toothpaste out of its tube and smeared it all over my bed.

Sadly, there was no lockable space in our cramped bedroom, so my phone and wallet never left my side, residing inside my boxers even when I was asleep.

The rest of the barn came to life about four-thirty as other grooms came to start work.

The Preakness Barn itself was already a hive of activity when I went over to collect some bedding. I took the chance to walk up the shedrow.

'Morning, Tyler,' I said. 'How's Crackshot today?'

'Never better,' he said, showing me the gold molars.

The big bay colt certainly looked fine, sticking his head out towards me with a sparkle in his eyes.

'He's eaten up really well,' Tyler said. 'I reckon he'll win easy.'

Was I wrong about the EVA?

I thought back to Churchill Downs.

Three horses had become sick early on the morning of the Derby, with another showing signs of illness some five days later, most likely as a secondary infection.

If five days was the incubation period, and if Raworth had indeed squirted large quantities of the EVA virus up Crackshot's nose only fifty or so hours ago, then it would be quite likely that the horse would still look healthy. Whether he would be able to run full pelt for a mile and three-sixteenths in fourteen hours' time was quite a different matter.

I took the new bedding back to the other barn.

Debenture had also eaten up well, so I prepared him for his light exercise.

Jerry Fernando was due to ride the horse in the race that afternoon and he arrived to give Debenture a warm-up jog, once round the track with a lead pony in attendance. It was more to accustom the horse to his rider, and vice versa, than any serious training.

Ladybird, meanwhile, was having a day off after her efforts of the previous day. So I walked across and stood next to the track to watch the others at exercise.

Eight of the Preakness horses had opted to go out in what was an abbreviated training session. All of Raworth's three were there, with Jerry Fernando having swapped his saddle from Debenture to Fire Point for a steady half-mile trot followed by a brisk but conservative gallop over three furlongs to open the pipes and expand the lungs.

Crackshot was noticeable by his absence, but there was nothing sinister in that. Some trainers chose not to give their horses track exercise on the morning of a race, wishing to keep them fresh for when it mattered later in the day, while others might be walked for an hour or so to loosen any stiffness in the legs.

Keith had told us that, for the walkover to the track before the big race, Diego and Charlie Hern would take Classic Comic, while I would be looking after Heartbeat, assisted by Maria. Keith himself would be with Fire Point, along with George Raworth.

Diego had scowled when Keith had allocated Heartbeat to me and Maria.

'I don't mind swapping,' I'd said to him, but he had refused to answer. Diego clearly didn't want me doing him any favours.

That suited me fine.

Debenture tried his best in the Maryland Sprint Handicap but, as George Raworth had predicted, he was outclassed by the opposition, finishing seventh of the eight runners, some nine lengths behind the winner – a huge gap in a six-furlong sprint.

The owner didn't seem to mind one iota.

'At least we weren't last,' he said to me with a broad grin.

I was standing on the track after the race, holding the horse's head while the jockey's saddle was removed.

'OK, Paddy,' George said, 'take him back to the barn.'

I turned away but was stopped by a racetrack official.

'Take him to the testing barn,' he said to me. 'This horse has been selected for a random drug test.'

I happened to be facing George Raworth as the man said it, and I couldn't help but see the look of concern that swept across his face.

Perhaps it was only a natural reaction to being tested, like that insuppressible feeling of anxiety one has when being breathalysed by the police, even when you are certain you are not over the limit.

Or maybe, just maybe, those 'vitamin' injections Charlie had given to Debenture had not been quite as innocent as I'd been led to believe.

It would be ironic, I thought, if my investigation into what appeared to be a colossal Triple Crown scandal was derailed due to a positive dope test from a journeyman horse that had finished seventh out of eight in a relatively minor race on the supporting card.

George recovered his composure and told me to take Debenture to the testing barn as requested, and then to start preparing Heartbeat for the big race.

As Preakness race time approached, the excitement swelled towards fever pitch.

An enormous party had been going on for hours, especially in the infield where multicoloured tents of all sizes and shapes abounded, some acting as shade against the blazing sun, while others were beer outlets providing a continuous flow of the amber nectar to quench the heat-induced thirsts of the vast crowd.

And it wasn't only among the spectators that the anticipation was growing. Back at the Preakness

Barn, there was a highly charged atmosphere of hope and expectation, with nerves beginning to fray at the edges.

'Are we all ready?' George asked for at least the third time.

'As ready as we'll ever be,' Charlie replied, shifting his weight from foot to foot.

I thought they were in danger of transmitting their nervousness to the horses, and it was a great relief when a track official arrived to announce that it was time for the walkover.

The Preakness Barn was behind the grandstand, so the horses were walked right round the public enclosures and then back along the track in order to be paraded in front of the crowd.

For this race, there was a special mounting yard in the centre of the course opposite the finish line and beyond the turf track, and half the field were saddled in there, while the rest, including Raworth's three, went down the ramp into the indoor paddock.

'It's quieter inside,' George said. 'Helps keep them calm.'

It wasn't the horses that needed to be kept calm, I thought.

Crackshot was also being saddled inside and I looked over to where Tyler was placidly holding the horse's head while the trainer made him ready. There appeared to be no concern whatsoever over his health.

Eventually all was ready.

I led Heartbeat up the ramp to the track with Maria on the other side of his head.

She ignored me completely and I didn't speak to her. It was for the best, I thought, and safer for the both of us. It didn't, however, stop Diego glaring at me with his cold black eyes as he and Charlie Hern followed us up the ramp with Classic Comic. Fire Point, flanked by Keith and George, brought up the rear of the three.

Out in the mounting yard, Victor Gomez was waiting for Heartbeat, having been promoted from stable exercise rider to big-race jockey for the day.

'Just like old times,' he said as I gave him a leg-up. 'It is eight years since I had a ride in the Preakness.' He gave me a gappy-toothed grin like a kid with stolen candy.

I watched as George Raworth tossed Jerry Fernando up onto Fire Point's back and Charlie did likewise with the jockey riding Classic Comic. Then we led the horses back onto the dirt track and handed them over to the outriders on their lead ponies, to take them to the start.

There was nothing more we could do. It was up to them now.

I realised that, despite my firm intention not to become emotionally involved, I was actually getting quite excited as the race time approached.

A trio of top-hatted and scarlet-coated trumpeters walked out onto the track and played the traditional 'Call to Post', and then everyone joined as one in singing, 'Maryland, My Maryland', the official song of the state.

American sporting venues certainly knew how to wind the crowd up into a frenzy. By the time the starting gates swung open, the noise was so loud that I had absolutely no chance of hearing the race commentary from where I stood on the grooms' stand.

But I could see one of the big TV screens set up in the infield.

The horses broke in an even line with Crackshot on the inside rail and Heartbeat outside him. Victor Gomez immediately took Heartbeat ahead and to his left, squeezing the Florida Derby winner for space and forcing his jockey to take a strong pull on the reins to prevent a collision. The poor horse would have been confused with a 'go' message as the gates opened being followed by a 'stop' one only a few paces later. Not surprisingly, he dropped back sharply.

Fire Point, meanwhile, had a clear run from Gate 8 allowing him to establish a lead of some six or seven lengths over his main rival as they passed the finish line for the first time.

Crackshot's troubles continued round the clubhouse bend as he was boxed in by both Heartbeat and Classic Comic, who seemed to have nothing else in their game plan but to thwart the progress of the big bay colt.

By the time the lead horses were at the half-mile pole, and Crackshot had finally worked himself away from the rail and past his distractors, he was all but out of contention, having been forced to make up ground while the others were taking a back-stretch breather.

Not that it really mattered.

Crackshot would not have won the race anyway.

The horse was clearly labouring as they straightened up for the run to the line and, when his jockey asked him for a supreme effort, there was nothing left in the tank.

Fire Point, in contrast, was having a dream race. Always well placed on the outside shoulder of the lead horse, Jerry Fernando kicked for home off the final turn and sprinted away impressively from the pack to win by four lengths, much to the delight of George and Charlie who I could see laughing and embracing in the stands.

Crackshot trailed in a disappointing seventh, behind Classic Comic and Heartbeat, both of whom had repassed him in the final hundred yards.

The crowd were relatively subdued by the result, as no one enjoyed watching a horse finish a race in the sort of distress that Crackshot was clearly exhibiting. There was even a smattering of boos, as some rightly disapproved of the apparent Raworth tactics, but even the least discerning of them could not seriously argue that Crackshot would have won with an uninterrupted passage.

And George Raworth certainly didn't care.

He was smiling from ear to ear as he led Fire Point into the winner's circle alongside the horse's owner, who was equally delighted. Even an announcement over the public address system that the stewards would hold an inquiry didn't seem to bother him.

Maybe it was because he knew that, even if the stewards found Heartbeat or Classic Comic guilty of interference, they couldn't take the race away from Fire Point just because all three horses happened to be trained by the same man.

In the event, the stewards took no action at all, other than to give Victor Gomez a ten-day suspension for careless riding after he had admitted to accidently taking Crackshot's ground after the break from the starting gate. The fact that everyone knew it had not been accidental was irrelevant, there was insufficient evidence on the video footage to prove it, and the incident had clearly not cost Crackshot the race.

I didn't know how I felt about things. It was difficult not to be drawn into the celebrations among the staff in the Raworth camp over wins in the first two Triple Crown legs, but there was a huge part of me that despised the man himself for cheating his way to such a position, as I was sure he had done.

I led Heartbeat back to the Preakness Barn to find that there was much veterinary activity in and around Crackshot's stall.

'Take that damn horse outside,' someone shouted at me as I tried to hot-walk Heartbeat round the shedrow.

I took him back out into the hot sunshine, which wasn't ideal, and tied him to a fence in the shade of a large tree. Then I hurried back inside to see what was going on.

Tyler was standing in the shedrow, watching three other men busy in Crackshot's stall. There was deep worry etched on his face.

'What's up?' I asked him.

'Crackshot is sick,' he said in his deep bass tone. 'The veterinarians are worried that the race has affected his heart.'

I looked into the stall. The poor horse was dripping with sweat and clearly very unwell.

'It is very hot here today,' I said.

'Not as hot as he's used to in Florida,' Tyler replied.

That was true.

'Have they taken a blood sample?' I asked.

Tyler nodded. 'First thing they did.'

I wanted to tell them it wasn't his heart that was the problem.

They should test his blood for equine viral arteritis.

LEG 3:

THE BELMONT STAKES

'The Test of the Champion'

A mile and a half
Belmont Park, New York

Three weeks after the Preakness
Five weeks after the Kentucky Derby

First run at Belmont Park 1905,
previously run at Jerome Park and Morris Park
racecourses in New York, since 1867

26

The Triple Crown jamboree moved on from Baltimore to New York but, with three whole weeks between the Preakness and the Belmont Stakes, there was a slight pause for everyone to draw breath.

Fire Point arrived back at Belmont Park on the day after his great success at Pimlico, returning to his stall like some victorious Roman general through a guard of honour provided by the racetrack grooms, not only those from George Raworth's barn but seemingly from every other barn on the backside as well.

The signwriter had already added *and the Preakness Stakes* to the 'Home of Fire Point. Winner of the Kentucky Derby' board screwed to the outside wall.

The local TV news channels were there in force to cover the homecoming, something that would do no harm at all for the marketing of the final leg. A Triple Crown contender was guaranteed to add tens of thousands of extra spectators to the gate come race day.

For my part, I did not look forward to settling back into regular Belmont Park life after the excitement of the week at Pimlico. True, it was a huge improvement to be sleeping again in a room with only the regularly drunk and flatulent Rafael, rather than with both Diego and Keith trying to out-snore one another, but, somehow, the fun had gone out of this particular assignment.

I was beginning to find the daily drudgery of a groom rather monotonous. Perhaps my enthusiasm would return as the Belmont approached, but that still seemed like a long way off.

I suppose happiness in any job has a lot to do with one's expectation.

For Rafael, working as a groom in a top horseracing barn in New York City, where he was occasionally given overall responsibility, was the pinnacle of his ambition. He had escaped from the dismal poverty, appalling criminality and deadly danger of a Mexican slum to share a room with what he thought was only one Irishman instead of his whole extended family. He was quite obviously a happy individual, even when he was inebriated, smiling and singing his way through each day without a care in the world or an ounce of desire to do any better.

Diego, in contrast, was an angry young man.

No doubt he had originally travelled to the United States from Puerto Rico to seek his fortune, arriving in New York with an expectation that the streets would be paved with gold, only to have his hopes dashed by the reality. In his eyes, ending up as a mere groom at Belmont Park was living his life as a failure. Consequently, there was not an ounce of happiness to be found anywhere in his body.

And, sadly, after a few quieter days at Pimlico on his own, he was again supported by his Puerto

Rican compatriots and thus somewhat bolder. Ever since the truck had arrived through the gates, he had been mouthing at me what I presumed were Spanish obscenities, or threats. On the plus side, however, we had also returned to the jurisdiction of the New York courts, which meant that his trip to Rikers Island was very much back on the cards.

I spoke to Tony Andretti on my second night back, after consuming yet another dose of Bert Squab's extra-hot chilli con carne from the track kitchen.

'Crackshot has got equine viral arteritis,' Tony said. 'It was confirmed today.'

I was not in the least bit surprised. Indeed, I would have been astounded if it had been anything else.

'Bryson, Crackshot's trainer, is creating merry hell and the Maryland Jockey Club are running round in ever-decreasing circles trying to determine where the infection came from. Norman Gibson has even initiated a FACSA investigation. What do you want me to tell him?'

'Nothing,' I said. 'Not yet.'

I could tell from a snort down the line that Tony didn't like keeping information from his section chief.

'And there's more,' Tony said at length. 'The professor has also established that there *was* EVA virus in the semen sample, loads of it. I really think it's time to arrest George Raworth.'

'No,' I said. 'And for the same reason as before. Nothing concerning the semen sample would be admissible as evidence in court because it was removed from a locked place without a search warrant.'

'Let's get a warrant now, then,' Tony said. 'If we can find that cryo-flask, there will surely be some trace left in it we could analyse.'

'I doubt that,' I said. 'And I don't think the flask is even here. It's probably still in Raworth's Jeep. I haven't seen that since the day after the Preakness and the flask definitely wasn't in the truck with the other stuff when we returned from Pimlico.'

'But we surely have enough to get the New York Racing Association to ban him.' Tony was getting quite angry.

'You think so, do you?' I said rather sarcastically. 'Do you remember that NFL quarterback who was banned for allegedly deflating footballs?'

'Of course. Deflategate,' Tony said. 'Big news. Tom Brady of the New England Patriots. FACSA was peripherally involved with the investigation.'

'Yeah, that's the one. The NFL thought they had a watertight case but, even so, the ban was overturned by a US federal judge due to a lack of convincing evidence that Brady himself knew anything about it.

'Everyone appeals to law these days, and Raworth would be no exception because there's so much at stake. Never mind the individual race purses and the kudos of being a Triple Crown winner, there's also the small matter of the ten-million-dollar Triple Crown bonus, half of which goes to the winning trainer. Trust me, Raworth would fight to the death through the courts and, without that sample being admissible as evidence, you would surely lose, and look foolish.'

'So what *can* we do?' Tony said in exasperation.

'Nothing. Not yet. We watch and wait and hope he makes a mistake.'

There was silence from the far end, as if Tony was digesting that rather unpleasant pill.

'In the meantime can you check on something for me,' I said. 'Debenture was selected for a random drug test after the Maryland Sprint Handicap at Pimlico on Saturday. Raworth seemed quite concerned about it. Can you find out the result of the test from the Maryland Racing Commission and keep it from being publicised?'

'Why?' Tony asked. 'Surely, if the test is positive, we can use that to ban Raworth.'

'Maybe,' I said. 'But if it's a positive for, say, steroids or clenbuterol then, even with his record, the Maryland Commission will ban him for only a month or two at best, and only then after lengthy appeals. I want to nail him for something far more serious than a bit of doping and, in the meantime, I don't want him put on the defensive.'

'OK,' Tony said. 'I'll have a quiet word with their commissioner, but if the test is positive he'll want to do something about it.'

'Convince him otherwise,' I said. 'After all, the horse didn't win anything. It came seventh out of eight.'

'OK,' he repeated. 'I'll do my best. Anything else?'

'How about the Texas ranch?' I said. 'Did you find out anything?'

'I haven't yet but I've asked the chief of our Colorado Springs office to do some digging for me. Don't worry. I explained that it was to be confidential to him alone. He normally deals with corruption in the pro rodeo circuit and they use Quarter Horses so it's his area of expertise.'

'Pro rodeo circuit?' I said. 'Is there such a thing?'

'There certainly is. It's big business. There are hundreds of events each year and even a national final each December to decide the World Champion All-Around Cowboy. There's millions of dollars at stake and it is broadcast live on CBS.'

I marvelled at the way Americans claim to be the champions of the world at something that no one else does – like the winners of the Super Bowl who are officially crowned as the World Champions even though no other country is allowed to enter a team in the competition, not even Canada.

'So when do you expect to hear back from your man?' I asked.

'He said it might take a few days. He's been at a rodeo in Las Vegas and he won't return to his office until Wednesday morning.'

'Didn't you tell him it was urgent?' I implored.

'The guy has worked for us all weekend,' Tony said in his defence. 'So he's entitled to a couple of days off playing the slots and tables. He is still the best man for the job, so be patient.'

I had never been very good at being patient.

Playing the slots and tables, indeed.

If I was busting my gut here seven days a week, why wasn't everyone else?

Charlie Hern took morning exercise on Wednesday, standing on the platform by the training track with a stopwatch in his hand, while the horses were galloped in turn by Victor Gomez.

'Where's Mr Raworth?' I asked Victor as he came back to the barn to change horses.

'He gone visit family,' Victor said.

'Where to?' I asked.

'El Paso,' Victor replied. 'He back Friday maybe, or Saturday maybe. Depends traffic.'

'Has he driven all the way to El Paso?'

Victor nodded.

It was 2,000 miles by road from Baltimore to western Texas.

'Perhaps he no like airplanes,' Victor said, before disappearing back to the track on Paddleboat.

Perhaps he no like airplanes.

Oh yeah? Who was Victor kidding?

Raworth was a man who regularly spent a third of each year in Florida, another third in California, and the rest of the time in New York, with training barns in each place. He would be as accustomed to getting on and off aircraft as most people were buses.

Was this the mistake we were hoping for?

I took a chance by going back to the bunkhouse to

317

call Tony immediately. All the grooms were at work so the place was deserted.

'Raworth is in El Paso,' I said. 'He went there by road from Pimlico.'

'That's a hell of a drive,' Tony said. 'Are you thinking what I'm thinking?'

'That he's driven all the way to El Paso to refill the cryogenic flask with EVA-infected Quarter Horse semen from the family ranch? No commercial airline would allow him to fly with liquid nitrogen in his baggage.'

'No way,' Tony said in agreement.

'We can't be sure about them having EVA at the ranch until your man in Colorado gets back to us.'

'I'll get him home from his gambling today,' Tony said decisively. 'Did you say Raworth has a Jeep Cherokee?'

'Yes,' I replied. 'A white one.'

'Registered in which state?'

I tried to conjure up a mental image of the vehicle registration plate.

'New York, I think. The Empire State.'

'I'll get the licence plate from New York Department of Motor Vehicles and then Homeland Security can track him across the country using their automatic licence plate recognition cameras.'

'How many of those do they have?'

'Lots, with hundreds more going up every month on every Interstate and in most cities across the country. Don't tell anyone though. The majority of Americans complain bitterly about their lack of privacy as it is but, if they really knew how much their government spied on them, they'd throw a fit. The cameras track people all over the country and match them to various databases such as known criminal, wanted person, gang member, missing person, immigration violator, even tax avoiders and those on the sex offender registry, not to mention terrorist suspects. The Los Angeles Police even want to use the camera data to send letters to the owners of all vehicles that enter areas of high prostitution to warn them to stay away.'

They ought to threaten to send letters to their wives, I thought.

'Could they also find out if Raworth has driven to El Paso before?'

'Probably. It depends on how long ago. They don't keep the data indefinitely.'

'It won't be very long,' I said. 'There was still liquid nitrogen in the flask at Pimlico, so it had to be only a few weeks ago at most.'

'I'll get it checked right away,' Tony said. 'Call me later.'

We hung up and I walked slowly back to the barn, thinking.

'Where the hell have you been?' Keith shouted at me, making me jump. 'Paddleboat has been back in his stall for ages.'

'Sorry,' I said. 'I've been to the jacks.'

'Well don't,' Keith said. 'The horses' comfort comes before yours.'

319

I hurried off down the shedrow to deal with Paddleboat.

'Raworth's Jeep left the hotel parking lot at the Hyatt Regency in Baltimore Harbor at five after eight, Eastern Daylight Time, last Sunday morning, overnighted at the Garden Tree Motel east of Memphis, Tennessee, and joined I-10 from I-20 fifty miles short of the family ranch at 8.52 p.m., Mountain Time, on Monday evening. That was the last camera he passed. Raworth was the only person on board throughout. He stopped for gas five times. I have the names of the gas stations if you want them, and their closed-circuit footage showing him there along with copies of his credit card receipts for both the gas and the motel.'

I was impressed.

'How did you get this so fast?' I asked, worried he might have used his own FACSA agents.

'I was at detective school with the current Director of Homeland Security. I asked him for a favour and he ran it this afternoon as a training exercise for his staff. They are good – very good. Even I think so. And, you were dead right. They also picked up that Raworth's Jeep had recently taken that journey before. He started out from his home in New York April twenty-fifth and arrived El Paso the twenty-seventh. On that occasion he left for Louisville April twenty-ninth, then drove back to New York May tenth, three days after the Kentucky Derby.'

'It all fits,' I said.

'So now can we arrest him?'

'Only if he has the cryogenic flask with him when he turns up back here at Belmont and we're absolutely sure it is full of frozen sperm containing the EVA virus. Then you can hang him out to dry, but I really want to get your mole as well into the bargain.'

'And how are you going to do that?' Tony said excitedly.

'I'm working on it.'

27

George Raworth arrived back at Belmont Park shortly after nine o'clock on Saturday evening.

I knew he was coming.

I had spoken to Tony after my supper on Friday and he'd told me that the Jeep was again on the move.

'It is amazing how it can be tracked in real time,' Tony said. 'If Raworth were a terrorist they could call in a drone strike to take him out.'

He'd been watching too many movies, I thought. A drone strike directed at a vehicle on home soil might have raised a few awkward questions in the US Congress.

Tony gave me two other important pieces of information as well.

The first was that Debenture had indeed failed the drug test after the Maryland Sprint Handicap.

'He had excess cobalt in his system,' Tony said.

'Cobalt?'

'Just so. Not a huge amount, mind. The test found seventy-two parts per billion of cobalt while the permitted threshold level in Maryland is only fifty.'

I'd heard of the use of excess cobalt before, in particular in Australia where a trainer had been disqualified from racing for fifteen years for giving it to his horses, and I'd done some research on the subject in London.

Cobalt is a trace element needed by bacteria in the human digestive tract to produce the vitamin B12, which in turn is essential for the production of the hormone erythropoietin that stimulates bone marrow to produce red blood cells.

Erythropoietin is known as EPO for short; it was regular injections of a synthetic form of EPO that allowed the cyclist Lance Armstrong to win seven consecutive Tours de France. Attempts to cover up positive tests had been instrumental in triggering Armstrong's dramatic fall from grace, an almost overnight transformation from sporting hero and cancer survivor into demonised cheat.

The injecting of cobalt is assumed to increase the amount of vitamin B12 produced, and hence the quantity of natural EPO in the blood. That, in turn, should increase the number of red blood cells created, and hence the amount of oxygen that could be delivered to the muscles, thus improving stamina and performance.

However, the jury was still out on whether it actually made any difference at all in horses.

Raworth had obviously been experimenting with a horse that he had not expected to win, and so he had not anticipated that it would be tested. The random selection had been his bad luck. And our good.

'Has the Maryland Racing Commissioner agreed to sit tight on the findings?'

'Reluctantly, for the time being,' Tony said, 'and only because the level is low. Some tests in the past have shown concentrations of many hundred parts per billion, even thousands.'

'What's the penalty for excess cobalt in Maryland?'

'For a first offence, especially one this low, it is fifteen days' suspension and a five-hundred-dollar fine, plus loss of purse money for the race.'

'The horse finished second to last,' I said, 'so he didn't win any purse money. And fifteen days hardly seems enough of a deterrent. That's just a holiday, and five hundred dollars is mere peanuts in this sport. I want to get Raworth for far more than that.'

'But the fifteen-day suspension might mean that he couldn't act as the trainer of Fire Point for the Belmont Stakes.'

'Don't you believe it,' I said. 'He would surely appeal and any suspension would be deferred until after it was heard.'

However, remarkable as all that was, it was Tony's second piece of information that I found the more interesting.

His man in Colorado Springs had turned up a two-year-old insurance claim for a stallion infected during an outbreak of equine viral arteritis in American Quarter Horses at the Raworth family ranch, the Crazy R.

'Why is it called the Crazy R?' I asked. 'Strange name for a farm.'

'That's their brand,' Tony replied. 'Crazy R means an

upside-down R. They brand an inverted capital R into the hides of their cattle with a red-hot branding iron.'

'Not these days, surely,' I said.

'Of course. It mattered more when stock ran free but, even now, it is still the best way of determining ownership – if an animal has your brand on it, then it's yours, no more questions asked. It continues to be the most important tool we have in the fight against cattle rustling.'

'I thought cattle rustling disappeared with the demise of the Wild West,' I said with a slight laugh.

'The West is still wild, let me tell you,' Tony replied, 'and cattle rustling is very much alive and well.'

'But branding the skin with a red-hot iron sounds so cruel,' I said. 'There must be better modern methods of proving ownership. How about microchips?'

'They're slowly making inroads and hot branding will probably disappear eventually, but it remains a legal requirement in many states.'

'Do people still brand their horses as well?'

'Less so these days,' Tony said. 'There's a new technique called freeze branding that's becoming more common for horses. Instead of using a red-hot iron, an extremely cold one is held against the horse's side. It is far less painful because instead of burning a vivid scar into the skin, the intense cold destroys the pigmentation cells, making the hairs grow totally white. That's what provides the unique mark.' He laughed. 'Not much good though, I suppose, if you have a white horse to begin with.'

326

'How cold does the branding iron have to be?' I asked.

'About minus three hundred degrees.'

'How do they get it that cold?'

There was a long pause from the other end of the line.

'With liquid nitrogen,' Tony said.

Raworth's white Jeep Cherokee pulled up alongside his barn just as it was getting dark, at the same time as I was making my way back from the recreation hall to the bunkhouse.

I stepped quickly behind one of the huge grey steel manure skips and peeped around the edge.

Charlie Hern came out of the barn to greet George and the two men shook hands. I was too far away to hear what they were saying but their body language was relaxed and friendly.

George went round the Jeep and opened the rear passenger door. He then stood back and looked all around him. I ducked behind the skip but there was no real chance he would see me in the rapidly deepening darkness.

I carefully placed only one eye around the side in time to see George and Charlie lift the white CryoBank flask out of the vehicle and carry it swiftly into the barn. From the way in which they were moving I could tell that it was heavy.

It had to be full again with liquid nitrogen.

But did it also contain more EVA-tainted frozen semen?

I reckoned so, but I would still have to check.

Never mind the coldness of his liquid gas, maybe it was time to turn up the heat on Mr George S. Raworth.

'What you doing?' said an accusing voice behind me.

I nearly jumped out of my skin.

'Nothing,' I said, turning round to find Rafael standing there. But it was pretty obvious what I'd been doing, even to Rafael.

'You pick lock,' he said.

It wasn't a question. It was a statement and I could hardly deny it.

I had sneaked into the barn after George and Charlie had both driven away in the Jeep. Keith was in the office busily watching a film on the TV and I'd thought that all the grooms were either in the recreation hall or already in their beds.

I'd been wrong.

Rafael found me crouching down next to the feed-store lock listening for the pins to be moved into the correct position by my rake pick. He had arrived just as the door opened, his footsteps making absolutely no sound on the loose dirt floor of the shedrow.

He looked from me to the open door and then back to me again.

'You bad man, Paddy,' Rafael said. 'I go tell Mr Keith. You get fired.'

He turned and started to walk away.

'Rafael,' I said clearly to his back. 'If you tell Mr Keith, then I'll also tell him that you are drunk most nights. Then we will both get fired.'

He stopped and slowly turned round to face me.

'Why you do this?' he said, pointing at the open feed-store door.

Think, I said to myself. Think – and fast.

'I was only practising picking the lock,' I said. 'It's my hobby.' I pulled the door shut so it locked again. 'Here, you have a try.' I held out the two metal lock picks.

He hesitated.

'You,' he said, pointing at me.

So I opened the lock again, showing him exactly how I did it.

He was amazed when the cylinder turned once more and the feed-store door opened.

'You thief?' he asked seriously.

'No. Of course not,' I said, laughing. 'I just like opening locks.'

I pulled the door shut again and grinned at him. He smiled back but it didn't quite reach his eyes.

'Come on,' I said, putting my hand on his shoulder and forcing him away. 'It's high time we were in bed.'

I steered him out of the barn and towards the bunkhouse.

Damn it, I thought. I'd have to have another go tomorrow.

*

'Paddy,' Keith said, 'Paddleboat is running in the second race this afternoon, off at one-fifty. Make him look nice. The boss wants him claimed.'

It was half past four on Sunday morning and I had again reluctantly dragged myself from my bed in the darkness. How I longed for a Sunday-morning lie-in – even to only six o'clock would be bliss.

'That's a bit sudden, isn't it?' I said.

'Late decision,' Keith replied. 'He was always entered but we had expected him to be scratched. But Mr Raworth has decided that he should run after all.'

Interesting, I thought.

Today was eight days after the Preakness. I had travelled down to Pimlico on the horse-transport truck a week last Monday – thirteen days ago.

To my sure knowledge, at that time, Paddleboat had still been getting a large dose of clenbuterol in his daily feed and had been expected to continue doing so for the rest of that week, although, to be fair, he had not been given any since my return to Belmont Park a week ago.

But that meant there had been a maximum of thirteen days since his last dose and possibly as few as seven.

The New York Racing Association rules stated that no horse could run within fourteen days of receiving clenbuterol.

Was this another mistake?

A combination of the drug and some hard work on the training track had certainly made a noticeable

330

difference to Paddleboat. He had bulked up considerably since I'd first arrived at Belmont.

Not that it necessarily made the horse any faster. George Raworth clearly didn't think so, not if he still wanted him claimed and out of the barn.

I did my four, mucking out the stalls and preparing Paddleboat for some light morning exercise, just a gentle pipe-opener before that afternoon's race.

After the horse returned from the track, I washed him down and made up his bed, then I set to work making him look as beautiful as possible. If I could help in getting the old boy claimed then he might have a happier existence with a new trainer, without the continual threat of a one-way trip to the knacker's yard hanging over him, deferred only by the application of large doses of clenbuterol and other drugs.

I polished Paddleboat's coat, plaited his mane and combed out his tail. Then I picked out his feet, blackened his hooves, and finally brushed a checkerboard pattern onto each side of his rump using a template.

He looked like a million dollars, even if the claiming fee for the race was only twelve and a half thousand.

If Paddleboat didn't get claimed today, he probably never would.

Rafael came to see me as I was finishing off and he was clearly impressed by my handiwork.

'You done really good job, Paddy,' he said.

But he hadn't come to compliment me on my grooming.

'No more play with locks,' he said sternly.

'OK, Rafael,' I said equally seriously. 'I promise. No more playing with locks.'

'You give me lock picks, now,' he said, holding out his hand, 'and then I say nothing to boss.'

I thought that Rafael was getting rather above his station, but he *had* been put in charge of the barn when Charlie Hern was at the Preakness, and he clearly believed he had authority over me.

I had no choice.

I put my hand into my pocket and handed over the two small pieces of metal. Rafael took them, nodded, and then turned and walked away.

Damn it and double damn it.

What the hell did I do now? New lock-picks were hardly things you could buy at the local convenience store.

28

Paddleboat finished fifth of the eight runners, which was an improvement by one position over his previous run.

And he was claimed.

I removed his race bridle and handed him over to a groom from his new barn. I had surprisingly grown quite attached to the horses in my care and, when I went back to the now empty Stall 1, it was with a heavy heart. But, I supposed, it was for the best. At least the horse hadn't been injured or killed.

Pull yourself together, I told myself; it was only a horse, and a not very good horse at that.

I walked down the shedrow to the office to find Keith leaning back in the chair with his feet up on the desk watching a rerun of *Friends* on the TV.

'Paddleboat was fifth,' I said. 'And he was claimed.'

He took his feet off the desk and sat forward, clapping his hands together. 'Wow! Who by?'

'I've no idea,' I said. 'I just handed him over to his new groom.'

'That's great news.'

'Why is it?' I asked. 'Surely there is one less set of training fees coming in?'

Keith shook his head. 'Paddleboat was owned by Mr Raworth. He claimed him in January at Aqueduct on behalf of an owner who then never paid up. We've been trying to get rid of him ever since. I wonder which mug claimed him.'

I turned to leave but Keith called me back.

'Hold the fort a minute will you, Paddy, while I go to the john? Saves me locking up.'

'Sure,' I replied.

He dashed off out the door and down the shedrow to the WCs in the centre of the barn.

The stable drug register was lying closed on the desk.

I opened it and skimmed through the recent entries, in particular looking for the drugs given to Paddleboat and Debenture.

According to the records, Paddleboat had stopped receiving clenbuterol in his feed on the Thursday before I had left for Pimlico, seventeen days ago.

I knew that to be untrue, but how could I prove it?

And, from what I could see, there was no record of Debenture ever having being given any cobalt salts. But then there wouldn't be, would there? Cobalt was a banned substance.

Keith returned to the office but I had already closed the register and made sure it was back exactly as I'd found it.

'Thanks, Paddy,' Keith said, settling down again in front of the TV.

'No problem.'

I went off in search of a quiet corner to call Tony on the non-smart phones.

*

'I think it is time to start setting our trap,' I said.

'How?'

'Who do you communicate with on your private email?'

Tony clearly thought it was an odd question.

'Friends and family, you know, and other private stuff.'

'Do you ever send emails to anyone involved with FACSA using your private account?'

There was a pause while he thought.

'I'm in touch with my predecessor as Deputy Director. I worked under him for thirteen years and we're still friends. I occasionally email him about FACSA matters, especially if I need some advice.'

'He'll do very nicely,' I said. 'I assume you trust him?'

'Without hesitation.'

'Will he keep things confidential from everyone, including the others at FACSA?'

'I am sure he will if I ask him to.'

'Right,' I said. 'Call him, but not from your office or your home phones, and certainly not with your own cell. Use the one you're speaking on now. Explain that you believe your emails have been compromised and you are trying to set a trap for whoever has done it. Give him as much detail as you think is necessary but make it clear to him that he should never call you, or send you anything unless you have called him first.'

'Do you really think my phones are bugged?'

'Probably not,' I said, 'but it is better to assume they

are than to get caught out later. After you've spoken to him, send him an email saying that you are now convinced there is someone in the FACSA setup who is leaking confidential information to potential racing targets. That should get our mole's attention.'

'Is that enough?' Tony asked.

'To start with, yes. It will put our mole on alert but not to the extent that he, or she, thinks we know who it is.'

'Which we don't,' Tony pointed out.

'I'm well aware of that,' I said, slightly irritated. 'But, in time, we might try to make him, or her, believe that we do, in order to flush them out into the open.'

'Do you want my friend to reply to the email? I would, if I were him.'

'Yes, tell him to send a reply asking why you believe there's a problem. But don't answer until tomorrow.'

'Why not?' Tony said.

'Because I'm still working on what and how much we should divulge. If we do too much too quickly, our mole will smell a rat.'

'Can moles smell rats?' Tony asked with a laugh.

I laughed too. It eased the tension.

'There's something else I would like you to do,' I said. 'Tell Norman Gibson officially that the Maryland Racing Commissioner has informed you in confidence that a horse failed a dope test for excess cobalt at Pimlico on Preakness Day. Say that the information is not being made public yet because you have decided that FACSA should conduct a review into the misuse of cobalt in American racing and you do not want to send everyone into hiding. When that gets around your office there will be even more for our mole to think about. He'll be desperate to find out which horse failed the test.'

'So I don't say which horse?'

'No,' I said. 'I'd be worried about our mole immediately alerting George Raworth. He might then remove the liquid nitrogen flask and we would end up with nothing.'

'Have you found out whether there's any semen in it?' Tony asked.

'No,' I said. 'And I'm unlikely now to get a chance.'

I explained to him that I had lost my lock picks, without actually giving him the details of how. That would have been too embarrassing.

'I could easily get a search warrant,' Tony said. 'We can't risk that Raworth will infect any more horses with EVA.'

He was right. Of course, he was right.

'But if we move too soon then we might lose the chance of catching your mole, and that's the reason why I'm here in the first place. Today is Sunday. The Belmont Stakes horses won't be gathering here until the end of this week at the earliest. If I don't have the mole by the coming Friday, then you can get your warrant.'

I could tell that Tony didn't like having to wait, but he liked having a mole in his organisation even less.

My only problem was working out how I was going to find the FACSA mole in just five days.

On Monday afternoon I had Tony write another email to his friend listing the reasons why he was certain that FACSA had a mole.

I asked him to explain how some trainers had been clearly pre-warned about upcoming raids, and also how he had brought forward the raid on Hayden Ryder's barn at Churchill Downs by three days, only to discover that the trainer had arranged for the horses to be moved out on that very morning due to a tip-off.

'Also tell him all about the journalist Jason Connor, including his trip to Laurel and how he died on the way home,' I said. 'Say that you don't believe the medical examiner's report and you are convinced the mole in the organisation is somehow responsible for Connor's death.'

To be honest, by doing this, I thought we were moving things along a bit too fast, but my timescale was limited.

'I need the mole to know that we are chasing his tail.'

'But surely it would be better if he didn't,' Tony replied. 'Then we could catch him unawares.'

'Yes, ideally,' I said, 'but how would we? We need him to come out into the open and, this way, he knows we know, but he doesn't know that we know he knows we know.'

'Eh? What was that? Can you run it past me again?'

'By reading your emails, the mole will know that we are aware we have a mole in the first place. But, I'm hopeful that he, or she, doesn't also know that we are aware that your private emails have been compromised, so that he is unaware that we are giving him the information that we know about him on purpose.'

'What if he does know?'

'Then we will probably never discover who it is. That's why we need to be very careful about what you should write to your friend. We absolutely must not let on to the mole that we know he's reading it. Otherwise we'll never catch him out.'

Life in Raworth's barn went on as normal during Monday's evening stables, except that Diego had decided that his self-imposed truce of the last few days should come to an end.

I couldn't understand why. He had clearly so scared Maria that she hadn't said a word to me in over a week and she had even ignored the other young grooms, choosing to eat her meals either alone or with Diego and avoiding the recreation hall altogether by returning to her room immediately after.

But that didn't seem to deter Diego in his vendetta.

Twice he tried to knock feed out of my hands in the shedrow and, when I went to sidestep him, he kicked out at me, causing me to stumble into the dirt.

'What's your problem?' I shouted at him from my knees, but he didn't reply. He only stared down at me with his cold black eyes.

Things only got worse when I went for my supper. I had hung back in the hope that he would go to eat with the others, and I would come along later and avoid him.

But my plan didn't quite work out that way.

Diego was waiting for me outside the track kitchen, together with his three Puerto Rican lieutenants, and he had a knife in his right hand. I could see it glinting in the late-afternoon sunshine.

I'd been stabbed before, badly, and it had so nearly been the end of me. On that occasion there had been two of them, and now there were four. But these didn't have the element of surprise that the others had had.

This time I saw my would-be attackers early so I turned and ran for my life, shouting as I did so.

'Help! Help!' I screamed at the top of my voice, dispensing for once with the Irish accent.

I could hear their footsteps chasing me as I sprinted down the roadway but people were coming out of the barns to see why someone was disturbing their horses.

The footsteps behind fell away to silence and I chanced a glimpse over my shoulder. My pursuers had disappeared. Too many witnesses, no doubt.

I eased my pace slightly but I didn't stop. I decided I would forgo my supper tonight and, in future, I would make certain that I was surrounded by Raworth's other grooms at all times.

I kept going right down to Belmont Park's huge grandstand, to where the last few of the Memorial

Day holiday race crowd were still making their way back to their cars or to the train station.

Safety in numbers was my goal and I milled around among those waiting outside the clubhouse entrance for the valet-parking boys to bring their vehicles to them, all the while keeping my eyes open for a quartet of unwelcome Hispanics.

So intent was I at watching the roadway that I walked straight into the diminutive jockey Jimmy Robinson, almost knocking him over and causing him to drop the bag he'd been carrying.

'Can't you watch where you're going?' he said angrily, bending down to pick it up.

I'd last seen him five weeks ago in the lay-by north of Oxford, when he'd been mistakenly arrested for drug dealing, but had actually only been buying diuretics and laxatives.

Nigel Green in London had warned me he was coming to ride in New York. I should have been more careful.

I quickly turned so he wouldn't see into my eyes. I had grown a beard since he had last seen me and I was also wearing my ever-present LA Dodgers baseball cap. Perhaps he wouldn't recognise me.

'Some people,' I heard him say loudly behind me as I walked briskly away. 'Not even an apology.'

I ignored him and kept going, against the human traffic, through the doors and into the grandstand.

It was high time I got out of here and went back to England.

29

Tuesday morning dawned with a dark and menacing sky. The humidity was up in the 90 per cents and the temperature wasn't far off the same in degrees.

'We have storm,' Rafael said as we walked to the barn from the bunkhouse.

I was sure he was right. One could almost feel the electricity in the air.

'No horse exercise early,' Rafael said. 'They go later.'

He was almost right about that too.

'It's dark here today,' Keith said, referring, not to the weather, but to the fact that there was no racing at Belmont Park on Tuesdays. 'So the horses can go out later. The track is closed anyway until at least nine, when this storm is forecast to be through.'

The chance of anyone being struck by lightning was always slight but why take the risk? That was obviously the opinion of the Belmont track authorities; or, more likely, they didn't want to get sued.

Some years ago, a 22-year-old Australian jockey had been hit when out riding morning exercise on a racecourse near Perth. He'd died instantly, along with the gelding he'd been on. The fact that the horse had been wearing metal shoes hadn't helped.

There was a dazzling flash of lightning followed almost instantaneously by a deafening clap of thunder, and the heavens opened, huge drops of rain initially making dents in the dirt outside before everything was overwhelmed by the huge volume of water falling from above.

For the next three hours, the Raworth grooms, plus Maria, walked the horses in turn round and round the shedrow in order to give them at least some exercise. We did our best to keep the animals calm but the repeated flashes of electricity and accompanying crashes of thunder put them all on edge, and us too.

By eight o'clock we were hanging around outside the office waiting for the elements to improve. Rafael went up the ladder to the bedding store and tossed down half a dozen bales of straw for us all to sit on.

Diego sat facing me, watching my every move.

He had made no comment about his attempted attack. Indeed, he made no comment to me about anything, not that communication of any sort was easy due to the incessant hammering of the torrential downpour on the barn's metal roof.

The previous evening, I had remained in the grandstand for almost three hours, until the very last possible moment before it was closed up for the night. I had taken the opportunity to have a good nose around all the hidden nooks and crannies, especially in the four separate kitchens, where I had conducted a fruitless search for some leftover food.

Still hungry, I had eventually made my way back

to the bunkhouse using a roundabout route to avoid Diego and his henchmen.

He was a distraction I could have well done without.

The weather forecasters had been rather optimistic. Nine o'clock came and went with the electrical fireworks still in full swing above us.

Keith came out of the office at ten.

'All track work is cancelled for the day,' he shouted over the din of the thunderclaps and the endless rain. 'Even if this blows over soon, the track will be too wet.'

No one moved. None of us fancied going out into the biblical-style deluge, even for a late breakfast at the track kitchen.

My non-smart phone rang, its piercing shrill ringtone cutting right through the other noise.

Everyone's eyes swivelled my way. Everyone, that is, except Diego, who hadn't taken his eyes off me for the past hour anyway.

I took the phone out of my pocket and looked for a number on the screen. There was none, just the single word 'withheld'.

No one knew this number, I thought. No one other than Tony and I'd given him the strictest of instructions never to call me.

'Hello,' I said, answering.

'Jeff, it's me,' Tony said. 'I have to speak to you.'

'I'm sorry,' I said loudly, 'you must have the wrong number.'

I hung up and put the phone back in my pocket.

Perhaps I should have had it switched to silent but then the alarm wouldn't sound to wake me in the mornings.

It had to have been really important for Tony to have called but there was no way I could speak to him with all the others listening. And I wasn't going to get up and go somewhere else to make a call back. That would have been too obvious.

Instead, we all went on sitting on the bales in the shedrow, waiting for the rain to pass.

But I sat there fearful that the atmospheric high jinks above my head wasn't going to be the only storm I had to deal with today.

It was not until well after midday that I was able to get any privacy. The rain had pretty much stopped by then and, when all the others went to lunch, I walked round the barn to the bunkhouse to call Tony.

I went right through the building to make sure everyone else was out, then I shut my bedroom door and placed the back of the wooden chair under the doorknob so I couldn't be disturbed. Even so I kept my voice to a minimum.

'We have a problem,' Tony said.

Houston? I thought, with a smile.

But our problem was, in fact, nothing to laugh about.

'Someone called the Maryland Racing Commissioner's office at eight o'clock this morning saying he was from FACSA, wanting to know the name of the horse that had failed the post-race cobalt test at Pimlico.'

'Who?'

'They don't know,' Tony said. 'The commissioner hadn't yet arrived at his office, so the man spoke to his PA.'

'What was he told?' I asked with trepidation.

There was a slight pause as if Tony was preparing me for bad news. My heart dropped.

'He was told it was Debenture,' he said miserably.

'How could such a thing happen?' I said angrily, hissing the words down the line. 'Surely they should have checked who was asking. It could have been a journalist for all they knew.'

'Apparently the man used my name and he was very persuasive, telling the PA that he had spoken to the commissioner last week, who had told him the name of the horse but had since mislaid the piece of paper on which he'd written it down. The PA knew the information was highly confidential. She had even been instructed by the commissioner not to tell anyone else in their own organisation, not even his deputy. It was partly because of the confidentiality that she assumed it had to be me calling as no one else knew anything about it.'

'What time did you call Norman Gibson to tell him about the test result?'

There was another pause. More bad news?

'I didn't call him,' Tony said. 'I sent him an email.'

My heart sank again.

'From your private account or from the FACSA one?'

'The FACSA account, obviously,' he said,

somewhat affronted. 'All FACSA emails are encrypted. They're meant to be totally secure between sender and recipient. The mole shouldn't be able to read them.'

Not unless he had access to your work computer and your password, I thought wryly. Or if the mole was Norman Gibson himself.

'When did you send it?'

'Late yesterday afternoon,' he said, 'after we spoke.'

'So how did you find out that someone had called the commissioner?'

'When he arrived for work at nine this morning, he called me only to make sure I had been given the right name. I knew nothing about it, of course.'

It had been a huge risk for the mole, but it had narrowed our search.

'At least we now know that our mole is a man,' I said. 'That reduces the field somewhat.'

'What are we going to do?' Tony asked.

'How quickly could you arrange a search of Raworth's barn if you had to?'

'It would probably take us at FACSA at least twenty-four hours to put everything in place but, if it was really urgent, I could call in the FBI or, better still, the local Nassau County Police Department. They could be on site almost immediately. Getting a warrant would mean finding a judge but they usually have one of those on standby. I might even make some calls now and get a warrant issued in case we need it.'

'Good idea,' I said. 'Do that. But, for now, we do

nothing. We sit tight, while I watch and listen. If things start to happen, I'll call you straight away.'

'Just like in England,' he said.

'What?'

'That day back in England,' Tony said, 'when we set that trap by the road. You didn't call in the police until well after I would have done. As I remember saying then, you have nerves of steel.'

'Do you want to find your mole or not?' I asked.

'I'll make those calls.'

'Fine,' I said. 'But don't send any emails.'

Tony didn't laugh.

I made it to the track kitchen for lunch just as the clock in the dining hall moved on to two minutes past two.

Bert Squab was already closing up.

I hadn't eaten anything since my lunch the previous day, having missed supper due to Diego and his chums, and then breakfast because of the rain.

My stomach was beginning to think my throat had been cut.

'I'm shut,' Bert announced, spreading his considerable bulk as wide as possible and folding him arms in front of him, so that they rested on his protruding belly. 'You're too late.'

I could see several steaming dishes of food behind him.

'Come on, Bert,' I said imploringly, holding out one of the plastic meal tokens. 'Give me a break. It's only two minutes past.'

'Two o'clock is the cut-off time for the groom meal scheme,' Bert said adamantly as the clock clicked over to three minutes past. 'You can still buy some lunch if you want it – for cash.'

He smiled at me.

Bastard, I thought.

Capitalism was alive and well, and living at Belmont Park.

For many people, and Bert was clearly among them, making a bit of extra money on the side was more important than making friends, even if the first actively hindered the second.

I'd done my utmost to be sociable towards him in the past but, far from being a friend, Bert Squab was now my sworn enemy.

Could I last until supper with no food?

I'd have to. I was damned if I was going to give anything extra to this obstinate oaf for food that was already there and paid for. And I knew for sure that any cash I handed over would go straight into his own pocket.

'I'll have to have words with my guv'nor,' I said, turning away and walking towards the exit.

I hadn't really said it as a threat, but I had quite expected Bert to soften and apologise, and then call me back to eat, but he didn't.

It was only food, I told myself. Some people in the world regularly go without food for days on end. I could surely manage it for another four hours.

*

I went back to Raworth's barn and hung around there, keeping my eyes and ears open for any unusual activity.

The storm of the morning had completely cleared away and the sun was now shining brightly in a near cloudless sky. I sat down on an upturned bucket at the end of the barn and watched as the puddles outside slowly evaporated away and the thick mud turned back into dry earth.

What should I do?

Tony had said that I had nerves of steel but it didn't feel like it at the moment.

What was the worst thing that could happen?

Even if Raworth were to get away scot-free for infecting his rivals *and* the FACSA mole remained undiscovered, it wouldn't be the end of the world as I knew it.

Sending in the Nassau County Police with a search warrant might secure the first objective but would, pretty much, rule out the second, at least for now, and that's the one I wanted the more of the two.

So much more.

That was the reason I had been living like this for these three long weeks, busting my arse by day, sleeping in a lookalike prison cell with a flatulent Mexican by night, and sharing a bathroom, not only with the other eight human occupants of the building but also, it seemed, with half the cockroach population of North America.

I surprised myself by how badly I wanted to catch this mole.

In fact, I decided that I'd stop at nothing to get him.

I stood up and walked a little distance from the barn to call Tony.

'Send an email to your predecessor friend telling him that you may have a lead on one of Adam Mitchell's former grooms who, you understand, knows how Mitchell was tipped off about the raid last October and is prepared to talk about it. Make a joke of the fact that you have found out partly by accident because it appears that the groom in question now looks after a horse that tested positive for cobalt at Pimlico on Preakness Day. But don't tell him the name of the horse is Debenture. We don't want to make it too obvious.'

'Don't you look after Debenture?'

'Yes,' I said.

'It could be dangerous.'

'I know,' I said. 'But I can't see any other way of getting our mole to show himself, and certainly not by this coming Friday. He may not buy it, of course. It is rather like waving a scarlet cape at a bull. Maybe he will charge, or maybe he won't. But surely it is worth a try.'

And as the matador, would I get gored by his horns, or could I deliver *la estocada*, the final coup de grâce?

'I thought male moles were called boars, not bulls,' Tony said.

I ignored him.

30

I stayed close to Raworth's barn right through until evening stables, waiting and watching, but nothing happened.

The horses spent the time in their stalls, alternately snoozing in the afternoon heat or munching from their haynets.

I wondered what dried grass tasted of, and how hungry a man would have to be to try it. I had certainly seen news items on the television where starving people had tried to sustain themselves by eating boiled leaves.

Thankfully, I wasn't yet at that stage, although a dull ache of hunger had settled into the pit of my stomach and I was really looking forward to my supper.

At about three-thirty I stood up and stretched my legs, walking round the shedrow to stay in the shade. I could hear canned laughter from the office where Keith was again watching a comedy show on the TV.

I didn't really want to have to chat to him so I avoided going past the open office door and retraced my steps down to the other end of the barn.

I tried the feed-store door.

It was locked. Of course it was locked.

The feed store was always kept locked except when Charlie Hern or Keith were actually issuing the horse nuts from the feed bins.

And the drug store within would also surely be locked, quite likely with frozen EVA-contaminated semen in the cryogenic flask hidden away in its bottom corner.

How I could have done with my lock picks to check.

Evening stables started at four o'clock under the close eye of Charlie Hern. With the departure from the barn of Paddleboat, I had been allocated another of the equine residents, a four-year-old gelding called Highlighter who was housed in Stall 15, close to the office and well away from my other three and, somewhat inconveniently, sandwiched between two horses cared for by Diego.

I had done my best all day to avoid him, but now I found myself right on his doorstep, even sharing a water tap at that end of the barn.

I left Highlighter right to the end in the hope that Diego would have given up waiting and gone to supper.

No such luck.

He came into Stall 15 after I had done the mucking out and just as I had finished brushing Highlighter's coat to a nice shine. But he wasn't intent, this time, on physical violence. Maybe that was because I was bigger than him, and he wasn't accompanied by his back-up team. So, instead, he simply threw a full bucket of muddy water all over Highlighter's back.

So juvenile, I thought.

Charlie Hern was already on his tour of inspection around the other side of the barn, and he certainly wouldn't have been pleased to find one of the horses caked in mud. I didn't have long enough to take Highlighter outside to the wash point, so I did my best to scrape the mud off his coat and out of his mane, brushing each vigorously with a stiff dandy brush. But, in spite of my efforts, the horse was still not looking very good by the time Charlie arrived.

'Come on, Paddy,' Charlie said, clearly irritated. 'Get a move on. You know better than to present a horse to me in this state.'

'Sorry, Mr Hern,' I said meekly. 'I'll make sure he's right before I go.'

'Damn right you will,' Charlie responded.

He felt down over the animal's legs and tut-tutted under his breath, but not so quietly that I wouldn't hear. Then he moved on to the next stall as I went back to my brushing.

'Damn you, Diego, damn you,' I repeated over and over in time with my brush strokes as I repaired his damage.

Consequently, I was the last in line as Charlie issued the correct quantity of concentrated feed for each horse.

'Have you cleaned up Highlighter?' he asked as he poured the feed into bowl 15.

'Almost, sir,' I said. 'I just need to finish him off.'

'Be sure you do,' Charlie said sternly. 'And check he eats up his supper.'

'Yes, sir,' I said, taking the bowl of feed and making my way back towards Stall 15.

I could do with eating up my supper as well.

I was still brushing out Highlighter's mane and tail when I heard George Raworth arrive. He came into the barn shouting loudly for Charlie Hern, who was still down in the feed store.

They went into the office.

'Keith,' I heard George say, 'go and make sure all the staff have gone to supper and then go yourself, will you? I need to talk to Charlie alone.' I could hear him clearly through the wooden partitions between the office and the stall I was in.

'OK, boss,' Keith replied. 'I think they've left already.'

'Have a look anyway,' George said.

I slipped out of the stall but, instead of leaving, I quickly climbed the ladder up to the bedding store and hid myself, lying down silently between the straw bales stacked above the office with my ear to the floor.

I glimpsed the top of Keith's head as he made a complete circuit of the barn beneath me, without once looking up.

'All clear,' I heard Keith say as he went back to the office.

'Right,' George said. 'You get going too.'

'OK, boss,' Keith said. 'How long do you want?'

'Give us a good half an hour,' George said. 'Come back after your meal.'

I heard the office door close and there was a pause, presumably for Keith to walk away.

'Check, will you?' I heard George ask.

I heard the office door open, then it closed again.

'He's gone,' Charlie said. 'Now what's this about?'

'I've had a call on my home phone from someone demanding money,' George said, hissing it hardly louder than a whisper. But I could still hear him clearly.

'What for?' Charlie asked.

'He told me I had a horse fail a dope test at Pimlico and ten thousand dollars in cash would make it all go away.'

'Which horse?' Charlie said.

'He didn't say but it has to be that damn nag Debenture for cobalt. Nothing else has had anything. Why did we ever think it was a good idea? The damn animal is useless and we should have recognised that.'

'It should have been clear of his system before that race,' Charlie said. 'I was told he'd pee it all out in only a day or two.'

'Well he obviously didn't.'

'It doesn't matter,' Charlie said. 'I looked up the Maryland sanctions for cobalt before I even suggested it. They're pathetic – a slap on the wrist and a five-hundred-buck fine, nowhere near ten grand. Just ride it out.'

'So what do we do about tomorrow?' George said.

357

'In what way?'

'Debenture is due to run in the last race. We'd better scratch him.'

'No,' Charlie said quickly. 'That's ideal. It's been over a week since he ran at Pimlico. The cobalt will have surely gone from his system by now. Let's insist they do another test on him. He'll be clear. That would help our case.'

'It is not really the damn cobalt I'm worried about, it's the other stuff.' George was sounding agitated.

'Relax,' Charlie said. 'No one can possibly know about that.'

How wrong he was.

'But what if NYRA do a search?'

'They won't. The positive was not even on their watch and no one would do a search for a single positive for cobalt. Others have been done for far more than that, and they've laughed it off. It wasn't as if we used much of the stuff anyway.'

Well done, Charlie, I thought. Keep talking George out of moving the flask.

'Look,' Charlie said. 'I'll get rid of what's left of the cobalt, just in case. But relax. All will be fine.

No it won't, I reflected.

My hungry stomach rumbled loudly.

I held my breath. Had they heard? It had seemed very loud to me. I went on lying as still as I could, silently berating my noisy stomach, without actually telling it that it was now unlikely to get any supper as well.

'What time was the call?' Charlie asked beneath me, seemingly unruffled. Even if he had heard a noise, he would likely have thought it was one of the horses.

'About four o'clock.'

'What did you say?' Charlie asked.

'I told him that I had no idea what he was talking about.'

'And?' Charlie prompted. 'What did he say to that?'

'He told me to think hard and he'd call me again in the morning.'

'And did he tell you how you were meant to pay him?'

'He said to get the cash together and take it with me to the track tomorrow. He'd find me there.'

'What, here at Belmont?' Charlie said.

'Yes. Here. During racing.'

'I reckon it's some smart-assed lab technician after a fast buck,' Charlie said. 'He's probably acquired a bit of information and is trying to make some easy dough on the back of it. He almost certainly couldn't make the Maryland charge go away, anyway. What are you going to do then? Complain that your ten-grand bribe to some mystery man didn't work? You'd get laughed at. Ignore him.'

'Maybe you're right,' George said. 'But do you think we should dispose of the other stuff, just in case?'

'No. We might need it. There's a piece in today's *Racing Form* that says Amphibious has recovered from his fall in the Santa Anita Derby and will run in the Belmont Stakes. It seems his trainer has been mouthing off that Fire Point is not good enough to be a Triple Crown winner and he intends to make sure he isn't. We've come this far, George, and I don't intend to give it all up now.'

'OK. But maybe we should move it.'

'Where to?' Charlie said. 'Do you really want your wife and kids asking what's in the funny tank in the garage? And I can't keep it. Not with Sophie sniffing round everything. Like I told you before, it is safer locked away here.'

George Raworth might have been the trainer, the big boss, while Charlie Hern was only his assistant but, in this venture, Charlie was definitely in charge. Everything about their conversation indicated so.

'If he calls you again in the morning, which I doubt, you tell him to take a hike, we're not paying.'

'What if he's not a lab technician but someone important? It might be worth ten grand to us not to have him create any trouble. After all, look at the prize we're after.'

I assumed he meant the five-million-dollar bonus to the trainer of a Triple Crown winner.

'But who's to say he won't then come back for more,' Charlie said.

'We might need to take that chance.'

'OK, string him along a bit,' Charlie said. 'But don't pay him anything unless you talk to me first. Got it?'

'Yes,' George replied. 'I'd better get back home in case he calls again. I don't want the kids answering, especially as George Junior now sounds exactly like me on the telephone.'

I heard the office door open and, presently, I could hear as the Jeep Cherokee was started and driven away.

Annoyingly, Charlie Hern appeared to stay exactly where he was.

Hence, so did I, hardly daring to breathe in case I was heard in the evening stillness of the barn. But I was well used to lying completely still. I'd had to do it in wet ditches before now, so a bed of soft straw was relative luxury.

After an anxious five minutes or so, Charlie stood up, scraping the legs of the chair on the floor. I chanced a look down as he came out of the office and watched his bald pate as he went along the shedrow to the far end of the barn jangling his keys. Off to the drug store, I thought, to remove the rest of the cobalt.

I gave him enough time to reach it, then I moved swiftly to the ladder and went down, leaving the barn quickly in the opposite direction from the track kitchen. The last thing I wanted to do was to meet Keith coming back from his supper.

I looked at my watch. Twenty minutes to seven.

I'd missed my fourth meal in a row and now I was really hungry.

I took a roundabout route down towards the grandstand and then along to the main gate of the racecourse, crossing over the Hempstead Turnpike at

361

the traffic lights to the Belmont Deli & Grill to spend some of my pitiful wages.

Never had a cheese-and-ham sandwich tasted so good. I even splashed out on a cold beer to help it down. Fabulous.

Next I called Tony.

'The fish took the bait,' I said.

'Huh?' he replied.

'Someone called George Raworth this afternoon demanding money to keep Debenture's positive test for cobalt quiet.'

'You're kidding me.'

'I am not. I overheard him not half an hour ago telling his assistant trainer. The man apparently demanded ten thousand dollars to make the test results disappear.'

'But who could do that?' Tony asked. 'Only some-one in the Maryland Racing Commission could make that happen.'

I thought back to what Charlie Hern had said earlier. 'Perhaps it's someone who couldn't actually make the test results disappear but is simply using the information to turn a quick profit by selling a promise he can't keep.'

'Then it could be anyone,' Tony said. 'How about someone in the testing laboratories?'

He was grasping at straws, even now not wanting to accept that one of his team had been so blatant in asking for such a bribe.

'I doubt that,' I said. 'If it is anything like in

England, samples are coded only with numbers so the lab staff don't know the names of the horses that provide them. The only people who knew were you and me, the Maryland Commissioner and his PA, plus your mole. And you can guess who my money's on.'

Tony took a second or two to digest that fact.

'What else did you hear?' he asked.

'That the man would collect the cash from Raworth tomorrow afternoon during racing here at Belmont. Who from the FACSA racing section is due to be in New York tomorrow?'

'I'll check the roster right away. The weeks between the Preakness and the Belmont are fairly quiet, racing-wise, hence it's a popular time for staff to take vacations, especially for those without kids who want to get away before the schools finish for the summer and all the prices are hiked.'

'How about if you call all of them on their cell phones, even if they're on vacation, and get your contact at Homeland Security to use his technology to find out where they are when they answer? You probably don't even need to call them. Some new smart phones are trackable even when they're off.'

'I'll try.' He didn't sound too hopeful. 'He stuck his neck out for me when he tracked the Jeep from El Paso. I'm loath to ask him for something again in case he says no. It is our problem not theirs.'

'I thought we were all on the same side,' I said, slightly exasperated.

'We are, but it is not always that easy. Each agency

has to answer separately to congressional committees and many of their members have political agendas. If we're too cosy with one another, they don't like it. They then think we have too much of the power that they want for themselves.'

'That's crazy,' I said. 'Surely it's for the greater good.'

'Maybe, but I'm also not sure I want Homeland Security asking awkward questions, which they would surely do. Tracking Raworth's Jeep was one thing, but helping us to monitor our own agents is quite another.'

Ah, I thought. Here was the real reason. Tony didn't want to have to admit to other government agencies that he had a bad apple in his organisation.

'Then we will have to catch your mole on our own,' I said.

31

'Paddy,' Keith said. 'Debenture runs in the last today.'

It was five o'clock on Wednesday morning and he came into the stall when I was with the horse in question. 'Mr Raworth confirmed to me last night that he'll definitely run. Make sure he's looking his best, the boss is quite keen that he should be claimed.'

'OK,' I said.

It wasn't a surprise. Not after what I'd heard between trainer and assistant the previous afternoon, but it did present a considerable difficulty. How was I going to keep an eye on George Raworth all afternoon if I also had to look after Debenture?

Tony had decided that, whatever happened, this would be my last day as a groom.

I had called him again before I went to bed to discover the whereabouts and roster of his agents, and he had given me the news.

Whether we managed to catch the FACSA mole today or not, the local Nassau County Police would execute a search warrant at Raworth's barn at seven o'clock on Wednesday evening, looking for the flask of frozen semen.

Tony had actually wanted to move in first thing this morning but I had managed to talk him into giving me until after the afternoon's racing. I had wanted longer but he was adamant that the raid had to be today.

That was because he had learned that Amphibious, the colt from Santa Anita, would be arriving at New York by air from California early on Thursday and he wasn't prepared to take the risk that he could purposely be infected with EVA.

I couldn't really blame him. It would be indefensible to allow another horse, a hugely valuable potential stallion, to have a future stud career ruined when we already knew the mechanics of how it was done, and by whom.

Try explaining that to a congressional committee, or to the jury in the civil lawsuit.

'I'm not feeling too good,' I said to Keith.

'What's the matter?'

'My stomach's bad,' I said, holding a hand to my abdomen and pulling a face. 'It must be something I ate.'

'Soldier on for the time being,' Keith said, not displaying any sympathy whatsoever. 'We'll see if you're better later.'

So I soldiered on, mucking out my four horses and getting them ready for morning exercise.

Twice I rushed off to the lavatory, both times when I knew Keith would see me, and did my absolute best to make myself appear sick.

I remembered reading the book *Day of the Jackal*, where the assassin chews on cordite to make his skin go grey and clammy, in order to fake illness. I had no cordite to hand but, after finishing my morning duties at nine, I ran on the spot very fast for five minutes, out of sight in one of the stalls, in order to make my face flush red and to produce some sweat.

Then I went to see Keith in the office.

'I'm really not good,' I said, again clutching my abdomen.

'I can see that,' he replied, standing up from his chair.

'Feel my forehead,' I said. 'I think I've got a fever.'

From Keith's reaction, you might think I'd asked him to put his hand into the open mouth of a starving lion. He shrank back against the far wall of the office, putting his arms up in front of his face.

'But you might be infectious,' he said nervously. 'Stop by the track medical facility and get yourself checked out.'

'What about Debenture?' I said. 'He runs later.'

'I'll tell Diego to deal with him.'

'Thanks,' I said. 'I'll go see the medics right now.'

I walked out of the office and went back to the bunkhouse. I needed a few things from my locker.

By midday I was positioned close to the grandstand entrance nearest to the barns, waiting for George Raworth to arrive.

I had used the time since leaving Keith to perform a transformation in my appearance.

First I collected my disguise kit from my room.

My plastic wash bag may have been cheap but it contained some seriously expensive hair dye, hidden in one of the two shampoo bottles. I also selected a disposable razor, a can of shaving cream, some cotton balls, a comb and my dark sunglasses, along with my one collared shirt and the only pair of trousers I had with me that were not made of denim.

I stuffed the lot into a Walmart plastic grocery bag and walked down to the grandstand just as the turnstiles were opened for the early arrivals.

With my groom's ID pass firmly in my pocket, I paid the clubhouse entrance fee and made a beeline for the nearest disabled toilet, locking myself in.

For most of the next half-hour I worked on my hair and beard.

By the time I emerged, my fair locks had turned jet black and my wispy yellow beard had been converted into a matching black goatee. The cotton balls had been lodged tight between my teeth and gums to change the shape of my face and the faded T-shirt and scruffy jeans had gone into the waste bin, replaced by more respectable wear. I even tried, mostly in vain, to bring some semblance of shine back to my faux leather black loafers.

To top it all, I added the dark glasses and looked at myself in the mirror.

Not perfect, I thought. My sister would have still known me but it was the best I could do under the circumstances. I hoped it would be enough.

Now I stood near the entrance, apparently studying

the day's racing programme but actually keeping my eyes fixed on the turnstiles.

The current structure was built half a century ago but, at almost a quarter of a mile long and nearly a hundred yards deep, it was still the world's largest single grandstand for Thoroughbred racing with well over a million square feet of floor space, twelve bars, five restaurants, eighteen escalators, nine lifts, and enough capacity for up to a hundred thousand people. There was even a five-bed hospital tucked away in one corner.

The place would be full to bursting in ten days' time for the Triple Crown showdown in the Belmont Stakes but, on the Wednesday after Memorial Day, a crowd of only a few thousand souls was expected. Consequently, two-thirds of the stand was closed off completely and even the rest felt cavernous and empty.

The first race of the afternoon was due off at twenty past one and, when the starting gates opened, I was still in the spacious grandstand lobby waiting for George Raworth.

Not that I hadn't seen a familiar face. I had.

Frank Bannister, he who had looked after me when I'd first arrived at FACSA, came swanning through the turnstiles at half past twelve, using his metal special-agent badge to gain entry.

Tony had told me the previous evening that Frank might be here.

'He has been detailed to be in New York by Norman Gibson,' Tony had told me, 'to make arrangements for other members of the racing section who will be attending the Belmont Stakes Racing Festival next week. There may be others too. It is largely up to them where they go when not actually scheduled.'

That hadn't been particularly helpful.

When I'd first seen Frank arrive, I had lifted the race programme up to my face and peeped over the top. He went from the turnstiles to an information desk where he spoke to a woman, who made a brief phone call. After a few seconds, a man appeared from the office behind the desk and shook Frank's hand. The two of them then disappeared into the office.

Nothing suspicious in that, I thought.

I went on waiting for George Raworth to arrive.

After about ten minutes, Frank emerged from the office and wandered off into the depths of the grandstand, in the opposite direction to where I was standing.

Much as I would have loved to follow him and find out what he was up to, my primary target still had to be George Raworth.

Only if he approached George would I be sure that Frank Bannister was our mole.

Not having heard the morning phone call, I wasn't totally sure if a rendezvous was actually in the offing. Maybe George had told the man to take a hike, as Charlie Hern had suggested, and he wouldn't appear at the track until it was time to saddle Debenture for the last race.

I went on waiting.

George arrived at five past two, but he wasn't alone.

I watched through the glass doors as he strode confidently across the open forecourt towards the clubhouse entrance, appearing for all the world as the self-assured trainer of a horse that had won the first two legs of the Triple Crown. However, fifteen yards behind him, and keeping slightly to one side, was a nervous-looking Charlie Hern.

That complicated the situation somewhat, I thought. So there would be two of us following George. I would have to be extra careful not to trip over his other tail.

But at least it meant that the handover of cash was probably 'on'.

George walked by without giving me a second glance and I stood waiting until his shadow was also well past me before joining the snake.

I tried to imagine myself as the mole.

If I were in his position, I would not simply walk up to George Raworth and demand the cash. First and foremost, I would want to ensure that I wasn't walking into a trap. I would be wary that George might have called in the police so I would check things out, gauge the lie of the land, and bide my time.

In fact, if I were the mole, I would follow George around for quite a while before making any contact, keeping my eyes peeled for others doing the same thing. So there might be four of us playing 'follow the leader', with George taking us on a merry dance for much of the afternoon.

The secret to being a successful tail was not to get so close to your target that you were spotted, but also not to be so far away that either you couldn't see what the target was doing or, worse still, you lost him altogether.

Clearly the best place was to be behind not only your target but also any others who were following him – to be at the back of the line, keeping an eye on all of them at once. It was easier said than done, especially if you didn't know what the other tails looked like, assuming they existed at all.

In this case, I did know what Charlie Hern looked like and, if the other tail turned out to be Frank Bannister, I also knew him. My advantage might lie in the fact that I was counting on neither of them recognising me.

And also I was good at my job. I'd been trained in the British Army Intelligence Corps by an instructor who had previously been a surveillance specialist with the elite UK police Special Branch. 'I know it sounds simple,' he had said, 'but the trick is always to be natural. If the target stops and turns round to check, don't you stop as well. That would not be natural and will instantly give you away. Keep walking, go past him and, if necessary, double-back behind later.'

Of course, when the Special Branch tailed a suspect, it was always done by a team. Here I was on my own so I couldn't afford to be seen at all, even if the target didn't realise I was on his tail. Being seen twice would surely give me away, even if he didn't identify me specifically as his former groom.

George walked briskly along the wide concourse and then back out into the open air towards the paddock, with Charlie never more than twenty paces behind him.

Charlie was being a fool, I thought. He was tailing George far too openly. Even if the mole didn't know what Charlie looked like, he couldn't fail to spot that he was following George, and hence know that George must also be aware of Charlie. My only hope was that the mole surely couldn't mistakenly believe that Charlie was the police, he simply wasn't good enough.

I stood on the concrete steps surrounding the paddock and leaned on the white metal railings. To anyone watching, I appeared to be studying the horses parading for the third race, occasionally consulting the race programme booklet in my hand. But, behind my dark sunglasses, I only had eyes for the people, in particular for anyone who was paying George undue attention as he stood on the grass close to a bronze statue of the great Secretariat.

Not that it was an easy task. As the trainer approaching a possible Triple Crown triumph, George Raworth was something of a racing celebrity and there were lots who wanted either to speak with him or get close enough to take a selfie with him in the background.

I scanned the faces of the other racegoers.

There was no sign of Frank Bannister, or anyone else I recognised.

The horses were led through the walkway under the grandstand to the track for the race and the meagre crowd followed, but George didn't budge an inch, almost as if he was making himself as conspicuous as possible. Charlie Hern didn't move either, continuing to lean on the white railings some distance to my right, all the while watching his boss.

I decided that, with everyone else moving through to watch the race, I would be too exposed if I stayed on the paddock steps, so I went back inside and continued to keep a lookout through one of the huge arched windows that ran down the rear of the grandstand.

George remained where he was for the next two hours, moving only slightly to his left to stand in the shade of the ancient Japanese white pine that dominated the Belmont Park paddock. He puffed out his chest and stood tall with his feet apart, facing the public enclosures.

His body language was broadcasting a very clear message. 'Here I am,' it said. 'You will have to come to me.'

As far as I could tell, nobody suspicious did, not that keeping close to him was easy for me. Both George and Charlie endlessly scrutinised the faces of all those around them, watching for some indication of understanding at what was going on.

Twice I became aware that Charlie was looking in

my direction. I was standing again by the metal rail, seemingly watching the horses for the fourth race. I didn't look back at him. Instead I lowered my head as if studying my programme.

There was no shout of awareness, no movement from him whatsoever.

Charlie may have seen me but he hadn't recognised me as one of the Raworth stable staff.

Without fail, for every waking moment since the day of my first arrival here, I had worn the blue LA Dodgers baseball cap with the peak curved down at the sides. It was the cap more than anything that had come to define me. Charlie had never seen me without it, not even at our first interview, and the fact that I was now bareheaded was thus an advantage in remaining unknown to him in the crowd. The variation in hair colour, the change in face shape and the dark glasses also helped.

Nevertheless, I decided that I shouldn't push my luck, so I again retreated inside the grandstand away from his gaze.

But watching George through the ground-floor windows was far from ideal. It was just about all right when there was no one else standing on the paddock steps, such as during the actual running of the races, but when the people returned they tended to obscure my view. That's why I had gone back outside in the first place.

So, after the next race, I moved my position again, working my way round to a hot-dog stand on the right-hand side of the paddock so that I was almost behind Charlie but still able to keep George in clear vision, albeit now with a profile view.

The afternoon wore on, becoming more and more overcast, and still there was no sign of anything close to being a handover of ten thousand dollars.

The horses for races five, six and seven appeared as if by magic through the horse tunnel from the barns, were saddled, mounted and then departed through the grandstand to the track, but George remained steadfastly in the centre of the paddock throughout, only occasionally glancing at the large TV screen to his left as the races unfolded.

He would have to move soon, I thought, in order to get Debenture ready to run in the ninth, and last, race of the day.

Frank Bannister appeared and I suddenly became very interested in *his* movements. But he wandered over to the left of the paddock area and never once went close to George Raworth. Indeed, he seemed more intent on watching the horses than keeping his eye on any of the people.

Or, maybe, that was what he wanted everyone to think.

So intent was I on watching Frank that I nearly missed it.

But not quite.

Something within my subconscious brain flashed a warning – a subliminal message sent from my eye to the cerebral cortex of my brain.

Gun!

It was hidden under a newspaper, which had slipped away only for a moment as the gun was thrust into George's belly. It had only been visible for the shortest of split seconds, but that had been long enough for my mind to register the shape – a Glock 22C with silencer, loaded, no doubt, with fifteen .40-calibre expanding bullets in the magazine.

All my concentration switched immediately back to George in time to glimpse a splash of white as an envelope was passed out of his hand and into another.

The whole exchange had taken merely a second or two.

No one else appeared to have seen it, certainly not Charlie Hern, who didn't move a muscle, continuing to lean nonchalantly on the white metal rail as he had for the preceding two and a half hours, yawning expansively into the bargain.

George himself, however, seemed totally shocked, standing there with his mouth hanging open in surprise, as his assailant turned and vanished into the crowd.

I, too, had been caught slightly unawares because the holder of the gun, the collector of the cash, had not been Frank Bannister as I'd been half expecting, nor any other man for that matter.

It had been a woman.

32

The woman with the gun was now my target and I set off in pursuit as she moved swiftly up the concrete steps towards the grandstand, both the gun and the envelope having been stuffed into the bag she was holding.

I hadn't seen her face, not even in profile, as she had a mass of long greying curls that hung down across both cheeks.

Wig, I thought, as I struggled to keep up.

The movement of her body was keen and athletic, not that of someone old enough to have grey hair.

My plan had been simply to watch and identify the mole, and then to report back to Tony Andretti. But now I was chasing her shadow, hoping to catch a glimpse of her eyes to make a positive identification.

She went through the doors into the grandstand and turned right towards the exit. I barged past the other spectators who were on their way from the paddock to watch the race.

'Sorry,' I shouted to one elderly man as I almost knocked him over, but I didn't stop to help. Instead I rushed forward, trying to keep the grey curls in sight.

The woman didn't make directly for the exit but veered off to the left in the main lobby and disappeared into the Ladies'. I didn't know whether she was aware that I had been following her. Quite possibly. It had certainly not been up to my usual high standard of covert tailing, more akin to a bull rampaging through a china shop. I didn't really care, but now I had a dilemma. Did I follow her into the Ladies'?

She was armed and might be waiting for me to appear. I had absolutely no intention of walking into a hail of .40 bullets, expanding or otherwise, but I was worried she might be escaping through a window.

The men's room was immediately alongside and I quickly went in there. Logic dictated that, if there were windows in the Ladies', there would also be some in the Gents'.

There were just solid walls and electric light, and not a pane of glass to be seen.

I went back out into the lobby and waited, finding a concrete pillar to lean against so that it wasn't too obvious that I was waiting for someone to emerge from the toilets.

There were loudspeakers in the lobby and I listened to the racecourse commentator as he described the horses making their way to the starting gate for the eighth race. Soon this deserted lobby would be filling with those leaving before the last race, making an early dash for the exits in order to miss the traffic jams. Watching the Ladies'-room door might then prove more difficult and I didn't want to lose our best lead yet to the mole.

I needed backup.

Tony had asked me earlier if I'd wanted some and I had foolishly said no, fearful that a cast of hovering hawks might have frightened away the prey.

I pulled the non-smart phone from my pocket and began to dial Tony's number.

'Turn it off,' said a man's voice close into my right ear. At the same time something hard was pressed into the small of my back.

I turned off the phone and the man reached forward over my shoulder to take it out of my hand.

'Move,' he ordered, pushing harder into my back.

I moved, walking forwards.

'Go left,' he said. 'Towards the elevator.'

He nudged me in the back again so I went to my left, towards the elevator.

I wondered how this could be happening.

Maybe there wasn't a crowd of nearly a hundred thousand as there would be in ten days' time, but this was no dark alley in some run-down city centre. It was a busy racecourse in broad daylight with security personnel within view.

Should I shout out to them?

'Don't even think about calling for help,' the man said as if he was reading my mind. 'You'll never live to receive it.'

I kept quiet and walked.

We arrived at the elevator. It had a *For Stewards' Use Only* notice stuck to the doors.

'"Up" button,' the man said.

I pushed it and I could hear the mechanism start whirring somewhere overhead.

'What's going on?' It was a female voice. 'Who's he?'

'He followed you,' the man replied. 'He was waiting for you outside the restrooms.'

Now I was in deeper trouble. I didn't like the odds. Two against one was bad enough but they also had guns while I had nothing more than my bare hands.

I dared not turn round but didn't actually need to. I could see them both reflected in the brushed-metal doors of the elevator. It was not a clear image but it was good enough.

Bob Wade and Steffi Dean.

The FACSA lovers.

Not one mole but two.

The elevator doors opened and a prod from behind implied I was to enter.

'Keep your face to the wall,' the man instructed.

If he thought it would stop me identifying them, then he was wrong. But maybe he didn't know that. Perhaps it was safer for me if he thought I didn't know them, so I went right in, almost pressing my nose up against the back wall.

It could also be that they hadn't recognised me. If so, I'd like it to stay that way.

The two of them followed me into the lift and the doors closed behind them. We started to go up.

'Did you get the cash?' Bob asked.

'Yes,' Steffi replied. 'Did you deal with the groom?'

'All done.'

'So what shall we do with this one?'

It was a question that I was quite interested to know the answer to as well.

'What do you suggest?' Bob said.

'Waste him,' Steffi replied.

That was not the answer I'd been hoping for.

'Not here,' Bob said.

The lift continued on its effortless way to the top of the grandstand.

I knew exactly where it was going.

I'd been up here before on Monday night when I'd been searching for food and avoiding the attentions of Diego and his chums. This was the lift used by the race stewards to make their way up to their exclusive viewing eyrie, which was attached precariously to the very front edge of the grandstand roof.

The lift stopped and the doors opened.

'Back out,' Bob said.

I did as I was told.

Where were the damn stewards when you needed them?

They were watching the last race, of course, looking for wrongdoing on the track when it was all taking place behind them.

What were my chances?

There was a little good news and plenty of bad news.

The good was what Tony had said about the accuracy of law-enforcement officers with their guns. He'd told me that the New York City Police hit barely a quarter of their human targets at distances up to six feet. However, the bad news was that he had also said that his special agents were trained to shoot multiple rounds to make up for that. And, at present, the distance between Bob's gun and my back was a lot less than six feet, more like six inches. He was hardly likely to miss from there.

How could I make the distance greater?

Running away might help, but not if he shot me before I had taken enough steps.

'Turn round,' Bob said, holding my shoulder so that I turned with both he and Steffi always behind me. That was a good sign, I thought. They were still trying to make sure I didn't see their faces.

'Walk.'

We were in a corridor that ran the full width of the grandstand from the lift at the back to the stewards' room at the very front. It had been built into the depth of the roof.

'Where are we going?' Steffi asked, a slight nervous timbre in her voice giving away her anxiety.

'There's a door into the roof space down here,' Bob said. 'We'll put him in there.'

Dead or alive?

I could hear the commentator trying to engender some excitement as the last race of the day drew to a close and I wondered how Debenture was doing. The stewards would soon be coming along this corridor on their way down to ground level.

I walked a little slower but Bob wasn't having it.

He prodded me in the back with his gun. 'Faster.'

I speeded up fractionally. If the stewards did come the other way, he could hardly shoot them all.

Sadly, we arrived at a door on the left before there was any sign of departing officials.

'Open it,' Bob said from behind me.

I did as he instructed.

Through the door was a world that the racegoer usually never sees – the void between the upper and lower skins of the grandstand's vast cantilevered roof.

I was expecting to find only the inside of the roof but there was far more than that. Apart from the vast labyrinth of steel girders that supported the huge structure, there was a maze of pipework providing drainage together with miles of wiring and a gigantic electrical switching box, similar to mine at home but about twenty times bigger.

Stretching away into the distance was a wooden walkway with metal-pipe handrails down either side. The walkway appeared to extend the full length of the grandstand and above it at about twenty-foot intervals were hung a series of naked light bulbs to provide illumination.

I started to move along the walkway and the two of them followed, closing the door to the corridor behind them.

'Stop,' Bob instructed. I stopped.

'Waste him,' Steffi said. 'Let's get out of here.'

'Hold on a minute,' Bob said. 'Let's find out who he is first.'

'Why?' Steffi said. 'Just waste him.'

I heard an automatic being cocked behind me.

Was this the end of the road? Was it time to play the only remaining trump in my hand?

'Tony Andretti and Norman Gibson know all about you two,' I said. 'You're finished. You kill me and you'll both be executed for killing a federal officer.' It was the first time I'd spoken and I had dropped the Irish accent.

There was a silence that seemed to go on for ever.

Had I misjudged? Was I about to get a bullet in the back of my skull?

'He's bluffing,' Bob said calmly into the stillness.

'I'm not bluffing,' I said quickly. 'Your names are Bob Wade and Steffi Dean and the cops are already on their way.'

Bob grabbed me by the shoulder and spun me round to face him. He tore off the dark glasses I was still wearing and stared at me.

'You?' he said, clearly seeing straight through my disguise. 'But you went back home to England.'

'No, I didn't,' I replied. 'I've been chasing your tails and now I've caught you.'

'You seem to be forgetting something,' Bob said, smiling and waving his silenced Glock 22C in my face.

'Are you really going to kill a federal agent?' I asked.

'You're not a federal agent,' Steffi said.

'As good as. I was invited here by your Deputy Director as a temporary member of FACSA. I am sure the jury will consider me as a federal agent when they choose to give you the death penalty.' I hoped it was so, even though I doubted it. 'Do they still electrocute murderers in New York?'

All the while I had been talking, I'd been moving myself further away from them, fraction by fraction, simply by rocking from foot to foot, shuffling an inch or so backwards each time.

'The death penalty is abolished in New York State.' Steffi sneered at me as she said it.

'Not for federal crimes,' I said. 'Sizzle, sizzle.'

'Shut up,' Bob shouted in my face. Another inch away. 'I tell you, he's bluffing about the cops.'

'And about the ten grand in Steffi's purse?' I said. 'George Raworth has been most helpful.'

He wasn't to know otherwise.

Another couple of inches away.

I looked at Steffi's thick black hair, tied back in a ponytail. 'They'll shave all that lovely hair off your head,' I said to her. 'To make a better contact. The current will fry your brain inside your skull.'

I was quite certain that 'Old Sparky' had, in fact, long been consigned to history, replaced by the banality of a lethal injection. Equally as effective, no doubt, but far less dramatic. Nevertheless, Steffi was clearly rattled.

'Shut him up,' she demanded. 'Or I'll do it.'

387

She reached into her bag, presumably for her gun.

Bob Wade began as if to say something and he took his eyes off me as he, too, looked down towards Steffi's bag. I didn't need a second invitation.

I reached to my left and grabbed the handle on the front of the electrical switching box and rotated it a quarter-turn from ON to OFF.

With a loud clunk, all the lights went out.

I turned and ran down the walkway into the darkness as if my life depended on it, which it probably did, at the same time bending down to reduce my target size.

I didn't hear any guns being fired behind me over the sound of my own footsteps, no doubt on account of the silencers, but I certainly heard the bullets as they whizzed past me before ricocheting off the steel roof girders.

I didn't stop but bolted onward at full pelt, guiding myself by running my hands along the handrails on each side and praying that no one had left anything on the walkway that I would trip over.

I was still running at top speed when the lights came on again, just in time for me to see the walkway ahead take a sharp zigzag to the left round a large vertical pipe.

As I negotiated the turns, I glanced behind me.

I had run a good forty yards in the dark and neither Bob Wade nor Steffi Dean had followed. They were standing where I'd left them next to the switching box, and they were looking in my direction.

I hoped and half expected that they would give up and leave but they clearly had other ideas as they both started down the walkway towards me. Steffi fired at me, not that I heard the retort of the pistol, but the bullet zipped past somewhere close to my left arm and I heard that all right.

It was all the incentive I needed to keep going along the walkway deeper into the roof space.

I looked to both sides for some sort of weapon but the only thing movable I could find was a five-tread wooden stepladder, no doubt left behind by some idle workman who hadn't returned it to its rightful storage place.

It was far too cumbersome to use as a club but I picked it up nevertheless and went on swiftly down the walkway using the ladder to break each light bulb above my head as I passed by. If they were going to find me, they would have to do so in the dark.

33

The walkway must go somewhere, I thought, as I continued to run down it. There surely had to be more than one way out of this roof.

I hurried on further, ever conscious that, as long as I stayed on the walkway, I was extremely vulnerable.

But dare I leave it? Was the skin of the roof below strong enough to take a man's weight? It was a long way down to the viewing seats far below if I got it wrong.

My instinct was to stay as far away from the two special agents as I could. Distance between gun and target was my friend. All handguns have short barrels and are pretty inaccurate at anything over twenty-five yards, but these two were marksmen, Steffi had said so on my first day at the FACSA offices.

As if to confirm the fact, a bullet crashed into the ladder over my head, sending splinters into my hair. Too close. Much too close.

At last I came to the end of the walkway and that was all it was, a dead end. No door. Nothing. No way out. The walkway was only there to service the pipework and electrical fittings in the roof, not as an access to anywhere else.

I now had no choice other than to leave it but, before climbing over the handrail, I spent a second or two taking a mental image of the pattern of steel girders that held up the roof. Then I used the ladder to smash the last remaining light bulb, plunging the whole end of the roof space into near darkness.

I climbed away from the walkway using the girders like a climbing frame.

In a modern structure the steel beams would have had a circular cross section and be welded together like those visible in new airport terminals, but this roof had been constructed in the 1960s and was all made from H-beams held together with nuts and bolts, like a gigantic Meccano set.

But that was an advantage as it provided me with plenty of hand and foot holds as I quickly moved away from the walkway towards the back of the grandstand until I was up against the far edge of the roof.

The problem with the lack of light was that, even though Bob and Steffi were unable to see me, I couldn't see them either.

So what was my plan?

Staying alive was uppermost, but I couldn't stay here forever, waiting for them to find and shoot me. I had to get out.

I could hear the two of them talking but could snatch only the odd word.

I thought I heard something about a flashlight. That was not good news.

However, even with the broken bulbs, it was not totally black.

The lights were still on near the exit door, where I had run under them before finding the ladder. As far as I could tell, that was the only way out and my foes had clearly grasped that fact as well. In the pools of light beneath the remaining bulbs, I could see Steffi striding back along the walkway towards the exit door to cut off any escape bid.

Being as silent as possible, I started again climbing through the steelwork, also making my way back towards the door but keeping in the deep shadow close to the far edge, well away from the walkway. It was a dangerous strategy but I could see no alternative.

Where was Bob?

I looked back over my shoulder and strained my eyes looking for him in the gloom. I could just make out his shape on the walkway and he seemed to be standing on the stepladder that I had used to break the light bulbs.

A light came on above him. He had obviously moved an unbroken bulb from further along. I watched as he went back along the walkway, set up the stepladder and reached above his head to unscrew another, which went out. It came on again down the line.

At this rate, he would soon have enough light to see me, especially if he followed me into the girder maze. One advantage, however, was that with every bulb he moved, it got progressively dimmer near the door.

It began to rain. I could hear it beating on the upper skin of the roof.

It was quite clear that Bob Wade and Steffi Dean had no intention of giving up. They were determined to get me. Maybe I would have been too if I'd been in their shoes. Contrary to what I had told them, no one else knew. Silence me and they might very well get away completely undetected.

It was such a prospect that made me all the more resolute to get out of here alive. Of course I didn't want them to kill me but I was absolutely damned if I would allow them to get away with it and to carry on undermining the work of their anti-corruption agency.

But how could I?

I edged closer to the door, making sure that I kept some of the larger girders between Steffi and me. My eyes were becoming accustomed to the dimness and there was enough light for me to plot a route in my head for the quickest way to the exit.

'I still can't see him,' Bob called out from the far end. 'He must be down here somewhere.'

His voice was partly drowned out by the noise of the rain and Steffi moved three or four steps down towards him before replying.

'Maybe he's hiding under the walkway,' she shouted back.

I had thought of that and now I was glad I'd rejected it.

'I wish we had a damn flashlight,' Bob said, almost to himself.

'I can't hear you,' Steffi shouted.

She moved forward another five paces.

I had to move. Not only was it likely to be my only chance to get to the door but, if she took another stride or two, she would be able to see me clearly.

I eased myself around the girder I was clinging to, trying to keep the metal between us.

The rain got harder, and louder.

Steffi walked forward another few paces.

'Do you need any help?' she shouted.

There was no audible reply.

She went further down the walkway.

'Do you need any help?' she shouted again.

She was now some thirty or forty yards from the door. Indeed, I was already behind her. It had to be now or never.

Once I started there would be no going back. My rapid movement would give me away, even in this light.

I swallowed hard and tried to generate some moisture into my mouth. This was it, and I was scared, bloody terrified in fact, but I was not petrified by fear. Indeed, it was the fear that drove me on.

I almost ran across the roof grid, giving a good impression of a monkey as I swung from girder to girder in a straight line for the exit.

I was almost back at the walkway before Steffi realised. Only five yards to go.

I leaped over the handrail and fairly sprinted for the door, yanking it open.

Something punched me hard in the right arm, almost knocking me off my feet. I'd been shot.

But I could still run – out through the door, along the corridor and back towards the lift.

I could hear Steffi shouting behind me.

My arm hurt like hell and I was dripping blood from my fingers, but I found I was laughing. I was out of that damn roof and I was still alive.

I pushed the lift button but the doors didn't open. The bloody thing was down the bottom and I didn't have the time to wait for it.

I'd be dead before it arrived.

I dived through a door marked 'Emergency Exit Only'.

This *was* an emergency.

I bounded down the stairs, but they didn't go all the way to ground level, rather they exited through double doors into one of the restaurants in the closed-off section of the grandstand. It was deserted.

The restaurant exit was at the far end of the room and I could already hear footsteps on the stairs behind me. So I went through the door into the kitchen only to be confronted with a mass of stainless steel – half a dozen rows of chef workstations with long preparation worktops interspaced with gas hobs and ovens below and extraction hoods and open storage shelves above. Even the ceiling was lined with stainless steel.

But there were no chefs. No kitchen staff at all. And no obvious route to an exit.

Damn it.

I was leaving a trail of blood droplets, a dead give-away to my whereabouts, so I grabbed an apron that was lying on a work surface and wrapped it round my hand. Maybe it wouldn't stop the bleeding, but it should prevent the blood from dripping onto the floor, at least for a while.

I had a quick look at my upper arm. The bullet had missed the bone, slicing through the flesh about three inches above my elbow. It was very painful but, thankfully, I was still able to use it.

I looked around for a knife. This was a kitchen, right? There had to be knives, but all I could find was a small vegetable knife with a blade about three inches in length. I'd have much preferred a nice heavy meat cleaver, but three inches was better than nothing. At least it was sharp.

I saw the door begin to move so I ducked down beneath one of the worktops, many of which had stainless-steel cupboards beneath.

'He's in here,' Steffi said. 'There's a blood trail.'

'How could you have missed him?' Bob said, breathing heavily.

'I didn't miss him,' Steffi said, clearly pained. 'Do you think he bled spontaneously? Of course I hit him.'

'But you didn't stop him though, did you? You let him get out.' Bob was clearly in no mood to be kind to his lover. 'I told you to guard the goddamn door. If you'd done what you were told, we wouldn't be in this mess.'

My eyes were down at floor level and I could see their feet under the cupboards, over by the door. I watched as Bob's moved. He started walking slowly down the first line of workstations. I crawled the other way.

For some reason, it reminded me of the children hiding from the Velociraptors in the *Jurassic Park* movie.

Who would be the T. rex that would come to my aid? No one. The racing was all over for the day, and everyone had gone home.

If Bob and Steffi had worked together as a team they would have caught me easily. But, they didn't.

'You stay by the door,' Bob said sternly to Steffi. 'And don't move this time.'

'All right.' She sounded cross. 'But there must be another way out of here. The door to the restaurant can't be the only one. How do the staff get in and out?'

That was a good question, I thought. Could I find it?

There followed a game of cat and mouse, where I was definitely the mouse, scampering around on all fours.

Bob moved up and down the lines of chef workstations, slowly advancing across the room. I did the same on my hands and knees, always keeping at least one line ahead of him. But I was running out of space – and of time.

Whenever I crawled round one end or the other of the workstations, I looked for the exit. Get it wrong and I'd be finished. There would be no prizes for trying to escape into a dead end.

I took a big gamble and doubled back. Instead of crawling down the last line, I turned the other way and went back where Bob had just been. It was another dangerous strategy as it put me between the lovers, hence there was definitely now one of them between me and any exit. But the alternative was no more attractive – guessing where to go and ending up with a bullet in the head if I were wrong.

'Where the hell is he?' Bob said, sounding so close that it was as if he was standing on top of me.

'He must have gone out another exit. He certainly didn't come past here.' There was something of a sarcastic edge to Steffi's voice, as if she was still somewhat miffed by Bob's earlier comments.

'You wait here,' Bob instructed. 'I'll go check.'

I heard Bob walk away, his shoes making a slight squeak on the scrubbed tile floor with each step. He soon returned.

'The only other exit door is locked from the inside,' he said. 'He must still be in here.'

Bugger, I thought. This isn't going well.

Where could I hide?

Nowhere.

Most of the worktops had cupboards beneath, which were all shut with sliding doors, and there was no way I could open one without Bob or Steffi hearing. But, at a few places, there was just a single shelf about six inches from the floor that stretched right through from one side of the worktop to the other. Most of them were covered in pots and pans, and there was no chance of moving those silently either.

However, on my crawling travels I remember spotting one empty shelf. It was where I had seen Bob not just from the ankles down but everything below his knees.

'I knew this was a bad idea,' Bob said.

'But we need that extra money if you're going to divorce Angie and marry me,' Steffi said. 'She'll take you for everything she can.'

Good old Angie, I thought. I wished she'd take him right now.

'I need to talk to you about that,' Bob said.

'About what?' Steffi demanded.

'Not now. We'll talk later. Let's find him first.'

'Not changing your mind are you?' Steffi was getting quite agitated.

'No, of course not,' Bob replied, but his tone suggested the completely opposite answer. He very clearly had changed his mind. 'Come on. Let's find him.'

'What if he's managed to escape?' Steffi said, panic audibly rising in her voice. 'Then we're done for. You heard what he said about the death penalty.'

'Shut up,' Bob replied sharply. 'He can't have. He must be here. In one of these cupboards.'

I heard him slide open one of the cupboard doors.

'But what if he has escaped?' Steffi's voice had risen so that it was little more than a squeak. She was now in full panic-attack mode.

'Shut up, woman,' Bob said angrily. 'And help me find him.'

Perhaps he thought it was better for her to be occupied than standing by the door dissolving into jelly. But it was more bad news for me. With two of them looking, they were bound to find me now.

'I think we should go,' Steffi said suddenly. She hadn't moved. I could still see her feet over by the door.

'What do you mean, go?'

'Go. Leave. Get out of here before the cops arrive.' All her earlier bravado about wasting me seemed to have evaporated. My talk of electrocution and Bob's change of heart over a divorce had clearly unnerved her.

Bob was far more relaxed. 'If the cops were coming they'd have been here by now. He was lying about that, and about everything else.'

'I still think we should leave, now,' Steffi said determinedly.

Go on, Steffi, convince him.

'No way,' Bob said. 'We finish this.' I heard him slide open another cupboard door.

'But I don't want to get arrested for murder,' Steffi said.

'You won't,' Bob said. 'He was lying, I tell you. We find him and kill him. And then we get out of here.'

All the while they had been talking, I had been crawling until I found the empty shelf.

Silently, I eased myself onto it so I was lying with my back to the metal, with my knees drawn up. Maybe Steffi would pass the end of the workstation and not see me. I would then be behind her again, and closer to the door into the restaurant.

My plan almost worked.

As I had hoped, she walked right past the end without spotting me.

Now all I had to do was roll off the shelf in the direction she had come from. Then I'd be behind her. Easy.

But it was at that point when things started to go badly wrong.

In *Jurassic Park*, it was a falling soup ladle that gave away the children's position to the Velociraptors. In my case it was a large metal saucepan lid.

It had been standing vertically on its edge on the far side of the large saucepan to which it belonged. I only touched the pan fractionally with my foot as I manoeuvred myself back onto the floor but it was enough to upset the equilibrium.

I watched in horror as the lid rolled gently off the shelf away from me and clattered to the floor, going round and round like a coin dropped onto a granite top, only ten times louder.

'Get him,' shouted Bob.

I stood up and ran.

A bullet zinged off the extractor hood next to my ear causing me to duck involuntarily. I reached the end of the line to find Steffi, but she was facing away from me and towards where the noise of the lid had come from.

I grabbed her from behind, holding her tight to me

with my left arm and placing the vegetable knife up against her windpipe with my right hand.

'Drop it,' I shouted into her ear.

She wriggled and squirmed so I cut her neck. Only a little cut but enough to draw blood. She gasped and went very still, dropping her gun with a clatter to the floor. I used my foot to slide it backwards but I had no chance of bending down to get it because Bob was standing right in front of us, about ten feet away.

'Drop your gun,' I shouted at him, 'or I'll slit her throat.'

He did nothing of the sort. Instead he took two steps closer and pointed the barrel straight at me, lining up his right eye with the sights.

Steffi was shorter than me by a couple of inches so I ducked my head down behind hers so as not to give him a clear target to shoot at.

'I said drop your gun,' I repeated. 'I will cut her if you don't.'

A strange look came over his face, almost one of indifference to the plight of his mistress. Was he thinking only of his own skin, or had he decided there was another way out of his matrimonial predicament?

He took another step forward and shot Steffi from no more than three feet away in the chest.

The force of the impact threw us both backwards off our feet, Steffi landing heavily on top of me.

My first instinct was that I had also been shot but my mind and body were still operating normally.

For some reason I remembered what Bob himself

had said to me on that very first day in the FACSA offices in Arlington. *Expanding bullets are less likely to pass right through suspects and into innocent bystanders behind them.*

How right he was.

But I feared that my relief was likely to be short-lived. I would be next.

I realised that I had landed on Steffi's gun. It was sticking into my back. I grabbed it and dived behind the next line of workstations. Now things were a little more even.

But why had he shot Steffi? It didn't make any sense.

And there was little doubt in my mind that she was dead. She hadn't been wearing her FACSA bulletproof vest and her chest had been ripped apart by the expanding bullet.

She lay there on the tile floor in front of me, a pool of bright-red blood spreading out beneath her, with non-seeing eyes still wide open as if in surprise.

I crouched behind the workstation, gun at the ready, watching for the moment that Bob appeared.

He didn't.

Where was he?

I lowered my head down to the floor and looked under the cupboards. All I could see was his ankles and feet. He was standing just the other side of the worktop.

He was a professional marksman, regularly practised, and I had only fired a gun once since I'd left the army, many years before. However, one never forgets how to aim and pull a trigger.

I reached under the cupboard with my arms fully extended, holding the Glock 22C as still as I could. The end of the silencer was only twenty-four inches or so from Bob's feet. Surely I couldn't miss from here.

I closed my left eye, looked along the sights with my right, and squeezed the trigger as smoothly as I could manage.

The gun leaped in my hand with the recoil as the round went off. It all seemed a bit surreal without an accompanying deafening bang, the only sound being the mechanic clanging as the gun's mechanism automatically ejected the empty cartridge and reloaded. However, the scream from Bob was amply loud enough to make up for it.

I hadn't missed. The bullet appeared to have caught him square on the right ankle bone and its subsequent expansion had almost torn his foot clean off.

I didn't go to his aid. He still had his gun and I was in no doubt that he'd use it.

Instead, I ran for the door to the restaurant before he too worked out he could also shoot me at floor level.

Logic told me that Bob couldn't have run after me with only one functioning foot but, nevertheless, I sprinted across the deserted restaurant, through the empty cavernous betting hall beyond, and down the stairway towards the grandstand exits.

Indeed, I didn't stop running until I reached a lone

uniformed guard at the security desk in the main lobby.

'Call the cops,' I shouted at him. 'There's been a murder.'

'I know,' he said. 'And the cops are already here investigating it.'

I stared at him. He knows? How does he know?

'So where are they then?'

'With the body,' the guard said somewhat matter-of-factly.

'Whose body?'

It was his turn to stare at me, as if I was the idiot.

'The groom who was murdered. Over in the barns.'

Did you deal with the groom? Steffi had asked.

All done, Bob had replied.

'No,' I said to the security guard, finally understanding. 'There's been another murder. Here in the grandstand. In one of the kitchens. Call the cops again.'

34

Everything considered, it turned out to be quite a busy night for the Nassau County Police Department. Almost their total on-duty manpower ended up at Belmont Park for one reason or another.

There was considerable confusion and I seemed to be the cause of most of it.

Initially, in spite of my protestations that I was all right, I was dispatched by ambulance to the emergency room of a local hospital to have my arm dealt with. The bleeding had decreased to a mere ooze, but there was still a nasty gash that required treatment.

It was while a doctor was cleaning and stitching the wound under local anaesthetic that more police turned up at the hospital to arrest me for the murder of one federal special agent, namely Stephanie Dean, and for the grievous bodily harm of another, *viz* Robert Wade.

Try as I might to explain to them that it had been Robert Wade who had killed Stephanie and that I had been the one they had shot at first, I was eventually handcuffed and frogmarched out of the hospital and into a waiting squad car.

At the police station, I was photographed and fingerprinted, plus I had a swab taken of my saliva for DNA. However, it was the discovery in my pocket of a groom's ID card in the name of Patrick Sean Murphy that caused the greatest excitement, and not only because the photograph on it didn't resemble me as I now was.

It transpired that the said Patrick Sean Murphy, an Irishman, was being sought as the prime suspect in the murder of the dead groom.

My repeated pleas to the lead detective that I was, in fact, one Jefferson Roosevelt Hinkley, an Englishman, on loan from the British Horseracing Authority to the Federal Anti-Corruption in Sports Agency, fell on deaf ears.

'Call the Deputy Director of the agency,' I told him. 'He'll vouch for me.'

But the detective didn't believe me and the discovery of an United States Permanent Resident Card in my wallet, also in the name of Patrick Sean Murphy and with my matching thumbprint, was all the proof he needed that I was lying.

He kept asking me the same questions over and over again, and I gave him the same answers on each occasion.

'Why did you kill a federal law-enforcement officer?'

He clearly took a very dim view of that.

'I didn't.'

'Why did you shoot at another?'

The police had already done a powder-residue test on my hands. I was sure it had registered positive. And my prints would be on Steffi's gun.

'Because he was trying to kill me.'

'And why would that be? Was it because you had already killed his colleague?'

I told him the whole story from the beginning at least four times but it was quite clear he didn't believe me. It sounded too improbable, even to my ears.

'Go and look in the roof space,' I said. 'You'll find the broken bulbs and a bullet hole in the stepladder. And who do you think shot me?'

I showed him the stitches in my arm, which were now hurting again as the local anaesthetic wore off.

The detective changed tactics.

'Why did you kill the groom?'

'I didn't. I don't even know which groom has been killed.'

The detective consulted his papers.

'Mr Ríos, a US citizen from Puerto Rico. Diego Manuel Ríos.'

I stared at him.

'His cousin, Miss Maria Quintero, says that you and Mr Ríos had an ongoing feud and she claims you killed him.'

She was right. I had killed him.

I had asked Tony to email his Deputy Director predecessor stating that he had a lead on how trainers were being tipped off: the groom who looked after Debenture was prepared to talk. That would normally have been me but, due to my feigned illness, Keith had detailed Diego to look after the horse instead.

And because of that, Bob Wade had killed Diego and not me.

'Where was he found?' I asked.

'Where you left him – in a barn, with a pitchfork stuck deep in his chest.'

Bob Wade must have acquired that idea from Hayden Ryder, who had tried to do the same to him at Churchill Downs. But Diego hadn't been wearing a bulletproof vest or a special agent badge as protection.

'I've already told you, I didn't see Diego Ríos at any time this afternoon. I was over at the racetrack, not at the barns.'

'Can you prove that? Do you have any witnesses?'

No, of course I didn't. I had spent the afternoon trying to be as inconspicuous as possible.

'So why did you kill him?'

'I didn't.'

'The murder weapon has your fingerprints all over it.'

Hell, I thought. That wasn't good.

'All the grooms have used all the pitchforks at one time or another. They will have all our fingerprints on them.'

'What was the feud between you and Mr Ríos all about?'

I was not going there. It would sound far too incriminating if I told him it was over advances I had made towards his cousin. It was not a feud anyway. A true feud needed animosity in both directions. Diego's had all been one-way.

I decided it was time I asked for a lawyer. Probably well past time.

'I want a lawyer,' I said.

'Why?'

'It is my right,' I said.

'Only guilty men ask for lawyers,' he responded, and I'm sure he believed it. In his eyes, suspects were all guilty until proved not to be and, even then, he'd probably still have had his doubts.

'I'd also like to make a phone call,' I said, ignoring his remark. 'I think I have a right to that as well.'

He obviously didn't like it but he shrugged his shoulders in acceptance. 'OK,' he said. 'One call.'

I made it to Tony Andretti.

'Where are you?' he asked angrily. 'There's been a disaster at the track.'

'What sort of disaster?'

'I've lost two of my best agents,' he said gloomily. 'One is dead and the other is currently in surgery to save his foot.'

'They were your moles,' I said to him. 'Not one mole, but two. Both of them. Bob Wade and Steffi Dean.'

There was a long pause from the other end of the line.

'Tony?' I said eventually. 'You still there?'

'Yes,' he replied slowly. 'I'm still here.' He sounded shocked. 'Are you sure?'

'Positive.'

He was not happy. 'I wanted you only to find our moles, not kill them.'

'I didn't,' I said. 'Steffi Dean was shot dead by Bob Wade from a range of about three feet. She didn't stand a chance.'

'Bob Wade says an unknown assailant did it, a man with a black goatee.'

No wonder the cops had come looking for me at the hospital. They would have readily believed a federal special agent. Who wouldn't?

'Check the ballistics. The bullet that killed Steffi came from Bob's gun.'

But I wondered if there would be enough of the expanded bullet remaining to test for barrel marks and scratches.

'Can you get me out of here?' I asked. 'The Nassau County cops have arrested me for murder.'

'I'll see what I can do.'

He didn't sound too hopeful or, indeed, particularly eager.

What had he expected? Perhaps he'd thought that I would silently expose his mole, only then for the villain to be discreetly retired from the service, rather than to face the full force of the law. Something nice and quiet that would keep the reputation of his agency intact. Maybe even to accept the death of Jason Connor as the accident that the Maryland Medical Examiner believed it was.

What he clearly hadn't intended was having to wash FACSA's dirty laundry in public. For the Nassau County detectives to be investigating the violent death of a special agent under the intense scrutiny of the intimidating New York City media, hungry for another fatal-shooting story, especially one tinged with more than a whiff of official corruption.

'Can you at least find me a decent lawyer?' I asked.

'I'll see what I can do,' he repeated, without giving me much confidence that it would happen.

The thought crossed my mind that maybe Tony Andretti would be perfectly happy leaving me to my own devices, at least for a while. The media scrutiny would then continue to be directed solely at me as the suspect in custody, rather than at him, asking difficult questions like, 'Why had I been released without charge?' and, if so, then, 'Who really had shot Steffi Dean?'

Part of me even worried that he might be quite happy to sacrifice me permanently, for the good of the agency. Steffi was dead and Bob could be declared medically unfit to continue. The cancer would have been excised from the body and no one need be any the wiser that it had ever existed.

The only problem would be what to do with me.

After his magic trick in getting me a Green Card from the State Department within twenty-four hours, I'd put nothing past the resourceful Deputy Director of FACSA.

I spent a restless night in a hot and airless police holding cell, in which the bright overhead lamp never went out and the toilet in the corner flushed itself automatically every fifteen minutes.

My arm throbbed and the stitches itched, but I couldn't complain about the breakfast.

A segmented metal tray arrived at six o'clock loaded with copious quantities of crisp bacon, scrambled eggs and fried potatoes but, thankfully, with not a single grit anywhere in sight. I ate the bacon with my fingers and the rest with a white plastic spoon – the officer who delivered it having explained that knives and forks, even plastic ones, were considered too sharp to issue to violent offenders.

I was pleasantly surprised, and hugely relieved, to find that Tony had sent a lawyer.

His name was Marty Mandalay and he arrived as I was finishing my breakfast. He was young and brash, with a snazzy three-piece suit and slicked-back black hair, held in place by copious quantities of wax. I wasn't sure I would have bought a second-hand car from him but his business card stated that he was a graduate of Harvard Law School and I assumed that, in spite of my earlier concerns, Tony wouldn't have sent me a dud.

'Don't say anything at the interview,' Marty instructed seriously in my cell. 'Nothing at all. I will answer all the questions for you. Got that?'

'OK,' I said, nodding.

'Not a word,' Marty reiterated. 'No matter what I say. Zilch! Keep those lips of yours tightly zipped. And don't ask to speak to me privately. Trust me. Just sit on your hands and keep schtum. I know what I'm doing.'

'I've got the message,' I assured him.

'Good.'

This time, the interview was conducted by the same detective as before but with someone from the State Prosecutor's office sitting alongside him.

'Now, Mr Murphy,' said the detective, 'let's start again from the beginning, shall we? Why did you kill the groom Diego Ríos?'

I would have thought a simple 'No comment' would have been adequate but Marty clearly had other ideas.

'My client, Mr Murphy, exercises his right under the Fifth Amendment of the US Constitution not to answer that question on the grounds he might incriminate himself.'

Marty had told me to keep my lips tightly zipped but, instead, my jaw hung open in surprise. For a start, I wasn't Mr Murphy, I was Mr Hinkley. And surely one 'took the Fifth' only in court, not in a police interview. If I knew that, then my Harvard-trained attorney undoubtedly should have known it as well.

I wanted to say something – to complain that my lawyer was an idiot – but he had also said to trust him, he knew what he was doing.

I closed my mouth again and kept it that way.

The detective, meanwhile, wore a semi-satisfied expression as if he felt he was getting somewhere.

'Why did you kill Federal Special Agent Stephanie Dean?'

'My client exercises his right under the Fifth Amendment of the US Constitution not to answer that question on the grounds he might incriminate himself.' Marty said it again without any trace of emotion in his voice.

And so the interview progressed.

Question from the detective, same answer from Marty.

Neither of them seemed to tire of the game as question after question was answered in identical fashion.

I remained seated throughout on Marty's right, stock-still and stony-faced, while all the time squirming inside at the guilty picture the answers were painting in everyone's mind, mine included.

Finally, after about two hours, the detective stood up and went outside with the prosecutor.

'What the hell do you think you are doing?' I said to Marty.

He didn't answer. He just put a finger to his lips, pointed at the mirror to my right and raised his eyebrows.

Yes. Stupid of me. I understood, all right.

One-way glass and, no doubt, a microphone picking up everything we said.

We sat in silence for a good ten minutes, until the prosecutor returned.

'Patrick Sean Murphy,' he said formally, 'I am indicting you for the first-degree murders of Diego Manuel Ríos and Stephanie Mary Dean and for the malicious wounding of Robert Earl Wade.'

He went on to outline the date and time of the alleged crimes, and then he read me some further rights, but I wasn't really listening.

First-degree murder.

There had to be some mistake.

35

It wasn't Diego who made the trip to Rikers Island in chains.

It was me, as Patrick Sean Murphy.

I spent a second night in custody, this time in what was appropriately named the 'County Lockup', a metal cage made of inch-thick steel bars solidly embedded into the concrete floor and the ceiling.

I had complained to Marty Mandalay, my so-called lawyer, that, in my opinion, his bizarre replies to the detective's questions had done nothing but make it more likely I would be indicted for first-degree murder.

'I thought lawyers were meant to help their clients,' I'd said to him sarcastically.

'Trust me,' he had replied. And then he'd winked at me, leaving me totally confused. I now wondered if, far from trying to get me released, he had actually been doing his best to get me charged.

The time seemed to drag on for ever, not helped again by having the bright overhead light blazing away all night. There was an electric fan situated behind a grille in one corner of the cage but either it didn't work or the staff refused to turn it on when I asked them to.

Probably the latter.

I was not the flavour of the month with the lockup staff. 'Cop killer,' I heard one of them say to a colleague, so I would clearly receive no acts of kindness from this lot.

When I'd first arrived from the police station, I had been issued with a faded orange boiler suit with 'County Lockup' stencilled on the back in large black letters. Then I had been made to strip naked in the centre of a room full of correctional staff, before being thoroughly examined by them to ensure that I had no drugs, mobile telephones or other contraband hidden in any of my bodily orifices.

If the process had been designed to totally humiliate the prisoner, then it had succeeded admirably.

How could this be happening to me? I kept asking myself. I had done nothing wrong. Yet everyone else seemed to think I had, apparently including Tony Andretti. Perhaps I should have used my one permitted telephone call to ring Paul Maldini in London rather than Tony. But the Nassau County cops probably wouldn't have let me make an international call anyway.

Was Paul Maldini even aware, I wondered, that one of his senior integrity officers was currently locked up in a New York jail? Somehow I doubted it.

At around nine in the morning I was told I would be going to an arraignment hearing at the county courthouse.

I had to stand with my hands behind my back

through a gap in the cage door while manacles were applied to my wrists. Then leg irons were placed around each ankle with only a short length of chain between them so I had to hobble.

'Is this all really necessary?' I asked the uniformed officer as he none-too-gently locked everything in place.

'You're a Category A prisoner,' he answered, whatever that meant.

I suddenly realised that he was more frightened of me than I was of him. I jangled the manacles and made him jump backwards in alarm. It was a minor victory in an otherwise dire situation.

I was loaded into a prison van for the short journey from the lockup to the courthouse and then escorted by two burly correctional staff to a holding cell in the basement. Here, after about an hour, Marty Mandalay came to see me.

'Just answer yes to your name when asked,' he said.

'Which name?' I asked. 'Patrick Murphy or Jeff Hinkley?'

'Patrick Murphy,' he said.

'But . . .'

'No buts. Do as I ask and you'll be out by tonight. Or maybe tomorrow night.'

'Tonight,' I said firmly. 'I can't stand another night of this.'

'I'll try,' he said, but I could tell he wasn't very optimistic. 'The judge will ask if you want to plead. Say nothing. I will do the talking.'

'How about bail?' I asked.

'You won't get it,' Marty said. 'Killing a federal law-enforcement officer is a capital offence. Add to that you're a foreigner, so there's absolutely no chance of bail and I won't even ask for it. It will prevent the judge having to deny. Better not to have asked than have it denied.'

I had to trust his judgement. What else could I do?

An arraignment hearing was similar to an appearance at a magistrates' court in England. It was the start of the legal process.

The accused was presented before a judge to confirm his or her name and address, and also to ensure that the charges, or indictments, were understood.

'Are you Patrick Sean Murphy, residing on the backside at Belmont Park racetrack?' asked the judge.

'Yes,' I replied.

I wondered if that constituted perjury.

He then read out the indictments: two counts of murder in the first degree with premeditation and malice aforethought, plus one count of malicious wounding. It didn't sound at all good.

'Do you understand the indictments?' the judge asked.

'Yes, sir,' I replied.

'Do you wish to enter a plea?'

Marty Mandalay stood up next to me.

'Not at this time, Your Honour.'

The judge paused for a moment, looking at Marty,

as if he was waiting for him to apply for a bail hearing.

He didn't.

'Remanded to New York City Correctional Department. Next appearance two weeks from today. Take him away.' The judge banged his gavel to indicate that proceedings were at an end.

The whole hearing had taken less than five minutes but it hadn't passed unnoticed by the media, who were squeezed tightly into the courtroom press area. It seemed that I was quite a celebrity.

But I was not the only newsworthy felon making his first court appearance on that Friday.

As I was being led away, the defendants in the next case were being brought in. George Raworth and Charlie Hern didn't take any particular notice of me but I did of them. They also wore matching orange boiler suits but were neither manacled nor chained. They were obviously not Category A prisoners.

The sight of them cheered me up no end.

The planned Nassau County Police raid of Raworth's barn had obviously gone ahead as planned, in spite of the murders, and here was the proof that the two had been indicted, although what for I didn't know. What would be the charge for cheating one's way to a Triple Crown? Fraud, maybe.

No doubt I would find out eventually from Tony Andretti. Assuming that he would get me out of jail as Marty had promised.

*

Rikers Island was as foreboding a place as I had ever set foot in.

The atmosphere was hugely intimidating but that, I realised, was the intention.

Somehow British jails at least gave the impression that rehabilitation of offenders was the highest priority. Here, it appeared, it was the punishment and dehumanisation of the inmates.

I was subjected to yet another strip search and my lockup orange boilersuit was exchanged for one of a similar hue with CONVICT in large letters on the back, in spite of the fact that I hadn't yet been convicted of anything.

But it was the assault on one's senses that was the most extreme.

Everyone seemed to be shouting at once – either the prison officers barking orders, or the unseen unfortunates incarcerated behind the cell doors yelling for attention. And the smell of stale sweat and rancid body odour hung like a fog over everything. It was as much as I could do not to retch.

I was processed once more – name, address, photo, fingerprints – and then I was finally placed in a stifling cell in the solitary block.

The cell had two doors, one inside the other. The outer door was solid with only a small glass window while the inner one was made of vertical bars with a single horizontal slot across in the middle.

I was pushed forward into the cell and the inner door was closed and locked. I then had to put my hands out through the slot in this door to have the manacles removed. The outer door was then slammed shut with a loud clang.

I almost cried in despair.

My court appearance had been at eleven but the transport to Rikers had not departed the courthouse until the end of the day's proceedings. Six others had made the journey with me in the prison van but, sadly, none of the six were George Raworth or Charlie Hern.

They must have secured bail, I thought. Lucky them.

I had no watch and there was no clock in the cell. Time dragged.

I'd been in a cell before but not one like this. If I stood up facing the door and put my arms out to each side, I could easily touch both walls at the same time. At the foot of the narrow bed was a stainless-steel toilet bowl, with no seat, and a small stainless-steel sink, complete with a single cold tap that only worked if you held it down.

I'd had my fill of stainless steel for one lifetime.

Opposite the cell door was a small window made of solid glass bricks. It let in the natural light but it was impossible to see through.

Time dragged some more and, presently, a tray of food was offered through the slit in the inner door. I took the tray and, to my surprise, the food wasn't too bad, although it was only lukewarm and rather lacking in taste.

How I longed for a bowl of Bert Squab's extra-hot chilli con carne at the track kitchen.

It took me all of two minutes to eat the meal and then I sat on the bed and tried not to think about anything much in particular. It was too depressing.

My job at the BHA suddenly seemed rather attractive, but anything would be better than this. What would Faye say if she knew where I was? She would certainly have given the prison guards what for about my treatment.

The square of light in the window slowly faded away to darkness.

It must be nearly nine o'clock, I thought. Another day gone.

I lay down on the bed and stared at the concrete ceiling. Amazingly, in spite of the constant bright electric light, I drifted off to sleep.

I was woken by the outer cell door being opened by two prison officers.

'On your feet, Murphy,' said one of them loudly. 'Hands.'

I put my hands behind my back and out through the slot in the inner door. The manacles were reapplied to my wrists.

'What's happening?' I asked.

'You're being transferred,' he replied without any further explanation.

The two officers escorted me from the solitary wing back into the main part of the prison. Oh God,

I thought, I'm going to have to share a cell. All those horrific stories of life in American jails came into my mind and a touch of panic came along with them.

But we didn't go to any of the other cell blocks. Instead, we headed to the reception area where I had arrived earlier. A clock on the wall showed it was three in the morning.

'Patrick Sean Murphy?' asked another uniformed officer, consulting a clipboard.

'Yes,' I said.

'Transfer to Sing Sing Prison.'

'Now?' I said. 'But it's the middle of the night.'

'So?'

Clearly transfers between prisons at such an hour were not unusual.

Leg irons were reapplied and I hobbled my way out to the prison van, a blue truck with 'New York State Department of Corrections' painted along each side. I was locked into one of its internal cells and I could hear as the engine was started and we set off.

I didn't get to Sing Sing.

Almost immediately we were clear of the Rikers Island prison gates, the cell door was opened.

'Come on,' said Tony, jangling a bunch of keys at me, 'let's get you out of those irons.'

I almost cried again, this time from relief.

'You took your bloody time,' I said.

36

How an hour can change a man's life.

At three o'clock in the morning I had been in leg irons and manacles in one of the most intimidating places on earth yet, by four, I was stretched out in a luxurious leather armchair aboard a US government private jet, en route from LaGuardia Airport in New York to Andrews Base outside Washington, DC.

I had also swapped the prison-issue orange boilersuit for a check shirt, chinos and slip-on leather brogues that Tony had thoughtfully brought with him from my stash of clothes in his guest-room closet.

Tony clearly wasn't eager to talk about the happenings in the grandstand on Wednesday evening. Twice he ignored my inquiry about ballistic tests on the bullet that had killed Steffi Dean. It was as if he was somehow embarrassed by it all.

So I asked him about the other events of the evening instead. 'How was Diego Ríos found?'

'The horse he was with never turned up at the paddock from the receiving barn.'

'Debenture,' I said.

'Yes. That's it. It seems George Raworth sent someone to find out where he was and they found Diego Ríos with a pitchfork through his heart, and the horse

427

still in the stall. Needless to say, the race went ahead without Debenture.'

And I had wondered in the roof how the old horse was doing.

'I'm surprised it went ahead at all.'

'The others were at the gate before Ríos was found.'

'Tell me about the raid on Raworth's barn,' I said.

'It all went like clockwork,' he replied, smiling broadly. 'The Nassau County Police turned up with their search warrant and went straight to the barn drug store, as you had suggested. They bagged up everything including the cryo-flask. Raworth and his assistant ...'

'Charlie Hern?' I said.

He nodded. 'They were both arrested on suspicion of fraud, and of animal cruelty.'

'Animal cruelty?' I said. 'That was imaginative.'

Tony laughed. 'It was the best we could think of at the time.'

'Unbelievably, I saw them at the Nassau County Courthouse yesterday morning. I was leaving my arraignment hearing as they were coming in for theirs. I presume they both got bail as neither went to Rikers with me.'

'Indeed they did,' Tony said. 'A hundred-thousand-dollar bond each, plus a condition that they may not go within five hundred feet of any racetrack or any horse barn. NYRA have moved quickly to revoke his trainer's licence so he can't act as a trainer for the Belmont Stakes. His horses have already been transferred to other stables.'

'Including Fire Point?' I asked.

'Especially Fire Point. He's gone to another trainer at Belmont Park. Someone called Sidney Austin.'

I nodded. I'd heard of him.

I wondered about Raworth's staff. He had three barns across the country but it was those at Belmont I was concerned about, in particular Keith, Victor, Rafael, Maria and Chuck, the yard boy. They would have lost not only their jobs, but their homes and keep as well.

I could only hope that, like the horses, they would soon be taken on by other trainers. I feared most for old Chuck and his trusty broom. I had been told by Keith that Raworth had acquired Chuck along with the barn when he'd first arrived at Belmont, but maybe his time would now be up.

There was nothing I could do for them but that didn't stop me worrying.

Maybe Bert Squab would give them a meal or two for free.

But probably not.

We landed at Andrews just before five, as the sky was lightening in the east. Harriet was there to drive us back to their place. Tony sat up front while I was in the back.

'What about Bob Wade?' I asked. 'How's his foot?'

'He lost it,' Tony said.

Was I sorry? No, not really.

At least I'd left him alive, which is more than he would have done for me.

'Is he under arrest?' I asked.

There was a pause from the front seat.

'He's not, is he?' I said.

'Not at this time,' Tony said in his official 'Deputy Director' tone.

'Why not?' I asked, but I already knew the answer.

It was much more convenient for FACSA if everyone believed that both Steffi Dean and Diego Ríos had been murdered by the Irish groom, Patrick Sean Murphy. Public confidence would not be compromised, as would certainly be the case if it became known that one of the Agency's own had been responsible. A high-profile trial, and all the media attention it would generate, would not be very welcome.

'We may not have secured a conviction,' Tony said.

'Surely there's enough evidence.'

'The ballistics are inconclusive and it would largely be your word against Bob's. Could we take the chance? It is sometimes pretty difficult to get a jury to convict even when the evidence is overwhelming.'

Ask O.J. Simpson's prosecutor, I thought.

'So what happens to Bob now?' I asked.

'He's been retired from the service,' Tony replied. 'Supposedly because he's medically unfit, but he knows the true reason. He has effectively been dismissed, losing his benefits and his pension.'

By benefits he meant government-funded medical insurance for life.

'Did you question him about warning people of upcoming raids?'

'We certainly did.'

'And how about Jason Connor? Couldn't you at least arrest him for that?'

There was a short silence.

'We decided that such an arrest would not be in the best interests of the Agency.'

'Who is *we*?' I asked.

'The Director and I.'

'Why?'

'Other than the collection of cash from George Raworth at Belmont Park on the day Steffi Dean was killed, we had no real evidence of racketeering and absolutely nothing concerning the death of Jason Connor. So we cut a deal.'

'What deal?'

'That Bob would leave the agency and face no criminal charges but, in return, he would tell us everything that had been going on.'

Tony paused and I waited patiently for him to continue.

'Over the years Bob had set up quite an operation with nearly a hundred trainers and breeders. Anyone that he came into contact with during his normal agency work.' Tony laughed. 'He effectively sold them insurance. They paid him monthly premiums on the understanding that he would warn them if there was a planned FACSA raid, or even if any out-of-competition drug testing was due to take place at their stables.'

'How much was this monthly premium?' I asked.

'Not a lot. It depended on the trainer, but it was

always less than a hundred dollars, sometimes only fifty. Not enough for anyone to worry about.'

But even fifty dollars a month was six hundred a year. Times that by a hundred trainers and the sum would soon add up.

'Was Hayden Ryder one of the trainers who paid?'

'Yes,' Tony said.

So that was why Ryder had been angry enough to go for Bob with a pitchfork. It had been his bad luck that Trudi Harding had seen it and shot him.

'What did Bob say about Jason Connor?' I asked.

'He refused to speak about him. He knew he was on firm ground as the Maryland Medical Examiner had already declared that Connor's death was an accident.'

'But you still don't believe it?'

'No,' Tony said. 'There was something rather cocky about Bob Dean's demeanour when I was questioning him about it, as if he knew we knew but there was nothing we could do about it.'

And there wasn't.

'Where did the money go?' I asked. 'That sort of cash doesn't appear anywhere on Bob's bank statements.'

I knew because I'd checked.

'His elderly mother has dementia,' Tony said, 'and Bob has power of attorney over her affairs. It all went directly into her bank account.'

'But then where?'

'The mother is in a nursing home. The money paid

for her care. Bob claims that was why he set the scheme up in the first place but he was making more than was required. He withdrew the balance in cash.'

'So why were he and Steffi trying to get ten grand out of George Raworth?'

'Raworth was not one of his regular clients and Bob claims it was Steffi's idea to get some quick extra. It seems she wasn't happy that most of the other money went to the mother.'

I bet she wasn't. Steffi had been the greedy one. It had been their undoing.

'Did Bob give you the names of all the trainers and breeders who were paying him?'

'That was part of the deal.'

'What are you going to do to them?' I asked.

'There's not much we can do. It's hardly illegal to help pay for an old lady's nursing care. According to Bob, that's what they were told – a *contribution*, he called it.'

'You could always send in the drug testers unannounced.'

Tony laughed. 'We already have plans to do just that.'

I looked out of the car window as we sped westward along the DC Beltway towards Fairfax. Washington was waking up and the roads were already busy.

'I heard Bob and Steffi talking when I was hiding from them,' I said. 'Steffi was expecting Bob to leave his wife and marry her. I was amazed when he shot her.'

'We interviewed Mrs Wade yesterday. She told us that those plans had been put on hold. Bob had promised her to give their marriage another chance, for the sake of their daughters. Not that it will survive now. She was apoplectic with rage when we told her that Bob had spent two nights in a New York hotel with Steffi Dean earlier in the week. He'd told his wife he was on an official agency assignment, when he'd actually taken three days of his annual vacation.'

'Did she know about his other little sideline?'

'She said not. She thought the nursing home was paid for by Medicare. She is absolutely furious with Bob about that too.'

So Bob Wade had lost his job, his benefits, his pension, his marriage and his right foot, but not his liberty.

Was it enough?

It seemed it would have to be.

I flew back overnight to London on a British Airways super-jumbo.

'Mr Hinkley, you've been upgraded to first class,' said the man behind the check-in desk.

'Thank you,' I said, and wondered if Tony had anything to do with it. I expected so. For someone who could arrange a Green Card in twenty-four hours and spirit an inmate out of Rikers Island, fixing an upgrade would have been child's play.

I relaxed into my first-class seat with a glass of chilled champagne and thought about my future.

Would I stay with the BHA?

I wasn't sure.

Paul Maldini had been keen to have me back – *stay for as long as you need, provided you come back eventually.*

I'd been away for over five weeks – five weeks of excitement and danger. Would I be able to settle back into my old routine?

I put off the decision by taking a week's leave, spending much of it with my sister. The renewed chemo had made Faye feel ill again and her skin looked pale and almost transparent when I first went to see her. But her spirits were high.

'It is good news,' she said, forcing a wan smile. 'My doctor thinks we caught it just in time.'

Good, I thought. But both of us knew it would be back, and that we wouldn't always manage to catch it *just in time.*

The following week I went back to work at BHA headquarters in High Holborn.

'Had a good holiday?' asked one of the admin staff.

'Great, thanks,' I said.

I went along the corridor to my office and sat down at my desk.

There were hundreds of unopened emails in my inbox. I sighed and set to work replying to some of the most urgent.

At noon, the phone rang.

'Hello,' I said, answering.

'Hi, Jeff,' said a familiar voice. 'How are things?'

'Great, Tony, thanks.'

'Did you see the Belmont on Saturday?'

'Sure did,' I replied. 'It was on late here.'

I had watched the race live on television. Fire Point, now trained by Sidney Austin and ridden by Jimmy Robertson, had won the Belmont Stakes by five lengths from Amphibious, going away.

'Makes you think, eh?' Tony said.

'It sure does.'

The irony was not lost on either of us that maybe, just maybe, Fire Point had been good enough all along to win the Triple Crown without the need for George Raworth and Charlie Hern to nobble the opposition. Perhaps they would then have deserved the kudos and won the five-million-dollar trainer bonus fair and square. As it was, they were facing financial ruin due to the expected lawsuits from the owners of the five EVA-infected horses, plus a long stretch on Rikers Island for fraud and animal cruelty.

'Any other news?' I asked.

'Angie Wade has officially filed for divorce.'

She who would take Bob for everything she could.

'Anything else?'

'Yes. One other thing. I thought you might be interested in the following piece that appeared in today's *New York Times*.'

He read it out to me:

Irishman Patrick Sean Murphy, aged 33, indicted and awaiting trial for the first-degree murders of fellow Belmont Park groom Diego Manuel Ríos and Federal Special Agent Stephanie Dean, was found hanged in his cell at Sing Sing Prison, Sunday morning, in a suspected suicide. Murphy was pronounced dead at the scene. Police sources confirm that no one else is being sought in connection with the murders.

But you should never believe anything you read in the newspapers.

'So Patrick Sean Murphy is officially no more,' I said. 'Is the case now closed?'

'Indeed it is,' Tony replied. 'How are you settling back into life as Jefferson Roosevelt Hinkley?'

'I'm working on it.'